THE
AMISH
BRIDE

THE AMISH BRIDE

MINDY STARNS CLARK
LESLIE GOULD

HARVEST HOUSE PUBLISHERS
EUGENE, OREGON

Cover by Garborg Design Works, Savage, Minnesota

Cover photos © Chris Garborg

THE AMISH BRIDE
Copyright © 2012 by Mindy Starns Clark and Leslie Gould
Published by Harvest House Publishers
Eugene, Oregon 97402
www.harvesthousepublishers.com

Library of Congress Cataloging-in-Publication Data
  Clark, Mindy Starns.
  The Amish bride / Mindy Starns Clark and Leslie Gould.
      p. cm. — (The women of Lancaster County ; bk. 3)
   ISBN 978-0-7369-3862-4 (pbk.)
   ISBN 978-0-7369-4282-9 (eBook)
   1. Amish—Fiction. 2. Lancaster County (Pa.)—Fiction. I. Gould, Leslie, 1962- II. Title.
PS3603.L366A77 2012
813'.6—dc23
                                                                    2012005745

Printed in the United States of America
        12 13 14 15 16 17 18 19 20 / LB-CD / 10 9 8 7 6 5 4 3 2 1

"I sing in the shadow of your wings."
Psalm 63:7

ACKNOWLEDGMENTS

Mindy thanks

My husband, John, whose input on this story was invaluable. You are my story-shaper, my love, and my best friend.

Our daughters, Emily and Lauren, who help in ways too numerous to count.

Vanessa Thompson, Stephanie Ciner, and Helen Styer Hannigan, the best office support team a writer could ask for.

Leslie thanks

My husband, Peter, who was the first reader of this story, even though he was commanding a field hospital in Afghanistan at the time. (I can't imagine life without you, more so now than ever.)

Our children: Kaleb, Taylor, Hana, and Thao, for their endless support.

Laurie Snyder and Tina Bustamante, for reading the manuscript in its early stages and offering invaluable advice and support, and Libby Salter for reading later in the process.

My writing group members: Kelly Chang, Melanie Dobson, Nicole Miller, and Dawn Shipman. Jenna Thompson for insightful ideas into this story. And Kylie Naslund for sharing her passion for all things culinary.

Jeff Kitson, executive director of the Nappanee, Indiana, Chamber of Commerce, for his assistance and direction; the many good people of Elkhart County that I encountered while researching this story; and the staff of the Menno-Hof Amish/Mennonite Information Center in Shipshewana, Indiana for an outstanding experience.

Mindy and Leslie thank

Our agent, Chip MacGregor, for his vision for this series; our editor, Kim Moore, for her dedication to our stories; and the exceptional folks at Harvest House Publishers for giving such care and attention to every detail of the publishing process.

Also, thanks to Dave Siegrist for his expertise; the Mennonite Information Center in Lancaster, Pennsylvania, for their invaluable resources; Erik Wesner, author of amishamerica.com, for his insightful view of the Amish; and Georgia Varozza for mouthwatering inspiration through her book *The Homestyle Amish Kitchen Cookbook*.

PROLOGUE

My grandmother was stalling like a little kid at bedtime. I bent down to kiss her a second time. "*Mammi*, I really need to go. Ezra's waiting for me." He was at the end of the lane on his motorcycle.

"But I have something for you." She forced her recliner down and struggled to a standing position. "It's important."

Afraid she might fall, I hurried to her side. "Tell me where it is," I said. "I'll get it myself."

She plopped back down into her chair. "Let me see...it's a book..."

Oh, boy. This wasn't a good time for *Mammi* to start on a new topic. I sent Ezra a quick text as she spoke, telling him to give me another minute, knowing it was bound to be even longer than that.

"I think it's in my room," she said. "On the dresser. Or maybe the nightstand."

"I'm on it." I hurried down the narrow hall, darting into her bedroom. It was tidy as a pin thanks to my Aunt Klara, who lived in the big house on the property. The dresser was bare except for *Mammi*'s hairbrush. On the nightstand was her Bible and another leather-bound book, one equally big and thick.

There was nothing on the worn cover to indicate what it was, so I picked it up and looked inside, surprised to see that this was no printed tome but instead something homemade, done by hand. Cool.

On the first page was a list of names, four in a row, one in block letters and the other three in cursive. The first one, printed in a child's hand, said "Sarah Gingrich." Under that, although the handwriting of the script was small and oddly slanted and difficult to decipher, I made out the name Sarah Stoll. Then, below that, Sarah Chapman, and finally Sarah Berg. If I was recalling my family history correctly, Sarah Berg was *Mammi*'s mother. My great-grandmother. I knew she was born as a Gingrich and ended up as a Berg, but I'd never heard of her having the last name of "Stoll" or "Chapman" in between. Weird.

I carefully flipped through the book as I moved back up the hall, intrigued by the quirky things I saw inside. It held a mix of drawings both large and small, recipes, an occasional journal entry, and other miscellaneous writings. Every word was in English, which surprised me. As a first-generation immigrant, it seemed as though she would have written in German, at least when she was younger.

The whole book was offbeat, but some of the pages were especially so. They held an odd mix of numbers and letters—or at least I thought they were letters at first glance. Pausing in the hallway to take a closer look, I realized they weren't letters at all but instead some sort of intricate, squiggly lines. Bizarre.

"*Mammi*, this is so cool," I said as I closed the book and entered the living room. "Did this belong to my great-grandmother?"

"Yes, and I want you to have it."

"Seriously? Wow. Thanks, *Mammi*." I held the book against my chest. "I can't wait to read it. I'm glad it's not in German."

She seemed surprised at the thought. "Well, my mother spoke German, of course, but she never learned to write it. She was taught to write only English in school."

"Oh. Duh." I opened the front cover. "What's the deal with the three last names here? Did your mom marry more than once?"

"It's a long story…"

My phone beeped. Ezra! I'd forgotten all about him.

"…and obviously you don't have time for it tonight."

"You're right. I have to go, but I'll be back soon."

"Good. Next time you're over, I'll tell you more about her. My mother was quite the…oh, how would you say it?"

I shrugged. Since her stroke I'd grown used to helping her find the words she wanted, but I had no idea what she was looking for now.

Her faded blue eyes lit up. "Free spirit."

I smiled. "Thank you, *Mammi*." I held the book close. "I can't tell you how much this means to me."

"You're welcome, dear."

"Why me, though? Instead of Lexie or Ada, I mean. I'm honored, but I just don't understand."

Mammi met my eyes and smiled. "Because of who my mother was. Not just a free spirit, but stubborn and feisty too. Sound familiar?" Her eyebrows raised, but when I chose to ignore her implication, she added, "Just like *you*."

"I'm not sure that's a compliment."

"Oh, it is. You're smart like her too, and oh, so pretty. You have her thick hair and lovely skin. You're even gifted creatively the way she was. Mostly, though, you have her spunk."

I wasn't used to receiving compliments from family members and felt too awkward to respond.

Mammi didn't seem to notice, though. Instead, her eyes moved to the book in my hands. Gazing at it, her face began to cloud over, and I could see she was troubled.

"There's another thing, about the book," she said.

I glanced toward the door, feeling bad for Ezra, though I didn't protest lest she give me one of her disapproving looks. Neither his family, which was entirely Amish, nor mine, which was a mix of Mennonite and Amish, made any secret of the fact that they weren't thrilled about our relationship.

"This is just between us," she continued, oblivious to my impatience. "There's something unique about it that you have to understand. And there's something important I need you to do for me."

Her odd tone brought my attention back to her. Curious, I lowered myself to the chair on her left and waited for her to elaborate. She gestured toward the book, so I opened it up and flipped through it, angling it so that she could see the pages.

"All of those tiny drawings at the tops and bottoms…" Her voice trailed off.

"These nifty little doodles?" Glancing down, I tilted the heavy tome my way. "It's funny, but they kind of remind me of icons. You know, like for a phone app?"

She stared at me blankly. Of course she didn't know what a phone app was.

"They're symbols," she said. "Each one represents something."

"Oh, yeah?"

I flipped through more pages and saw that the various icons weren't just random—they were repeated the exact same way in different places. She was right. Symbols.

"What are they for?"

"I'm not sure. But there's more."

She again gestured with her hand, so I tilted the book back toward her and continued to flip through it.

"There." She placed a pointed finger on the page to stop me.

Glancing down, I saw that she was indicating the middle part of the book, the pages of weird squiggly lines. They reminded me of letters or numbers but were completely unreadable, like a foreign language that used a completely different alphabet.

"What is this?"

She sat back and clasped her hands in her lap. "It's a code."

My eyes widened. "A code?"

She nodded. "My mother didn't want just anyone reading her journal. So she invented a code to keep parts of it private."

"Cool." I was really starting to like my great-grandmother Sarah.

I was studying the squiggles more closely when I realized *Mammi* was leaning toward me in her chair, her expression intense.

"Ella, I need you to decipher that code. Figure out how to make sense of it. The symbols too. I want you to translate the code and the symbols into words. I need to know what it says."

My first reaction was to giggle, but her face was so serious I held it in. What was this, the CIA or something?

"I'm not exactly good at this sort of thing. I mean, Zed's way smarter than I am. Why don't you ask him?"

Mammi placed a hand on my arm and gave it a firm squeeze. "Never mind him. I'm asking *you*, Ella. You can do this. You *have* to do this."

"But why?" I looked into her eyes and was surprised to see pain there. Deep pain. "What is it, *Mammi*? Why is this so important to you?"

Without responding, she broke our gaze, released my arm, and let herself fall back against the chair. Then she gave an elaborate shrug and spoke in an odd, singsongy voice. "Oh, I've just wondered over the years what she wrote, that's all."

I stared at her. An actress she was not.

"I'm not *that* dumb, *Mammi*. I can tell there's way more to it than mere curiosity."

My grandmother's eyes brimmed with sadness. She turned her face away and spoke in a soft voice. "Just let me know when you figure it out, will you? It's important to me." Clearly, she wasn't going to elaborate.

I sat there for a long moment, trying to decide whether to insist she explain or just let it go for now. It was no big surprise that she wouldn't tell me, nor that she'd asked me not to tell anyone else. Our family was known for its secrets. I hadn't imagined there were any left, but it looked as though I was wrong.

"I...I'll give it a shot, *Mammi,* but I'm not making any promises."

She nodded. "If it would help, maybe you could even go visit the Home Place. It's still in the family. One of your distant cousins lives there now, and I'm sure she'd be happy for you to come out."

Visit the Home Place? In Indiana? It was a neat idea, but there was no way I could take a trip like that any time soon. There were other things in my life that were much more pressing.

"My mother grew up there, you know," she said dreamily, not catching the reluctance in my expression. "Lived there on and off as an adult. Ended up raising a family there. Died there."

The Home Place was legendary in our family, built by Sarah's parents in the late 1800s when they emigrated from Switzerland to Indiana. *Mammi* had grown up there, and though she moved out when she married, she and her husband had lived on a farm nearby. Once he died, *Mammi* and her three daughters moved away from Indiana entirely to start life anew here in Lancaster County, but it wasn't hard to see she'd left a piece of her heart behind. I'd heard her stories of home. I even had a very special wooden box with an image of the Home Place carved onto the lid.

"You'll see she drew it in the book a lot. Sometimes the whole farm, sometimes just a particular tree or piece of furniture or view from a certain window. I don't know the significance of those drawings, but they are obviously tied in with the symbols and the code somehow. Maybe if you went there yourself, it would be easier to figure it all out."

I looked down at the book in my hands, feeling the weight of my grandmother's request—and her memories—pressing down on me.

"Let's take this one step at a time, okay? I'll see what I can do here first. You never know. I might just crack this baby wide open without having to go anywhere at all."

Mammi's eyes met mine. "Thank you, Ella" she whispered.

"No problem."

My cell phone buzzed in my pocket with a text. Poor Ezra had to be going stir-crazy by now. I closed the book—which was taller and slightly wider than even my biggest school textbook—and wiggled it into my backpack for safekeeping. Then I stood and gave *Mammi* a quick kiss on the cheek. As I turned to go, she wrapped a hand around my wrist, her fingers cold, her grip surprisingly strong. I paused and looked down at her.

"Do whatever it takes, Ella," she said, her voice tinged with desperation. "I'm an old woman, and the Lord has numbered my days, but before it's too late, I simply must know what my mother wrote in that book."

One

Once I was out of sight of the house, I rolled down the cuffs of my jeans—which I already had on under my clothes—and removed my skirt. Folding it quickly, I shoved it into my backpack and zipped it shut. I tucked my shirt into my jeans.

At the end of the long driveway, waiting for me, sat Ezra on his motorcycle. I gave him a small wave, and just the sight of his smile in return made my heart flutter.

"There you are." He handed me a jacket and an extra helmet.

With a quick "Thanks" I pulled off my *kapp*, stuffed it in my pocket, and strapped on the helmet instead. Then I climbed on behind him and wrapped my arms around his broad chest, ready to zoom through Lancaster County on his motorcycle.

Holding on tightly, I leaned with Ezra as he steered his bike around a sharp curve toward the covered bridge, and then I braced myself against the jolt as we jumped onto the wooden slats. A moment later he brought the bike to a stop next to the railing. We both climbed off, removing our helmets and holding them in our hands.

It was unusually warm for January—no snow or ice, which was why Ezra wanted to be out on his motorcycle. However, it was still crisp and cold, and even more so on the bridge, with the creek rushing below us. He grasped the railing with his free hand and leaned over, dangling his helmet above the water.

It was our special place. Over the past two years we'd stood side by side in the same spot many times, but tonight was different. I'd taken the last of my high school finals yesterday, finishing my senior year a semester early so I would be able to work and save money until next fall, when I planned to start taking college-level classes. In three months I would be eighteen. Our lives were no longer on hold. Finally, we could make decisions about what lay ahead.

"Can we talk?"

Ezra leaned a little farther over the creek, his brown eyes sparkling, his red hair pushed up at his hairline. "About?"

"Our future."

"How about if we take off for Florida?" He grinned.

"I'm serious."

He stood upright, his hands resting on the railing, his eyes connecting with mine.

"I know what I want to do," I said. "Go to baking school and then open my own business."

"I know," he said. "You've told me a dozen—make that a baker's dozen—times."

I wrinkled my nose. I probably had. "So what about us?"

He shrugged. "Time will tell, *ya*?" He reached up and touched my hair. "I like it when your *kapp* is off," he said. "You're so pretty." I was used to compliments from him. I stepped closer. As he leaned over to kiss me, I pulled my hand from my pocket, accidentally pulling out my *kapp* too. As I reached for him, it fell to the railing, and before I could snatch it back, it went over the side.

We both leaned forward, watching it float downstream for a few seconds, a white vessel bobbing along in the darkness.

"Will you get in trouble?"

I shrugged. "Not much. I have another at home."

"Want me to jump in after it anyway?"

"And make it miss the adventure of a lifetime? Who knows where that *kapp* might go?"

Before Ezra could reach for me again, my phone rang. It was Mom. I knew if I ignored it, she would grill me later.

"I need you to come on home," she said.

I assured her I was on my way and hit "End."

"Your mom?" He stepped back.

I nodded.

"Let's go."

I followed him to the bike, put on my helmet, and climbed on behind him, wrapping my arms around him again. Even through his coat I was aware of his muscular shoulders and back. He was everything I'd ever wanted—handsome, adventurous, and strong.

In no time we were back on the pavement, rolling through the hollow and then up the hill to the driveway to my house. As he turned, we both leaned in unison again and came to a stop in front of my cottage.

I climbed from the bike, pulled off the helmet and then the jacket, and gave both back to him. "Thanks." I leaned toward him just as the front door opened. My brother, Zed, stepped onto the porch. The fringe of his blond bangs nearly hid an odd, befuddled look on his face, but as he flicked his hair from his eyes, I could tell something was troubling him.

"Give me a minute, would you?" I called to him, though I consciously kept my voice kind. In the past I'd been a bit of a brat, but lately I'd really been working on being nice to everyone, even my little brother. Make that younger brother, by three years. I still couldn't get over the fact that he was now taller than me.

In spite of my effort, a hurt expression passed over Zed's face, and he stepped back inside and shut the door.

I felt a twinge of regret that I'd put my brother off, but still I turned my attention back to Ezra. Before I could say anything the front door opened a second time. I spun around, expecting Zed again, but it was my mother.

"Hello, Marta," Ezra quickly said, his back stiffening.

"Ezra." She nodded, and then her eyes fell on me. "Come on in, Ella." She stood, sure and solid, with her arms crossed over her chest. She wore a kerchief over her graying hair instead of her customary prayer covering, which meant she was tired, stressed, or had been cleaning. Maybe all three.

No matter. I knew not to argue with her. I gave Ezra a wink. "See you soon."

His deep brown eyes flickered in agreement, but he didn't say anything more to me. He called out a goodnight to my mother, secured the extra helmet, and by the time I reached the open doorway, he'd swung the motorcycle around and was gunning it toward the highway.

Mom appeared more serious than usual as she directed me to sit in the wingback chair next to the woodstove. Zed sat on the couch, and she sat down beside him.

She didn't ask me where my head covering was or tell me to change out of my jeans. Instead, she launched right in with, "I need to tell you something."

I could see that it was something big. Eyes wide, I glanced at my brother.

"Zed already knows. He overheard me on the phone the day before yesterday."

"And you're just bringing me into the loop now?" I knew my voice sounded petulant, but I hated it when people kept secrets from me.

My mother nodded. "I wanted to tell you, but not during finals, and then last night, with me being out on a birth and all, I didn't have a chance."

I leaned forward, wondering what in the world she was talking about.

"I had a call—"

I nodded my head impatiently.

"From your father."

I fell back against the chair. No one ever talked about him. Especially not my mom. Never, ever.

"He's ill." My mother turned her head to the side, profiling her tired face. She took a deep breath. "He wants to come back to Lancaster County."

Zed had known this since Thursday and hadn't told me? I shot him a disapproving look and turned back toward Mom. Her gaze was fixed on the darkened windowpanes below the half-closed shade.

"You told him not to, right?" My voice was raw. So much for trying to be nice.

She didn't respond, but the look on Zed's face told me she hadn't. And that he hadn't asked her to.

"Why do you care?" I blurted out to Zed. "He's not your real father."

Zed flicked his bangs out of his brown eyes and stared me down. I'd never seen such a challenging look on his face—at least not directed toward me. Me, he had deferred to his entire life.

"Actually…" Mom's head turned toward me as she spoke. Her features looked more weathered than usual. And sadder. "It's time for you to know the truth, Ella. I told Zed Thursday night. I'm telling you now. Freddy Bayer *is* Zed's father, as much as he is yours." She leaned forward, placing her elbows on her knees.

"Yeah, of course, legally and all," I replied with a wave of my hand. "But he's not his *birth* father." Mom and Dad had adopted Zed when he was just an infant.

"Actually, he is. Freddy is Zed's *biological* father. By a woman other than me."

I barked out a frustrated laugh, but neither of them smiled. Closing my mouth, I stared at her for a long time as her words tried to make their way into my brain.

Freddy is Zed's biological father.

By a woman other than me.

I shook my head. None of it made sense. "How could a father adopt his own child?"

"He didn't, Ella. We let others believe we were *both* adopting. But the truth is that the only one in our marriage who actually adopted Zed was me. Freddy was already Zed's father, so there was nothing else he needed to do."

Again, all I could manage was to stare. What was she saying? That my father had a child outside of my parents' marriage, a baby boy, and then he took that boy from his own mother and forced his wife to raise him? All while pretending the child wasn't even really his in the first place?

I ran a hand over my face, telling myself to breathe. Zed and I shared the same biological father. *Breathe.* He wasn't just my brother legally; he was my half brother biologically. *Breathe.*

This was insane.

"What about his birth mother?" I managed. "Who was she?"

"An unwed young woman, as I've always said. No need to know more than that."

"But how could Freddy make her give up the baby? Even if he was the father, she was the *mother*. Don't the courts favor—"

"Ella, he didn't make her do anything. She loved her baby. She loved him enough to want to give him a better life, one with two parents, where he wouldn't have to endure her shame and grow up under the scorn of the community."

I closed my eyes for a moment, trying to understand. "What about you? How could he make you raise that baby, the result of his"— I spat out the word—"*affair?*"

"Ella, he didn't make me do anything either. I *wanted* the child, desperately so, regardless of how he came to be."

I opened my eyes to narrow slits. "So you weren't forced to do this?"

"Absolutely not."

"And the birth mother really wasn't either?"

Mom shook her head. "No. She loved the babe enough to give him up. And I will always be grateful. I loved him enough to make him my own. It's that simple, Ella."

As her words finally began to sink in, I found myself curling up in a ball, my hands grasping my knees. I tried to breathe normally, but instead gulped for air.

I felt more deceived than I ever had in my life.

Not that I'd ever had any big delusions about the kind of person my father was. After all, he'd abandoned us when I was just three years old. But now, to learn that not only had he done that, but he had also had an affair, taken in the result of that affair, and created a lie about it for the world to believe, was a shock.

I looked at Mom and then at Zed. Both suddenly appeared as strangers, sitting before me. Calmly.

Where was their outrage?

I concentrated on my brother, whom I'd coddled and bossed and nagged and loved the last fifteen years. I looked at his blond hair, so different from my dark auburn waves. Sometimes, people who didn't know he was adopted said we looked alike, but I knew it was just coincidence. All these years I thought my baby brother and I didn't share a single genetic cell, and yet we did. I felt as if I'd been kicked in the stomach.

"I'm sorry," Mom said, rising and stepping toward me. "I know this is a surprise, but—"

I found my voice. "You told him none of us would see him, right?"

She leaned forward as if to reach out to me, but I recoiled.

She shook her head. "I told him to do as he wished, as God led."

"As God led?" I bolted from the chair, my voice bouncing off the walls of the tiny living room. I grabbed the backpack at my feet. She reached for me again, but I swung around the newel post of the staircase before she could touch me. I bounded up the wooden stairs and into my room, but even before the slam of my door finished echoing through the little cottage, I regretted it. Now I was stuck. Why hadn't I dashed out the front door instead and sent Ezra a text to come get me?

I expected Mom's quiet knock, but it never came. Neither did Zed's tentative voice, asking if I was all right. I paced around my room, around the path I'd worn into the braided rug, round and round. It was an Amish rug. The quilt on my bed was Amish too, made by *Mammi*, with the typical blocks of green, blue, maroon, and black. As a little girl, I'd wanted pink. But these were the more common Amish colors.

Amish colors, Amish quilt, Amish rug.

My mother's forgiveness of my father was most likely Amish as well. Which made sense because she'd grown up in that faith. We had the same deep roots, but Mom had raised us as Mennonites, not Amish.

Still, I used to think I understood the whole Anabaptist forgive-and-forget thing, but clearly something was missing when it came to my father. He had never once, in all these years, contacted me. Not on a birthday or on Christmas. Not for any reason at all. And he'd never acknowledged what he'd done. He'd never asked for forgiveness.

Half an hour later, I sent Ezra a text. I told him I'd had an argument with my mother and could really use some cheering up, but he didn't respond. He must have left his cell phone in the barn, as his parents had been requesting for a long time. Feeling even more lost and sad and alone, I set my phone aside and closed my eyes.

For years I was out of place not having a father, but by the time I was in high school I'd kind of liked the mystery of him disappearing. Here I was, an ultraconservative Mennonite girl with a mother who was a social misfit and a geeky younger brother who wanted to make films but wasn't even allowed to have a camera. The missing father added a little intrigue to who I was, which I sorely needed.

At times I made up little stories for myself. Maybe he'd done something heroic and was in a witness protection program in Alaska. Sometimes I pretended he was a famous actor or politician. I imagined he would come back someday, loaded with money.

But tonight, with this new information—and his return a real possibility—I hated what he'd done. Though Mom had always drilled into me to hate the action and not the person, that wasn't happening here. If I was honest with myself, I'd have to admit that I didn't just hate what he'd done; I hated *him*.

And why shouldn't I? He'd abandoned me. He'd cheated on my mother and then abandoned her. And now it turned out he'd abandoned Zed too.

As for Zed himself, I didn't know what to think. All these years I'd been so smug about the fact that even though my father had left, at least I knew who he was. Zed hadn't known who either of his birth parents was. That thought would have driven me crazy were I in his shoes, but it had never mattered to him at all.

Gritting my teeth in frustration, I opened my eyes, got up, and went to my closet. As I changed into my nightgown, I remembered Sarah Berg's book in my backpack. I took it out, curled up on my bed, and pulled the quilt to my chin. I started at the beginning, hoping this would help take my mind off my troubles.

The book began with an entry on the first page dated January 12, 1898, and from the look of the handwriting, I would have guessed her to be a young girl, maybe eight years old or so. It read:

Opa Abraham sent me this book from Switzerland because he liked the drawing I sent him for the box he carved. He said I should draw more, but Mamm says I should use the book to write down recipes, which, unlike my drawings, I'll actually need.

Ouch. Sounded as though little Sarah's creativity hadn't exactly been encouraged around the house. That was a shame, because she was clearly talented. On the very next page was an excellent drawing of a young hen. It was a good rendition with lots of texture and shading, but what was most striking were the eyes, which weren't those of a chicken, but rather more like an intelligent human. Sarah had been a gifted illustrator, especially for her age.

On the next page, carefully printed across the top were two words, "My Recipes." Below that was a recipe for making sugar cookies, including an ingredient list followed by the instructions. I scanned it quickly but then slowed down and read it again, sure that this was the very same recipe *I* used when I made sugar cookies. Just the thought filled me with some emotion I couldn't name—not exactly joy, but close—like an intense sort of wonder at the connection of it all.

The next page had a piecrust recipe, followed by one for berry pie filling, with drawings of different leaves all around the border. Then a couple of more pie filling recipes. I was getting hungry just reading them.

Interrupting the recipes was another journal entry, dated August 2, 1898. Still scrawled in a childlike hand, it read, *Opa Abraham passed away. He was planning to come visit, but then he died.*

Those sad words were followed by a page covered with tiny drawings of birds and plants. But then she must have put the book away and forgotten about it for a while, because the next entry was dated five years later, June 17, 1903. Headed "Recipes for Life," the handwriting there was in a tight script, much messier than before, which made it more difficult to read.

I think the word "recipe" can mean many different things. A drawing follows a sort of recipe. So does the behavior of birds. So does drying herbs and making a quilt. So does a song. I think other things do too, like friendships and marriages. Brothers don't seem to follow recipes, though. They seem to do whatever they want, whenever they want, in a far more random fashion. My brother Alvin is especially hard to figure out. Mother says God has a special blessing for all of us through Alvin and that I must be more patient. She says it is a sin for me to ridicule him for his sloppy ways.

A smile crept across my mouth. Clearly Sarah Gingrich had a desire for order, not to mention a mind of her own.

Feeling impatient, I stopped going page by page and began flipping through the whole thing, skipping over the sections written in the weird script-and-number code *Mammi* wanted me to figure out for her.

There were recipes for chocolate sauerkraut cake, lemon tart, and trifle.

The last few seemed downright fancy, especially for that time and place. Reading them, my mouth began to water. The book was quite thick, and as I made my way through it, I noticed that most of the recipes had a symbol at the top. A flower. A crow. A hawk. An alpine horn.

I went back to the scripted code, taking a closer look, but, again, I had no idea how to decipher it. I skipped ahead to an entry about halfway through the book that was dated October 3, 1920, and featured drawings of a vine and leaves encircling the words: *Hang bird feeder. Finish quilt. Sort herbs. Marry D.* I smiled as I read the entry a second time.

My eyelids were growing heavy, so I decided to save the rest of the book for another day and turned to the very last page instead. It featured a hand-drawn maze with a symbol at every correct turn, leading to the middle. First there were mountain peaks, a small flower—probably edelweiss—and the alpine horn again, then a flock of crows, a chicken, a hawk, a city, and an owl. Next was an eagle, the chicken again, but this time with chicks too, and then a small bird. At the very center of the maze was a daisy, and in the center of the daisy was a tiny drawing of a farm.

A little more than a year ago, my cousin Ada had given me a beautiful wooden box that had originally been carved by our Great-Great-Great-Grandfather Abraham. The carving on the box's lid showed a farmhouse and a barn amid wheat fields, and I knew he had based that carving on a picture Sarah had drawn for him.

I was positive this drawing was of the same farm that had been featured in the carving of my box. Underneath, in a cursive script that was shaky and hard to read, was written "the Home Place."

I shivered. What a beautiful illustration. What beautiful words. I wanted something like that in my life. A place where I belonged.

I traced my finger above the ink, working my way through the maze again, thinking about my own life. Mom was at one turn. Zed at the next. My father at the end of a blocked-off pathway.

Ezra was at the end of the maze, waiting for me at our own someday place. He was my daisy. I grabbed the spiral notebook I used for my journal and flipped to the next blank page. I picked up a pen off the bedside table and drew my own maze with a cottage and a motorcycle, a box and a book. I put a daisy in the middle with a question mark at its center.

Like Sarah, I wrote "Recipe for Life" at the top. I flipped back to her list: *Hang bird feeder. Finish quilt. Sort herbs. Marry D.*

I wrote my own list. *Find job. Go to school. Open bakery. Marry E.* And then, on a sudden impulse, I added one more item.

Visit the Home Place.

Then I sat back and smiled, knowing my words had less to do with *Mammi*'s request than they did with my own deepening curiosity.

Two

A month later I still hadn't found a job, let alone made any progress on the rest of my plan. It wasn't that I hadn't looked for work. I had—every day. First, I applied at my favorite bakery, a place called Nick's. Then I applied at a few cafés. Finally, I even applied at five fast-food places. I took the bus downtown and crunched through the frozen snow day after day in my worn boots, checking back at the places I'd applied to, but I hadn't even had an interview in all that time.

I'd also done more research on culinary schools, finding possibilities across the country, several that I would absolutely die to go to. But the local community college offered classes at a very reasonable price. I was sure that was the direction I would take, starting next fall. As long as I could find a job to add to my savings from all the babysitting I'd done through the years to pay for it.

On a Sunday morning in mid-February, Mom knocked on my bedroom door. "I have a mother in labor and don't have time to get you and Zed to church," she said. Public transportation was limited on Sundays and not an option. "Be sure to do your chores."

I called out a groggy "Okay." I waited until the putter of her car disappeared before I crawled out of bed, collected my clothes and head covering, and went to the shower.

The day loomed ahead of me, monotonous and boring. Zed would insist he had homework to do so he could spend time on the computer, which was only supposed to be used out of necessity. Still, Mom had recently upgraded our Internet service to help him with his schoolwork—something she hadn't done for me, even though I'd asked multiple times.

Zed had been avoiding me as much as possible due to my constant pestering about his birth mother. Mom hadn't said another word about any of the family drama since the night she revealed that dear old Dad planned to move back to Lancaster County, and Zed had been just as tight lipped as she.

It had been a bleak stretch of days, to be sure. The weather had turned cold and icy, which meant Ezra hadn't been able to ride his motorcycle and I hadn't seen much of him since our night on the covered bridge.

Yesterday, the weather had finally warmed above freezing, but he would be going to church with his family today.

The cold rain began to pelt the bathroom window as I dressed, and when I came back to my room and was making the bed, my eyes fell to Sarah's book on the nightstand. Feeling listless and in need of a distraction, I got myself comfortable on top of the covers, grabbed it, and opened it up.

I'd spent quite a bit of time the last couple of weeks studying the book, and every time I looked through it I saw something new. It was fascinating—at least, what I could read. Whole sections were in that coding system Sarah had used, which I hadn't yet been able to figure out. I'd even done some research on breaking codes and tried to play around with the numbers in the first few entries. I couldn't see any correlation between the numbers and letters they might represent.

That wasn't my only problem, though. Even sections not in code were hard to read because the handwriting was so small and flowery. It took a lot of time to go through it with a magnifying glass, and I had to review those sections several times to figure out what she'd written.

At least some of my questions about her multiple husbands were answered. One section talked about her first husband and how he was killed in a hunting accident—shot by one of Sarah's brothers, of all things—not long after they were married. It was so sad. Another was about her second husband, who died too. He was originally from Great Britain, which explained the recipes for trifle, scones, and Irish soda bread. She met him after her first husband's death, when she moved to Indianapolis to go to nursing school. He was a doctor who ended up going off to serve with the Red Cross in the Great War and died from the 1918 flu pandemic while on the western front. This poor woman, twice widowed at such a young age.

Besides the recipes, I was fascinated to see that the book also had herbal remedies written out, plus notes about how she used the same herbs in other ways. Lavender in pound cake and soap. Clove oil for a toothache and to "help a marriage." I could only guess what her meaning behind that was.

Mammi had said the images were symbols, and she was right. I was certain they represented people, places, or her way of life. For example, I felt pretty sure the edelweiss was for her mother and the alpine horn her father. The mountain peaks looked like the Swiss Alps and most likely represented her grandfather, Abraham. The first three symbols all ceased to appear after about the middle of the book, probably as those people passed away. I had a feeling that all of the birds represented people, mostly because of the eyes she'd given each of them. They weren't the eyes of birds, that was for sure.

A lot of her recipes had symbols at the top, and I felt pretty sure that was her way of indicating who liked that recipe or who had given it to her, depending on whether the symbol was on the right side or the left.

Only one symbol was carried throughout the entire book, and that was the hen. It changed from the young one at the beginning to an old one at the end. The quality of the drawings improved over time, but what was especially interesting were the eyes. Although the eyes drawn on the first hen were amazing, each rendition grew more and more realistic, until the last few were absolutely full of life and pain and joy. It was odd that such detailed eyes were wasted on a hen, unless it represented a person.

Toward the end was a page entitled "Home Place Recipe." On it she had drawn all of the various symbols used previously in the book, plus the words "hope," "trust," "love," "cherish," "believe," and "forgive." Though the placement of the words and symbols seemed random, I couldn't know for sure because they showed up in the middle of a long string of entries written in code.

The more I read, the more I wanted to understand—and the more I really did want to visit the Home Place, not just for *Mammi* but for myself too.

My stomach growled for some breakfast, so I put the book back on my table and went downstairs. Despite the pleasant diversion from the past, by the time I reached the dining room my mood had again turned as dark as the dreary winter day. Sure enough, Zed was on the computer, but when I turned to see what he was doing, he minimized the screen.

"Did you find out who your birth mother is?"

I'd asked him the same question several times over the last two weeks when Mom wasn't around. I'd wanted to know for years, ever since I comprehended that his mother and my mother had been two different people. Then, when my cousin Lexie came searching for her own birth mother, I wanted all the more for Zed to do the same.

He didn't answer me.

"Zed…" I cajoled.

"It's none of your beeswax," he answered matter-of-factly, using one my favorite phrases and keeping his eyes glued to the screen.

Certain he knew her identity by now, I decided to try a little nectar to get him to reveal the name to me. Mom had been around pretty regularly lately, and I hadn't had a chance to speak with Zed alone for more than a few minutes at a time. Today was my chance.

"What do you want for breakfast?" I turned toward our closet-size kitchen. "Waffles? Dutch babies? Deep-fried French toast with ice cream?" I'd seen that on an online cooking show.

"I already had oatmeal," he answered, and then he stood and stretched. In the last year he'd grown and grown, and he'd started shaving too. Not every day, but at least a few times a week.

His blond hair had darkened a little and so had his eyebrows. His eyelashes had grown thicker, and he'd lost his baby fat.

"Are you done with the computer?" My voice dripped with sarcasm.

"No. Just taking a break."

"Because you have so much homework to do, right?" It was too early in the semester for him to have too much.

His face stayed bland. "I'm getting started on my German project."

"When is that due? A month from now?"

"Two weeks," he answered as he headed into the living room.

I heard him on the stairs, probably on his way up to our one bathroom. That gave me a couple of minutes to snoop for what he'd been looking at. I popped into the Internet history. The last item was an article from the local newspaper. I clicked on to it. It was about the legal case against Mom from two years ago, when she was the midwife for Lydia Gundy. She and the baby had both died under her care during childbirth. Mom had been exonerated when it was determined that the cause of Lydia's death had been an undiagnosed heart condition and had nothing at all to do with any of my mother's actions during labor and delivery. Of course, that never made the front page of the paper the way the other articles had—it was buried in the back. I couldn't fathom why Zed was looking at it.

I jumped as I heard him on the stairs. By the time he reached the computer again, I was in the kitchen. "Even though you already had breakfast, I thought I'd make you a Dutch baby. You'll be hungry again by the time it's done." I'd found the recipe in Sarah's book and copied it onto an index card. I'd been doing that with all of her recipes I could read. That way I didn't risk ruining the book in the kitchen, and I only had to decipher the words once instead of each time I used the recipe.

I beat the eggs with the wire whisk I'd purchased with my hard-earned babysitting money. It was stainless steel and weighted. I loved the feel of it in my hand and the way it blended the ingredients together so swiftly and smoothly. I added milk to the eggs and then gradually whisked in flour, nutmeg, and salt. The way the ingredients came together to create something entirely new thrilled me every time. Years ago Aunt Klara made Dutch babies for breakfast one time when I was visiting. All we ever had at my house was oatmeal, and I thought what she whipped up—sort of like a pancake but fluffier and baked in a skillet in the oven and then sprinkled with powdered sugar—was absolutely divine.

I hadn't thought to ask for her recipe back then. Now I wondered if it had been passed down from Sarah.

Twenty minutes later, as we ate I smiled at Zed between bites, hoping to make up for my earlier attitude.

"Stop it," he said, his lips covered in powdered sugar.

"What?"

"Smiling. You're creeping me out."

I pretended I didn't know what he was talking about. After I was done eating, I asked him again about his birth mother. He just shook his head and then shoved in another bite.

I folded my arms.

He ignored me.

I leaned toward him, the ties of my head covering falling forward.

"Zed, you're my brother. You always tell me everything."

"Who says?"

"I say." I tried to smile, but it came out more like a snarl. He'd always been so compliant. Until now.

"Thanks for the Dutch baby." He shoved the last bite into his mouth, sending a puff of powdered sugar down his chin.

"Baby," I said, "is the key word. You as a baby is what we need to talk about. Come on Zed." Now I was whining. "Tell me. I've wanted to know, like, forever."

He swallowed hard, his Adam's apple bobbing around on his neck. He shook his head then, a little sadly, and took his plate into the kitchen. A moment later, I heard the water running. He was washing his dishes. Something was really bothering him.

As much as I resented the secrets in our family, I couldn't help but marvel at the decisions around those secrets that had been made so long ago. I was certain that Mom forgiving her husband's sin, accepting his child with another woman, and adopting Zed could have only come from her Anabaptist roots. Some women would hold the child's origins against him. Not Mom. Although she wasn't much for physical affection or expressions of endearment, I knew she absolutely loved Zed. He'd been her own since the day she brought him home.

After I fed the chickens, nagged Zed to clean the ashes out of the woodstove, and scrubbed the kitchen, it was nearly noon. My phone beeped with a text from Ezra. *Just got done with church. Singing at the Benders' tonight. Want to go?*

I answered immediately, overjoyed that I would get to see him for the first time in days. *That sounds great!*

I caught myself humming after that. Zed may have turned on me, but at least I had Ezra.

By the time Mom came home, I had a pot of vegetable soup simmering on the stove, a broccoli salad made, and biscuits in the oven. She'd delivered a nine-pound baby girl, the first for a couple near the village of Paradise. She stretched out on the couch and closed her eyes while I set the table.

I couldn't understand why anyone would want to be a midwife. Some weeks Mom wouldn't have a single birth. Others she'd have four or five. Some years nothing went wrong. Others years lots went wrong. Sometimes she got a full night's sleep. Other times she didn't sleep at all.

She lived by faith, is what she said. When we were little, she had to scramble to have someone stay with us when she was gone, hiring widows from our church mostly. But by the time I was eleven, she let us stay home alone. By then I was pretty much running the house. I'd grown up fast compared to my non-Plain friends at school, as far as responsibility and household duties went. Then again, I was about on a par with the Amish girls I knew, who also mastered such skills at a much younger age than their English counterparts.

On the other hand, I was sure I had far more of an independent streak than any Amish girl ever would have. How could I not? I had more options. I'd be able to drive a car—although I didn't have my license yet. I attended high school, and now I could go to baking school—or at least take classes. I could marry a man of another faith—if I wanted.

The problem was I wanted to marry Ezra, who, despite his rebellious ways, was set on joining the Amish church. Once he did that, he wouldn't be able to marry me unless I joined it as well. It would be a huge change for me, but at least I was familiar with the lifestyle, because *Mammi* and half of my family were Amish. I felt I could live as they did. And I was willing to do so for love—but only *after* I'd gone to baking school.

Putting that out of my mind for now, I set the last spoon down on the table and told Mom it was time to eat. I had an hour before Ezra would be by to get me.

I'd been sitting for a minute before she shuffled into the kitchen to wash her hands and then join me. She cleared her throat, getting Zed's attention. He quickly popped up from the desk chair and joined us too. After a silent grace, I dished up soup for everyone.

As Mom started to dig into hers, her cell phone rang. I hoped it wouldn't be another baby, not tonight. Then again, if she *did* leave, that would make it easier for me to go with Ezra. It wasn't that she would tell me I couldn't. She'd just give me that look of hers.

She stood and walked into the living room as she said hello. It didn't sound like a mother in labor by her tone.

"You're here already?" There was a pause. "I thought you were coming in a few weeks."

I groaned. Zed smiled.

"That would work." She sounded as if she were talking to an old friend, not the husband who had left her. There was another pause. "I know where that is. We're just eating…" After another pause, she said, "Oh, no. It's fine. We'll see you in an hour."

We? I pushed my bowl and plate toward the center of the table as she came back into the dining room, her face calm and serene.

"I have plans," I said. What I didn't add was that even if I hadn't had plans, I wasn't about to stick around for this.

"Can't you change them?" She looked at me with expectant eyes.

"No." I looked from her to Zed, who also had a hopeful expression on his face. They were fools. Absolute fools. "Have you no pride?"

A confused look passed over Mom's face, and then she touched the bridge of her nose with her finger. "I guess not," she said. And then she laughed a little.

"He cheated on you! He left you!"

"Yes, Ella." She wasn't laughing anymore. "I know."

Ezra arrived right on time. Because we were going to a singing, he was in his courting buggy, which was open on all sides. He brought plenty of blankets, but I knew it was going to be a cold ride. At least we weren't on his motorcycle—which he would never take to a church-sanctioned event—as that would have been an even colder ride.

By the time I was sitting beside him, I'd worked myself into a dither over the matter of my father. *Dither*. That was one of my mother's words for me: "To act nervously or indecisively." So it wasn't completely true tonight. Yes, I was nervous. But there was nothing indecisive about what I was going to do. I'd had an epiphany. Ezra and I could get married first and *then* join the church. Doing things in reverse that way would not go over well with our families or the church leadership, but at least it was better than running away to Florida and never coming back.

I snuggled closer to him and tucked the lap robe in a little tighter. We rode in silence, me trying to solidify my plan as the horse trotted along at a brisk pace. I no longer wanted to go to baking school in Lancaster County. Not now. Not with my father moving back.

I needed to convince Ezra to leave Lancaster County with me. We could go to Chicago, where there was a great baking school. Or somewhere else. Or even Florida if that was really what he wanted. I didn't care. Just anywhere but here. We could marry. He could work. I could go to school. We could join the church together when I was done. But first I had to get away from home. And I had to go to school. That was non-negotiable. It wasn't about earning some certificate or degree—those things didn't matter to me. It was about *learning*. I needed to learn everything there was to know. I needed to master everything there was to do. And for that I had to go to school.

Most importantly, though, we needed to leave *tonight*.

He pulled the horse to a stop at the crossroads. A big truck zoomed by. The horse nickered. Ezra turned his head toward me and smiled slightly.

"I've been thinking—" we said in unison, and then we both stopped and laughed.

"Ladies first," he said as he urged the horse onto the highway.

I took a deep breath. "Well," I started "now that I'm finished with high school…" I reiterated my goal of going to baking school and then described the school in Chicago, my absolute first choice. When he gave no reaction, I added there were schools in Florida too. I'd wanted to be a baker since I made my first batch of peanut butter bars when I was six. It wasn't that I didn't enjoy all sorts of cooking. I did, everything from ambrosia to ziti, but I especially enjoyed baking—bread, pies, big cakes, fancy desserts. All of it.

"How would you pay for it?" he asked.

"Well, I would work...and maybe have a little help."

"Help?" He looked straight ahead as he said the word. "From your mother?"

"No." This was turning out to be harder than I thought. "From...you."

"How so?"

I narrowed my focus. "I thought we could go together. We both could work. I'd go to school."

"What are you getting at, Ella?" He was looking at me now. "We couldn't afford that, both of us living on our own."

I pursed my lips together, realizing that it was an expression I'd seen a million times on my mother.

"Well." I concentrated on keeping my tone even. "We could marry."

An amused expression fell on his face, but then a semi blew its horn and the horse jolted a little, causing Ezra to grip the reins tightly as the truck passed.

He was as silent as the night was dark. I tried to match his thoughtfulness, but I finally couldn't stand it any longer. It wasn't like him to be so serious.

"Talk to me, Ez."

"I don't know what to say." His voice was flat, but then he smiled at me, flashing his killer, gazillion-dollar grin. The one that reminded me that out of all the girls in Lancaster County—Amish, Mennonite, and *Englisch*— he'd chosen me, Ella Marie Bayer. "Let's talk more after the singing." He turned the horse into the Benders' driveway.

As much as I enjoyed being with Ezra, singings weren't my favorite thing. The Amish girls in Ezra's district looked at me funny, and I always felt that they were probably talking about me behind my back. Even though I would wear my most conservative dresses, the printed fabric and the round shape of my head covering, compared to solid fabrics of their clothes and the heart shape of the Lancaster Amish *kapps*, always gave me away.

Worse, it was as though everyone pretended I wasn't there, as though Ezra and I weren't together. Sure enough, when he parked the buggy in the line by the barn, a girl called out to ask if he'd brought anyone, even though she could clearly see me sitting right there next to him!

"*Ya.*" He kept his head down as he spoke, but even in the faint light I could see he wasn't smiling.

Three

The singing was in the Benders' shed, which had been cleaned from the cement floor to the high rafters. The host family had placed propane heaters strategically around the room to make it warm and cozy. Long tables and wooden benches had been arranged, and the boys sat on one side and the girls on the other. Ezra and I both faced forward at our separate tables, straight across the dividing aisle from each other, me on the left with the girls and him on the right with the boys. I had the urge to reach out and hold his hand, but I could only imagine what the Amish girls would say about me then.

As the songbooks were passed around, a young woman named Ruth Fry walked in with a group of other girls. She spotted Ezra and sat one row in front of me, shifting in her seat so that she was facing him directly. She and her friends whispered and giggled. Ezra grinned at me but didn't say anything. She was the little sister of Ezra's sister-in-law Sally, and it was no secret that Ruth had been crushing on Ezra for years. I'd had no idea she was visiting from Ohio right now.

The chaperones milled around in the back of the barn as we got settled, putting out snacks and drinks. I heard my cousin Ada's laugh and turned around. Sure enough, she and her husband, Will, Ezra's older brother, were in the back, by far the youngest of all the adults. I tried to catch her eye to give her a wave and a smile, but before she saw me I realized Ruth had probably come with them. My own smile fading, I turned back around and gave Ezra a questioning look. He shrugged his shoulders, but not with surprise.

We started out with a hymn in High German. Everyone sang the same notes—there were no separate parts and no one sang harmony. I didn't even try to follow along. I thought of Sarah's book and how she said singing a song was like following a recipe. Some of these songs were pretty bad. When we were on our third hymn, a group of younger, mischievous boys came in poking and shoving each other. Will cleared his throat and they straightened up, filing onto a bench at the front table, the only available place left.

Halfway through the singing, the women chaperones handed out pitchers of water and glasses, and when we started up again we sang "What a Friend We Have in Jesus" in English and then a German song to the tune of "Amazing Grace." As the evening went on, the tempos grew livelier and the volume louder. I kept thinking about Great-Grandmother Sarah, who probably would have appreciated the more spirited numbers.

When the singing ended, Ezra and I followed the others to the back of the building for refreshments. Ada didn't seem to pick up on my irritation with her and Will about bringing Ruth, so I let it go for now. Ada gave me a hug, her brown eyes as bright and lively as ever. Her face was a little pale, though, and I wondered suddenly if she might be pregnant. I knew it wouldn't be polite to ask. Growing up with a midwife for a mother, I had always been surrounded by talk of pregnancy and birth, but I'd been taught to hold my tongue and not speak of such things so freely with others.

The chaperones had put out spiced cider, fresh pretzels, popcorn, and orange slices. Pinwheel cookies with a vanilla and chocolate swirl were also on the table, and they looked absolutely delicious. I sampled one, judging the texture and taste against my own and deeming the one I was eating to be much better. I'd have to try to get the recipe.

I took a cup of the hot cider and wrapped my hands around it, trying to ward off the chill of the cold evening. I was ready to go, but Ezra seemed happy to stay and chat with the Amish men forever.

Gradually, the courting couples began to leave, most to go to the girls' houses for a snack and some privacy. Then a group of single girls left together, followed by some of the single boys.

"We should get going," I whispered to Ezra. I was anxious to finish our discussion.

"Let Will and me take you home," Ada said, reaching for my hand. "I've hardly seen you lately."

I must have looked alarmed because Will laughed and said, "We won't bite, Ella. Ezra has some finishing up to do back at the greenhouses before bed."

"Thanks anyway." I hoped my voice didn't sound too alarmed. I gave Ezra a pleading look.

"I'll hurry," he said to Will. "I can take her home and still get it done, I promise."

Will looked at Ada, who was yawning. "Are you tired?"

"Just a little." She had to be pregnant. Maybe she'd already seen Mom. Maybe everyone in the family knew but me. That seemed to be how things were going. Will put his arm around his wife, his lips brushing the top of her head covering and then her blond hair. I glanced away, embarrassed. Amish couples rarely showed affection in public.

"I guess I'm ready," Ezra said to me.

I told Ada and Will goodbye and then approached Amanda Bender, praising her pinwheel cookies. She rattled off her recipe. It sounded just like mine, which made no sense because hers were so much better. I asked what kind of chocolate she used, and when she named a more expensive brand, I had my answer. Her food budget obviously had more leeway than ours. I thanked her and followed Ezra out the door into the cold night, where we were met by Ruth and her gaggle of girlfriends, all wrapped in their capes.

"I thought Will and Ada were giving Ella a ride home," Ruth said, her bottom lip protruding in a tiny pout. Then she smiled up at Ezra. I hadn't noticed how pretty she was getting until that moment, under the moonlight. Her hair was coal black and her eyes bright blue. Her lips were red and shiny, as if she'd put gloss on them, but perhaps it was from the cold.

"Not tonight," Ezra answered.

"Oh," she said. "I was hoping you could give me a ride."

"Will and Ada have room," I said sweetly. "Ask them." I took Ezra's arm and waved goodbye.

"Here's the deal." We hadn't even driven out of the barnyard when Ezra started talking. I glanced around, wondering if anyone was listening.

"I can't go to Chicago with you." His voice was monotone, as if he'd been rehearsing what to say in his head all evening. "And I was only joking about Florida."

The buggy wheel hit a rock and I lurched forward. Ezra reached out and steadied me, his hand against my arm.

"It's already been decided." He put his hand back on the reins.

"What's been decided?" I whispered.

"I'm going to learn to be a dairy farmer."

I lurched forward again, all on my own. But he didn't reach out to steady me this time.

"Will and *Daed* have their eye on a farm—the one on Oak Road. The owner doesn't have anyone to pass it down to. His sons left the church decades ago. He's thinking about selling in a year." His voice was still monotone. "So the family wants me to learn the business."

"Oh," was all I could manage to say. As the horse picked up speed on the paved lane and the icy wind hit my face, I felt my dreams freeze. I was all alone, a solitary figure in a winter landscape. Ezra had his entire family. And his church. And now a dairy farm. While I had nothing. *Correction*, I thought. *I have my mother, a brother who is, apparently, now a half brother too, and a birth father who wants to come back after abandoning all of us fifteen years ago.*

I wound my scarf tightly around my neck and stared straight ahead.

"Ella." He glanced at me, holding the reins tightly. "We both knew it would come to this sooner or later. I'm sorry. All along I hoped we could make it work. I could become Mennonite, I thought. But I need my family—"

"I don't want you to become Mennonite, really. I'm more than willing to become Amish after I take some baking classes. Then I'll join." I just needed to learn enough to open and operate a successful bakery, but that wouldn't be possible once I was a member of Ezra's district. For some reason, even though they allowed some job-related education, culinary training was not acceptable.

"That would be too hard for you, to become Amish."

Tears stung my eyes.

"It's not that I don't want you to," he added quickly. "I just don't think it's realistic."

Now the tears were falling down my face. Embarrassed, I brushed them away as my cheeks stung from the cold.

"Ella, I'm sorry." His voice had an edge of defensiveness to it.

"It's not just this." That wasn't entirely a lie, but I wasn't going to grovel in front of him, even though the evening wasn't turning out anything like I had planned.

I put on my brave face and told him about my father, about Mom and Zed going to see him, about Zed and I being half siblings, about Mom keeping it from us all along. "That's why I have to get away from here. I don't want to be around to see my mom and Zed cozy up to Freddy Bayer. I need to have my own life—one that makes sense to me."

We were on the highway by the time I took a breath.

I rushed on. "I can't believe my family is even more messed up than I thought. You're so lucky to have your folks and brothers and sister. And sisters-in-law."

He nodded but did not reply

"So will you work at the dairy on Oak Road to learn the business?" I finally said, trying to bring him back. "Is that the plan?"

"Not to learn the business, no," he said. "The plan is to own and work that dairy eventually, but for now my folks—and Will—want me to go somewhere else to train for it. They think it would be good for me to experience life in an Amish community outside Lancaster County."

My eyes narrowed. It was obvious what was really going on here. They wanted to get Ezra away from me.

"Like where?" I tried my hardest to keep my voice even. "Ohio?" I was certain he had some relatives there. Probably next door to Ruth's family.

"Maybe," he said.

"How about Indiana?" I asked, thinking of my own desire to visit the Home Place. "I have relatives in that area. If you went there, I might be able to come out too."

His face didn't exactly light up at the notion. Instead, he just shrugged and said, "I have no idea where I'll end up. Will's sent out a few letters so far, but that's all."

Refusing to be deterred, I leaned down a little, putting my hand to my forehead, and continued working the idea through in my mind. If we could find a dairy for Ezra to work at in Indiana, not only could I go out there for a visit to the Home Place, but maybe I could even find some way to stay and go to baking school.

"At least Indiana is a possibility, right?" I persisted.

He stared straight ahead, not saying a word, but his eyes flickered as if he'd heard me. Judging by his expression and his lack of response, our conversation had veered into dangerous territory.

This was the closest Ezra and I had ever come to breaking up, and I didn't want to cross that line, that point of no return. Trying not to panic, I decided to change the subject and lighten things up a bit instead. As I did, I could hear myself growing chatty, turning my earlier outburst about my mother and Zed going to see my father into a joke, as if I really didn't care.

"Maybe I'll see him next week," I said. "I don't look a thing like Mom. I guess I should see if I at least look like him."

Ezra nodded and smiled, but I could tell he was deep in thought. Was he thinking about Indiana? Considering that we could marry? We crossed the covered bridge in silence. The horse lunged forward, taking the hill quickly and then heading toward the curve in the highway.

I'd grown up with a car and a computer and a public education. Now I had jeans and a stash of makeup and a stack of bridal magazines under my bed. I wanted desperately to get more schooling. But still, for him, in time, I would make the sacrifice and become Amish. If anyone could do it, I could.

As we turned into my driveway, I noted Mom's car wasn't back yet. Feeling sick to my stomach, I imagined her and Zed with my father, talking through the last fifteen years, laughing and sharing stories. I groaned, but Ezra didn't notice.

"So you'll think about Indiana?" I asked again as he pulled the horse to a stop. "I really do have family connections there. I bet we could work something out."

"I don't know if that's one of the locations Will is pursuing or not. You could ask your mom."

My smile faded. "My mom?"

"*Ya.* She gave Will leads on a bunch of people she knows who own dairy farms all over the country."

Ezra was turning his horse and buggy around before I stepped into the dark and empty cottage. I stood for a moment, listening to the horse's hooves as they reached the pavement. Once they had faded away, I shut the door firmly, leaned against it, and slid to the floor.

It was becoming clear as day. Not only did the Gundys want to get Ezra away from me, but so did my mother. And because of her business, she had contacts from all over. She knew midwives from other counties and states. She had clients who moved away from the area but kept in touch because they felt endeared to her. From the sound of things, she was using those connections to help Will separate Ezra and me as much as possible.

I heard the car in the driveway and struggled to my feet, but Zed pushed the front door into me before I had stood up all the way.

"Ouch!"

"What are you doing?"

"I just got here." I retreated toward the woodstove and fed it a piece of pine, hoping to take the chill off the room.

Mom's footsteps were heavy on the porch, and then she flicked on the light as she came through the doorway. "You're home early."

"Ezra had some work to finish up."

A brief smile flashed across her lips and then disappeared. She took off her cape. "Your father said to tell you hello."

"I don't consider him my father," I retorted.

She took a deep breath. "He would have liked to have seen you."

I turned to face the stove, putting my hands out in front of me.

"He's ill."

"I don't want to hear about him."

"Ella." She was making her way around the couch, moving toward me.

Zed retreated to the dining room, his coat still on. "I know you have a lot of bitterness toward the man, but some compassion right now would be appropriate too."

"Compassion?" I crossed my arms, my hands warm against my sides. "You're a fine one to talk about compassion, Mom. Especially to me."

She stopped in the middle of the room. The strip of hair showing in front of her head covering was almost completely gray. She was shorter than me by a couple of inches. And though she'd always been stocky, it seemed that she'd grown even thicker over the past few years.

"Ella," she finally said. "I'm afraid I don't know what you're talking about."

"Dairy farms? From all over?"

She raised her eyebrows.

"Ezra?" My tone was accusatory.

"Oh, that." She took another step toward me. "Will asked me if I knew anyone who owned a dairy, and I gave him some names."

"From how far away?"

She flinched, as if I'd hit her, confirming my suspicions.

"Why can't Ezra work on a dairy farm in Lancaster County?"

My mother shook her head a little. "That's not our business, is it? That's up to the Gundys."

"It might not be your business, but it's mine. They are trying to make me disappear from Ezra's life. That's why they don't want him in Lancaster County."

Mom closed her eyes for a moment, as if to gather strength. Finally she said, "He's twenty years old, Ella. He needs to start making solid decisions. It's not like the two of you have a future—"

"You don't know what you're talking about."

That condescending smile of hers started to creep back over her face. "Ella, you can't join a church—especially not the Amish church—for a man."

A dead silence hung between us.

My mother didn't get it. She didn't get anything, ever. Nothing about me. Nothing about love. Nothing about life.

I was stomping up the stairs when she added, "Joining a particular church can't be based on whom you want to marry. It has to be because of your relationship with Christ."

I spun around and peered down at her. "Didn't you join the Mennonite church because of a man?"

She blushed. "That was different. It wasn't his church. Or mine. It was a compromise, a new one for both—"

I bolted up the rest of the stairs and was in my room before she'd finished.

I was pretty sure the majority of Amish youth who joined the church did so primarily because they had found a mate they wanted to marry. So what would be so wrong with me joining the Amish church to marry Ezra?

I could hear Mom's footsteps on the stairs. I anticipated her quiet knock on my door, which came as expected.

"What?"

"Klara invited us to dinner tomorrow. The Gundys have been invited too."

"Will *Freddy* be there?" I spat out his name like a poison.

She was quiet for a moment. "Of course not."

"How about Ezra? Is he coming?"

"I don't know. I imagine so."

"Then are you sure you want me there? Maybe I should hop on a bus to the next state or something instead. He and I can't be too close, you know."

I hated the sarcasm I could hear in my own voice, but I just couldn't help it. When my mother replied, she ignored the question completely.

"Ella," she began, her voice tired, "essentially, you're an adult now. Done with school. Nearly eighteen. I know you're applying for jobs, but you and I need to sit down and talk about what your long-term plans are besides dreams of marrying Ezra or going to baking school."

In other words, you want to crush those dreams before they have a chance of happening, I thought but did not say. She was right about one thing. I was an adult now. I needed to sound rational, not petulant.

The problem was, I knew what she wanted for me. She'd said so several times. She thought I should go to nursing school, something I was certain she wished she'd done if she'd had the choice way back when. But being a nurse would only be a little better than being a midwife. Neither appealed to me. Not even knowing my great-grandmother Sarah had worked as a nurse, for a while at least, had any sway on me at all.

"Can we do it some other time?" I said, trying to be mature about it. "I'm very tired."

"Of course. It's much too late for any more discussions tonight."

After a minute I heard Mom's door open and close. I thought of the photo on her nightstand, the only one in our house, of her and my father. I rarely went in her bedroom at all and could hardly remember the photo, but I knew it was there. Nothing in her room ever changed. An Amish quilt over the double bed. A small bureau with nothing on top. Four dresses on pegs. Two pairs of shoes in a corner.

When I heard her door open again and the sound of her steps going down the hall and into the bathroom, I hurriedly slipped from my room and dashed over to hers. Once inside, I headed for the nightstand, where the photo had always been. The light was dim so I picked it up to see it better.

She looked so young. Her hair, what I could see under her *kapp*, was close to the auburn color of mine. Her gray eyes were lively, even though there was only the hint of a smile on her lips. He was tall and blond, and his brown eyes sparkled as he grinned.

I heard a bump in the bathroom, and then the sound of the running water stopped.

I put the frame back down and hurried from the room, wondering why she'd kept it all these years. She wasn't adamantly opposed to photos, but she wasn't in favor of them either. She'd never owned a camera. When someone from our Mennonite church would give her a photo of Zed or me, she would thank them for it and bring it home, but then it would disappear. I'd looked before, several times, but could never find any pictures in our house at all except for this one.

I slipped into my room and pulled the door tight as my mother stepped into the hall.

Not only had she kept a photo of him, but she had kept it beside her bed all these years. There were about a million and a half things I didn't understand about my mother. Could she possibly still be in love with the man?

My face contorted at the thought.

I knelt down on the floor and fished under my bed, past the stack of bridal and fashion magazines, all the way to the back to the wooden box with the farmhouse from Indiana carved on the top. There was no reason for me to hide it, not really. Zed wasn't interested in it and neither was Mom. Still, I liked the thought of it under my bed. My hand landed on it and worked it forward until I had it in both hands and pulled it out. I stayed on the floor, crossing my legs and running my fingers over the carved surface. It was a little bigger than a laptop. The farmhouse was on a little rise and was two stories high, with what looked like additions on both sides. It was big, probably close to the size of Aunt Klara and Uncle Alexander's house. A field was in front of it, and there was a stand of trees behind it. On the sides of the box were shafts of wheat.

I opened the lid and pulled out a copy of Sarah's drawing. It had symbols of pies and shafts of wheat around it, in the same style as the symbols in her book, although she was much younger when she did the drawing.

I picked up her book from my bedside table and slipped it into the box.

I would talk to *Mammi* tomorrow about the relatives in Indiana. I'd see if she knew of any dairy farms in the area, ones that might be close to the Home Place.

Already, a new plan was forming in my mind.

Four

The Gundys used to be in the same church district as *Mammi*, Aunt Klara, and Uncle Alexander, but that district had divided long ago. Because the population of the Amish was continually expanding but districts were limited to a certain size, splits were sometimes necessary. Ever since the one that had separated the two families, they tried to get together several times a year anyway to fellowship and catch up with each other. Just because they didn't worship together anymore didn't mean they were willing to give up those ties.

And the ties did indeed run deep, much deeper than just church membership. Our two families had been friends for generations. In fact, when Ada and several others went to Switzerland last spring, they learned how the families had first been connected way back in the 1800s. Apparently, my great-great-great-grandfather Abraham Sommers had been next-door neighbors with Ezra's great-great-great-grandfather Ulrich Kessler. Abraham had helped finance the Kessler family's emigration to America when the Mennonites came under persecution in Switzerland. Abraham hadn't been Mennonite himself, but his daughter Elsbeth had joined, and she and her husband had made the trip to the States with the same group the Kesslers were in. Elsbeth was friends with Ulrich's daughter Marie, and the two women had stayed in touch for the rest of their lives.

Once in the United States, Ulrich settled in Lancaster County, but Elsbeth and her husband, Gerard, moved out to Indiana and built the Home Place. That separated the families for a time. But then, several generations later, Elsbeth's granddaughter Frannie moved back to Lancaster County. A young widow with three daughters, Frannie knew of her family's earlier connections with the Kesslers and had contacted Marie's granddaughter Alice, whose married name was Beiler, when she got here. Frannie and Alice had become acquainted and soon were fast friends. Now that Frannie's granddaughter Ada had married Alice's grandson Will, five generations down from the original next-door neighbors of Abraham and Ulrich, our families had finally even been joined by marriage.

That thought should have given me joy, but instead it gave me more than a twinge of irritation. Ezra and I should be free to marry too, without objection and without interference. My cousin Ada was Amish, so everybody had been thrilled with the news of her engagement to Ezra's brother Will, especially considering how their union bound us all together. But thanks to my mother's break with her Amish heritage years ago when she got married, I had been raised Mennonite, which was a huge sticking point. At least we were able to have a relationship with our Amish family and friends, thanks to the fact that my mother hadn't yet joined the Amish church when she made the switch and thus was never shunned. But the way they saw it, maintaining friendly ties was one thing; marriage, quite another.

Along the way from nineteenth-century Switzerland to twenty-first-century Pennsylvania, plenty of our forebears had switched back and forth between the two faiths. Despite that fact, when it came to Ezra and me, the families just wanted us apart, all because Ezra was raised Amish and I was raised Mennonite.

Give me a break.

We left for dinner at Aunt Klara's at four thirty, just after Zed arrived home from school. On the way, after we had crossed the covered bridge, the rain started to come down in buckets, casting a pall over the darkening landscape. The swishing of the windshield wipers, even on high, could barely keep up with the rain coming down.

"Maybe we shouldn't be going out tonight," Mom said.

"We'll be fine," I answered, hoping Ezra would be there. He hadn't sent me a text all day, even though I'd sent him several.

When we reached the highway, Mom turned right toward Aunt Klara's. Sheets of rain bounced against the pavement. It was so dreary, I hoped *Mammi* hadn't gone back to bed. Some days she did that, even though she was much better than she'd been a few years ago, before my medically trained cousin Lexie had come into our lives and discovered some dosage issues with the prescriptions *Mammi* had been taking.

Lexie's visit here had had a huge impact on our family in many ways. Before then, a lot of secrets had been kept under wraps, secrets that had to do with why she'd been given up for adoption years before to a childless couple who lived out in Oregon. Lexie had come here searching for the identity of her birth parents and ended up blowing the lid off a whole shocking web of lies and secrets. That had been a painful time for all of us, but in the end the truth really had set us free.

Since then, we'd all seen a lot of healing take place. Aunt Klara wasn't so bitter. Aunt Giselle was no longer so estranged from the family. Uncle Alexander stood taller and spoke stronger than he ever had before. And *Mammi* seemed far less burdened and remorseful.

I turned toward the window. Here I thought that time was all about the truth, the whole truth, and nothing but the truth, and yet Mom hadn't said a word about my father being Zed's father too. I'd thought that all of our family's secrets had been brought into the light during that great come-to-the-truth meeting, as Lexie liked to call it, but in fact one of the biggest secrets of all had stayed in the dark—and right under my own nose, no less.

Mom turned down the lane and the car bounced through puddle after puddle until my aunt and uncle's white house with the balcony finally came into view. The wisteria that wound its way along the railing was as bare and ominous as a skeleton. Up ahead, I spotted a carriage headed toward the barn. Perhaps it was Will's. Or his parents'.

Mom parked under the pine trees, and then she and I dashed toward the house, holding our capes tight to keep our hoods on our heads. Zed came along behind us at a more leisurely pace.

My mom's older sister, Aunt Klara, had the door wide open before we reached the porch.

"Come in before you drown," she called out. She motioned to us to hurry and then stepped over the threshold, peering around us. "Come on, Zed!"

As we stepped through the doorway and paused to take off our shoes, I was greeted by Ada and her stepdaughters, thirteen-year old Christy and three-year-old twin girls, Mel and Mat. Izzy Mueller was with them too, a young teen who had been working with Ada as a mother's helper. She'd grown tall and willowy since the last time I'd seen her, and her hair had darkened to a deep chestnut.

Standing near the kids were Ezra's grandmother Alice, and his parents, Ben and Nancy. Ezra himself, however, I didn't see anywhere. I didn't see Will either, for that matter, and wondered which one of them had been driving the buggy around to the barn. I called out a hello to everyone as I shed my cape and gave a hug and kiss to *Mammi*, who was standing in the midst of the fray.

Zed closed the door behind himself, flicking his wet bangs from his eyes. When he also hugged *Mammi*, I noticed he towered over her now.

"Oh, how you've grown," she gushed, reaching to pat his shoulder. "You're going to be well over six feet, aren't you?"

I stepped back, taking in the two of them and wondering if *Mammi* knew whom Zed's father was.

Alice and *Mammi* sat down in the living room. Ben said he would go out and help Uncle Alexander finish his chores, and Mel and Mat grabbed Zed's hands and led him over to the stack of puzzles on the bookcase by the fireplace. Izzy joined them. Mom and I followed Aunt Klara, Ada, Christy, and Nancy into the kitchen. The table, extended for tonight, was already set, and the scent of roasting chicken filled the air.

"I just need to mash the potatoes," Aunt Klara said. "Then we'll be ready to eat when the men come in." If Zed and I weren't around, they would have all been speaking in the German dialect of Pennsylvania Dutch instead of English. We'd picked up some through the years—Zed probably more than me because he seemed to have a knack for languages—but I hesitated to speak it because I was sure I was getting it wrong.

The thing was, Mom never spoke it at home, not even when I was little. Because my father hadn't grown up Plain, he didn't know the language at all, and Mom said she didn't want to teach me something he couldn't understand and had no reason to learn. Given that I was just three years old when he left us, it seemed a little silly for her to have persisted with that notion even after he was gone. I gasped, my mind filling with one very disturbing thought: *Was it possible that she did so because she thought he'd be coming back soon? Had she wanted him to come back?* Last night I wondered if she'd ever really stopped loving him. Whether she had or not, surely once he was gone, she had closed off her heart to any possibility of his return. Hadn't she? That's what I'd always thought, but maybe I'd been wrong. Maybe she'd been pining for ol' Freddy since the day he took off fifteen years ago, a ceaseless yearning that had never abated. Maybe his reappearance now was the answer to her prayers, her dream come true.

The thought made me so sad.

Trying not to go there, I wandered to the back door and peered outside, even though I couldn't see the barn from there, just a corner of the garden and the lawn.

"How are those grandbabies of yours?" Mom asked Nancy.

Nancy laughed. "Do you mean all of them or just the youngest three?" She had eight altogether, ranging in age from two months to thirteen years. Mom had delivered every single one of them except for twins Mel and Matt, who had been born in the hospital.

Nancy began to talk about the newest baby in the family, and as she did, I noticed Aunt Klara glance at Ada, who smiled in return and shyly ducked her head. I knew it! Ada *was* pregnant. I tried to catch her eye, but she avoided my glance and focused her attention on retrieving a pitcher from the cupboard and filling it with water.

"Here, Ella," she said, handing me the pitcher and gesturing toward the empty glasses on the table.

I took it from her and started pouring as I made my way around the large rectangle. Aunt Klara had put out her wedding china, the same she used at holidays. Ada handed Christy a stack of napkins, and she, too, began quickly zipping around the table.

"How's school?" I asked.

"Fine. I have one more year after this one, and then I'll be done."

I cocked my head as I looked at her. "Already?"

She grinned. "What do you mean 'already'? It's been the longest seven years of my life." She groaned dramatically. "I don't know how I'll manage to suffer through eighth grade. That's another whole year!"

I was surprised to hear her say that, as most Amish kids I knew lamented the end of their formal education. Then I remembered how Ada had been hired to tutor Christy on their trip to Switzerland last year, and I realized the book learning probably wasn't her strong suit.

Still, Christy was as sharp as a tack, not to mention pretty and feisty too. With her bright and lively brown eyes and beautiful strawberry blond hair, Will was going to have his hands full a few years from now.

The back door opened and I spun around. Uncle Alexander came through first, followed by Ben. Then Will appeared, his eyes finding Ada's immediately. I knew he'd been happy with his first wife, Lydia, but he seemed absolutely enchanted with Ada. Sure, they had only been married a few months, but I'd never seen a couple so enamored—except maybe Lexie and James. My cousins were both lucky when it came to love.

Ezra popped through the door after Will.

I turned back toward the table and picked up the next glass, filling it slowly, trying not to look flustered.

Christy was directly across the table from me, placing a napkin under a fork.

"How's your new cousin?" I asked.

"He cries all the time," she said. "Alice Elizabeth was such a good baby, but he's a little pain in the neck."

"Christy," I scolded, chuckling. "You might end up with one of those at your house, you know."

She rolled her eyes. Then her expression changed as she smirked at someone over my shoulder. Ezra was behind me. I knew without her little antics. I could feel his presence.

"Hi, Ezra," I said without turning around.

"Fancy seeing you here." He stepped to my side.

Christy put the last napkin down and then made a funny face at her uncle. "I thought you were hanging out with Ruth today."

"Ruth?" The word slipped from my mouth before I could stop it.

"You know, Sally's little sister from Ohio." Christy was clearly enjoying herself. "The one who's just crazy about Ezra. The one who went to the singing last night, just because *he* would be there. She's back again because Aunt Sally is—"

"Christy, that's enough." It was Ada, stepping toward the kitchen. "Please go tell the little girls to wash up."

"I need to as well." Ezra held out his dirty hands, giving a valid reason for his escape.

I filled the last of the glasses. So Ezra's sister-in-law Sally was pregnant again. I wasn't surprised Ruth had come to help out. She'd come the last time Sally was pregnant too—and stayed for at least six months that time, during which she'd made no secret of the fact that she had a major crush on Ezra. Maybe there was one advantage of him being sent away to learn the dairy trade now. He wouldn't be anywhere near Ruth, who, it seemed, was planning to stick around Lancaster for a good long stretch to come.

I refilled the water pitcher, put it on the table, and noticed that both Nancy and Mom were standing idle, which meant Aunt Klara had fewer jobs than people. I decided I was no longer needed in the kitchen and went in search of Ezra. Moving into the living room, I saw Alice at the card table helping Mat with a puzzle and, across the room, *Mammi* sitting by herself on the couch. As soon as *Mammi* spotted me, she waved me over, and I could tell by the conspiratorial glint in her eye that she wanted to seize the opportunity to speak privately about Sarah's journal and my attempts at code breaking.

Though I would have preferred to share a few quiet minutes with Ezra before the meal instead, I didn't really mind talking with *Mammi*.

After all, I had some questions for her too.

"Well?" she whispered eagerly as I settled onto the couch beside her. "Have you made any progress with the code and the symbols?"

"No. I've been trying really hard, but so far I haven't figured out either one."

I knew she would be disappointed to hear that, but I wasn't prepared for the absolute devastation that came over her features.

"Hey, don't give up hope yet," I said, sounding more optimistic than I felt.

She squeezed my hand, sighing heavily. "Oh, Ella. Thank you for trying at least."

She looked so sad that I wished I could cheer her up somehow. "Even without knowing the code, the book is awesome. I love it. The recipes are great. And Sarah's artwork is amazing."

Mammi smiled in spite of herself. "She definitely had a gift. I remember sitting out in the garden with her and watching her sketch the chickens." She shifted toward me and lowered her voice even more. "I don't know why anyone would draw those crazy birds."

"Did she ever draw people?"

Mammi shook her head. "I don't think so. That would have been in violation of their *Ordnung*, I feel sure."

"That's too bad." Lowering my own voice, I added, "I don't know if you ever noticed, but there's something really strange about the eyes on those chickens. They look more like human eyes. If she'd drawn pictures of the people she knew, I could compare the eyes in those pictures with the eyes on the hen and maybe figure out who it represents."

"I never noticed before, but now that I think about it, you're right." *Mammi* turned to look at me, her face considerably brighter than before. "You see? I knew you were the right person for this job. You'll figure it out one way or another, won't you?"

I nodded and smiled, though I was again discomfited at hearing a compliment from one of my own family members.

"I'm pretty determined to crack that code. Though in the end, you may be right, *Mammi*. It might take a trip out to the Home Place to do it."

I was glad no one else was looking my way right then, or they would have wondered why my cheeks were flushed and my eyes downcast. I felt so guilty! Was I really going to do this? Was I really going to take advantage of an old woman desperate to learn some truth about her mother and use that to get closer to my boyfriend? I took a deep breath and let it out slowly, reminding myself that I also wanted to break the code. I really would love to see the Home Place for myself now that I'd read so much about it in Sarah's journal.

Besides, for my big plan to work at all, several really important elements would need to fall into place first.

That job would have to be located within a reasonable distance of the Home Place.

Mammi *would have to help me get permission from the current owners to come visit the Home Place.*

I would have to figure out how to get there and where I would stay once I did.

My family would have to get over the realization that Ezra and I would be together again, despite their best efforts to keep us apart.

That was a lot of contingencies for somewhere I knew next to nothing about. Settling into the couch more comfortably, I decided to back up a few steps and do some information gathering before I got too carried away. In lieu of pen and paper, I pulled out my cell phone and opened a text to send to myself. Then I asked *Mammi* what I needed to know to get the ball rolling, just in case—the address of the Home Place, the name of the people who lived there, stuff like that, ready to type what she told me into the text.

Unfortunately, she didn't have many specifics herself. She said the Home Place was located outside Nappanee, Indiana, which was apparently near the Michigan border. The best she could give me for an address was "Willow Lane," though she had no house number.

As for who lived there now, she said the last she heard it was owned by her niece, Rosalee Neff, though the woman had been widowed at a young age and had probably remarried since then, in which case her last name wouldn't be Neff anymore.

Frustrated, I pressed send and was about to give up completely when *Mammi* volunteered the single most important piece of information she'd given me yet.

"Of course, I feel sure the dairy farm next door to the Home Place is still owned by Neffs," she said absently. "If Rosalee's name has changed and we can't find her in the phone book, we could contact them and see if they can connect us to her."

I gasped and then covered it with a fake cough.

"So there's a dairy farm right next door to the Home Place?" I asked, hoping I sounded at least somewhat nonchalant.

"Of course, dear. *My* dairy farm. I sold it after Malachi died and I decided the girls and I would move to Lancaster County to live with my brother."

Sitting up, I turned toward her, my heart pounding. "I didn't know the farm you owned with your husband was a dairy farm."

"Oh, yes. My, that was a hard life. Back then we milked by hand. Your mother never told you about that? She sure milked her share of cows growing up."

My mother hadn't told me a single thing about Indiana. I shook my head as Aunt Klara stepped into the living room.

"Time to eat," she called out to everyone.

Mammi started to struggle to her feet, but I wasn't finished just yet. "It'll take a few minutes for everyone to get settled at the table," I told her softly, a hand on her arm to keep her there. "Just real quick, explain this to me again. You and your husband owned a dairy farm right next door to the Home Place, where you grew up?"

She nodded, glancing toward the dining room. "Yes, well, 'next door' being relative, of course. As the crow flies, the houses weren't too far apart, I suppose, but these were big farms, bigger than what we have here in Lancaster County. To drive a buggy from my house to my mother's, we had to go way around a big loop on the road, nearly a mile, if not more. Most of the time, we just walked over so we could use the shortcut instead. But even that was probably a quarter of a mile."

Next door. Short cut. Dairy farm. I could hardly breathe, I was so excited.

"And the people who own that dairy farm now," I said. "Do you know them?"

"If they are still the same owners, I do. I sold it to the Neffs, a nice family in our church. Last I heard, their daughter Cora and her husband were running the place."

It was hard to keep everything straight. "Okay, and how are they related to us?"

"They're not."

I pinched the bridge of my nose, listening to the shuffle of chairs being pulled out around the table. "But you said they were Neffs, like your niece Rosalee, who is also a Neff."

"Oh, right, I see what you're asking. Well, we are related by marriage, I suppose. Rosalee is a Neff because she was married to Cora's uncle. Now that I think about it, though, Cora's maiden name was Neff but now she's a Kline. So actually, it's the Klines you would contact if you want to track down Rosalee."

Mammi looked toward the dining room and again tried to stand. This time, I had no choice but to stand as well and take her arm, gently helping her up.

"So, Kline is the name of the people who own the dairy farm?" I whispered urgently. "What's the husband's first name? Do you know?"

Steady on her feet at last, *Mammi* took a moment to brush her hands across the wrinkles of her skirt.

"Darryl. Cora married Darryl Kline. He was a fine fellow, maybe twenty when we left. I used to think he'd make a good husband for one of my girls. But that was not God's will for their lives. And I'm sure he and Cora have been very happy."

She began walking to the dining room, which had grown nearly still. As we rounded the corner, we got a glare from Aunt Klara, who was seated at one end of the table.

"Hurry up, you two," she chided. "The food's getting cold."

"Like a pair of whispering hens in there," Alice teased with a wink.

I was blushing furiously, trying to think of some explanation when *Mammi* simply grinned and said, "'The last shall be first, and the first last.' That means Ella and I have dibs on the biscuits."

Everyone chuckled as we took the two remaining seats, both on the same side of the table. *Mammi* was on the end, next to Mom, who was next to Zed. I was in the middle between him and Christy. Nancy and Ben rounded out our side. On the other side sat Will, Mat, Ada, Alice, Ezra, Mel, and Izzy. The twins did better at mealtimes when separated from each other and seated between attentive adults.

Uncle Alexander and Aunt Klara were at the head and foot of the table, and as I looked around at the group gathered there, I suddenly found myself getting kind of choked up. Except for Izzy, whom I didn't really know, I realized almost all of the people I loved most in this world were around this table. If only Lexie and James were here too, my joy would be complete. I put my hands to my face, willing my tears to stop.

Zed poked me with his elbow. "What's with you?"

"I have a speck in my eye." I pretended to be fishing for one with my index finger.

Uncle Alexander asked us all to bow our heads, and we prayed silently. I wanted to ask God for a favor—that Ezra would love me, that he would marry me, that I could handle joining the Amish church—but it didn't feel right, and I couldn't pull a coherent prayer together. Instead, I silently recited, *Our Father which art in heaven, hallowed be thy name. Thy kingdom come. Thy will be—*. I stopped. Was I truly willing for God's will to be done? If His will matched mine, of course…but what if it didn't?

Uncle Alexander stirred, and one by one heads were raised, including mine.

Thy will.

I looked around the table. *Mammi's* life hadn't turned out the way she expected it would. Neither had Mom's, nor Aunt Klara's, nor Will's. Ada was off to a good start, but she was still young. Who knew what lay ahead for her? Just the thought of it made me shiver.

I took the bowl of mashed potatoes that appeared in front of my face. Next came the chicken, salad, applesauce, steamed chard, and homemade biscuits, distracting me from my thoughts. Aunt Klara was an exceptional cook. She'd sprinkled dried rosemary from her summer herb garden over her roasted chickens, which made them more than perfect. The birds were fresh, from her own coop, moist and flavorful. The potatoes were beat to perfection, and the chard was probably from her garden, frozen last summer to be used through the winter. The biscuits were freshly baked. In fact, they were still warm. I savored each bite. I couldn't wait to see what was for dessert.

With my plate fully loaded, I had taken just a few bites when Mat knocked over her glass of water.

"Uh-oh," she said, in her cute, going-on-four voice. Ada sprang to her feet and rushed to grab a towel as Will scooped up the little girl before the liquid cascaded over the edge onto her lap. Ada was back with the towel, sopping up the water on the table and then the floor. In record time they had everything cleaned up. It was obvious they had done this before.

"What about your table cloth?" Ada turned toward Aunt Klara.

"It's just water. It'll be fine until we're done eating." She smiled at Mat, whose glass was half empty now. No one offered to pour her any more, and as an afterthought, Izzy grabbed Mel's glass, carried it to the sink, and poured some of hers out too. Watching as she brought it back to the table and set it down in front of the child, I was embarrassed that I hadn't thought of potential spills when I'd dispensed the water so fully earlier.

"Ella was asking about the Home Place," *Mammi* said out of the blue, turning toward Ada. "It's in Elkhart County, but now I have to wonder how my mother's people ended up there. Didn't you tell me that they settled in Adams County when they came to Indiana?"

I held my breath, hoping this conversation didn't take any bad turns. While I was interested in getting more information, I certainly didn't want her to bring up anything about my going out there. That would have to be kept under wraps until after I found out if a dairy job at the Kline farm could be arranged for Ezra.

"They weren't in Adams County long. That was just the first stop when they emigrated to Indiana," Ada said. Ever since her trip to Switzerland, she had become our ad hoc historian. Her friend and tour guide, Daniel, had done a lot of research about our families and had encyclopedic knowledge of our ancestors, much of which he'd imparted to her.

"From what I understand," she continued, looking toward *Mammi*, "your parents learned that land was cheaper a little farther north and west, near the Michigan border, so they ended up there with the financial help of their sponsors. They wanted to farm wheat and needed a good-sized piece of land to make a go of it."

Mammi nodded, her eyes sparkling with memories. "They started with wheat, but through the years that changed to corn and soy. Of course, when I was growing up, we had the usual livestock too. Chickens and a few head of beef. Some pigs. A nice garden, of course."

"So the farm where you grew up was real big, *Mammi*?" Christy asked.

She'd been part of the group who went to Switzerland with Ada, and I'd noticed that she also had taken a genuine interest in our family's history ever since.

"One hundred and ten acres with a woods behind the house," *Mammi* replied proudly. "We were a few miles northeast of Nappanee, not too far from the road to Goshen, so in the summer we would sell produce from a little shed just off the highway—and sometimes baked goods and flowers too. We'd drive our pony cart with all of our things in it and set up shop."

I glanced at *Mammi*, still worried she might say the wrong thing but gratified to see such a spark in her eyes. She didn't glow like this when she talked about her life there as a wife and mother—not surprising, considering she'd had an unhappy marriage to a mean husband—but the memories of her childhood were clearly happy ones.

"Did you have many brothers and sisters?" Izzy asked shyly before popping a forkful of chicken into her mouth.

"No sisters," *Mammi* replied. "I had one half brother and two full brothers, and I was the youngest."

One half brother. Just like me. I was tempted to poke Zed under the table, but the topic was still a little too raw.

"I did everything I could to keep up with the older kids," *Mammi* continued, shaking her head with a smile. "Not just my brothers, but also tons of cousins. My mother had eight siblings, so you can imagine how many cousins I had by the time I was born."

Izzy nodded, genuine interest on her face. "And they lived close by?"

Mammi nodded. "The nearby Mennonite district was made up almost entirely of my aunts and uncles and cousins."

"Mennonite?" I glanced across the table at Ezra. "I thought they were Amish."

"No, my mother was the only one on her side of the family to change over to Amish. My grandparents and aunts and uncles all stayed Mennonite, as far as I know."

"Oh." My mind raced. That meant Sarah had been raised *Mennonite* but had ended up joining the *Amish* church instead. My exact situation.

"Why did she become Amish?" Zed asked, the first words he'd spoken since the meal began.

Mammi tilted her head to the side. "That's a good question." She was quiet for a long moment, and then she said, "My father was Amish, so I suppose she did it because of him."

My heart began to race. "Wait a minute." I put down my knife and fork and let my hands fall to my lap. "Your mother joined the Amish church so she could marry the man she loved?" I looked toward *Mammi* as I said it, but my eyes met those of my mother instead, who gazed back at me with dismay. For a moment I realized the face she was giving me was the same one I had given Christy earlier, when she'd been talking about Ruth's crush on Ezra under the guise of feigned innocence, as if she didn't know such news would upset me. Christy hadn't been fooling anyone then, and neither was I now.

Even as I felt my cheeks flush with shame, I couldn't help but persist. "That's really amazing, *Mammi*. Imagine that. A Mennonite woman falls in love with an Amish man, and their families don't try to stop them from becoming the same religion and joining together in marriage."

I shifted my gaze across the table to look straight at Ezra, but his face was tilted downward, eyes glued to the table, cheeks and forehead a vivid red. My first thought was, *Shame on him for being too chicken to support me in this moment.*

My second thought was, *Shame on me for ruining a lovely gathering because I don't know how to keep my mouth shut.*

Clearing my throat, afraid I might suddenly start to cry, I pulled the napkin from my lap and excused myself, tossing it onto my chair and heading for the bathroom. Once there, I locked the door and just stared at myself in the mirror for a long while. I wasn't wrong to want to marry Ezra and embrace his church. They needed to hear the truth, but maybe this wasn't the place and time.

I knew my mother was probably furious, Ezra clearly mortified, and everyone else either scornful or disgusted or just plain embarrassed for me.

Eventually, once I had gained control of my emotions, I went back to the table. I was still torn between feeling half stubborn and half repentant, but no one seemed to notice either way. They didn't watch me as I took my seat nor even pause in the conversation. Their discussion had moved on to the topic of cheese making, and they continued with that as if nothing unusual had happened at all. Right or wrong about what I'd done, I was relieved to see that the moment had passed.

The rest of the meal, right down to Klara's delicious blueberry cobbler made from filling she said she'd canned last summer, progressed smoothly. *Mammi* and Alice were tired by the time we were all finished and retreated to the living room, where they settled on the couch. I began clearing the table while Izzy and Christy took Mel and Mat upstairs to put on their pajamas, and Will, Uncle Alexander, Ben, and Ezra, with Zed tagging along, all went outside to check on one of the cows that my uncle thought was in preterm labor. I wished I could go with the men. I really didn't relish the thought of having to face my mother just yet.

Ada soon disappeared, I assumed to check on the girls, leaving me alone with Nancy, Aunt Klara, and Mom. I just kept cleaning and ignored all of them until Nancy addressed me directly.

"So, Ella," she said as she took a stack of dishes from me and lowered them into the sink of sudsy water, "what are your plans for working now that you're done with school?"

"I've been doing a lot of babysitting, but I'd like to find a real job, any job. Then, once I've saved up enough money, I'll be going to baking school."

Mom gave me a pointed look but didn't say anything.

I wasn't as fortunate when it came to Nancy. "Baking school?" Her voice was incredulous. Amish women invariably learned to bake from their mothers and grandmothers. The thought of going away to school and paying a lot of money for it had to sound ridiculous to them.

"I'd like to be a pastry chef," I said, trying not to sound defensive. "But I'd settle for basic classes, if need be."

Nancy and Aunt Klara exchanged one of those looks. Fanciful Ella—that was me. I returned to the table for another stack of plates. When I came back with them, Nancy asked if I planned to go away to school or if there was one locally I could attend.

"I'm looking into both options," I said, retreating to the table for the glasses. I wasn't about to tell her I wanted to leave Lancaster County or why.

Aunt Klara and Nancy began talking about a recipe that had been in last week's *Budget*, the Plain newspaper all of us subscribed to, and I continued clearing the table. I'd tried the recipe they were talking about last Saturday. It was for a caramel pie. Aunt Klara said she thought it was too sweet. I kept my mouth shut, but I agreed. I was thinking about experimenting with it, maybe adding a chocolate-and-nut layer, perhaps make it resemble a sundae minus the ice cream. I tuned out the rest of their conversation as I thought about my recipe ideas, but after a while Ada came downstairs and began helping Mom dry the dishes while Aunt Klara continued to put food away.

At one point, they got on the subject of Zed's ever-increasing height.

"He's getting so tall and strong," Nancy said to my mother as she slipped a plate into the rinse water. "I think he's looking more and more like his *daed* all the time."

There was an awkward pause, which caused Nancy to glance around, bewildered. "Did I say something wrong?"

I placed the butter dish on the counter, near the stove. "It depends on how many people in the room know who Zed's father is." Each woman's face was expressionless. I turned to Nancy. "I think it's unanimous. Up until a couple of weeks ago, *I* didn't know. But it looks like everyone else did." My eyes landed on my mother. "And did you hear that Mom and Zed saw him last night? Spent the entire evening with him. He's moved back to Lancaster County, apparently."

"Marta?" Aunt Klara moved quickly from the refrigerator to my mother, her arm around her shoulders in an instant. "What's going on?"

Mom, in her typical fashion, stood statue still and answered, "Zed wanted to see Freddy, that's all. Ella chose not to."

I crossed my arms. "So now it seems there's just one mystery remaining. And that would be, who is Zed's mother?"

Instantly every face in the room went slack again.

"So how is Freddy?" Aunt Klara asked, turning her back to me.

"Don't do this," I stammered.

"Ella." It was Ada's sweet voice. Her sickening, annoying voice.

"Don't 'Ella' me!" My hands landed on my hips. "You all know something I have the right to know. Don't do this."

"There are no 'rights' here," Mom said, her head still turned away. "And now is not the time to discuss it. We'll talk about it later."

I spun around and stomped from the room as a wave of despair swept through me.

"I have to go. Tell Mom I'm walking home, would you?" I said to *Mammi* as I reached the door in the living room and slipped on my boots.

"Ella—" Alice was struggling to her feet. "It's cold and wet out there, not to mention pitch-black."

I nodded as I put on my cape. Mom would be leaving soon, but I wasn't going to sit around in the dark, so to speak, any longer. Besides, I had my cell phone, which would serve as a flashlight.

Izzy and Christy were descending the stairs with the little girls. At least they hadn't been present to see me humiliated.

Swallowing my fury for a moment, I kissed *Mammi*'s wrinkled cheek, gave Alice's hand a pat, and then hurried out the front door. By the time I was halfway up the lane, using my cell as a flashlight, Ezra was calling my name.

Without looking behind me, I pulled my hood down farther on my head and marched on. In no time, his running steps encroached on me.

"Ella!" He was a little out of breath. "Wait! We need to talk."

I waved my gloved hand, gesturing for him to leave me alone.

He was beside me now. "Where are you going?"

"Home."

"It's freezing out here."

"Not like it is inside."

"Come back and I'll get the buggy. I'll give you a ride."

I shook my head and picked up my pace.

"I feel bad about last night," he said.

I kept my head down.

"I didn't explain myself very well."

I lifted my face, meeting his eyes. "You heard *Mammi* in there, Ezra. My own great-grandmother was Mennonite, and then she joined the Amish church to marry her husband. It happened for them. It could happen for us."

"You're serious, aren't you?"

I nodded.

"It was different back then," he said. "Switching from Mennonite to Amish wasn't that big of a change. They didn't even have cars."

"They did. It was nineteen twenty."

Even in the darkness, I could see Ezra smile. "Maybe Model Ts. But no computers. Or baking school. And I certainly can't imagine you without your cell phone."

Before I could answer, Mom's car pulled up beside us, and Zed rolled down the window.

"Let's go," he called out.

As I opened the back door of the car, Ezra tipped his hat toward me, the rain dripping off the brim.

"I'll call you," he said. "Tonight. I promise."

I nodded curtly and climbed onto the backseat, realizing I'd said too much to him in the last two evenings, even for me. To counterbalance my deluge of words, I didn't say a thing to Mom or Zed. The rain was coming down in torrents and, again, the windshield wipers were having a hard time keeping up with the sheets of water slamming against the car. Mom slowed and then finally pulled over under the willow tree not far from Aunt Klara's. The defroster worked about as well as the stupid heater, and soon the car windows were completely fogged over. I leaned my head back against the seat.

Finally, Zed turned around. "Lydia Gundy," he said, his eyelids heavy.

"What?" I sat up straight.

"Lydia Gundy was my birth mother."

I gasped. "Will's first wife?"

He nodded.

My mind was spinning. Lydia had been a patient of Mom's, the one who had died during childbirth and nearly ended my mother's career. Lydia had been Christy and Mel and Mat's mom. How could she be Zed's birth mom too? How could I have not known that all of these years?

"Everyone knows?" I was whispering.

He nodded again. "Even Lexie."

"Ezra too?"

"Maybe." He glanced at Mom.

"I'm not sure," she said.

I sank down in the seat and crossed my arms. So I'd made an even bigger fool of myself in front of the Gundys than I'd thought. Worse, they had all kept this from me. I'd never felt so humiliated in all my life. My only hope was that Ezra didn't know.

Because if he had known and didn't tell me, I would never forgive him for that.

Five

Once we got home, I changed into my nightgown and robe, waited for Zed and Mom to go to bed, and then sat down at the computer to reread the articles about the deaths of Lydia and her baby. No wonder Zed had accessed them that day.

I didn't understand how Will and Ada and Ezra and everyone could pretend as if nothing had happened. Why were we still friends? Didn't they feel the shame of all of this? Back before Lydia was married to Will, she had become pregnant by Freddy, my own father—while he was still married to my mother! At least Lydia had then given that baby over to them to raise as their own once he was born. But no matter how well things turned out in the end, the way it all started was still a major disgrace.

Once I was done reading, I was more determined than ever to leave Lancaster. I would come back eventually, of course, but not until after my father was healthy and had gone on to greener pastures.

I searched the online white pages for a Darryl Kline in Nappanee, Indiana. Of course there would be a gazillion Klines, but I hoped just a handful with the first name of Darryl. There were two. I printed out the names and addresses. I'd have to ask *Mammi* which address was for her old dairy.

Then I searched for Rosalee Neff. There was only one—and she lived on Willow Lane! There was also a business listed under her name, Plain Treats. Was that a bakery? No way could that be possible. I jotted down the phone number, along with the address, wondering if I should call or write.

Next I went to Google Earth and typed in the address for the Home Place. As the image became larger and larger, I saw that the two properties bordered each other and the houses, as the crow flies, were less than a quarter mile apart, just as Mammi had said. I smiled, imagining Ezra working at the dairy and me working at the bakery. It was a possibility that was too, too good to be true. It had to be God's doing. Nothing less could explain it.

Even though my first choice was the French Pastry School in Chicago, I did a search for cooking schools in Indiana. A pastry school in Indianapolis popped up, and then classes at a Goshen grocery. Next I tried South Bend, which wasn't too far from Nappanee and the Home Place. The University of Notre Dame offered culinary classes, but that wasn't exactly what I had in mind. There were a few restaurants offering a series of classes, but none of them were schools.

I kept going down the list, stopping at Pierre's *Culinaire* Classes. I read the description, which said that Pierre was French, no surprise, and had trained at Cordon Bleu. He had a bakery and restaurant in town called Petit Paris. It sounded as if his cooking school was located behind the restaurant. He only took ten students at a time, and the site said the program was "perfect for those looking to open their own bakery someday. Business plans and practices are covered in the course work." The program was only three months, running from January through March, May through July, and September through November. It was quite the clever schedule, with time off at Christmas, in the spring, and summer. Maybe someday I would have a bakery and could offer similar classes. It would definitely be a way to generate more income. I couldn't find a "Tuition" link, but it was probably far more than I could afford.

I clicked on the "More Information" button and requested a packet. Though I was taking a slight risk by having it sent here, Mom had a post office box for her business, and I was the one who brought in the mail from the box at the end of our driveway. Chances were she would never see it—or, if she did, she would lump it in with all the other cooking schools I'd received info from and not notice the Indiana in the return address. As I logged off the computer, my phone vibrated in the pocket of my robe.

It was Ezra. *Finally.* I hurried up the stairs to my room, not answering until I was behind my closed door, a towel pushed against the bottom to muffle my voice, thinking about when Zed used to sit on the top step and eavesdrop on my conversations.

We chatted for a few minutes before he blurted out, "I can't imagine my life without you. I don't know what to do."

Come away with me to Indiana! was what I wanted to say, but I bit my tongue. For once I wasn't going to say too much.

"Really, Ella," he continued. "You make me crazy, you know? You're always scheming and pushing and testing."

I remained silent, hoping there was a "but" in there somewhere!

"But all of that is worth putting up with because you're also so alive and eager and determined. I've never known anyone who keeps coming out and swinging at life the way you do. For such a beautiful girl, you sure are tough and feisty, but you have a big heart. I love that about you. I love you."

"I love you, Ez," I whispered, glad I'd gotten my "but" and then some.

"Are you really serious about joining the Amish church?" His voice was a little shaky, which surprised me.

"Yes," I answered. I asked when he was going to start taking classes to join.

"When I get back."

The timing could work out perfectly. We could marry after he finished his stint on a dairy farm and I'd finished school.

"When are you going?"

"That depends on what Will finds for me, but probably soon."

I wasn't ready to share my crazy Indiana scheme with him yet, not before I had a chance to talk with *Mammi* again. For my plan to work, it would be best for it to look as if it wasn't my idea at all but hers instead. I didn't like being disingenuous, but I figured as long as I accomplished what she needed me to once I got there, I didn't owe anyone the whole truth about my reasons for wanting to go. Instead, I told Ezra I would check back at our favorite bakery in downtown Lancaster to see if they still had a position open.

He said he was going to be working hard for Will all week in the greenhouses.

I wanted to ask him if he knew who Zed's birth mother was, but I wasn't sure how to broach the topic. Finally he asked if I planned to meet my *daed* while he was here.

"No," I answered firmly, and then I saw my opening. "I'm afraid if I did, all I'd think about was his relationship with Zed's birth mother."

"Why? What does that have to do with you?"

"Are you kidding? It has everything to do with me. It has to do with—" I was about to say "with you too," given that Zed's birth mother was Ezra's late sister-in-law, but I changed course and said, "Well, you'd understand if you knew who she was. Do you know?"

There was a long pause. Then he said, "No. Why would I?"

"Because some of the people in your family do. I thought maybe they had told you."

"Of course not. That's not any of my business."

My face grew warm. "So you really don't know who she is?"

"No."

"And you don't want to know?"

"No."

"Even if it had something—"

"Ella, I said no."

"Okay." I grinned

"I'll try to call tomorrow night."

I imagined him outside in the barn, in the freezing cold.

"Sounds good," I said. "I'll talk to you then."

I held the phone in my hand for a moment, staring at the screen, overcome with loneliness. For comfort, I grabbed my magnifying glass and opened Sarah's book, flipping to the first drawing of the hen. The next entry wasn't dated, but it was after June 1903. She would have been thirteen or older. She wrote in cursive, *I found Alvin looking through this book today. He ran and showed it to Mamm before I could get it back. I can't draw* in code—but at least I can write in one. I told Mamm I wished Alvin would grow up. She told me I needed to accept God's will—and accept Alvin too.

Next was a lemon cream pie recipe, then a bread recipe, and then a recipe for cabbage chowder. The next three entries were written in code. I reread the next one, not in code, dated December 27, 1910.

Mrs. Gus Stoll. With no Alvin around, I won't need to use my code anymore.

What is the recipe for a good marriage? Women have told me to keep the house tidy…to cook a delicious meal every night…to never to go to bed angry… to put my husband before myself…to never criticize him in public. Respect is what Gus needs most, I think.

Then three months later she wrote, *Gus is always on the alert. Always has a plan. Always moving. Sometimes I just want him to sit still, but he is like a hawk, always circling around. Always absorbed in a task.*

I sat back, thinking for a moment.

He is like a hawk.

A hawk.

The symbol for Gus was the hawk! I grinned, feeling like a code breaker.

Still smiling, I continued reading, the next entries dated more than a year later.

June 28, 1912—Recipe for a baby… The wise woman near LaGrange told me to use red clover blossom. I've been making a tea and drinking it every morning. I am ready to be a hen with a brood of babies. Gus prays for a baby for us. Still no baby.

September 5, 1912—The wise woman recommends black cohosh now too. I'm taking it along with the red clover blossom. Still no baby. Mother Stoll asked me the other day if I had any unconfessed sin. I love my husband, but I have to say I don't love living on his parents' farm.

October 10, 1912—Gus was injured in a hunting accident. Please God, I don't care if You never give me a baby. Just let my husband live. I've been caring for him night and day, doing all I can.

October 17, 1912—We buried Gus in the old cemetery outside of town. Alvin feels horrible. I almost think it's harder on him than on me. His gun discharged as he jumped down from a boulder. He thought Gus was behind him and wasn't as careful as he should have been, but Gus had circled around in front of him. The bullet entered Gus's back and then out his stomach. At least he was conscious until the last day. He forgave Alvin, who is still beside himself with grief. Gus was so kind to him.

I strive to follow Gus's example, but my heart is so heavy.

I will never remarry. Never be a mother. (I was still hoping, but I know for sure it's not meant to be, now that Gus is gone.)

November 28, 1912—I've moved back to the Home Place. Steeping a cup of sage, hoping it will help me rally. No one has told me to stop feeling sorry for myself, but if I don't snap out of it pretty soon, they probably should. Alvin mopes around worse than I do.

November 3, 1912—I caught Alvin with my book. He's twenty-five and much too old for that. I guess it's back to the code. I do wish he would grow up. I think he feels somehow responsible for me now, but the truth is I'm much more capable than he is.

The next entries were all in code, even the dates. I felt as heartbroken as I did the first time I read it. Her husband, dead, at the hands of her brother. Sure, it was an accident, but what a tragedy. It made me all the more curious as far as Alvin. What was up with him?

I didn't understand how Sarah could marry again after losing Gus. If Ezra died, I knew I'd never marry. I closed the book, not able to bear going on to read about her second husband again. I fell asleep thinking about the Home Place, longing to visit it more than ever.

The next morning I called Plain Treats, hoping it really was a bakery as I suspected. No one answered, so I left a message, saying I was thinking about moving to Indiana and wondered if they were hiring. I decided not to say I was a relative, afraid Rosalee might spill the beans to someone back here.

In the evening she left a message in return. I was babysitting for a family in our church and changing a diaper when she called, so I couldn't answer. Her voice was soft and somewhat tentative, typical of an older Amish woman using the phone. She said the bakery wasn't hiring but might be in a couple of months. She told me to check back then.

The *bakery* wasn't hiring. While I was disappointed that she had no openings at the moment, I was thrilled to learn that I'd been correct. Plain

Treats really was a bakery, and it was located at the Home Place, right next door to a dairy farm.

Thank You, Lord, for making Your will for Ezra and me so clear.

I spent the next stretch of days looking online for jobs and researching Indiana more when Zed wasn't home. Mom had two births that week, so she was out quite a bit. When she was home, I mostly tried to avoid her. It was easy to avoid Zed. All I had to do was stay away from the computer, which he monopolized day and night when he was around.

On Thursday Mom had several appointments near *Mammi's* so I hitched a ride with her and spent the morning with my grandmother. I'd made cranberry scones the night before using a recipe from Sarah's book, and I brought some along to have with our tea. She was in a chatty mood, telling me about a visit the day before with Ada and the twins.

"Those little girls." She laughed. "I think they take after their Uncle Ezra. They're always up to something."

"Speaking of, I'm not sure you heard, but Ezra's parents are thinking about buying a dairy, and before they do, they want Ezra to work on someone else's dairy farm to learn the trade."

"Yes, I believe Klara and Alexander were talking about that just the other day," *Mammi* replied. "Alexander has a cousin with a dairy farm down near Chambersburg, and he was thinking that might make a nice option."

I looked at her, wishing I knew if she'd heard the real reason they were sending Ezra away or not. I hoped not.

"Actually, I was wondering if you thought *your* old dairy farm would be a possibility. Maybe he could go out there and work for the Kline family."

Her face fell into a frown. "All the way to Indiana? That's so far."

"That's what the Gundys want—to send him far from Lancaster County so he can broaden his horizons."

"I see. Well, at least that explains why Klara was skeptical of the Chambersburg idea. That wouldn't take Ezra very far at all."

I exhaled. Judging by that remark, *Mammi* obviously hadn't heard the full story, thank goodness.

I took out my piece of paper and explained that I'd been doing some research on the computer. "There are two Darryl Klines near Nappanee, but I figured out which one lives next door to the Home Place. Do you think I should give his name and address to Ezra?"

Mammi squinted at me. "I think it's up to his family to find a place for him."

I folded the paper and put it back in my apron pocket, feeling a little sheepish. I'd fallen to a new low.

Then she surprised me. "I'll talk to Alice."

"No," I said. "I shouldn't have brought it up." I regretted trying to manipulate her.

"She's coming over this afternoon. I'll mention it and see what she thinks."

I went to pour the Earl Grey and serve the scones. *Mammi* wouldn't remember what we'd talked about by the time Alice arrived—at least, that's what I told myself. While we were waiting for the tea to cool, I pulled Sarah's journal from my backpack. I asked her about the little flower, saying I was sure it was edelweiss.

"Oh, *ya*."

"I thought so. It looks like the edelweiss carved into the side of the wooden box Lexie has."

Lexie and Ada both had carved wooden boxes just like the one I kept under my bed. All three boxes had been made by our ancestor Abraham Sommers, and though the carving on the lid of mine featured the Home Place, Lexie's showed Abraham's residence in Switzerland, a gorgeous mansion called Amielbach. Ada's featured his childhood home and business, a bakery, in the Swiss town of Frutigen.

"How about this?" I pointed to the drawing of the alpine horn, hoping she could see it. "Did your grandfather have one of these?"

"He brought his with him from Switzerland."

"How big was it?"

"As tall as he was," she said. "I don't know how he had room for it on the ship, much less once they got here and had to make their way across the country to Indiana." She leaned back and closed her eyes. "I remember it as a child. He used to play 'Amazing Grace' on it, out in the pasture, under the willow tree by the pond."

"Wow."

She opened her eyes and met my gaze. "Wow is right. It wasn't still at the Home Place by the time I was grown. I don't know where it ended up. Maybe one of his older sons got it."

I held the book open to one of the recipe pages that had symbols drawn in across the top and bottom.

"Remember when I said I thought the symbols represented people?" I asked.

Mammi nodded.

"Well, I've been pursuing that line of thought, and I think I've figured some of them out."

She gasped, her face lighting up like a lantern with a sparkling clean globe.

Grinning, I pointed to the page and explained. "See this hawk? It represents Sarah's first husband, Gus Stoll. This owl is her second husband, Clive Chapman. I'm guessing the eagle is David Berg, her third husband. Can you think of some reason she would have chosen an eagle to represent your father?"

"I have no idea," she said. "What about the hen? You mentioned that before."

"Right." I flipped through the pages. "It's the only symbol Sarah included through the entire journal from beginning to end. I'm guessing it represents her. An ongoing self-portrait of sorts."

"Oh, Ella. I think you're figuring this out. We need to get you to the Home Place—and soon."

"I would really like that," I said, calmly, "though let's not share that idea with anyone else just yet, okay?" That was all I needed, for her to blab to Ezra's grandmother about sending me to Indiana!

Mammi nodded, a faraway look in her eyes. "*Ya.* Of course, dear."

"When was the last time you had contact with anyone from Indiana?"

"Rosalee wrote to me faithfully for a while, but then she had some troubles of her own and I didn't hear from her as often. I can't remember the last time I received a letter from her…" Her voice trailed off. "And I really didn't keep in touch with anyone else."

"What about your uncle Alvin? Did he have any children?"

"No, he never married."

"Do you remember him?"

"Oh, no. He died long before I was born. He lived at the Home Place his entire life, and my mother spoke quite fondly of him."

I couldn't help but think of Alvin's snooping when it came to Sarah's book. "Really? She was positive toward him."

"Oh, *ya*. But also with regret. She said she didn't fully comprehend until much later than she should have that there was something different about him. She said he was always childlike, and it took her years to accept and appreciate him for who God made him to be."

I wondered when Sarah's opinion of her brother changed.

Mammi yawned, so I closed the book and asked if she needed a rest.

"Yes, but I'd like to have tea first. And one of whatever that is you brought. I always look forward to your treats."

"Well, then, you'll appreciate these especially." With a grin, I unveiled the plate of scones. Eyeing them expectantly, she chose one and took a bite. Her eyes widened with delight.

"Oh, Ella, God bless you! These are the exact scones my mother used to make! You must have followed her recipe."

"To the letter." I sat back and watched as she relished the confection. Despite the many years that showed in the wrinkles on her face, it wasn't difficult at all to picture her as a little girl, enjoying her mother's treats.

Thinking of that little girl, regardless of my own ulterior motives at play here, I really did want to break the code for her sake.

I wanted to bring her whatever truth of her mother's she'd waited a lifetime to learn.

The next evening my cousin Lexie called.

"Just to check in," she said, but I was certain Mom told her Zed had revealed his birth mother to me.

I was touched that she cared, really, but I was still feeling raw.

"Why didn't you tell me?"

"I'm sorry," she said. "It wasn't my place."

"How long have you known it was Lydia?"

"Since that day at *Mammi*'s, when James led the family come-to-the-truth session."

"You mean the family come-to-just-part-of-the-truth session?"

"Ella, that's not fair. This other information was Zed's. Your mom couldn't tell you before Zed was ready to know."

"Freddy Bayer is my father too." I winced. Now I was sounding as if that was a good thing. "I had a right to know."

"I know it's hard. I feel for you, I really do."

I muttered a thank-you.

"So when are you going to see Freddy?"

"I'm not."

"Why?" Her voice was incredulous.

"Because I don't want to."

"Aren't you curious?"

"No," I answered. "And what's up with you? You never met your birth mother."

"That's different. She's thousands of miles away. If she showed up in Oregon, you bet I'd make a point to see her."

"How's James?" I asked, changing the subject.

"Good."

"When are you two going to start a family?"

"Ella." Her voice was soft but firm.

"Oh, come on. It's not like you're Amish. I can ask you things like that. You're a nurse-midwife, for goodness' sake."

She changed the subject anyway, asking how my job hunt was coming along. Because there wasn't much to report, we only talked for a few more minutes before wrapping up the call.

A little while later, Ezra sent me a text, asking if I wanted to go for a ride on his motorcycle. The rain had finally stopped, and it was unseasonably warm, even though snow was predicted for the next day. I kept my emotions in check as I said yes.

I undid my bun and shook out my hair, changed into my jeans and a sweater, and put on my warm down jacket. I stayed in my room until I heard his motorcycle turn into the drive, and then I rushed down the stairs and nearly got out the door before I heard Mom's voice from the kitchen.

"Ella!"

"I'll be home soon." I slipped through the front door, jumped down the steps, took my helmet from Ezra, and climbed on behind him.

"There's a party down by the canal," he said. "Want to go?"

I shrugged and then pulled my helmet on my head.

"How about you?" I usually didn't defer to him.

"Not really."

"You know what sounds good?" I fastened the helmet.

He shook his head.

"Hot chocolate." I positioned my arms around his waist.

His face was still pointed toward me and a look of relief passed through his eyes. "At Nick's?"

I nodded. We hadn't been there together for a couple of months, although I'd been in twice since then looking for a job. It was hard to put my finger on exactly what was so appealing about the place. It was a strange mix of Italian and American desserts, soups, and breads in an old brick building with lots of charm, but the decor was a little outdated and actually pretty tacky.

Thankfully it was open well into the evening.

Ezra usually liked parties. At the first one I went to with him, I drank too much and really regretted it, but after that one bad experience, I learned to enjoy them. I met a lot of people—both Amish and *Englisch*. I met kids from my school I never would have known before, kids who, once they saw me at a party, thought of me in a whole different way. At least they noticed me after that, even if before then I'd been absolutely invisible to them.

Everyone loved Ezra. He was funny and friendly. He didn't drink much, and he seemed to get along with everyone. If a hot topic came up, he'd change the subject with a joke. People were drawn to him, including the *Englisch* girls. "You're so lucky," they would say to me. "He's the best guy around."

I snuggled closer to him, trying to stop shivering. It was too cold to be out on a motorcycle, even if it was warmer than it had been. In a couple of months it would be motorcycle weather, though. I wondered what it would be like to take his motorcycle to Indiana but then caught myself. There was no reason for me to get my hopes up.

By the time we reached Nick's Bakery, I'd stopped shivering. It really would be the perfect place for me to work, somewhere I could get both baking and waitressing experience. I led the way into the shop, my helmet under my arm. I didn't recognize the girl at the counter, so I asked if she was new. She said she was, hired just last week.

I tried not to pout as I placed my order for a cup of hot chocolate and a *pain au chocolat*. Ezra mimicked my French accent as he ordered, shooting me a teasing look.

"What does she have that I don't?" I asked as we sat down at the table.

Ezra pulled a napkin from the dispenser. "Experience?"

I slouched against the bench. "How much experience does it take?"

He shrugged and smiled. I glanced around the eating area. It was as boring as could be. Old vinyl booths lined the walls. Cheaply framed posters of European landmarks—the Eiffel Tower, Big Ben, the Coliseum, and the Pantheon—hung on the white walls above the booths, but that was it as far as decor. I had no idea if Nick was French or Italian or maybe even Greek. We actually only saw girls around my age working in the bakery.

"If I owned this place—"

Ezra interrupted me. "I know, I know. You'd paint."

"And add plants."

"And better display cases." Ezra smiled.

I nodded, aware that I spouted off my ideas every time we visited the bakery. I focused on the Eiffel Tower. What would be really cool would be to study in France, but if I couldn't study there, a French bakery in Indiana would be—

"Ella?"

"Sorry," I said, turning my attention back to Ezra.

"I was telling you about Will."

"I'm listening."

"He got on my case about a sprinkler."

He continued to complain about his big brother chastising him for not fixing it properly. "But I had. It turned out the pipe had broken." He loved Will, but sometimes his big brother was much harder on him than their *daed* was.

When the waitress brought our hot chocolate and pastries, Ezra thanked her warmly. He didn't have to be so nice, especially not to the person who had gotten the job I wanted.

Once she'd walked away, I asked Ezra who was going to be Will's right-hand man after he left.

"That's a good question." His mouth spread into a grin. "Maybe he'll finally appreciate me after I'm gone." His grin faded. "I think he found a place for me."

"Really?" I wrapped my hands around my mug.

"Will called the guy yesterday, and it looks like it might be the one."

"Oh?" I took a sip of hot chocolate, hoping he couldn't hear the pounding of my heart.

"I think Will likes the idea of this particular place because it's so far away."

I raised my eyebrows as I put my mug down. "Where is it?"

"Indiana."

It took everything I had to hold in my glee, but he didn't even seem to notice.

"Do you know what town?"

"No," Ezra replied, "but I think the info came from your grandmother. That's how Will made the connection. The name of the owner is Kline. I remember you said you had family out there."

"Yeah." I took another sip of hot chocolate.

My plan was actually falling into place! Now, if only I could get myself out there too, before anyone found out the full scope of what I had in mind.

Surely I could make that happen. Ezra probably wouldn't be leaving for a few months, long enough for me to hunt for a job long distance and earn some more money here in the meantime. I already had a fair amount in my savings account from all the babysitting I'd done through the years.

I half listened as Ezra chatted away, realizing my first two contingencies had been met:

Ezra's dairy job would have to be in Indiana.

That job would have to be located within a reasonable distance of the Home Place.

Check and check. That left just three more:

Mammi *would have to help me get permission from the current owners to come visit the Home Place.*

I would have to figure out how to get there and where I would stay once I did.

My family would have to get over the realization that Ezra and I would be together again, despite their best efforts to keep us apart.

The more I thought about things, the more the whole plan solidified in my mind. This wasn't going to be just some extended visit on the pretense of helping out *Mammi* with her search. This would become my life for a time, for as long as it was Ezra's life. We would go out there together. We would live separately while in Indiana, but we would come back home the same way we'd gone. Together.

That meant I would need a job, an apartment, and enrollment in a baking school. All of the above in Indiana and near the Home Place.

What had felt impossible before suddenly didn't feel like a very big deal at all now. We'd already crossed the biggest hurdle, which was to get Ezra all set up to work and live at the Kline's dairy farm in Indiana.

Now that we had that, nothing could stand in our way.

Six

I began spending every moment I wasn't babysitting or cleaning houses at the library, so much so that Mom came to expect it. I told her I was researching and applying for jobs, which was true. It was also true I could have done ninety-nine percent of it at home on our computer, but it was nice to be out of the house—and not have anyone looking over my shoulder to see that the jobs I was applying for were all in Indiana.

I'd take my lunch and sometimes, if the weather was warm, sit on a bench outside the library to eat it. I began to notice a man hanging around across the street. He was tall and wore a ski parka and a baseball cap pulled down so I couldn't see his eyes. Even so, I had a feeling I knew exactly who he was.

One evening, when Ezra picked me up at the library, as I pulled on my helmet I noticed the man walking toward us, but then he stopped abruptly. As I climbed on the back of Ezra's bike, he just stood, staring at us. Ezra revved the engine and then pulled out into the light traffic. As we passed the man a few feet away, he turned from us so I still couldn't see his face. I shivered as the wind took my breath away, ducking my head against Ezra's back.

I saw the man lurking across the street a few more times over the next several weeks. I couldn't help but think it was Freddy. According to Zed, he was renting a room in downtown Lancaster.

"Like at a cheap hotel?" I stirred the gravy with my good whisk as we talked.

"No. Like in someone's house. It's an old lady with an extra bedroom. She rents it out to him."

"Creepy." But as I spoke I decided it was a brilliant idea. That's how living in Indiana could actually be affordable. That night, when Mom returned home, I asked her about Freddy and if she'd told him I spent a fair amount of time at the library.

"I suppose I did," she said, taking off her cape.

I slumped down on to the couch and told her about the man I'd seen a few times downtown.

"He's curious, that's all. I asked him not to approach you. I told him you're not ready."

She went into the kitchen. I heard the refrigerator door open and close. And then the water running. It was past ten. Zed was already in his room.

Mom settled down at the dining room table, a bowl of yogurt and a glass of water in front of her.

"There are leftovers," I said.

"Thanks, but I'm not very hungry." As she bowed her head, I thought of Zed as a baby. It was funny, but I had no memory of Freddy. However, I clearly remembered sitting on the sofa, my legs out straight with Zed draped over my middle while I held his bottle. I loved him so much. Mom always said I had mothering down, right from the beginning, and what a big help I was to her.

I honestly couldn't imagine my life without Zed. Our home would have seemed so empty with just Mom and me. For the first time, I questioned whether I should leave. I managed most of the cooking, cleaning, and washing. How would they get along without me? And when Mom was gone on a birth, Zed and I always had each other. What would he do alone?

When she raised her head, I leaned toward her. "Why do you think Zed feels okay with seeing Freddy while I don't?"

"You were older—three when he left. You have subconscious memories of him."

"Was I close to him?"

A faint smile crossed her face. "You were more of a mama's girl. And he was distracted a lot of the time by his own self-made misery. But, yes, you were fond of him. He adored you, in his way, and you loved him, the way a three-year-old loves her daddy."

Daddy. I winced at the word.

Mom pushed her chair away from the table as if she were ready to go. "Any other questions?"

I shook my head.

"I'll ask Freddy to keep his distance." She stood, as if it took great effort, and then put her things in the kitchen and said goodnight. I followed her upstairs a few minutes later.

The next day I found a couple of rooms for rent in Nappanee and also in Goshen. The Mennonite college was there, so I figured I would fit right in as far as my age and looking for a place to stay in someone's house. South Bend was also an option. Nappanee was by far the closest to where Ezra would be living and to the Home Place. I sent emails requesting more information from three different homeowners.

There were several waitressing jobs listed in that area, including one at a café right downtown. They weren't taking online applications, but I jotted down the address so I could mail an inquiry right away.

And I still hadn't broached the subject of going to Indiana with Ezra. Sure, I'd introduced my idea in theory, but I hadn't let him know I really was serious about it, that I had been spending a lot of time actually trying to make it work.

My opportunity came in early March. Ezra sent me a text on a Sunday afternoon and asked if I wanted to go to a singing. I accepted the invitation, but when we were on the way there, he got a phone call from Will. Ada wasn't feeling well, and Hannah and her family all had the flu, as did Christy. They had sent Izzy home, hoping she wouldn't get it, so Will needed Ezra to come watch the twins.

We headed straight to Will's, but when Ezra drove the buggy up their driveway, I was surprised to see Mom's car in front of the house. It only took me a second to guess what was going on. Ada was pregnant—I'd been right about that. Or maybe she had been. Something was wrong for Mom to be there on a Sunday evening.

I hesitated as Ezra stopped the buggy and told me to go on in while he unhitched the horse and put him in the barn.

"I'll be along shortly," he said.

I knocked on the kitchen door and stepped inside. Will was at the stove, stirring a pot. Mel and Mat were at the table.

"Ella," Will said, obviously surprised to see me. The little girls scampered down from the table, rushed toward me, and hugged my legs. For the first time ever, it struck me that they were as related to my brother Zed as I was. He and I shared a father, but he and they had shared a mother. Suddenly, my heart was filled with gratitude that Lydia had been willing to give up custody when Zed was born, and that my mother had been willing to adopt and raise him despite the facts of his paternity. That must have been incredibly difficult for both women. As much as I didn't understand Lydia's decision, and as crazy as my mother made me sometimes, I would always be grateful to them both.

"We were on our way to a singing," I explained. "We were closer to here than my house, so Ezra brought me along. He'll be in as soon as he deals with his horse."

Will nodded. "I was heating up soup for the girls." He handed me the spoon. "If you don't mind taking care of this, I'll go back in with Ada."

I put the spoon down on the counter and wiggled out of my cape, hanging it by the back door, and then told the girls to go wash their hands. I hoped they wouldn't get the flu too—or give it to me. I ladled up the soup. It was thick, with tender noodles and lots of chicken. When the girls returned, I told them to blow on the hot liquid to cool it down. By the time Ezra joined us, they were nearly done.

As they finished up, he told me how much he would miss Will's girls when he was in Indiana.

"I spend more time here than at my *mamm* and *daed*'s," he said.

I knew they would miss him too. The twins carefully carried their empty bowls and spoons to the counter and then headed down the hall to wash their hands again.

"I wish I had a brother my age who was going too. It would be so much easier if someone I knew were going with me."

I glanced around, glad we were alone. "I could go."

He looked startled. "No, Ella. We already talked about that—"

"I found a room to rent online," I said quickly, interrupting his protest. I'd heard back from all of the landlords and decided on which one I thought would be the best fit, a really nice-sounding woman named Penny. "And several waitressing jobs that are open. I have quite a bit in savings already. I'm certain I could pull it off."

"But I'm not going to get married before I join the church."

"Of course not. And I'm not going to get married before I go to baking school. I found one in South Bend, which is less than an hour's drive from Nappanee." I didn't say I didn't have any idea if I could figure out how to get there. Or how I would pay for it. The packet still hadn't come in the mail, so I had no idea how much it would actually cost. "That's as far as I'm thinking. But it would be nice for both of us to have a friend." I wouldn't have a problem, especially if I was in the same town as Ezra.

"I just want to get out of here," I said. "I'm feeling more and more pressure to deal with my dad. And I've wanted to go to Indiana to meet my relatives ever since Ada came back from Switzerland and gave me the box. It's the perfect opportunity, Ezra, for both of us. Besides, my grandmother wants me to go there for her sake too."

As I finished, the little girls came running into the room. Before he could respond, they were up on the bench and crawling on his back.

Seven

I left with Mom without seeing Ada. Will walked both of us out to the car, thanking my mother and then adding a nod of gratitude to me. I hadn't done anything except dish up soup. Ezra was the one who read the girls book after book after book. He was the one who told them to put their pajamas on and brush their teeth. He was the one who told them jokes and then tucked them into bed.

Mom was silent until we reached the highway. Then she let out a sigh, and even though it was dark I could tell her eyes were teary by the sound of her voice.

"Did Ada have a miscarriage?" I asked.

"You know I can't answer that," she responded, and then she swiped her index finger under her eyes. It would be breaking confidentiality if she told me, even though Ada was my cousin. "Actually, I'm not sure."

It was pretty clear what had happened. She was probably just trying to be vague because she felt as if I already knew too much. I couldn't remember how long it had been since I'd seen her cry.

"I'm turning into an old softie," she said. "A lot of things hit me tonight."

I gazed out at the pastures still covered in snow. Poor Ada. I knew how much she loved being a mom and could only guess how much she wanted

91

to add another baby to her and Will's family. She must have gotten pregnant soon after her wedding.

As Mom neared the covered bridge, my phone beeped. It was a text from Ezra. I quickly opened it.

Thought through what you said about Indiana. I'd like it if you came along. I'm leaving in a week. Let's talk more. Ez

I quickly closed my phone and did my best not to smile, but Mom was so lost in her own thoughts that she didn't notice my change in expression or even ask me, as she usually did, whom the text was from. I waited an hour until I texted Ezra back, and then I simply sent one word. *Cool.* Another ingredient for my "recipe for life" was coming together.

Two days later, Ezra came by the library on his motorcycle and asked if I wanted a ride home. It was a warm March day. As I walked beside him out to his bike, I noticed that his hair had been cut, back into the bowl shape he'd avoided for the last four years. He probably thought that would go over better in Indiana.

"How about if we go to the park first?"

"Sure," I said, although I would have rather gone somewhere more private.

The green shoots of daffodils were managing to emerge, even though winter had hung on so late. I gulped in the air, happy to be on Ezra's bike again. I felt such freedom as we zipped around the block and down the street. A sense of hope filled me as we sped along.

The park was filled with people, but Ezra led the way to a bench near the playground. The voices of children clanged around us. I watched a mother carrying an infant while chasing a toddler. Another mother was trying to wrestle a little boy into a stroller.

"Have you made the arrangements to rent a room?"

"I told the woman I was interested."

"And you talked to your mom?"

"I'm eighteen, Ez."

"Not for another month," he answered. "Marta Bayer is the last person in the world I want to offend."

I wrinkled my nose. "You know how hard she is to talk to."

Ezra stared at me, a frown on his face.

Feeling chastised, I said, "I'll do my best."

We sat there for a moment, both staring off at the playground, me wondering why I felt so unsettled about something I wanted so badly. Chalking it up to nerves, I broke the silence.

"You know what would be cool?"

He shook his head.

"If we could take your bike."

He laughed. "I'd have to hire a driver with a trailer. That wouldn't go over well with the family."

"Or, if the weather is good, we could drive it out."

"It's a long trip, Ella. Almost ten hours. Something like that. And I doubt if the family I'm staying with would be thrilled to have me show up on my bike."

I pulled my knees to my chest, my feet flat on the bench, my dress tucked around my legs. "Maybe we could store it at wherever I end up staying."

He shook his head. "As usual, you've thought of everything."

"Not everything. I just like to brainstorm, that's all." I hugged my legs tighter. "We could wait to decide, once we know what the weather's like."

We talked a little longer and then Ezra put his arm around me. I snuggled closer. With all of the angst of figuring out our futures, we hadn't had much time for us, not like we used to. He leaned toward me, his chin brushing the top of my head. I turned my face toward his, and then, to my surprise, he leaned down and kissed me, tenderly. In the park. In public. In front of all of Lancaster if, in fact, anyone was watching. When he pulled away, he had a grin on his face.

"Thank you," he said.

"For?" I stammered, sure he wasn't referring to the kiss, but I had no idea what he meant.

"Going with me."

It was my turn to smile. "Isn't it amazing how everything has fallen into place? Obviously, it's what God wants for us."

Ezra gave a little nod and then popped up from the bench, taking my hand and pulling me up beside him.

"We'll have the adventure of our lives," I said. "Just wait and see."

That evening I sent an email of confirmation to Penny, and then I checked the online job listings again. The waitress job at the café was still open. I decided I would call in the morning about it. I finished filling out an application to another restaurant, online, as Zed came up behind me. I turned around and glared at him, wondering if he'd seen anything. If so, was he going to rat me out to Mom?

"Give me a minute," I barked.

Once I was done, I turned the computer over to him and then looked at what he was doing. He'd saved clips of different videos to a program he'd managed to scrape enough money together to buy. He had footage from Lexie's wedding, clips of the three wooden boxes our ancestor Abraham Sommers had carved, and footage of Aunt Klara's house. He'd also shot footage of horses and carriages around the county and the covered bridge near our home.

I knew he'd used the camera on my phone at Lexie's wedding.

"How'd you film all of this?"

"Your phone."

I nodded. "And?"

"A friend's phone." He lowered his voice. "Sometimes Mom's phone."

"Zed!" The thing was, Mom probably had no idea she had a video camera on her phone. I looked him in the eyes. "What are you going to do with all of it?" As I asked the question, a video of the man I was sure was Freddy came on the screen. I leaned closer to the monitor. "Is that him?" He wasn't any clearer than he'd been on the street corner. It was the same coat and cap, but I still couldn't see his face. He was in downtown Lancaster though, walking toward the camera.

"Yep."

"You see him without Mom?"

"I have a couple of times."

I made a face.

"He's on disability, Ella. He gets lonely—although he helps out at the soup kitchen on weekends."

I hadn't listened very carefully the few times Mom had tried to talk with me about Freddy. It sounded as though he had some sort of digestive problems that made it hard for him to work.

Zed clicked on another clip. It was of me on Ezra's motorcycle. You could see my face but not his.

"What are you going to do with all of these?" I asked.

He shrugged. "I just like to play with the clips. Rearrange scenes, that sort of thing."

I'd been annoyed with Zed ever since Freddy returned, but I grew teary at the thought of how much I would miss him. He was a constant, steady presence in my life. There was no doubt I'd taken him for granted his entire existence.

I wouldn't be around for the end of his freshman year. Or for his sophomore year. And maybe ever again. I always thought he was much too responsible to get into any kind of trouble, but now that I knew he was Freddy's son, that added a whole new set of ingredients. What if he took after his father? What if it turned out he hadn't fallen far from the family tree?

On Sunday afternoon I talked Mom into dropping me off at *Mammi's* while she went to check on a first-time mother who had been having contractions on and off for a few days. *Mammi* was happy to see me and asked me to make us a pot of tea. Aunt Klara and Uncle Alexander were still away at church. *Mammi* had been fighting a cold and had chosen to stay home.

After I served her tea, I positioned a straight-back chair close to her recliner and sat down.

"How goes the code breaking?" She leaned toward me, a twinkle in her eye.

I smiled. "Well, we're not there yet."

Her face fell, and I realized that when she saw me show up this afternoon, she must have assumed I had come with big news. I felt terrible.

"Don't look so sad," I told her quickly, "it's not like I haven't made any progress at all."

"No?"

"No. I've been working on it. Besides, we knew this would take time. Be patient, okay? I really feel as though I'll have a breakthrough on this stuff very soon."

I bit my lip, wanting so badly to tell her everything, to tell her I was about to do exactly what she'd been hoping for all along, go to Indiana. To the Home Place. Once there, I had no doubt I would find some clues or leads or explanations or something that would help me figure this out for her.

Changing the subject before I gave in to the urge to spill all, I pulled the carved box from the flannel pillowcase I'd stashed it in.

"I brought this," I said. "I'd like to hear more about the Home Place, and I thought having the image of it might help."

Mammi reached out for the box and I passed it to her. She handled it with such care. She knew as well as I did that all three boxes—mine, Ada's, and Lexie's—had been carved from sycamore wood well over a century ago.

"What can you tell me about the different buildings in the picture?" I prodded.

She studied it for a long time, carefully running her fingers over the carved ridges and dips of the wood. Finally, she began to talk, saying that the first part of the house had been erected in the late 1870s—and that the original tile roof was still on it a hundred years later when she left Indiana. The big barn had been built first, then the one-room front part of the house, but within a few years the structure was turned into a two-story house, and later the two wings were added. A *daadi haus* had been built as a separate structure for her grandparents when her parents had purchased the property.

Once I'd received the architectural run-down, I asked more questions about the people who'd lived there, and soon she was off and running again.

"We were a small family, just six total," she said, "though there was a seventh, a baby who died. As you know, I was the youngest, and the only girl. My oldest brother, Caleb, left home when I was still little and moved to Lancaster County, so I never knew him all that well when I was growing up."

"How about the other two? Were you close to them?"

I saw a flash of something in her eyes, some pain of long ago that for a moment bubbled to the surface. Then she answered my question. "Of the three, the brother I was closest to was Gerry, the father of Rosalee, the niece I was telling you about who lives there now."

Feeling guilty as I held in the fact that Rosalee and I had actually played phone tag with each other just recently, I asked what made her decide to leave Indiana and move to Pennsylvania.

"When Caleb first came to Lancaster County, the woman he married had no brothers, so it was arranged that he would run his in-laws' farm. Many years later, after Caleb's wife died, he needed a housekeeper, so my mother urged me to come out and work for him that way. It ended up being a good move. He was kind to me. After he died, of course, the farm still belonged to his late wife's family, who had no obligation to my children or me. But they were also kind. They let me lease the property, and eventually I was able to buy it from them."

I nodded, knowing that out of all the descendants of Abraham Sommers, *Mammi* had been the one to inherit Amielbach, the old family mansion back in Switzerland. When she sold it, she'd used the proceeds to purchase this farm.

"Did you ever go back to Indiana, at least to visit?" I crossed my legs to get more comfortable.

"No. Once we left there, I never looked back."

"Why?"

"Oh, Ella…We've gone through hard times here in Lancaster County too, but nothing like back in Indiana." She took a raggedy breath and then stared off toward the window. "There was too much pain there. I know I speak glowingly of my time at home when I was a little girl, but every childhood eventually comes to an end. The realities of adulthood can be far more cruel…" She turned back to meet my eyes. "For one thing, I'm sure you're aware that my husband was…well, that he was difficult."

Difficult? From my understanding, he was downright abusive to her and to their children. But of course I didn't say that out loud. Instead, I just nodded.

"And there were other hurts, other sorrows. It would have been too hard to face all that again. I didn't even go back for Gerry's funeral." Her voice trailed off, her eyes growing moist. "He died ten years after we left. He had a heart attack out in a field." She sighed, glancing down at her wrinkled hands, dotted with age spots. "Maybe I was wrong to stay away, but I was weak."

"*Mammi*, can I ask you something?" I said softly, leaning forward and fixing my eyes on hers.

Looking back at me, she nodded.

"Why is it so important that I break this code for you? What is it you want to learn from Sarah's book?"

Mammi studied my face solemnly, and for a minute I thought she was going to tell me. But then that urge seemed to pass and she merely shook her head.

"If I do break the code, I'll find out anyway."

Her eyes narrowed. "Well, then. Let that be your incentive," she replied stubbornly, pursing her lips.

And there we sat for a long moment, her lips pursed, my chin jutted out, both of us digging in our heels. Suddenly, the absurdity of the moment came clear and we began to laugh.

"Sarah and I aren't the only feisty ones in this family, you know," I teased, getting up to refill her tea.

"I suppose not."

When I sat back down she was still smiling, but she made it clear that the subject was closed. Instead, she asked me about my job hunt, so I told her I'd been cleaning houses and babysitting while I looked. I didn't add that I'd been looking in and around Nappanee, Indiana.

"That's needed work, but you should be baking." She squeezed my hand. "My mother loved to bake too. The other women in our district thought she was fancy with her pretty desserts, and sometimes she'd do things like put lavender in her pound cake. Oh, and the way she'd dress up her pies. She'd draw birds and trees, things like that, in pie dough with the tip of a sharp knife, and then she would cut them out and then bake them onto the top crust. She'd end up with a whole picture."

I tried to imagine it, the symbols from her book on top of a pie. "Was the Amish church okay with her art?"

Mammi held the book at arm's length. "I really don't have any idea." She sighed. "I'm sure the bishop wouldn't have approved of all the time she spent drawing and painting, had he known. But it was our family secret."

"Did your *daed* approve?"

"Not exactly, but Mother didn't draw as much when he was around." *Mammi* had a faraway look in her eyes.

"What happened to all of the artwork she created?"

"I don't know." She leaned her head back against the recliner and closed her eyes. "She had many finished canvases and full sketchbooks back then, which she kept in a big closet in the front upstairs bedroom. Though, at some point, she must have taken them out of there and hidden them away somewhere else, because I don't recall seeing them anywhere later, once I was an adult."

"So they're just…gone?"

Mammi shrugged. "I suppose so."

"What a loss," I said sadly.

An odd expression crossed *Mammi*'s face. "Maybe. Maybe not. She was Amish, Ella. She had no business indulging in any endeavor—no matter how talented she was—if that led her to commit the sin of pride. I don't think she was prideful of her artwork, but she may have been, at least privately so. Perhaps getting rid of it in the end was her way of asking for God's forgiveness."

Sobered by the thought, I patted *Mammi*'s hand and said I would make us lunch. Though the Mennonite faith stressed humility, the Amish made a huge deal out of it. And while I understood what she was saying about Sarah's sin of pride, I still didn't think a confession would warrant the destruction of a lifetime of art. But I let the subject drop.

After we were finished eating our sandwiches, *Mammi* said she was going to take a nap as she settled more comfortably in her chair.

"I wish I could have known Sarah," I said, feeling nostalgic. I knew lots of people who had relationships with their great-grandmothers, the way Christy did with Alice. Never mind that mine would have been absolutely ancient if she were alive now. I still would have liked to have known her.

"She loved life, that was certain," *Mammi* said. "She was much more joyful than me. She saw beauty in absolutely everything. You can see that in the drawings in her journal." She closed her eyes, and because I couldn't think of how to respond, for once I didn't.

Mammi had never been fun loving, that was for sure, or one to gush over people or nature, but she had been steadfast and hardworking—at least until a few years ago, when she'd had her stroke. Stroke or not, I always knew she loved me and that she was dedicated to me and to our entire family. I stood perfectly still and watched her for a few moments as she drifted off to sleep.

Next to Zed, I knew I would miss her the most. But then my mind leaped to the Home Place, and I couldn't help but wonder if something was there that really could help me break the code in the book. Maybe Sarah hadn't ditched her artwork after all. Even if the art really was gone, there had to be papers or something she'd left behind that might help me decipher it. Because the place was still in the family, chances were Sarah's things were still there somewhere, probably boxed up in an old attic or forgotten down in some basement.

All I had to do was get to Indiana, get to the Home Place, and get a good look for myself.

Eight

I never did receive the packet from the cooking school in South Bend. When I called to follow up, a machine greeted me, so I left a voice mail message requesting another packet to be sent. It never arrived either, so the day before Ezra and I left for Indiana, I called a third time and left a message requesting that a packet be sent to Penny's house in Nappanee.

That afternoon Ezra again picked me up at the library. Will had given him the day off to prepare to leave.

"The weather's cooperating," I shouted into his ear as we zipped along.

He nodded his head.

"So we're going to take the bike?"

He nodded again. "I canceled the driver this morning."

I was feeling giddy by the time we reached the cottage. Mom's car wasn't in the driveway, and Zed wasn't home from school yet.

"Want to come in for a minute?" I asked.

He hesitated.

"Come on, Ez. Just for a minute."

He followed me inside and I poured him a glass of water. I started telling him all about *Mammi* and Sarah's book and the Home Place. I hadn't mentioned any of it to him before because *Mammi* had asked me to keep her request to myself. But now that he was going to be a part of my adventure in cracking the code, I thought he needed to know.

"I'll go get the book," I said once I'd finished explaining.

Upstairs, as I was fishing for the box under my bed, I heard Mom's car turn into the drive. I must have pushed the box, still wrapped in the pillowcase, farther back than where I usually positioned it. I got down on my hands and knees and was finally able to retrieve it. I hurried to the stairs, hoping to be back in the dining room before Mom came inside, but she must have noticed Ezra's bike because she hustled into the house in a hurry. I was halfway down the stairs and Ezra was at the bottom when the front door opened and Mom called out my name.

By the time I reached Ezra, it probably looked as if we had both just raced down the stairs. Mom didn't say anything. She just gave us one of her killer stares. We shuffled over to the couch and sank down onto it. I hated how suspicious she always was, especially when she had nothing to worry about. Sure, I could be headstrong and stubborn, but I wasn't stupid. You don't grow up with a midwife for a mother without fully gasping the consequences of certain choices. More importantly, though, Ezra and I were both committed to waiting for marriage—whether my mom believed it or not—and that's all there was to it.

I took the box out of the pillowcase and then took the book out of the box. Ezra leafed through it briefly, shrugged, and handed it back. Then he took the box, turned it over, and looked at the construction of it as much as at the carving.

As he handed it back, he said, "Cool."

I don't know what I expected from him, but I was disappointed. Then I decided he was probably so ho-hum because Mom was in the dining room. He stood, saying he should go, but he wanted to tell my mother goodbye first. Terrified he would say something about my going, I told him that wasn't a good idea.

"She and I still have a few things to work through," I whispered, and then I walked him outside and down the steps to his bike.

"I'll see you tomorrow morning," he said.

I nodded. I had to tell Mom what I was up to because I hadn't mustered the courage to discuss it with her before now.

I walked to the highway and watched Ezra go, tracking his motorcycle as it dipped down the hill and then out of sight.

When I returned to the cottage, Mom was in the dining room.

"Come here," she said.

I obeyed.

"Ella Marie Bayer, don't you dare interfere with that young man and his future." Her voice was calm, but her face reddened as she spoke. "He's leaving tomorrow. It's the beginning of his new life."

"I was just showing him the book and the box of the farm in Indiana because he's going to be right next door to it." I met her gaze. "Because he's been my friend for as long as I can remember."

It was as if she hadn't heard me at all.

"You have no right," she barked.

I spun away from her and fled to my room to pack. How could she care so deeply about the man who cheated on her and abandoned her, and not care about me, her only daughter? She acted as if I had no right to my feelings. She acted as if I had no right to my life. There was no way I was going to tell her about my plans to go to Indiana now.

Shutting my door, I scanned my room. I'd already mailed a box to my new address a week ago. I had filled it with clothes and toiletries, including the hand mirror I used to use when I was a little younger and sometimes wore makeup. I had also included my magnifying glass to continue reading Sarah's book. And though I would have liked to add the book itself, just because it was so bulky, I didn't dare. Being irreplaceable, it wasn't worth the risk of mailing. For the drive out, Ezra had bought saddlebags for the motorcycle, and I would have my backpack. I planned to carry the book with me in there.

I pulled my stack of wedding magazines out from under my bed and leafed through one after the other, tearing out photos of cakes. I folded the pages and slipped them into my backpack. Next, I pulled my remaining two dresses and my cape off the pegs along the wall, rolled them to keep the wrinkles to a minimum, and then put them in my backpack too. My mother never came into my room anymore, but I definitely needed to keep her out today. If she noticed that all of my things were down, she might get suspicious.

I'd wear my jeans, of course, and warm coat. I had a stocking cap to wear under my helmet and warm gloves.

After a while I went downstairs and started vegetable-beef soup for dinner. Aunt Klara and Uncle Alexander had given us a quarter beef last summer, and I used one of the last pounds of hamburger. Zed came in the door as I was chopping carrots. It seemed he'd grown another couple of inches in the last month.

"Where's Mom?"

"In her office." At least I assumed that's where she was because she wasn't in the cottage, and her car was still in the driveway. "What's up?"

"One of the teachers at school is offering a filmmaking seminar, and I want to take it."

"Good luck with that," I muttered, scooping up the carrots and dropping them into the pot of broth.

He sat down at the computer without taking his jacket off. "I need her signature to do it. We're going to meet before school."

"Starting when?" I tried not to panic, imagining Zed up at five thirty tomorrow morning as I tried to slip out the door.

"Next week." His answer hardly alleviated my anxiety because I realized then that Mom could be just coming home from a birth or just leaving. She could hear Ezra's motorcycle. She could be getting up to go to the bathroom. Or she could simply be up already.

I began chopping the celery, but the knife slipped and I yanked my hand back just in time, annoyed with Mom's cheap knives. That was the first thing I was going to buy when I had some extra money—a decent knife.

By the time we sat down to eat, I was too anxious to get much down. After Zed and I finished the dishes, I told him goodnight. He grunted at me. I gave him a quick hug, fighting back the tears.

"What's with you?" He pushed me away.

I wrinkled my nose. "It's called a good night hug, okay? I won't see you in the morning. I'm leaving early." I knew both he and Mom would assume I had an early babysitting job, as I did now and then.

He shrugged and folded his lanky frame into the desk chair.

I headed up to my room, taking the stairs slowly. Mom was out in her office again. I was afraid if I went out there to tell her goodbye that she would become suspicious, so I didn't.

In less than twenty-four hours, once she knew I'd left, she was going to be furious with me anyway. It would only pour salt on that wound if I went out and told her goodbye now without giving her the full story.

I contemplated leaving a note but decided against that too. What if, for some reason, she found it in the morning and came after us? I honestly didn't think she would ever chase after anyone, especially me, but I didn't want to risk it just in case. The more time we had before she even knew we were gone, the better.

The thing was, I was sure she wasn't going to be that upset about my leaving. It was my leaving *with Ezra* that she was going to be the angriest about, afraid I was going to ruin his perfect life. It wasn't that I didn't feel bad about deceiving her. I did. I just didn't know what else to do.

The next morning I was up by three forty-five. Truth was, I'd hardly slept at all, tossing and turning and checking the time on my cell phone half the night. At one point, I'd even talked myself out of going. But then I thought of Ezra going alone. All those hours on his bike by himself after I'd talked him into taking it. Then all alone in Indiana.

By the time I crawled out of bed, I was determined—again—to make it work.

I showered, dressed in my jeans and sweater, and grabbed my boots and backpack and the carved box with the book safely inside. I tiptoed downstairs, grabbed a banana and a muffin from the kitchen, and walked out the door into the darkness, sitting down on the edge of the porch to firmly pull my boots on before heading down the steps. I could hear Ezra's motorcycle in the distance, and I began to run to the road, not wanting Mom to hear his bike. I glanced back at my childhood home one more time, blowing a kiss over my backpack that was bouncing on my shoulder.

I made it to the road as Ezra crested the hill.

"Hey," he said. Then he looked past me to the cottage. "Your mom isn't going to see you off?"

I shook my head. "She said everything she was going to say yesterday."

His eyes clouded a little. "She's not too happy, I take it."

I shrugged, wedging my box, still wrapped in the flannel pillowcase, into the saddlebag. "She'll get over it."

I positioned my pack on the bike's rack, arranging it so I'd be able to lean against it.

"How about your family? Did they all tell you goodbye?"

He shook his head. "I talked with my parents last night and told them I was taking my motorcycle, which annoyed them. I spent the night at Will's. He did tell me goodbye this morning, but he's upset with me too."

I climbed on behind Ezra. "Did you tell them I was going with you?"

"No." His voice was raw. "Which I don't feel good about at all. They'll probably find out about it from *your* mom, and then who knows what they'll do?"

Sick with guilt, I didn't reply but instead just wrapped my arms around him and held on tight.

"Let's go," I said into his ear, and we jolted forward. He turned around in the middle of the highway and then headed back toward the covered bridge.

As we jumped over the wooden planks, I couldn't help but smile, regardless of all the anxiety I felt. As we passed out from under the shadow of the bridge and started up the hill, I saw our Amish neighbor putting her wash on the line by the light of a lantern, taking advantage of the warmer weather. Daffodils bloomed alongside their house, and her husband, a dark figure in the field, was herding the cows into the barn to be milked.

In a minute the idyllic scene was nothing but a blur, and we were turning onto the main road, bypassing the city of Lancaster as dawn broke. The emerald green pastures glistened from the morning dew. Cows raised their heads, chewing their cud as we zoomed by.

Ten minutes later we were on Highway 283, headed toward Harrisburg. As we crossed the county line, leaving Lancaster County behind, I couldn't help but grin.

The biggest adventure of our lives had just begun.

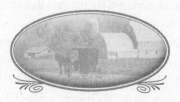

Nine

After three hours on the road, we exited the turnpike outside of Bedford and turned into a truck stop for breakfast. Ezra was quiet as we studied the menu.

"What's wrong?" I hoped it was just that he was tired.

He put down his menu and exhaled slowly. His chocolaty brown eyes were full of concern.

"I don't know about this, Ella." He looked nothing like the romantic young man who had kissed me in the park just a short time ago.

"About what?" I smiled, trying to be playful.

"If what we're doing is right. Upsetting my folks back home. You leaving like this without a job. Bringing my bike. All of it." He raised the menu before I could answer. Ezra had always been the one ready to take risks.

I cringed a little, fully aware I was in the wrong—being dishonest with both Mom and Ezra—but he was just being his usual sweet self, doing his best to accommodate me.

Honestly, I didn't feel good about deceiving everyone. Mom was one thing—though I would have told her if she hadn't been so ruthless with me. But the Gundys were another matter. It didn't help that I truly liked

Ezra's family. For the most part they were very reasonable people, but on this issue I knew they would never see it clearly.

After the waitress took our order, Ezra settled back in his seat and asked how far the dairy farm was from where I'd be staying.

I grabbed a paper napkin and then a pen out of my backpack, telling him it might be easiest just to draw a map.

"First, let me orient you to the area," I said, drawing three dots that, had they'd been connected, would have formed an upside-down triangle. The upper left dot was South Bend, the upper right dot was Elkhart, and the bottom dot was Nappanee. "As the crow flies," I explained, "these cities are only about fifteen to twenty miles apart, though driving it takes a little more than that because there aren't any straight shots. You have to kind of zigzag to get from one to the other."

"Makes sense," Ezra said, nodding.

"Now," I continued, adding another dot about halfway between Nappanee and Elkhart but just to the right of the imaginary triangle line. "This is Goshen, which is about twelve miles from Nappanee as the crow flies and maybe fifteen if you drive it."

"Okay."

Wishing I had more of Sarah's drawing ability, I sketched a tiny cow a little less than halfway between Nappanee and Goshen. "Here's the Kline's dairy, where you'll be living. It's about a five- or six-mile drive from there into Nappanee."

"And that's where you'll be living? In the actual town of Nappanee?"

I nodded. "Yep, just a couple of blocks from downtown, actually." I drew a little house about where I thought it should go.

"Five miles. That's not so bad."

"Here's the cool part," I said, drawing a little daisy next to the cow. "The Home Place is right next door to the Kline's farm. If I can get a job at the Plain Treats bakery, which is there on the property of the Home Place, I'll be working close to you."

"Cool." Ezra picked up the wrapper from his drinking straw, flattened it on the table with a finger, and began rolling it up from one end to the other.

"From what I could see on Google Earth, the dairy and the Home

Place are separated by woods, with a little creek in there somewhere, but according to *Mammi* there's a shortcut from one house to the other. Driving, you have to go the long way." I drew a line from the Home Place around to where I thought the road would be and then back to the dairy. "Either way, can you believe it? If I could get a job there, we'll be next to each other every day. I could bring you over a cupcake if I wanted to, no big deal."

"You're all the cupcake I need."

I laughed. "Oh, boy. Don't try that line on just anyone."

We shared a smile.

"Here, want to keep the map?" I extended it to him, relieved his anxiety seemed to have passed.

"Thanks," he said, brushing my fingers intentionally and making me shiver as he took it from me. Folding the napkin carefully, he asked when I thought I might get on at Plain Treats.

"Rosalee said to call back in a couple of months…"

"So where are you going to work in the meantime?"

I shrugged. "I'll find something." I put my pen away, wishing I felt as confident as I sounded.

Ezra tucked the napkin into the pocket of his jacket and leaned back against the booth, closing his eyes.

I rested against my backpack and started going through old text messages on my phone, erasing them as I did. Most of them were from Ezra. I wondered how long Mom would keep me on her cell plan. Zed had been asking for a phone—I had been allowed to buy one when I was fifteen—and his birthday was coming up in just over a month. Maybe Mom would let him get a phone sooner, especially with me gone.

Not that she had paid anything for my phone. I bought it and paid all the fees. And then paid to upgrade it and paid larger fees. Zed would be required to do the same, I was sure.

Ezra stirred when the waitress brought our food, opening his eyes by the time she left. We didn't talk as we ate. When we were finished, he paid the bill and then led the way to the bike, the saddlebags that contained all his worldly goods, probably just a couple of changes of clothes and his toiletries, in his hand.

Back on the Turnpike, the day grew warmer but I kept my coat on as a shield against the wind. I'd never been on the motorcycle for a three-hour stretch, and I was pretty sure Ezra hadn't either. My muscles were beginning to tighten. At the same time, the warm sun was making me sleepy, and I fought to keep from dozing. I was beginning to regret asking Ezra to bring his bike instead of hiring a car

By the time we reached the outskirts of Pittsburgh, traffic had increased and I was more wide-awake. It was almost noon and the lanes were packed with both cars and trucks. The exhaust was thick, and I tried to take little breaths. Ezra zipped in and out of traffic, and after a half hour, we were on our way again, nearing Ohio, but the delay meant we would arrive in Nappanee later than I thought.

When he turned into a rest stop an hour later, my body was so stiff and sore I was near tears. He pulled some dried apples, a bag of cashews, and a bottle of water from his saddlebag and handed all three to me. "Walk around for a few minutes," he said. "I need to check the bike." He pulled a little tool set out from the second bag. I marveled at all he'd managed to squeeze into them.

I drank from the bottle as I walked to the end of the parking lot area, my backpack slung over one shoulder, taking long strides, trying to stretch out my legs. I was guessing that people who went on long trips by motorcycle usually worked up to it. I stretched my arms too and my neck and back. Stopping at a picnic table, I took off my coat, wadded it up like a pillow, and then sat down, placing my head on it on top of the table.

I dozed but didn't realize it until Ezra approached me. I offered him the water and food, which he took. After he finished eating, I offered him my coat. He declined, but rested his head on his arms. I watched as the rise and fall of his breathing slowed. The breeze picked up a little but still I felt warm in my sweater. I put my head back down, thinking I would rest until Ezra was ready to go. But we both slept for at least an hour and when he woke me, he seemed a little impatient.

"We'd better get going," he said.

I gritted my teeth for the next four hours, except for when we stopped at a drive-in outside of Absolutely Nowhere, Ohio, for a hamburger. We cut down from the interstate to Bowling Green after that and then took the highway through Indiana for the longest two hours of my life. The terrain was flat, with an occasional small rise, unlike the hills I was used to back home. The fields were the same emerald green as in Lancaster, but there were more patches of woods interspersed across the landscape. I realized I wasn't gritting my teeth anymore. They were absolutely clenched shut.

It was after seven by the time we neared Nappanee. A freight train was chugging along the tracks that ran parallel to the highway. Several of the farms were obviously Amish. The clues included the usual things: no electrical wires running to the buildings, workhorses grazing in the field, laundry hanging on the lines, buggies parked here and there, and well-kept houses and barns. Although most of the buildings were painted white, as in Lancaster County, there was more of a natural look to the farms. Back home it sometimes seemed as if everything had to be perfect, with not a single weed or weathered board to be seen. Here, although everything was well cared for, it seemed as if there might be less of an emphasis on appearances. I wondered how much of that might have to do with the droves of tourists who visited Lancaster County every year. Although I was sure Elkhart County had its share, I knew it couldn't rival the numbers back home.

The sun was beginning to set directly in front of us. I was so stiff I could barely pull the directions to the house where I would be staying from my pocket as we passed an Amish buggy. I turned my head to get a glimpse of the driver—a young woman about my age, wearing glasses and a sweatshirt. Oddly, her head covering was round, like mine, rather than heart-shaped like the Amish wore back home. I knew that didn't mean she was Old Order Mennonite—it probably just meant the Amish here wore rounded *kapp*s.

Ezra slowed for the city limits, passing an Amish youth on a bicycle. That surprised me as the Amish back home weren't allowed to have bikes. Fast-food restaurants and stores were on either side of the four-lane highway, but they soon gave way to houses, many of them brick and all of them looking at least a century old. When Ezra stopped at a red light on

Main Street, I told him to turn right. Several blocks later I instructed him to turn right again and in a few more blocks I told him to pull over. The two-story house in front of us was painted ivory with cranberry trim, and it had a wide porch and an American flag. The lawn was as well cared for as the house. I climbed off the motorcycle and pulled my helmet from my head. Ezra kicked down the stand, positioned the bike, and turned off the motor. As he stood, I handed him my helmet and retrieved my box from the saddlebag. The front door opened and a woman stepped out.

"Is that you, Ella?" She was short and a little plump, probably around fifty, and her shoulder-length dark hair looked as if it were dyed. She wore a long-sleeved light-blue blouse and a pair of jeans. It had to be Penny, the woman I'd been emailing with back and forth. I greeted her and then introduced Ezra, saying he needed to hurry out to the farm he was staying at before it grew completely dark. I turned back to him.

"Do you want me to ask if you can leave the bike here? If she can give you a ride?" That had been the original plan.

He shook his head. "I'll just drive it out." He seemed resigned to it, and I actually thought that was a good idea. That way he could come back into town to see me when he was off work.

"Okay. I'll send you a text tomorrow about my job search."

He climbed back on the bike and then shook his head.

"What's wrong?"

"I'm not so sure about this," he said again.

"It'll be fine," I answered quickly. "Everything will work out." I tried my hardest to smile, but even my face hurt.

He rolled the bike backward, a frown on his face.

"It's going to be fine, Ez," I said again, my voice still low but as cheery as I could make it. "Trust me." My voice fell flat, though, betraying my fear.

He shook his head.

I slung my backpack higher on my shoulder.

"Ella?" the woman called out. "Is everything okay?"

I nodded. "I'll be right there." I gave Ezra a little wave. "Text me," I said. "Let me know you made it out to the dairy farm."

He grimaced, pulled around in the middle of the street, and then headed back the direction we'd come.

As I made my way toward the house, walking stiffly, I pulled my phone from my pocket. I had three missed calls from Mom and two from Zed, and several texts. Mom had expected me home by two—which was more than five hours ago. At first she might have thought I'd lost track of time, but when I didn't answer any of her texts or calls, I could see that she might have grown concerned.

As I reached the porch, my cell vibrated in my hand. This call was from Lexie. It looked as if the whole world knew I'd gone missing.

Penny led me straight up to my room, asking as we climbed the stairs if I'd found a job yet. I winced as I said, "No." Taking another step, I was sure I'd be bowlegged for the rest of my life.

"Are you okay?" She paused, looking back down at me.

I was going to make up some flip answer, but the concern on her face was so earnest that it stripped away my defenses.

"No, actually. I'm an idiot!" I laughed. "I have learned my lesson. Never, ever take an all-day motorcycle ride unless you're physically prepared for it. The longest I'd ever been on that bike before was an hour at the most. Trust me, after this, I may never walk normally again."

Penny chuckled. "Well, I've never ridden a motorcycle, but I did take a day trip on a horse once, during my honeymoon, so I know what you mean. It kinda took the 'honey' out of the honeymoon, if you get what I'm sayin'!"

It even hurt to laugh, but at least I finally reached the top of the stairs.

My room was simple—a twin bed, a chest of drawers with the cardboard box I'd mailed ahead on top, a small desk, a wardrobe in the corner—but it was neat and more than adequate. I put the pillowcase with the carved box and Sarah's book on the end of the bed and then slung my backpack beside it.

"I'll give you a few minutes," Penny said. "But then come down and chat. I have a job idea."

Falling onto the bed, I listened to Lexie's voice mail first.

"Your mom is worried sick, Ella. Call me."

I listened to Mom's messages and then Zed's. Neither one of them sounded worried sick, but in one of them, Mom offered to give me a ride if I needed it, something she never did. She must have imagined me hidden away somewhere in Lancaster County—not two states away.

As I deleted the last message, my phone vibrated again. *Mom.* I decided to get it over with and answered it.

After a terse hello, she said a packet came for me today with the return address of a cooking school in South Bend.

"Ella." Her voice was as suspicious as I'd ever heard it. "Are you, by chance, with Ezra in Indiana?"

"Yes and no. I'm not with Ezra, but I am in Indiana."

"*Were* you with Ezra?" she asked. It was so like her to be as specific as possible.

"I was earlier today, but he went on to the Klines' dairy farm."

"And where are you?"

"At Penny's." I knew I was sounding smart—as if she should know who Penny was.

"And where did you meet this Penny?"

"Online."

There was a long pause and then she finally said, "I see." That was all. She was absolutely quiet.

I quickly filled the silence with chatter. "You wanted me to be independent, right? To make my own decisions? Well, that's exactly what I'm doing. I'm renting a room."

"It sounds like what you're doing is manipulating Ezra and putting yourself in a potentially harmful situation."

I sat up straight. "Oh, no. He *wanted* me to come. And Penny is a woman even older than you, I swear."

Mom sighed. "Was it Ezra's idea for you to go with him?"

I didn't answer.

"And how do you think this looks to his family and community in Lancaster County, not to mention his new supervisor in Indiana? And the new community he's supposed to be a part of. Him running off with a girl?"

"We've done nothing wrong." I was adamant. "There's nothing to accuse us of. We've been beyond reproach." That was a term I'd heard used about other couples.

"I'm not accusing you. Listen carefully. I'm saying that you've presented Ezra in a bad light as well as yourself. And you've been determined all along to get what you wanted, not thinking once what's best for either of you."

I didn't answer that, either.

"Ella, if you get on a bus tonight and come home, there's a chance Ezra may still be able to salvage what was planned for him, but—"

"That's just it. All of this was planned for him. He didn't have a say—"

"Did he tell you that?"

I thought for a moment. Actually, he hadn't.

"Young lady." Mom's voice was low and firm. "The truth is, you're the one who didn't have a say in any of this. And that's what's been eating you up all along."

"No, Mom, that's not true." But even as I said the words, I knew it was. "I love Ezra..." I thought about saying more but then decided it wouldn't do any good.

I expected her to point out I hadn't acted in a loving way, but she didn't. Instead she said, "Get on the bus."

"I'll think about it," I said, standing as I spoke. "I'll send you a text once I decide."

There was another long pause. "In the meantime, I need to talk with this Penny person," she finally said.

I slumped against the headboard for a moment and then rallied myself. I limped out into the hall and then went down the stairs.

Penny was standing at the bottom. "I have more info about that job I mentioned." It was clear she didn't notice the cell phone I was holding to my ear.

"Okay," I answered. "But first my mother wants to talk with you." I handed her the cell and sat on the bottom step, shaky with exhaustion, both physical and emotional. Penny listened intently, glancing my way a few times and then wandering off around the corner into the next room. I stayed put.

After my mother was finished with her, my new landlady would probably drive me to the bus station herself.

I could hear the murmur of Penny's voice every once in a while, but it was clear Mom was doing most of the talking. It wasn't like her to be so open with a stranger, and I couldn't help but wonder what she was saying.

After what seemed like an eternity, Penny returned and handed me the phone, a look of deep concern on her face. I thanked her and scampered as best I could up the stairs as I listened to Mom say, "Well, it's hard to tell from a distance, but the woman seems stable enough. Of course, she was shocked you hadn't discussed your plans with me." There was definitely a twinge of hurt in Mom's voice. "She said you won't be able to get a bus out of town tonight, but she'll give you a ride to the depot in the morning."

"If that's what I decide to do."

Mom sighed. "Yes, Ella. In fact, I told her that because I anticipate you will be as stubborn as ever about this."

I didn't answer.

"Please call me tomorrow," she said. "One way or the other."

Reluctantly, I told her I would.

She told me she loved me, something she didn't say very often, before she said goodbye. As soon as I hung up, my cell began vibrating again. It was Lexie. I slipped the phone into my pocket and took the stairs slowly this time, running my hand along the polished cherrywood banister. I stepped into the living room, but Penny wasn't there. The room, with its rag rug, blue velvet-covered sofa, and two overstuffed chairs, looked as if it was seldom used. It was decorated in Americana, with wall hangings and picture frames all with stars and flags and colonial buildings painted on them. I headed through the dining room, around an antique table and hutch, and into the kitchen. Penny stood at the counter, filling a teakettle. The kitchen had plenty of counter space, plus a gas range, a heavy-duty mixer, a humongous refrigerator, and a dishwasher. What stopped me in my tracks was the bookcase filled with cookbooks and magazines.

"Do you like to cook?" Penny asked, noting my interest.

"Yes," I answered. "I especially like to bake." She had a series of *Gourmet* magazine, one of *Sunset*, and one of *Cooking Light*, plus all the classic cookbooks—*The Silver Palate, The Joy of Cooking,* Julia Childs, James Beard. French and Italian cookbooks. Greek. I squinted. She even had an Amish cookbook. I nearly laughed to see it on the shelf with all the others.

I turned toward Penny. "What a great collection."

"It's one of my many hobbies," she said, seeming a little relieved to be talking about it. "Buying cookbooks. Of course, I like to cook too, although now that it's just me I don't do it much anymore. Feel free to borrow any of these—anytime."

My gaze fell back on the books.

"Speaking of cooking…" Penny leaned against the counter. "I'm acquainted with the couple who own the café downtown. I called them a few minutes ago, after you told me you needed a job and before I spoke with your mother. They still have an opening, but now it sounds as if you'll be returning home."

"I'm not sure if I will or not," I said. "So I would like to meet your friends."

"But your mother—"

I wanted to say, "Can be a real pain," but instead I smiled and said, "She said she told you I might choose not to go."

"She did, but it seems to me—"

"Thanks," I said, "but I really am interested in the job. I wonder if it was the same place that had advertised for a waitress online."

"I don't know, but don't you think you should—"

"I'm definitely interested. In fact, I think I sent them a letter of inquiry. I'd love to talk with them."

Penny was quiet for a long moment. "Okay. I can give you a ride. Let's plan to go around ten, after their breakfast rush."

"Or I can walk," I said.

"It's no problem for me to give you a ride." She smiled. "I just don't want to get between you and your mom."

"We're good. We just had a little misunderstanding over all of this, that's all." I thanked her and then said I was exhausted. "I'll see you in the morning," I added, not wanting her to ask any more questions about my mother.

As I struggled back up the stairs, my legs growing heavier and heavier, my phone beeped. Thankfully it was Ezra and not Mom or Zed or Lexie again. I read the text slowly as I continued to climb. *At the Klines' place. Voice mail from Will. He's furious with me. I'm super furious with you. Can't believe you didn't tell your mom. You tricked me! You lied to me!*

I tapped in an answer as I walked down the hall to my room. *I know, I know. I'm sorry!!! I had no choice! You don't know what Mom was like there at the end!*

Heart pounding, I sent off that text and then followed it up a moment later with another. *We'll get through this. You'll see.*

It was too bad I didn't feel as confident as I sounded. Ezra didn't text me back—no big surprise there. After I took the carved box out of the pillowcase and put it in the top drawer of the dresser, I changed into my nightgown and collapsed into bed.

TEN

I didn't hear a thing from Ezra the next morning, either. He'd probably been up and working for hours, learning how to milk and run the machines.

I could see no reason to go home. With Penny's help, I would probably have a job in no time. In a couple of weeks I would check back with Rosalee to see if she had an opening at the bakery so I could be closer to Ezra. Then I'd figure out school. Ezra might have to sell his motorcycle if the Klines were opposed to it, but we could both get bicycles.

Things would work out. I really didn't want to return to Lancaster County. Freddy was there. Ezra was here. My choice was as clear as day. I sent Mom a quick text, ccing Lexie. *Job on the horizon. All is well. I'll call soon.*

Then I limped downstairs to tell Penny I'd be thrilled if she could give me a ride to the café and introduce me to the owners.

She seemed a little surprised at my dress and head covering.

"You're Mennonite?" She was wiping down the granite countertops as she spoke. Face coloring, she added, "I guess I shouldn't have made that joke yesterday about my honeymoon. Sorry about that."

"Don't be sorry. My mother's a midwife, so it's not like I don't know the facts of life."

119

She chuckled. "So the jeans last night were just for the ride out?"

I nodded, realizing I hadn't mentioned being Mennonite in any of my emails.

"Is that boyfriend of yours Mennonite too?"

"No," I answered.

Penny began to smile.

"He's Amish."

"Amish?" Her eyes widened. "On a motorcycle?"

"Well, he hasn't joined the church yet."

"Guess not. Around here some of the Amish kids drive mopeds before they join, but that's about it."

"And bicycles," I added.

"Of course," Penny said. "All of them ride bicycles."

"Even the adults?"

"Yes."

"None of the Amish do in Lancaster County. They ride scooters."

"Gas powered?" Penny looked quite surprised.

"No, foot powered."

She laughed again. "How about some breakfast? I can make you eggs and toast."

"Toast would be great." I didn't have much of an appetite.

She set right to work and soon placed in front of me two slices of whole wheat toast spread with butter and strawberry jam. I dug right in, hungrier than I'd thought I was.

Penny seemed like a nice woman, and I was thankful she was taking me under her wing. Having someone to feed me once in a while was great, but helping me to find a job was even better. With only babysitting and housecleaning experience, I needed all the assistance I could get.

"Let's go," she said when I was done.

I quickly rinsed my plate and glass and then followed her out the back door to the driveway. She drove a Volvo SUV, the kind of car Ezra considered "pretentious," given its price tag. But when I sat down on the leather seat, I knew I'd never been in such a fancy car in all my life. Pretentious or not, I was sold.

It only took us a few minutes to reach the restaurant. I could have easily walked, but then I wouldn't have had Penny to introduce me. She parked in front of an old brick building with a sign above a door that read Downtown Café. I followed her through to the inside, where the dining room was painted white and lots of light streamed in through the windows. Booths lined the walls, and several tables were arranged in the middle of the room. It was all very clean and simple.

"Good morning," Penny said to a waitress measuring out coffee. "Is Kendra around?"

"I'll go get her," the woman said.

Penny pointed to the last booth and I slid in to it.

Instead of a woman, as expected, a man wearing a paper chef's hat came out of the kitchen, wiping his hands on his apron. He was tall and lanky and greeted Penny with a wide grin.

"Did you sleep in?" He winked as he spoke. "I've never seen you roll in here for breakfast this late before."

She smiled. "No, I decided to bring Ella in after the morning rush. I'll be back on my regular schedule tomorrow."

The man turned his attention to me. "So you're looking for a job." He extended his hand, and I shook it. "I'm Wes. Got any experience?"

I explained that I'd been cooking since I was six, and then added my very limited job experience, saying I'd sent in a letter a few weeks ago.

"Yeah, well, we don't look at those too closely. Penny recommending you is much better. Did you say you're from Lancaster County, Pennsylvania?"

I nodded.

"You Amish?"

"Mennonite."

His eyes sparkled. "Close enough. The tourists like that. The cap and dress and all. And anyone interested in the Amish is doubly interested in Lancaster County." His eyes lit up even more, making me feel like a commodity. "Well, I can't give you full time, but probably thirty hours a week. Can you start tomorrow? Six a.m. sharp?"

I told him yes, even though I flinched a little at my clothes getting me the job. Still, I thanked Penny profusely as we left, and then, once we were back in her vehicle, I asked if she would mind taking me by the grocery store. She was happy to.

On the way I asked how she knew Wes.

"He went to high school with my son," she said. "Kendra is his wife. She went to school with them too."

"Where's your son now?"

Penny sighed heavily. "Denver. He manages a hotel there. I miss him like crazy."

"How about your other kids?"

She shook her head. "He's my one and only. I keep hoping he'll get married and give me some grandchildren." She chuckled. "He's nearly thirty. You'd think he'd be ready to settle down."

"What do you do? As far as a job?" I asked. She hadn't mentioned going to work, and it sounded as if she ate at the café every day.

"I'm not employed right now," she said. "I've worked at different things through the years, though. Interior design was the latest, but when the economy tanked business dried up. My husband left me a few months ago. Now he's in California, from what I hear." She turned onto the main street. "It seemed as though it was out of the blue, but now I can see there were warning signs the last few years."

"I'm sorry," I said, thinking of Mom.

She turned into the parking lot of the grocery store. "That's why I decided to rent out a room. I'm doing okay financially, although I'll need to figure out something soon, but I thought it would be good to have some company."

"What kind of work are you looking for?"

"Well, what I'd really like to do is start a business. A shop. Or a little diner. Something like that." She pulled into a parking place and turned off the engine. "I'd like something with lots of contact with the public. I need something for the next ten years or so. Once my divorce is finalized, I'll have quite a few investments to draw from. Then half my ex's retirement in the future. But I need something to keep me busy…"

I gave her a quick smile, not quite able to imagine the years ahead of her.

I didn't take long at the store. I bought oatmeal, eggs, bacon, whole wheat bread, sandwich material, pasta, lettuce, black tea, granola bars, apples, and milk. Penny said I could use her staples, no problem.

Once we were back at the house, I put my groceries away, ate a granola bar, and then decided I'd send Ezra a text, even though he was furious with me: *Found a job at the Downtown Café. Start tomorrow morning. Stop by if you have a chance to get into town.*

After I hit "Send," I settled down to take a nap.

The midday sun was streaming through the window, warming my room. I slept hard for several hours, still exhausted from the ride the day before. When I awoke, thirsty and groggy, I checked my phone immediately, hoping Ezra had called or texted. He hadn't.

Sitting up on the side of the bed, I felt a sick, sinking sensation in the pit of my stomach—and the long nap had left me out of sorts, which didn't help. I decided to eat something, and by the time I'd polished off a glass of water and a sandwich, I started to perk up. Surely once Ezra saw my text he'd feel better about my staying. Everything was bound to work out.

I watched Penny through the window of the front door as she sat in her wicker rocking chair on the porch, staring out on the street. I wasn't sure whether I should intrude or not, but then I received a text from Ezra, and wandered back through the house to the kitchen as I read it. *Finally caught a minute to myself. The two of us are in big, big trouble. At least I am. Why did you lie to me? I can't believe you did that!*

I headed out the back door and out into the yard, noting the patio lined by pots of plants. I sank down onto a plush lawn chair and closed my eyes. I hadn't exactly lied to him. I was very careful with my wording. Still, I'd obviously deceived him. And Mom.

I opened my eyes and texted back, *I'm sorry, Ez.*

Sorry? Will is saying he's coming out here.

Out here? What do you mean?

To straighten me out. And the Kline family is something else. Darryl already thinks I'm bad news as far as his kids are concerned, especially his daughter.

Daughter? I took a series of short breaths and then forced myself to inhale slowly. No one said anything about the Klines having a daughter. And I never guessed Will would come out after Ezra!

Before I could answer, another text flew in. *Gotta go. Not sure if I'll be able to see you in the next few days. Cell phones are a big NO-NO here. Don't come out here for any reason. That would only make things worse.*

Ouch. He was mad—but he would get over it. So maybe Will would come out and humiliate Ezra, but then he would go home and we would settle in. Sure, I might only get to see Ezra once a week or so, but once I figured out the baking school situation, I'd be plenty busy between work and classes anyway. Although I did want to get out to the Klines as soon as possible, even more now that I knew there was a daughter, but maybe I should go out to the Home Place first. At this point, I figured I would introduce myself to Rosalee as soon as I could and tell her I was a relative. Otherwise, it would just be more awkward later on.

I felt sorry for Ezra, with his big brother coming out and all. Even though others saw him as worldly and wild, mostly because of his motorcycle, I couldn't see him standing up to Will. Ezra hadn't been raised that way. I know Mom hadn't intentionally raised me to be so independent, but circumstances—or maybe just personality—prevailed.

"Everything okay?" Penny was standing in the doorway of the kitchen.

"Pretty much," I answered.

"Boyfriend problems?"

"Sort of."

"The Amish kid?"

I nodded.

Penny was silent for a moment, but a look of sympathy spread across her face. Then she gestured back toward the kitchen. "I'd like to cook you dinner tonight, as a welcoming meal. Would you be my guest?"

"Sure. Thanks." I wondered why I felt uncomfortable. "May I help?"

She smiled. "Oh, no. I hate to have company in the kitchen. We'll eat at six."

"Okay, thanks. That sounds like fun." I retreated toward my room. I'd never spent the night in anyone's home who wasn't Mennonite or Amish, let alone lived with them. Why hadn't I thought of that when I decided to rent a room? I hadn't even shared a meal with anyone that wasn't Anabaptist. I'd only gone to a classmate's home a handful of times in all my years of school, and that was to work on a project together, not to socialize or stay for dinner. I hadn't realized what a sheltered life I'd lived until that moment.

When I came down for dinner, Penny had the dining room table set with china and crystal goblets filled with what looked like cranberry juice. A basket of homemade rolls, a plate of grilled asparagus, and green salad with arugula were on the table.

"Right on time," Penny said as she came through the door with a platter. In the middle were two pieces of beef.

As we sat down, she explained the meat was rib-eye steak. "I don't fix it for just myself," she said. "It's nice to have someone to share it with."

I placed the linen napkin in my lap and waited to see if she would say a blessing. She didn't. I said a quick one with my eyes open, not wanting to draw attention.

The steak was delicious. "What sort of a marinade did you use?"

"It's a soy sauce–orange juice mix." She seemed pleased I liked it.

I told her about cooking sirloin steak, a tougher cut, in the Dutch oven back home with vegetables, and how that tenderized it right up.

Next we talked about the roasted asparagus and then her homemade salad dressing, a vinaigrette with regular mustard. I never would have guessed. She smiled at my praise. Clearly, I'd found a fellow chef. I told her about the baking school and asked if she'd heard of it.

"Oh, I've been to Petit Paris," she said, pronouncing Paris with the long *e* sound on the end, the French way. "It's one of my favorite cafés in South Bend." She squinted. "You know, I remember hearing that they offered cooking classes, but I never thought of it as an actual cooking school."

"I don't think it's accredited. I know they don't take many students at a time," I said. "At least that's what the website indicated. I never did receive a packet, although I asked them to mail one here too."

"Why are you interested if it's not accredited?"

"I want to open a bakery someday, back in Lancaster. I don't need a degree to do that, just the knowledge."

"I'll keep my eye out for it." She was quiet for a long moment and then said, "I'd be interested to find out more too. I could even give you a ride if you like."

I thanked her for the offer and told her I would let her know.

After I helped clean up, I said I was going up to my room.

"I can give you a ride to work in the morning," she said.

"You don't have to do that. I'll walk. It will help me wake up." I started to leave the kitchen but stopped in the doorway. "I was thinking I should buy a bike. Once I get my first paycheck." I didn't want to dip into my savings.

"I have an old one in the garage. I'm sure I'll never ride it again. I'll pull it out and leave it on the patio. You'll have to dust it off, maybe shoot air into the tires, but I'll leave the hand pump out there for you. Otherwise it should be okay. It doesn't have rust or broken chains or anything like that."

"Wow. Thanks, Penny."

As I headed up the stairs, it struck me how much easier my life would be if I had a car and a driver's license. At seventeen I was old enough now to get one, but I'd never even taken the classes. I knew Mom would never pay for my insurance or my gas, and I doubted she would have let me borrow her car all that often anyway, so it had always seemed a nonissue back home. Now that I was out here, it probably still wasn't worth pursuing, I realized, because even if I got the license, I couldn't afford the other stuff. Besides, why go through all of that just to give it up when I joined the Amish church anyway?

It had been a fun evening, but as I entered my room I wondered what Mom and Zed were up to. Maybe they were out with Freddy. Or visiting *Mammi*. Then again, *Mammi* was most likely asleep at this hour.

I slumped down onto the bed, evaluating how my plan was going. The housing situation was good. So was the job—at least so far. Missing Zed and even Mom wasn't so good. Neither was the situation with Ezra.

I texted Ezra back. *I really am sorry. At the time I was being really careful not to lie, but I can now see I tricked you. Please forgive me.*

The next morning I rode Penny's bike, a one-speed with a comfy seat, to work in the predawn light. As I came through the doorway, I was greeted by a woman who introduced herself as Kendra. She was tall, taller than Wes, and walked with confidence. Her blond hair was piled on the top of her head, which added another three inches to her height, and her heels were at least two inches high. I felt like a dowdy dweeb next to her.

I guessed that without her hair and heels, she was probably a few inches shorter than her husband.

She showed me around the dining hall and kitchen. I was to spend the day bussing tables, and then I'd start waitressing the next day.

I wasn't surprised when Penny came in around eight, ordered breakfast, ate it, and then told us all a cheery goodbye without engaging me in conversation. But I could tell she was happy to see me and pleased I was working at her favorite breakfast place.

By then the rush was long over and Kendra was scrubbing tables and I was filling the ketchup bottles.

"That Penny," Kendra said.

I expected her to elaborate, and when she didn't, I said, "What about her?"

"Oh, she comes in here every day, just like clockwork. I think she's lonely." Kendra smiled. "Not that I'm not happy for her business and her friendship. She's a great gal. I just think she's a little lost with her husband leaving the way he did." Kendra started for the kitchen. "I can't imagine…"

I finished with the ketchup and moved on to the salt and pepper shakers, thinking about Penny. I couldn't fathom living alone like that, cooking by myself, going out to eat by myself. Well, not when I was in my fifties, anyway. I hoped that wouldn't be the way Mom's life would be when Zed left. All alone in that cottage. She couldn't work forever.

In the midafternoon a young Amish man came into the restaurant. He held his straw hat in one hand and a slip of paper in the other. When he spotted me, his gray eyes lit up.

"Ella?"

I nodded and stepped toward him, a bussing tub in my hands.

He was tall, much taller than Ezra, and had dark hair with his bangs cut straight across in the typical Amish fashion. He smiled shyly, showing a pair of dimples on his lean face. He looked to be around twenty, but by the style of his hair I'd guess he'd already joined the church.

"I'm Luke," he said. "Luke Kline. Ezra sent me." His face was flushed as he extended his hand.

"Oh." I put the tub on a table, wiped my hands on my apron, and shook his hand, noting its roughness. "I'm pleased to meet you."

He nodded in agreement and then handed me the slip of folded paper. "Ezra's cell phone died."

My heart sank, wondering if he'd be able to get another one.

I opened the note. *I'm not allowed to charge my phone here—even though there's a generator in the barn. Will is coming Friday. He wants to see you. Got your last text—I read it before the battery ran out. I still can't figure out what you were thinking to lie to me—and to your mom.*

I looked up at Luke.

"Everything okay?" he asked.

"I think so." I gestured toward a table. "Would you like a cup of coffee? A piece of pie? My treat for delivering the note."

He shook his head. "I need to get going." He started toward the door and then stopped, turning around quickly. "I'm sorry things didn't turn out the way you wanted." His last statement stabbed at my heart, and I wondered how much Ezra had told him. But I was grateful for his words. He hurried through the open door, pulling his hat onto his head, wheeling his bike to the street, and hopping on as soon as he had it over the curb. I waved from the open door, wondering if I'd see him again.

When I turned around, Kendra was standing in the middle of the room, a smile on her face.

"Cute guy," she said.

I blushed.

"And your religion."

I shook my head. "He's Amish."

"Close enough."

"I just met him," I said. "This minute. Plus, I already have a boyfriend." I didn't add "maybe" or that he was also Amish.

"Oh, that doesn't matter." Kendra laughed. "Ask Wes."

"You had a boyfriend when the two of you met?"

"No. He had a girlfriend that he'd dated all through high school."

"Oh."

"Ask him sometime." She threw her head back and laughed. "Hey, Wes. Come here a minute."

I blushed. The last thing I wanted to do was talk to Wes about his past love interests.

He appeared, wiping his hands on a towel.

"Tell Ella about how I stole you away from your girlfriend."

He reached for his wife, putting his hand around her waist and pulling her toward him.

"What's there to tell? One look at you was all it took." He kissed her on the lips and headed back to the kitchen.

"He left out a few details," Kendra said.

"I guessed that," I answered, smiling. They were awfully cute. It was obvious how much they loved each other.

My shift ended ten minutes later. I retrieved my purse and cape and stepped out onto the sidewalk as a light rain fell. I pulled my hood onto my head as Luke's parting words rolled around in my head.

He was sorry things didn't turn out the way I'd wanted them to.

I climbed onto the bike, pushed down on the pedal, and settled onto the seat as I did. Now I had no way to reach Ezra. I desperately wanted to talk with him before Will came. I imagined Will chastising both of us together, and the two of us presenting a united front. I imagined Ezra standing up to Will, telling him to back off.

I steered the bike onto the street, staying as close to the parked cars as I could, wobbling a little as a car passed me.

Then again, maybe Luke knew something I didn't.

Eleven

I showed my box to Penny that evening as she sat in the living room, telling her the address of the house and asking if she was familiar with it. She said she'd lived in or around Nappanee her entire life and had never seen a house like it.

"I would definitely remember this place," she said.

She seemed a little overconfident, but I didn't say so.

"It may have burned down," she added. "Back when the Amish used kerosene, their houses burned down all the time. Now with gas and propane, from what I understand, there aren't nearly as many fires."

Some sort of house had to be there, or at least the bakery and outbuildings. I'd seen structures through the trees on Google Earth.

She took off her apple-red reading glasses and twirled them in her hand. "I can drive you out that way sometime, though, just to see what we can find."

I thanked her and mentioned the bakery I found online.

"That doesn't ring a bell either, but there are scads of little businesses around—shingle businesses. Someone puts out a sign and, voilà, a business!" She threw her hand up as she spoke. "But let's go visit. I'd love to find a new place to buy pastries."

Not only had she volunteered to take me to South Bend to visit the cooking school, but she was also willing to take me to the bakery too. The woman was kind and generous. This living arrangement was turning out to be quite nice. Sure, I'd rather be driving myself to find the Home Place and to South Bend, but God was good to provide a driver.

I held the box tightly as I climbed the stairs to my room, hoping Penny was wrong about the place burning down. I couldn't bear that.

That night, as I was drifting off to sleep, my phone beeped with a text from a number I didn't recognized. I opened it anyway.

Since you're not here, Mom let me get a phone. Thx!

It was Zed, of course. I could only imagine the film footage he'd be shooting now.

Cool! I texted back. *Now go to sleep.*

I couldn't help but smile as I closed my phone and tucked it next to my pillow. It would be so much easier to keep in touch with him now.

I half expected Will to show up at the café Friday morning, but he didn't. Near the end of my shift, I was feeling more unsettled than ever. I'd only been in Indiana for a few days, but it felt much longer, thanks to all the stress with Ezra and his family.

We had a bit of a midday rush and I didn't notice Penny at first, sitting in the last booth in my section. I was a little surprised to see her because she'd already been in for breakfast. I approached her with the coffeepot, thinking that was all she wanted, but she ordered a salad too.

Ten minutes later, as I served Penny her order, the front door opened, and out of the corner of my eye I saw Will holding the door for Ada and then Ezra.

Penny leaned to the side a little, staring. "Isn't that your beau?"

"And his brother, plus my cousin," I whispered.

Penny's eyes were full of concern. "Looks serious."

I ignored her comment and waved, doing my best to stay calm. Ada walked directly to me, taking my hand, her brown eyes tearing up.

"How are the girls?" I asked.

"Fine."

"They didn't come with you?"

"Christy's in school."

"Of course," I said.

"And it would have taken us days to get here with the twins." I was sure she was right about that.

Ada continued, "We had to leave at four this morning as it was." So they hadn't come partway yesterday. I felt for their driver, who was probably parked somewhere near the restaurant, taking a nap.

Will gave me a quick hug. Ezra didn't make eye contact with me. Instead, he ducked into a booth.

"Do you have a minute?" Will asked.

I glanced around for Kendra but didn't see her. "I'll ask."

I headed into the kitchen. It was only a few minutes before my shift was finished. I asked Wes if it was okay if I clocked out early, and he gave me the go-ahead. I took off my apron, collected my purse and cape, and walked back to the dining room.

As I passed Penny's table, she gave me an encouraging smile.

"Who is that?" Ada whispered as I slipped into the booth beside her. She still had her cape on and was hunched over a little, as if she was cold.

Before I could answer her, Ezra said, "She's the lady Ella's staying with."

"What?" Ada had a confused look on her face. "I thought you were boarding with a Mennonite family."

I shook my head, hoping Penny couldn't hear us, and whispered, "I rent a room from her."

Kendra approached, saving me from further questions, the coffeepot in her hand. Will said that was all we'd have, and she poured a cup for each of us. As she did, Penny approached and introduced herself. My face reddened, embarrassed that I hadn't thought to introduce her first. After everyone greeted each other, she turned to me and mouthed, "Everything okay?"

I nodded quickly, and then she said, "I'm going to Elkhart with a friend. Want to come with us when you're done here?"

I shook my head.

"Okay. Well, I'll be home late."

As she left, Ada reached for my hand that was lying flat on the table.

"Come home with us," she said. "We'll stop and get your things. Your boss here will understand. So will—what's the woman's name you're staying with?"

"Penny."

"That's right. She'll understand too."

"Understand? *I* don't even understand what's going on." I spoke directly to Ezra, who was across the table from me.

"We've come to collect Ezra," Will explained. "The Klines were concerned when he arrived on his motorcycle and then alarmed when they found out how the two of you deceived all of us back home. They told him to leave, and we agreed it was for the best."

"You're going home?"

Ezra crossed his arms and nodded.

"What about your bike?"

He jerked his thumb toward the window. There was a large white van parked on the side street, with a small flatbed trailer attached. Ezra's motorcycle was on top of it, held in place by canvas straps.

"Come with us," Ada said again.

I turned toward her. "Did my mother put you up to this?"

"She asked me to talk with you."

"Did she ask you to come?"

Ada shook her head. "Will asked me to."

I leaned back against the booth. "Did Mom consider coming?"

Ada tilted her head. "I'm not sure."

I turned my attention to Ezra. "That's it? You're going home, just like that?"

He met my gaze. "I don't have a choice." He wrapped his hands around his coffee cup. "I know you're disappointed in me, Ella, but I don't have a job or a place to live. And I really don't want to cause more of a rift with my family."

Ada put her arm around me, and as much as I wanted to pull away, I didn't. "Come home," she pleaded.

I didn't answer.

Will said they needed to get going. He pulled out his wallet and left a ten on the table. It registered then, that not once had Will asked me to come back. Neither had Ezra.

Only Ada.

"Are you coming?" Ada asked as we spilled out onto the sidewalk.

I shook my head. "Maybe in a couple of weeks. I'll probably take the bus home."

Ezra's head dropped, and Ada's eyes filled with tears.

"Ella, Ella," she whispered. "Please come home."

A year ago she would have insisted I obey her. Being a wife, or maybe it was being a mom, had changed her. Either that, or this was more about me, about the fact that she was finally realizing I was an adult and not a child.

I shook my head slowly. Ada's face was drawn, but she didn't say any more as she stepped beside Will, who tipped his hat to me. They crossed the street together, not touching but clearly joined.

That left Ezra and me on the sidewalk, not looking at each other.

"So," he said, speaking quickly. "I know I was mad a couple of days ago, but I've gotten over it, even though what you did really hurt." He sighed. "It was horrible staying with the Klines. Luke's great, but his *daed* is a real tyrant. I've never been so miserable." He exhaled. "Come home, okay? Join the church with me."

My voice was barely a whisper. "Are you proposing?"

His face was as red as his hair. "Kind of," he stammered. "Just come home. Then we can figure out what's next."

I closed my eyes. That's what I wanted—to marry Ezra. That's what I'd always wanted.

"Stay," I said, thinking of Freddy back home. I couldn't face my family, not yet. "You can find another job. I'll help you find a place to live. Penny probably has a friend…"

He was shaking his head. "Come back, Ella."

"I need to give notice here. I can't just walk out on Kendra and Wes."

And I hadn't seen the Home Place yet or found my answers to Sarah's book. I hadn't even started on that part of my plan.

"Then you'll come home?"

I took a deep breath. Going home meant dealing with Mom, Zed, and Freddy. Staying meant losing Ezra.

"I'm so sorry for making a mess of all of this," I said.

"Just come home."

"Give me a couple of weeks."

"Write to me and tell me when. I won't have my phone much longer."

"Your family will want you to marry someone else, Ez. Not me."

"Ella, I'm not going to marry anyone else."

Touched, I stepped forward to hug him, but as I did he leaned down and kissed me, even though Will and Ada were right there. The kiss took my breath away, and long before I was ready for it to end he pulled back, turned, and headed straight for the van.

I took a step to follow him.

"Ezra!" someone called out from behind me. I looked to see Luke speeding toward us on his bike.

"I didn't get a chance to say goodbye." He whizzed past me, toward the van. "*Daed* said you would be here." Luke brought the bike to a skidding stop and then climbed off. He seemed so much more assured and confident than he had when he'd come into the café. After they shook hands, they hugged and patted each other on the back. I hadn't realized they had forged a friendship in such a short time.

"Thanks for everything," Ezra said. "I don't know what I would have done without you."

After they let go of each other, Luke continued on his bike without looking back toward me. Ezra turned before he climbed into the van and waved.

I waved back and then winced as he slammed the door behind him. In the distance, Luke sped on down the street and then turned the corner, heading north.

I'd made a disaster out of things so far, but I still had hope—and with good reason, considering Ezra's goodbye. Maybe I could quickly resolve things here and then get home. I'd told him to give me a couple of weeks. That should give me enough time. I still needed to visit the Home Place—and to meet *Mammi's* niece Rosalee.

TWELVE

When I arrived at Penny's, I texted Zed, asking what he was doing.

Homework, he texted back.

Mom around?

No. She's out.

I didn't bother texting again. I called and then choked back my tears when he said, "Hello, Ella Pilla."

I stood quickly, doing my best not to cry. "Pilla?" He'd never called me that before. We'd never been big on nicknames in my family.

"Yeah. You're the biggest pill there is. You've really done it this time."

"Not you too…" I practically choked on the words. Was I that horrible? Probably…

"Mom's been on the phone with various Gundys, not to mention Lexie, nonstop. She even drove over to Aunt Klara's today. I think the two of them and *Mammi* had a big ol' discussion about you."

I shuddered at the thought. "I was surprised Mom didn't come out with Ada and Will."

"Nah," Zed responded. "The last thing she was going to do was beg you."

That sounded like Mom. "Is she out on a birth?"

"Nope."

I expected Zed to elaborate, but he didn't. "Where is she?"

"Out with Dad."

"Dad?" I barely recognized my own voice, it was so full of alarm.

"Back off, Ella. I mean Pilla."

"Since when did you start calling him 'Dad'?"

He didn't answer.

"Is Mom, like, dating him or something?"

He didn't answer.

"Zed?"

"Maybe you should talk to Mom about this, not me."

"No, maybe you should give me some straight answers. What is going on?"

"Maybe you shouldn't have taken off like you did at a critical juncture in the life of our family."

"Zed!" I used my firmest tone with him, the one that used to make him jump.

"That doesn't work anymore." His voice was as calm as could be. "You can't intimidate me the way you used to."

"Wow, that was harsh." I wasn't accustomed to him talking back. I began pacing around the room.

There was a long pause, and then he said, "I need to get back to my homework. Bye."

"Wait!"

But the connection ended.

I collapsed back on the bed. So much for my loving brother. I had no one, absolutely no one, left. No Mom. No Zed.

And now, no Ezra either. I was absolutely, utterly alone. Thanks to no one but myself. Another wave of loneliness overcame me. Who was I fooling? I was as homesick as could be. I'd give my notice to Kendra and be on a bus home in no time. I'd have Penny drive by the bakery and the address for the Home Place, but there was no reason for me to try to get a job at Plain Treats. Or to check out the cooking school in South Bend. I didn't have the money to pay for it, anyway. When I got back home,

I'd convince *Mammi* into letting me ask Zed to help crack the code. He would be our best bet.

I needed to get back to Lancaster County as soon as possible. So be it if I had to give up baking school.

I had Saturday off and dragged around the house. Penny was gone all day, shopping with a friend. By the time she arrived home, it was dark. She said she was going to church the next morning and then out for lunch with another friend. I didn't bother to ask when she could take me by the Home Place. Once again, I found myself wishing I had a license and a car.

The next morning I sat on my bed and watched the rain bounce off the leaves of the maple outside my window. Mom and Zed would be going to church and then maybe over to Aunt Klara's later. Or maybe they would spend the afternoon with Freddy. Maybe he would come to our house for Sunday dinner even. *Our house.* It wasn't mine anymore, not at all. I pulled one of the three pillows on the bed against my chest and hugged it tightly.

My mind jumped from one memory of Ezra to another. Then I started speculating what the talk about us was back home, who was saying what, how his *mamm* and *daed* would have reacted, what Ada would have said to other people about me, what Ezra was telling people about his short time in Indiana.

I didn't want to head out to the Mennonite church, the one Penny had pointed out when she drove me to the grocery store the week before. Though it was within walking distance, I had no desire to go out in the rain.

I stayed in bed.

A half hour later, my head still in an Ezra fog, I shuffled downstairs to make myself a couple of eggs. By the time I finished eating it had stopped raining and the sun had come out. I stepped out onto the patio. It was relatively warm. Penny had offered me the use of her bike anytime. I contemplated going for a ride.

I knew the Home Place was toward Goshen. It wouldn't hurt to ride the bike in that direction, looking for Willow Lane.

A few minutes later, I turned right on Nappanee Avenue, away from downtown and toward Goshen. The tires of the bike made a hissing sound over the wet pavement. I passed house after house, then a church, a school, and more houses. I pedaled harder. Even though the day was cool, I began to sweat under my cape. I missed Ezra. I missed his motorcycle. I missed the security of being with him.

The trip out on Ezra's motorcycle had made me more aware of the countryside, but being on the bicycle was that times ten. I noticed everything. A man was working on his truck in the driveway of his house while children played around him. A little girl holding a doll waved. A family piled out of a van in front of a house, looking as if they had just returned from church. A couple on the other side of the street strolled along, hand in hand. Everyone seemed to be with someone today, except for me.

I turned right, following the sign to Goshen. A horse and buggy came toward me on the other side of the street. I could make out the young family inside as they passed by. And then two bicyclists.

Finally I reached the outskirts of the town and the fifty-five mile-per-hour speed limit. I was now on Highway 119, and I winced as the cars and trucks picked up speed and whizzed by. I tensed up again, bracing myself against the force of it, gripping the handlebars to keep the bike steady, trying to stay on the edge of the shoulder but out of the gravel.

The other bicyclists I'd seen since I arrived in Nappanee made it look so easy. I kept glancing from one side of the road to the other, hoping Willow Lane would appear. As I rode, I studied each house. At first all of them seemed to be *Englisch* farms, but after a while I passed a decidedly Plain farm with no electrical wires in sight and a buggy with a horse hitched to it out front. After that, there were plenty of Amish-looking places. Lots of them had "No Sunday Business" signs up under placards advertising farm-fresh eggs.

After a while I stopped and pulled my cell phone from my pocket. I'd only been riding for half an hour. I decided to ride for fifteen more minutes and then turn around if I hadn't found Willow Lane. That would make it an hour and half total, a good long ride considering I'd hardly ever been on a bike before.

Not long after, however, I bumped over a sharp rock. As the air rushed out of the tire, I hobbled the bike to a stop. My stomach knotted. I had no idea how to fix a flat and even if I did, I had nothing with me to do so. I took out my cell and called Penny's home number. She didn't answer. I left her a message but decided not to call her cell in case she was still in church. Turning the bike around, I started pushing it, knowing I had a long walk ahead of me.

It was just after noon and the traffic had increased, creating a wind of pungent exhaust against my face and an occasional smattering of pebbles against my legs. I turned down the next county road I came to and cut back toward town on a less busy route.

I walked along, pushing the bike awkwardly. The road was narrow with hardly any shoulder, and I began to wonder if I'd made a mistake. A couple of times, when a car seemed too close, I stepped down into the slope of the ditch, holding the bike up as best I could. I called Penny's home phone again, leaving a message that I'd gotten off the highway, hoping she would come looking for me. As I slipped my phone back into my pocket, I heard the clopping of a horse behind me and turned my head.

Two young women were approaching in a buggy. The driver looked to be about twenty, but the passenger was a few years younger, probably right around my age. They both had dark hair and creamy complexions and were obviously sisters.

"Need some help?" the driver called out.

"Yes," I called out gratefully. "Where are you headed?" I hoped they were going into town.

"Home," the oldest girl said, reciting the county road number they lived on.

It was two over from the one the dairy was located on. "Do you know the Darryl Kline family? I think they are close by."

"Sure," the driver said.

"Could you take me there?" If he was home, maybe Luke could patch the tire for me.

"No problem," the younger girl said. "I'll help you with the bike. I'm Naomi, by the way. And that's Anna."

"Thanks so much. I'm Ella."

After we wrestled the bike into the back, I hopped up front, settling onto the bench.

Naomi asked if I was related to the Klines. I said I wasn't, but that I'd met Luke and hoped he could help me.

"Have you met Thomas?" Anna asked.

I shook my head.

"Anna thinks he's cute," Naomi said.

"You hush!" Anna was blushing.

"And he is," Naomi added, and then she laughed.

"As cute as Luke?" I asked.

Anna was laughing now.

"Oh, well, they don't look a thing alike," Naomi said. "Tom is bigger, more muscular. And taller, even though they're only a year apart."

Luke had appeared pretty tall to me.

"But she prefers Luke," Anna said, nudging her sister.

"He's definitely handsome," I said, but I felt uncomfortable in the middle of the girls' teasing.

After that we rode along in silence for a while. They didn't ask me where I was from and I didn't volunteer. We passed Willow Lane and I strained my neck trying to see if I could spot the Home Place. I couldn't.

I asked about Rosalee.

"*Ya*, we know her," Anna said. "She's in the same district as the Klines, over one from us. The older kids work for her some."

I perked up at that. Maybe Luke would introduce me to her.

A few minutes later, Anna maneuvered the buggy down a long driveway, bordered by pastures. Ahead was a weary-looking and quite small farmhouse. A wave of emotion swept over me at the sight of the farm where *Mammi* had lived with her husband, where they had raised their three daughters. If I had my dates right, my mother had spent the first eight years of her life here. Now I had come back to the very same place, bringing it full circle. Amazing.

"They might not be back from church yet," the younger girl said.

The place looked pretty quiet. Just as I was getting out of the buggy, intending to go knock on the front door, I caught a glimpse of a man by the barn. I headed that way instead.

"Hello," I called out.

A moment later I could tell the man was Luke.

"Ella?" He stepped toward me. "What are you doing here?"

"My bike has a flat tire. I was hoping maybe you could fix it for me."

"Sure," he said, leading the way back toward the buggy. Anna and Naomi were both smiling at him. He said hello and thanked them, and then he hoisted the bike from the back.

I thanked the young women too. As Anna turned the buggy around, Naomi kept her eyes on Luke, as much as she could, until they were headed back toward the road.

Luke told me to wait while he fetched a new tube. As he headed back toward the barn, I stood in the driveway, holding the bike and looking around. Next to the house stood a shed, a windmill, and then the barn. Past the house was a creek that came out of the woods. I knew from Google Earth that it bordered the Home Place.

As I was staring off into the woods, my eyes along the tops of the fir trees, Luke returned empty-handed.

"Someone used the last tube and didn't replace it."

"That's okay. I'll walk back to the highway. I'm sure I'll find a ride."

"No, I'll take you."

"But you're busy…"

He shook his head. "I came home from church before the others to check to see if we have any cows in labor, but we don't." He nodded back toward the barn. "I'll go hitch up the buggy."

"Are you sure?" I didn't mean to be such a pain.

"Of course," he said, blushing. He didn't seem as nervous as the first time I met him, but he wasn't exactly comfortable either.

I knew he probably had other things to do. Like courting a local girl. Maybe even Naomi. Or maybe they would see each other at a singing tonight. I sighed. It wasn't as though I had any other options, except to walk back to the highway and see if someone would stop.

"Thanks," I said. "That would be great."

Ten minutes later, as we were headed toward the county road, I asked him about Rosalee and the Home Place.

"The Home Place?" His expression was bewilderment. "I haven't heard it called that."

"Really?" How odd. "But you know Rosalee, right? Aren't you related somehow?"

"She's my aunt. Let me think. By marriage, yes. Her husband was my mother's uncle. Something like that."

I nodded. "I'm hoping to see the Home Place sometime. And meet Rosalee. That's where I was headed when I got the flat."

"She isn't there today."

"Oh?"

"She's off visiting. She went to another district's church service."

We were quiet for a few minutes. Finally, I turned toward him a little. "My mom lived on your dairy when she was little."

"Oh?"

"So it was really nice to see it. Maybe you could show me around some more sometime."

He nodded his head a little, but that was all.

I stared straight ahead. I thought of what Ezra said, about Darryl Kline being a tyrant. Maybe he wouldn't want me stopping by. Maybe that was why Luke was so eager to give me a ride away from the farm.

We rode in silence after that, except for me giving directions to Penny's house. When we reached our destination, I thanked him.

He blushed again.

"I hope this doesn't mess up your day too much. You probably have plans for tonight, right? Like a singing?"

He nodded his head but didn't, of course, elaborate.

Instead, he jumped down from the buggy and hauled the bike out of the back. I took it and thanked him again.

He nodded his head and climbed back into his buggy. As he pulled away, a wave of loneliness swept over me. It would have been nice to think Luke would be my friend and introduce me to Rosalee and show me around both the Home Place and the dairy, but that didn't seem likely at all. Nothing having to do with Indiana was going according to my plans.

I missed Ezra with all of my heart.

I would give my notice the next day and then ask Penny to take me out to Plain Treats so I could at least see the Home Place before I went back to Pennsylvania. I had little hope of making a connection with

Rosalee more than introducing myself, but still I wanted, more than anything, to see where Sarah had lived. Then I would return to Lancaster County, do my best to avoid Freddy, and hope to marry Ezra as soon as possible.

THIRTEEN

Penny didn't return until nightfall. I met her at the door, explaining the voice mails before she had a chance to listen to them and assuring her Luke had taken me home. She gave me a hug and said she was glad I was safe. I told her I was sorry about the flat and that I would get it repaired. I decided to wait to tell her I would be leaving until I gave Kendra and Wes notice. I did say I had Wednesday off and asked if it would work for her to take me to Plain Treats. She said yes.

When I arrived at the restaurant the next morning, Wes asked me to make biscuits while he whipped up gravy. I followed his recipe closely, adding the flour, salt, and baking powder together, and then cutting in the butter. After I added the milk, I mixed the cold dough with my hands and then started kneading it, pushing my very being into the bowl.

"Easy does it." Wes stood at the stove, a whisk in his hand. "You're going to upend the kitchen."

I backed off a little.

"Rough weekend?"

I nodded.

"Homesick?"

I nodded again.

"I would be too," he said, adding more flour to the gravy.

I swiped at my eye with the back of my hand, sure he would understand my giving two-weeks' notice. But I wanted to tell Kendra, not him. It wasn't until the breakfast rush had started that Wes told me she wasn't feeling well and that we'd have to handle the day on our own.

I was surprised when Luke came in and ordered coffee and biscuits-and-gravy as I scrambled to serve everyone. When I delivered his plate, he said he needed to talk with me about something.

Fearing it was serious, I sat down across from him in the booth. He'd been drawing on his napkin, a diagram of some kind of machine, but he covered it with his hand when he realized I'd noticed it. His face reddened.

"I got to thinking about your bicycle when I got home. Did you get it fixed yet?"

I exhaled with relief. So it wasn't anything serious. "No, not yet. But I will."

"You know how to fix a flat?"

I wrinkled my nose. "Not exactly, but I can figure it out."

"I can do it now."

"I don't get off until two."

"I just bought a bunch of tubes. I could go by that house where you're staying."

I imagined Luke working on the patio, startling Penny. "Okay, but let me call Penny first and let her know you're coming." She hadn't been in for breakfast yet.

I slipped into the kitchen and told Wes I needed to make a quick call. I retrieved my cell and dialed. This time Penny answered her landline. She was fine with Luke stopping by.

"It will be a pleasure to meet him," she said.

Luke blushed again when I told him what she said. I found him both endearing and annoying. I couldn't imagine why in the world he was so shy.

Later, just before the evening shift waitress came in and I would be leaving for the day, I gave Wes my two-weeks' notice.

"I'm so sorry," I added.

"Actually, we saw this one coming. At least Kendra did. On Friday, when that bunch of Amish folk came in. We knew you'd be heading home soon."

My face grew warm.

"No worries," he said. "We'll manage."

I thanked him profusely for all he'd done, and especially for giving me a chance to waitress even though I'd had no experience. I thanked him also for being so very understanding.

He held up his hand. "Sure, I understand, but I'm not happy about it. Now I have to start back through the pile of résumés we have."

When I reached Penny's, she went on and on about how sweet Luke was.

"What a thoughtful person," she said.

She invited me to share the minestrone she'd made for dinner, and over the meal she said, "Maybe you should give him a chance. It would be nice for you to get to know a local young man."

I resisted the urge to roll my eyes. "Too bad you didn't have a chance to get to know Ezra. You would have *adored* him."

"Oh?"

"Yes." I picked up my spoon. "Unlike Luke, Ezra is very outgoing, not shy at all. He has a great sense of humor. Children adore him. He has a wonderful family. And he's cute, cute, cute."

"That I noticed, but would he have come over to fix the bike?"

"Absolutely. And he would have had you laughing within a couple minutes of arriving." At least I thought he would have fixed the tire, although he wasn't very mechanically inclined. He even needed help sometimes when his motorcycle had problems.

She smiled at that. "A good sense of humor certainly makes life easier." She put a roll on her plate. "That was something my marriage could have used more of."

I reached over and patted her hand, my thoughts still on Ezra. Just picturing him made me happy. I would soon be home. Ready to join the church with him. Ready to leave my life as a Mennonite behind. Philosophically, the two churches weren't that different. I knew I would struggle with the High German, but I could learn that better with time. And

Pennsylvania Dutch. The biggest challenge for me would be no technology. I thought of my cell phone in my pocket.

"What's the matter?" Penny ladled more soup into her bowl.

"Oh, nothing," I said. "Except, speaking of Ezra, I need to tell you I gave my notice at work today. I'm going back home."

She put the ladle back in the tureen. "Oh, my."

"I'm sorry, Penny," I said quickly. "I hope I haven't put you out."

"It's just I've enjoyed having you here, that's all." She smiled. "But I knew from that first night you wouldn't be here long."

"I can pay you for another month."

She shook her head. "It's not that. It's been a pleasure having you around, is all."

"Thank you." I ducked my head as I spoke, suddenly feeling shy myself. For the first time I second-guessed my decision. I hoped she'd find another tenant soon.

After dinner I called Mom, but she didn't answer. I left a message, telling her I was planning to take the bus home in two weeks.

The next day, around two, an older Amish woman walked into the café, her cape around her shoulders. She had silvery hair under a black bonnet and smooth skin despite the fact that she was probably somewhere in her early sixties. She was a couple of inches shorter than I and seemed timid. She slid into a booth and then searched the room. When she saw me she nodded slightly but didn't smile. She turned the coffee cup in front of her right side up, and I hurried over with the pot and a menu.

As I filled her cup, she said in a quiet voice, "Are you Ella?"

I nodded.

"I'm Rosalee. Your grandmother's niece."

"Oh, my goodness," I said, my face breaking into a grin. "I was planning on coming out to your bakery tomorrow."

She smiled in return and a sweetness filled her eyes. "I heard you were interested in working for me. As it turns out, I need more help than I thought. I'm hoping you can start soon. You can live with me too, if you would like, to save on room and board."

"Seriously?" I answered, my antennae spinning. Something was up. I wondered if Luke had spoken to her about me. "But I'm heading back to Lancaster County in two weeks."

"Have you talked to your mother recently?" She stared at the table.

"I left her a message last night—"

"Call her again." Rosalee kept her eyes down.

"Why?"

She didn't answer me.

I couldn't fathom what Mom had to do with all of this, but I was desperate to find out.

Rosalee handed the menu back to me and said she would only have coffee.

I headed into the kitchen. My shift was officially over. I grabbed my purse and jacket from the closet, told Wes and Kendra goodbye, and then stepped outside, turning my back to the street so I was staring at the brick wall of the building. I dialed Mom's number and let it ring. Just as I was sure I was about to get her voice mail, she answered.

"Did you get my message last night?"

"Ella, Ella," Mom said. I knew her saying my name twice didn't bode well.

I swallowed hard. "Rosalee's here. She asked if I'd spoken to you."

"I was going to call once you were off work."

"I gave my notice yesterday, Mom. I'm coming home."

"But you wanted to get away…" Her voice trailed off.

"I did."

"And then you made your decision to stay in Indiana. That's what Ada said."

"Yeah, sure, but then I changed my mind." What was this? No one had ever taken me at face value before. Why should they start now?

"You need to give it more time." Her voice was firm.

I needed to…what?

She continued. "The Lord may have more for you to learn before you come back home."

I pressed the palm of my left hand against a smooth brick and leaned forward. I knew what this was about. With Ezra back there again, everyone now thought the best place for me was out here. Incredible. My mother was trying to force away her own daughter.

"You don't want me," I said. She was the most cold-hearted person I knew, as cold as the wall in front of me. My own mother.

"That's not it. You made a rash decision to leave. Now I wonder if you're making a rash decision to come back. Rosalee has a job for you."

So they had talked. "I can't ride a bike all that way to work."

"It's my understanding she has a place for you to live too."

Wow. Obviously, they had discussed my entire situation. The very thought made me furious. When were other people going to stop trying to run my life?

"It would be good experience for you," Mom added, "in your field of interest, no less."

I didn't respond. *Now* she cared about my field of interest? Give me a break!

"Ella, I want you to take responsibility. You can't be dashing here and there, working yourself into a—"

"Dither?"

"Exactly."

I bristled, telling myself to keep my voice steady despite the anger that bubbled inside of me like lava in a volcano.

"So, when do you anticipate me coming home?"

"It depends…"

"On?"

"On what you learn."

On what I learn. And everybody thought *I* was the dramatic one.

I took a deep breath and let it out slowly, trying to calm my anger and look at the situation rationally.

Truth be told, living at the Home Place would be amazing. I desperately missed Ezra, but what better way to discover who Sarah Berg really was than to live where she lived, bake where she baked, and try to decipher the rest of her "Recipes for Life" while living where she wrote them? I could even search around at my leisure for Sarah's missing artwork.

And the icing on the cake, so to speak, would be working at Plain Treats. Though I hated the thought of giving in to my mother's manipulations, when else would I ever get a chance like this, to work in a real bakery, one located on the property of an old family home, no less? Living at the Home Place and working at Plain Treats—getting to do both was a dream come true.

If only it didn't have to happen this way, with a whole gang of scheming Amish and Mennonite puppet masters pulling the strings from two states away.

"Let me think about it."

"Of course," she answered.

I managed a raggedy "Goodbye."

As I hung up she was saying, "I love—"

I never heard the "you."

My hand shook as I slipped my phone back into my pocket. She didn't want me. But she loved me. I shuddered.

Squaring my shoulders, I took in another deep breath and told myself I'd be a fool to turn these opportunities down, regardless of how they were coming about. On the other hand, I'd be a fool to stay here and let everyone succeed in keeping Ezra and me apart.

Guess it was clear: Either way, stay or go home, I was a fool.

Once I was back in the dining room, I took a deep breath and then approached the older Amish woman again as I clutched my cape and purse.

"I talked to my mother. When would you want me to start?"

"As soon as possible."

I glanced toward the kitchen. Kendra was standing in the doorway.

Rosalee spoke to me in Pennsylvania Dutch. I shook my head and said I didn't understand, even though I caught a few of her words.

In English, she said, "You can come with me today if you like." It was then that I spotted the buggy out the front window. Luke was in the seat, holding the horse's reins.

"Ella," Kendra called out. "A word in the kitchen?"

I followed her, feeling like a naughty puppy. She'd guessed right and explained what was going on to Wes, that Rosalee Neff had come here to offer me a job in her bakery—and that I was thinking about taking it.

"I thought you were going back to Pennsylvania, to your Amish beau," he said.

"I thought so too," I replied. "But then this popped up. So now the question is, do I stay here for a while and get the experience in a bakery I've been needing? Or go back home where my boyfriend is?" Feeling like that volcano inside was about to blow, I looked from one to the other and cried, "I don't know what to do!"

"Whoa." Wes turned to Kendra. "Babe, I'm going to let you handle this one." Looking to me as he held the spatula in front of himself, as if for protection, he added, "I don't do drama."

I smiled in spite of myself. "I'm sorry. I'm all worked up into a dither. At least, that's what my mom calls it."

"Yeah." His eyebrows shot up. "Good word." He turned back to the stovetop and started scraping the grill.

Kendra put her arm around me and led me aside. "Don't worry about working the two weeks, if that's what this is. I have a couple of gals coming in for interviews later this afternoon. I can have one of them start tomorrow as your replacement if this is really what you want to do."

"I…I don't know if it is or not."

"You're not sure?"

I swallowed hard. "No. Well, kind of. Maybe…maybe not."

Kendra chuckled. "You really *are* confused."

Glancing toward Wes, I lowered my voice and explained a little further, saying that while on the one hand living at the family home and working in a bakery were both dreams come true, on the other hand, the only reason these opportunities came up in the first place was because Ezra's family and mine were trying to keep us apart, thanks to our differing religions. So while I really was excited about the opportunity, I was reluctant to give in to the manipulations of others.

Kendra listened intently, her big sister face on. When I was finished, she thought for a moment and then spoke. "If I were you, I'd stick around and take that job no matter how I got it. The people back there may be trying to manipulate you, but the way I see it, you're the one who makes out in the deal. Swallow your pride, accept the job, and go home in a month or two, once everybody's had a chance to calm down."

She made a lot of sense. Wavering, I said softly, "But what about Ezra? I miss him so much."

She gave me a sympathetic smile. "So go home in a few weeks instead of a few months. Really, hon, in the big scheme of things, does it matter all that much? If your relationship is as strong as you think it is, this time apart will only make it stronger. Haven't you heard the saying? Absence makes the heart grow fonder."

I was quiet for a long moment, and then I looked over to Wes, who was still at the stove.

"How'd your wife get so wise?" I called out to him.

"Years of running interference on all the drama, I guess."

"Listen, don't be a stranger," Kendra said. "Check in with us from time to time until you go back home."

I thanked her and gave her a hug, called out another thanks to Wes, and I returned to the dining room, coming to a stop at Rosalee's table.

"Okay," I said. "I'll do it. And I can go with you today, if Luke will take me by Penny's on the way so I can collect my things."

I waited as Rosalee put the exact change for the coffee on the table. Then I led the way out, straight toward Luke and the buggy.

She climbed in first and I followed.

"Go to where Ella is staying," she said to Luke.

He looked straight ahead as he eased the horse toward the street. As we rode along, though this had probably been the right decision, the truths surrounding that decision began to close in on me.

My mother didn't want me.

My boyfriend was six hundred miles away.

My whole family had conspired to enforce what had simply started out as an impulsive whim.

It was as though they were all saying, *Okay, Ella. You made your bed, now lie in it.*

Thus, lie in it I would.

Or maybe I would smother in it instead.

Once we reached Penny's house, I told Luke and Rosalee to wait in the buggy. I found my landlady and friend at the kitchen table, leafing through a French cookbook. I quickly explained my situation, saying I was only stopping by to collect my things.

"Oh, I'm so disappointed," she replied. "I was at least looking forward to the next two weeks. We got along so well."

I agreed. "It's not you. It's just that—" I wasn't sure how to say it without sounding as if I were in junior high.

She smiled. "I can see this will be a good situation for you." She stood. "I'd still like to take you to South Bend to check out the cooking school."

I was touched, although there wouldn't be any reason for me to go to cooking school now. I wasn't going to stay in Indiana that long—just long enough to serve my sentence for being impulsive, just until Mom agreed it was a good idea for me to come home again. Maybe just until I'd solved *Mammi*'s mystery—though more for my sake now than hers. She'd probably been the one to suggest the arrangement with Rosalee in the first place. Once my secret ally, it now seemed that even my own grandmother had turned against me.

I thanked Penny and said I would call her sometime and then hurried up to my room. It only took me a few minutes to gather my belongings. With my backpack over my shoulder, and a cardboard box full of my toiletries and the carved box wrapped in its pillowcase in my hands, I walked down the stairs.

Penny went out onto the porch with me and then gave me a hug, reaching awkwardly around my things. She made me promise to call her once I was settled in with Rosalee. She stayed put as I hurried toward the buggy. Luke took the box and backpack and stowed them in the back while I climbed up on the seat next to Rosalee with the carved box. I waved to Penny. Just before we left she called out to me.

"Ella, take the bicycle."

"Oh, no. That's too much—"

"Luke, come get it," she said. "It's right where you left it."

He glanced at me. I shrugged and then looked at Penny. "I'll pay you for it."

"Hogwash," she said. "It's yours."

Luke did her bidding as I called out a thank-you. Soon he had the bike wrangled into the back and we were on our way. Neither of my companions spoke, and I, surprisingly, didn't know what to say.

My stomach churned, wondering what I'd gotten myself in to. Rosalee obviously had a bakery business, but that could mean just about anything. Maybe she made bread out of her kitchen. And maybe she had an outhouse instead of a bathroom. Even if Mom didn't change her mind soon, I might still go home anyway. It wasn't as though she could stop me, any more than she'd been able to prevent me from coming out here in the first place.

As we plodded along through town, I took the carved box out of the pillowcase and handed it to Rosalee.

"Look what you have," she said. Obviously she'd seen it before—her voice was a little more animated than it had been. Luke glanced down at it as he drove.

"My grandmother had it. There are three altogether. My cousin Lexie has the one with a carving of Amielbach, a big house in Switzerland. And my cousin Ada has one of the Frutigen bakery, which is also a place in Switzerland."

Rosalee ran her finger over the top. "They were carved by Abraham Sommers. This one is from a drawing by my grandmother."

"That's right. So you've known about the boxes all these years?"

"I remember two of them from when I was little—the place in Switzerland and this house. My father must have told your grandmother to take them when she left for Pennsylvania. But the third one is news to me."

"There's a book too." I took the box back and opened it, figuring she might know a thing or two that could help me break the code. "It was your grandmother's. She recorded recipes, drew all sorts of stuff, and wrote in a secret code." I handed the book to Rosalee.

"I've never seen this," she said, flipping through it carefully. "What a treasure."

"The pictures are symbols. They represent different people in her life. That I've figured out. I'm not so sure about the other stuff though, the odd code. Then there's her handwriting in general—it's so small and old fashioned. Some of the recipes I can read—and others I can't. Same with the entries."

"Oh, my," she said, lingering on the page with the maze. "Isn't this something? I wonder what she meant by all of it."

"I think it's a maze of her life."

"Could be," Rosalee said, squinting in the afternoon light.

"My *mammi* said Sarah did other artwork. Drawings and paintings."

Rosalee continued through the book. "I remember her drawing when I was little. I hadn't thought of it in years."

"Is any of her work still around? In the attic? Or somewhere else?"

The woman shook her head. "I haven't come across anything."

"Could I look around while I'm there?" I blurted out, and then I felt embarrassed for my blunder. That was far too forward, even for me.

But she didn't seem offended. "Sure. But I bet my *daed* got rid of all of it years ago after Sarah died. He didn't think it was right for her to be drawing."

My heart sank. I could see an Amish son cleaning out his mother's art, especially if he'd felt all along that it was too prideful.

"I'm so excited I'm finally going to be able to see the Home Place."

"The Home Place?" Rosalee gave me a sideways glance. "No one's called it that in years." She handed the book back to me.

"That's what Sarah called it. And my grandmother calls it that too."

A somber expression fell across her face. "She's probably the last one to do so since *Mammi* Sarah passed on."

As the horse picked up speed on the outskirts of town, heading toward Goshen, I carefully tucked the book inside the box and then slipped both of them back into the pillowcase. I held it securely against my chest, wondering at Rosalee's response as we rode along in silence.

Luke turned on the road past the one I took on the bicycle. At the next intersection was a simple sign that read "Plain Treats" and an arrow directing us up Willow Lane.

He made another turn, onto a gravel road this time, so the going was a little slower. In about a quarter of a mile, the lane curved. Ahead was a small building with a "Closed" sign in the window. I smiled at the sight of the bakery. A row of poplar trees partially hid the rest of the property. Even if Penny had been out this way before, she wouldn't have seen the house. The trees blocking it from view had probably been there for more than a hundred years.

Fourteen

As the buggy passed the bakery, the lane turned sharply to the right, and in the distance a large white house came into view. My first sight of it wasn't at the same angle as the image carved on the box, but it was definitely the Home Place. My heart raced. To think I'd actually been invited to live here! Sure, I would only stay a short time, but the very thought lifted my spirits immeasurably.

I could see one of the wings of the house and the front porch. A moment later the barn, off to the left, came into view. It was large, with a rounded roof and whitewashed, although in need of a fresh coat. Off to the right was a root cellar, dug into the slope of a slight hill, and then a small orchard of apple trees. The trunks were worn and gnarly, while the leaves were a tender green.

As we neared the house, Luke brought the horse to a stop. There were more outbuildings in back of the farmhouse and also a vegetable garden. Beyond were the woods and past that, I knew, the Klines' dairy farm.

Luke set the brake, and I jumped down, stepping around to the rear. Luke was already there, pulling out the bicycle. He handed me my cardboard box and backpack before turning toward the barn. I followed Rosalee.

The main house was big, two stories in the middle, with a one-story wing on each side.

On the way to the back door, I got a closer look at the outbuildings behind it. One was likely a toolshed and another was definitely an old smokehouse. I'd seen a few of those in Lancaster County, and they always intrigued me. I loved imagining the smell of smoking bacon and hams and the months the process took.

Seedlings poked up through the rich, dark soil of the garden plot. Beyond it was a chicken coop. In the middle of the side lawn was a tulip tree, already budding with blossoms. For years I'd wanted Mom to plant one by our cottage, but she'd never been interested.

I spotted an herb garden close to the house and stepped toward it. "Sarah wrote about drying herbs," I said. "And lots of her recipes and remedies use them."

Rosalee shuddered a little. "I remember those remedies well. When I was sick, my *daed* would send me down to the *daadi haus* for one of her 'treatments.' Ugh." She stepped toward the side door of the house.

A brown vine, probably clematis, wound its way around the railing and up the weathered steps. The roof above it sagged a little and was covered with moss. Rosalee led the way into a mudroom and then through that to a large kitchen. Pine cabinets lined the walls all the way around, and in the middle of the room was a table covered in a blue-checkered cloth with an old kerosene lantern sitting at the center. I was pleased to see a small propane refrigerator and stove. So at least Rosalee's district approved some modern conveniences, thank goodness.

"The bathroom is down this hall," Rosalee said, and then she smiled, probably at the look of relief on my face. "And where you'll sleep is too."

I followed her, poking my head into the bathroom. It had a toilet, sink, and shower, nothing fancy but more than adequate. To my relief, there was a propane lamp to the side of the sink.

Rosalee motioned toward the next open door, and I joined her in a few more steps. There was a twin bed, covered with a quilt. On the dresser was a set of sheets, two towels, and a washcloth. It was obvious she'd expected me to come. There were three pegs on the wall, next to a window with simple white curtains. I peeked out and could see the garden, the barn, and the woods in the near distance. It was a lovely room.

"Thank you." I slid the box on top of the dresser and set my backpack on the floor, wondering who all had slept in here through the years.

Rosalee turned toward the door. "I'll be finishing up in the bakery. Come join me after you've put your things away and had a look around."

I placed the torn pages from the bridal magazines and my jeans in the bottom drawer of the dresser. I knew I wouldn't need those for a while. I hung my dresses, coat, and cape on the pegs, and then I set my second pair of shoes next to the wall.

Once back in the kitchen, I headed around to the foyer, past the open staircase and over to the second wing, which was a large living room. It was as big as the kitchen and sparsely furnished with a sofa, a cabinet, a recliner, and three straight-back chairs. As with most Amish homes, it could easily hold a church service or even a wedding. There were two bookcases, both full, and a small table under the window facing the front porch.

I wondered if Rosalee had any children and where they lived, surprised one of them didn't live with her. Most Amish women her age would have a son running the farm and a houseful of grandchildren to help with.

Rosalee had said I could check out the place, so I headed up the open staircase. Nearly every step creaked, and I couldn't help but notice the dust bunnies in the corners. On the landing, I stopped to look out the window. It faced the woods. I was eye level with a canopy of new leaves, each one a different shade of brilliant green, contrasting with the dark needles of the fir and pine trees. Down the hall was closed door after closed door. Reminding myself that Rosalee had said it was okay, I opened the first one.

The room was empty. The walls were painted an off-white, as was the trim. The closet was completely empty as well. The next room had a bed and bureau, but it was obviously vacant. The next one was sparsely furnished too, but there were dresses and *kapps* hanging on the pegs. Realizing it was Rosalee's room, I shut the door in a hurry. I was surprised she slept upstairs and not down, closer to the bathroom.

Then the next door I opened dispelled that notion. It was a fairly new bathroom, probably added within the last ten years.

There were two more completely vacant rooms and then one filled with a bed, several bureaus, and two desks. Judging by how they were piled, she used it as a storage room. At the end of the hall was another door, which I opened and saw that it led to the attic staircase. I ventured upward. There was enough light coming in from a small window at the far end for me to make my way. I stood on the last step, squinting, and could make out several trunks and cardboard boxes. I opened the closest box to find a set of white dishes. The next box had a couple of quilts in it. And the third was full of clothing, mostly trousers and shirts. The trunks were all empty.

Puzzled, I decided I'd snooped around enough for now. If the drawings were in the house, they weren't in plain sight. One thing was obvious—Rosalee wasn't a pack rat. For the house being in the family so long, the place was practically bare. *Mammi's* tiny *daadi haus* had more things crammed into it than this entire building did.

I went downstairs and then outside. As I walked toward the bakery, I noted again the entrance to the underground cellar, a stone staircase leading down to a wood door. I would visit it later. Off to the side were raspberry and blueberry bushes and, beyond that, the orchard. Clearly, Rosalee raised far more produce than she needed for herself. I wondered how much of it she used in her bakery.

I walked around to the front of Plain Treats, impressed again with the clever name. The sign in the window still read "Closed," but the door was unlocked.

The smell of freshly baked bread and rosemary greeted me as I stepped inside. Everything was clean, though I could see immediately that the walls needed to be repainted and the seats of some of the gray vinyl chairs, pushed up against gray faux-marble tables, had little tears. There was a small glass case filled with pastries, sticky buns, and loaves of bread.

I heard voices coming from the kitchen. I recognized both of them.

"Can you bring Millie to help tomorrow?" Rosalee asked.

Luke said, "If you don't mind if Eddie comes with her. *Mamm* hasn't been feeling well again."

Rosalee didn't answer.

I stopped at the counter, unsure if I should continue.

Luke laughed. "So, is it worth it for Millie to come?"

"Has Eddie calmed down any?"

I couldn't make out his response, but I could hear the chorus of their laughter that followed. Though they had been nearly silent with me, neither one of them seemed shy talking with the other.

I took the opportunity to step past the counter and into the kitchen. "What can I do?" I asked.

Rosalee nodded toward the sink. "Wash up and then you can help us bag this bread."

They were both standing at a stainless steel table, slipping loaves into plastic bags, their hands in latex gloves. I stepped over to the sink and began scrubbing. The kitchen was much smaller than the one at the restaurant. There was a gas stove with two big ovens and an industrial-sized mixer, which to my relief was plugged into an outlet in the wall, meaning I'd be able to charge my phone here.

On the other side of the room was a rack with trays of rolls, pies, and pastries. At the far end were two closed doors, one with a "Restroom" sign on it.

"Did this used to be a house?" I dried my hands and slipped on gloves from a box by the sink.

"*Ya*," Rosalee answered. "It was the *daadi haus*. My grandparents lived here while I was growing up. We turned it into a bakery a year ago."

The other door probably led to what had at one time been the bedroom. This was where Rosalee came for her grandmother's remedies. I took a deep breath. Sarah had lived both here and at the Home Place.

Rosalee explained that one of the long-term goals for the bakery was to get orders to area stores, and this was their first one. The labels on the bags read "Amish Bread from Plain Treats, Nappanee, Indiana." Then there was a list of ingredients and the address in small print.

"You have a nice place here," I said. "The bakery. The house. All of it."

Rosalee didn't answer, and Luke kept his head down.

Feeling awkward that neither had responded, I rushed on. "How do you keep up with everything?"

"We manage," Rosalee said, glancing at Luke. "Although, Luke has had to spend more time at his *daed*'s dairy again. That's why we need you."

I blushed. It sounded as though Ezra having to go home had affected her too.

Wanting to change the subject, I asked if she got much business out this far.

"A little more each month," Rosalee answered. And then *she* changed the subject. "I understand you're interested in going to baking school."

I shrugged, not looking up as I slipped a loaf into a bag. I didn't want to talk about my desire to go to school. I was certain she'd have the same response as Aunt Klara and Nancy did back home, that it was foolish to take classes on something I should be learning at home.

"What's your schedule out here?"

"I get started at four thirty," she said. "Luke helps when he can, some in the bakery but mostly on the farm." She twisted a bag shut.

"Why aren't you open today?"

"I was. Until we came and got you," she said matter-of-factly.

Luke began placing the bread back on the racks, and just as we were completing the work, a deliveryman arrived. Rosalee counted the loaves of bread with him and then signed a form. We followed him out to his panel truck.

"Where's the bread going?" I asked as the driver put the trays in the back.

"Indianapolis," Rosalee answered. "It will be on store shelves by morning."

All three of us watched the truck turn toward the road, and then I followed her back up to the house, while Luke headed to the barn.

"I'm going to sit for a spell and then start dinner," she said when we reached the kitchen.

"I'll help."

"Give me a few minutes," she said, her brow creased under her *kapp*. "I need a little time to just be."

I shuffled down the hall, back into my room, wondering if I was an imposition. No matter. Rosalee wouldn't have to put up with me for long. And I intended to more than pull my own weight while I was here.

As I entered my room, I heard voices outside the window. I peeked through the gauzy curtain to see Luke standing a few yards away. I couldn't see Rosalee, but I could hear her voice. "*Ya*. Clean the coop. We can worry about the garden tomorrow."

I wiped my hands on my apron. Cleaning the coop was something I could help with and not be in Rosalee's way while she made dinner—as long as she had a pair of boots I could wear.

I stepped into the kitchen quietly. She was sitting at the table again, her head bowed. I wasn't sure if she was dozing or praying.

"I can help Luke," I said.

She opened her eyes but didn't look at me.

I quickly explained I didn't have any boots.

"There's a pair in the mudroom," she said, looking at my feet. "They should fit."

When I arrived in the doorway of the coop, Luke nodded his head and pointed to an extra shovel by the wheelbarrow as if he'd been expecting me. But after we'd worked for at least half an hour in silence—except for the five times I'd tried to get a conversation going—I was sure he thought I was an annoyance, maybe even a troublemaker. He seemed as interested in me as he was in one of the squawking chickens.

Finally I asked how sales were for the bakery. I'd sensed earlier that they were less than stellar.

He shrugged. "That's Rosalee's business, don't you think?"

Feeling chastised, I shut up.

Luke was a fast and hard worker. And strong. After we dumped the manure in a pile behind the barn, we put the shovels away in the toolshed. I stood in the middle, looking around in awe. It was full of hooks and pulleys. The wheelbarrow was hanging from the ceiling, as was a push lawnmower. Each shovel, hoe, and cultivator had its own hanger. The garden stakes and string each had a slot, and even the watering cans had a custommade shelf.

"Wow," I said, twirling around. "Who's the master organizer?"

Luke blushed, which I expected. "I like to tinker," he said.

"I'd say so."

I followed him toward the house, kicked the boots off on the back porch, and then greeted Rosalee in the kitchen.

"We'll eat in five minutes," she said, standing at the stove, the table set for three.

"I'll go wash up."

Luke still stood at the edge of the mud porch, but I had a feeling he was watching me as I walked down the hall.

By the time I returned to the kitchen, he was sitting at the head of the table and Rosalee was dishing creamed corn into a serving bowl. She directed me to sit to the right of Luke. Mashed potatoes, a plate of ham slices, and a bowl of chard were already on the table. She sat down and Luke led us in a silent prayer. A few moments later he picked up his fork and I followed suit.

The three of us ate in silence for several minutes. I chewed my dry ham for what seemed a near eternity. Then I took a bite of the chard, which was overcooked. The mashed potatoes needed more butter, and the creamed corn wasn't very hot. I hoped Rosalee was a better baker than cook.

I took a drink of the pinkish juice in my glass. It was a rhubarb punch, I was sure. I'd come across a recipe for it, although I'd never had it before. It was tart and sweet. I analyzed the taste, guessing it also had pineapple juice in it. It was delicious.

Neither Rosalee nor Luke said a word as they ate, and I began to grow anxious in the silence. Finally Rosalee cleared her throat. I looked at her expectantly.

"So tell me about this baking school idea of yours." She had an amused look on her face.

I sighed. So much for not wanting to broach the topic.

"Well," I answered. "There's one in South Bend I looked into, but it's not going to work out now." I paused, not sure how to say I didn't plan to stick around.

Rosalee concentrated on cutting her ham. After what seemed like quite a while, she said, "I know your grandmother has some money set aside for your schooling. And your mother signed you up for the class."

"I beg your pardon?" I looked from Rosalee to Luke, who had a blank stare on his face and quickly dropped his gaze to his plate, where he kept it, which only added to the awkwardness of the conversation.

"Your *mammi* is paying for school for you. For the course in South Bend." Rosalee dished up more corn, adding, "Although for the life of me I can't understand why anyone would pay to learn how to bake." She shrugged and then said, "So be it."

I tried to give *Mammi* the benefit of the doubt. While on the one hand, I was pretty sure she had come up with this living and working arrangement as a solution for the keeping-Ella-and-Ezra-apart problem, which was awful, I also had a feeling she was working things out so that I'd have an opportunity to decipher the code, which was fine. Ordinarily, I felt sure that *Mammi* agreed with both Mom and Aunt Klara that baking school was just a big waste of money, but now that such a thing would give me a reason to stick around Indiana for a while, at the Home Place no less, somehow she'd decided it was worth ponying up for. I didn't know whether to be furious at her or thrilled.

Maybe both.

"She's already sent a check to the school."

I wrinkled my nose, again, trying to give *Mammi* the benefit of the doubt, but how absolutely presumptive of her! I would rather take baking classes at the community college in Lancaster and be close to Ezra than stay in Indiana.

Then again, it looked as though *Mammi* and Mom had now cooked up an offer too good to refuse. I didn't know what to do.

We all fell silent once more. I was lost in my thoughts as I chewed another leathery bite of ham, thinking about Ezra and our future life together. Then, trying to distract myself from my loneliness, after I'd swallowed I asked Luke if he stayed for supper with Rosalee very often.

"Fairly so," he answered, the color rising in his face. "Except when I'm needed at home."

It wasn't unusual for Amish families to hire their youth out to work. I wondered if Luke was allowed to save his money or if it went to support his family. I'd seen it handled both ways among the Amish in Pennsylvania.

We spent the rest of the meal in silence until Rosalee served each of us a piece of coconut cake. I took one bite and closed my eyes. It was divine. The cake was moist and flavorful. The icing was a glaze, and the taste of coconut wasn't overpowered by sweetness.

"Oh, my," I said after I'd swallowed my second bite. "This is wonderful."

Rosalee didn't answer me, but Luke nodded in agreement. I ate every last crumb.

When we finished, Luke led us in a silent, after-the-meal prayer. I'd never heard of such a thing back in Pennsylvania, but he bowed his head again so I followed suit, as did Rosalee.

After he'd finished, he said he needed to go on home.

I stood and collected the three plates. "It's not far, is it?" I wasn't going to tell them that I'd looked up the distance on Google Earth more than a month ago, plotting how to be closer to Ezra.

"No, I just cut through the woods. It takes only a few minutes."

I glanced out the window over the sink, at the trees. How I wished Ezra was still that close! I'd be thrilled to stay in Indiana if he were, and even more thrilled to go to baking school here.

"I'll bring Millie and Eddie with me in the morning," Luke said to Rosalee.

"*Gut.*"

As I washed the dishes she disappeared, and a few minutes later she returned holding a large manila envelope.

"This came for you yesterday," she said.

Surprised, considering no one knew until today that I would be staying here, I couldn't fathom whom it was from. I dried my hands and took it from her. It was addressed to me in Mom's handwriting in care of Rosalee. I opened it up. Inside was a smaller envelope, addressed to me in Pennsylvania. There was no return address in the upper left-hand corner, but when I flipped it over I found, on the flap, a return address label for Petit Paris that had been broken and then re-taped. Obviously, my mother hadn't even tried to hide the fact that she'd opened my mail to look inside.

"It's the information on the cooking school," Rosalee said. "The next session starts the first of May."

I glanced at the front of the larger envelope Mom had addressed again. The postmark was dated the previous Thursday, four days ago, the day before Ada and Will had come to get Ezra. Mom and *Mammi* hadn't just come up with a plan this morning—they had been scheming since the moment they knew Will would be coming out here to take Ezra home. These people would do *anything* to keep the miles between the two of us. Incredible.

I headed down the hall, the packet under my arm, my cell already out of my pocket. I left messages on Mom's phone, Aunt Klara's barn phone, and Ezra's cell phone, even though I was convinced he no longer had his, as I sorted through the packet of information. It was the same as what was on the website, except there was no tuition list in the packet. Mom must have given that to *Mammi*.

Her partner in crime.

Her coconspirator.

My benefactor.

My traitor.

Fifteen

I tried to sleep but tossed and turned, wishing I could get comfortable on the hard bed. Moonlight shone through the window. Two cats were fighting around eleven. At three I woke to the hooting of an owl.

Rosalee knocked on my door at five. I was tempted to roll over and go back to sleep, but I struggled out of bed, planting my bare feet on the cold floor and then grabbing a pair of socks from the drawer. By the time I dressed and finished in the bathroom, the smell of bacon was making my mouth water. I hurried down the hall. Rosalee stood at the stove, flipping hotcakes on the griddle. Luke sat at the head of the table again, but he and Rosalee weren't alone. A young woman, a little older than me, and a boy of about six sat on either side of him.

"Morning," Rosalee said to me, the pancake turner in her hand. Then she introduced Luke's sister and brother, Millie and Eddie, in Pennsylvania Dutch. That much I could understand.

Both had dark hair like Luke's and striking gray eyes. Millie was beautiful—no wonder her father was worried when Ezra showed up. She was probably taken with him, like every other girl I knew. As for what he'd thought of her, I could only hope he listened to his heart and not his eyes.

Eddie smiled at me, showing off dimples identical to his brother's. My heart melted.

When he began chattering away in Pennsylvania Dutch, his voice loud and animated, I put up my hand to stop him.

"I'm not as smart as you are," I said in English.

"You are stupid?" He was absolutely serious as he spoke.

"*Ya*," I answered. "Just a little."

"Eddie." Millie's voice was quiet, like Luke's. "She's not Plain." She glanced at me and sighed. "Well, she's partly Plain."

Then she spoke to him in Pennsylvania Dutch. I made out the English words "Mennonite" and "Lancaster" but that was all.

"*Ach*," Eddie finally said. Then he whispered to Millie, "She's purty," and everyone, including me, laughed. There was nothing shy about Luke's little brother.

Rosalee stepped toward the table with a plate of hotcakes and a smile on her face. I noted she seemed more relaxed than she had last night. After she put the plate down, she patted Eddie's head and then settled onto her chair.

Again, Luke led all of us in a silent prayer, but that, and the fact the bacon was overcooked and the pancakes too doughy, was all this meal had in common with the calm and quiet one from the night before. Eddie, who kept jumping between English and Pennsylvania Dutch, didn't stop talking except when Millie insisted he give someone else a chance.

"You don't want to be annoying," she chastised.

He wasn't at all. He was highly entertaining. I found out all sorts of things, including that he was turning six in June.

"I'm going to be more than a handful then," he said, his eyes dancing. "And when I'm sixteen, I'm going to court you, Ella."

I nearly spat my coffee all over the table, but somehow I managed to swallow and say, "Sorry, Eddie, but I'll be an old married lady by then, nearly thirty. Besides, you'll find an Amish girl. Not a Mennonite one like me."

He pouted, so I added, "Don't worry, buddy, you'll have your pick. You're already a player."

"What's a player?"

I blushed, taking another forkful of doughy pancake followed by a bite of too crisp bacon, thinking if my mouth was full I wouldn't be able to answer.

"Like a volleyball player?" Eddie persisted.

Luke and Millie both looked straight at me. I chewed slowly and nodded.

As if on cue, Luke suggested that it was time for the end-of-the-meal prayer. Sometimes during a silent prayer I tried to focus on talking to God about my day or what was weighing me down. But sometimes I recited the Lord's Prayer instead, just as I'd done back in February at Aunt Klara's house. That's what I did now, but just like then, I found myself faltering when I reached, "Thy will be done…"

Was this God's will for me? To be at the Home Place and attend a baking school in South Bend? The course was three months long, but I wanted to be back in Lancaster much sooner than that. Ada told me once that when God closed one door, He always opened another. He'd certainly done that for her, but I didn't feel God working in my life the way He had in hers. In fact, I'd always felt God was far more interested in other people's lives than He was in mine.

When the silent prayer was over, Eddie started toward the door, but Luke called out, "Don't go anywhere yet except to fetch the Bible for me."

Eddie changed direction, hopped on one leg over to the hutch, and returned with a worn Bible.

"We didn't read last night," Luke said.

"*Ach*, I don't know how that slipped by," Rosalee said.

I was sure it was because of me. I'd upset their predictable world.

Eddie handed Luke the Bible, and, in English, he said he was reading out of Isaiah 40. But then he began to read—in German. I tried to follow along, but could only make out a few words. If Zed were with me, he would have comprehended the entire passage.

When Luke finished, Rosalee put her hand out flat on the tablecloth.

"There's something we need to talk about. We need to find a ride for Ella to South Bend so she can visit the cooking school."

I shook my head. "Actually, there's no need. Penny, the woman I lived with, will take me. I'll call her." I still wasn't sure if I would be attending the school or not, but I decided it couldn't hurt to pay it a visit. Maybe God was working in my life after all, even if He had chosen to do so through my manipulative, meddling family members.

Looking relieved, Rosalee instructed Millie to clean up the breakfast things, and Luke said he'd take Eddie with him for the morning and see how it went.

After I helped clear the table, Rosalee and I started toward the bakery. The morning was cold, and I was happy to have my cape around my shoulders.

"Today is pie day," she told me when we entered the bakery. She flipped the sign to "Open," and I followed her into the kitchen. The smell of cinnamon greeted us. Rosalee said she had popped sticky rolls into the oven before breakfast. She began pulling them out.

"The berries for the pies are in the cooler, and the recipe for the pie filling is on the board. Please prepare that, Ella." She motioned with her head toward a bulletin board on the far wall. "Wash your hands first."

I nodded, thankful to be here and not back at the house washing the breakfast dishes. Having a job at the restaurant had been good, but working in a bakery was truly what I wanted to do. Of course, I knew Rosalee's bakery wouldn't offer me the variety I craved. There certainly wouldn't be anything fancy here, but at least it was a start.

After I washed my hands I searched the board for the recipe. Finally I found it written on a card nearly hidden by several others. I took the tack out of the board and pulled the recipe card free. It was written in an old-fashioned hand and I held it carefully.

I turned toward Rosalee.

"This isn't Sarah's, is it?"

She squinted to see what I was talking about and then shook her head. "No. My mother's. Most of the recipes I use were hers."

"Oh." I started back to the worktable. "Did she get her recipes from Sarah?"

Rosalee wrinkled her nose. "No, she probably got them from her own mother. Though I imagine many of their recipes were the same—or at least similar. Sarah was my mom's mother-in-law, but they didn't get along very well."

My eyebrows shot up.

"'Tis true, I'm afraid. My father either. He and his mother weren't exactly what you might call close. It was a bit complicated for me, when I was a child, because I loved my parents and my grandmother, but there was always a lot of conflict between them."

"How about your dad's sister?" I asked, referring to my own grandmother. "She got along okay with her mother, right?"

From the wistful way *Mammi* always talked about Sarah, I had a feeling that was a stupid question.

"Oh, yes. Frannie and Sarah were very close. In fact, if you just went by the two of them, you would think we were all one big happy family. Sadly, we were not."

Surprised, I wasn't sure how to respond. Finally I said, "I'm sorry."

Rosalee chuckled. "Whatever for?" But then her voice grew serious. "By the time I married and moved to Michigan, it didn't matter anymore." She sighed. "But that's all water under the bridge. Now I'm back and happy to be here. The past is the past. I wasn't able to have children, so Darryl and Cora's brood is an extra blessing. But to keep all this going we need to concentrate on work now—and pray for customers."

The recipe in front of me was for blueberry pie and was written in English, thank goodness. It called for lemon juice and rind, just like the one I used at home. The ingredients had all been increased, enough to make five pies. Rosalee pulled uncooked shells from the refrigerator and delivered them to the worktable. She must have rolled them out before breakfast too.

A bell dinged.

"Customer," Rosalee said, wiping her hands on her apron before picking up a tray of the warm sticky buns. "Come with me."

She went through the door, pushing it open with her hip and holding it for me. An English woman stood on the other side of the counter.

"Hello," Rosalee said, sliding the tray into the display case.

"Oh, good," the woman said, a wave of relief passing over her face. "Everyone at my office will be thrilled. I'll take a dozen sticky buns, please."

Rosalee showed me where the boxes were stored under the counter. I put on latex gloves, grabbed a set of tongs, and started filling a box while Rosalee rang up the order. The register was similar to the one at the café, and the bakery took credit cards, which didn't surprise me. So did the Amish shops in Lancaster.

In just a few minutes the woman was out the door, and I was back in the bakery, washing my hands. Every time the bell rang I hurried out front. A couple of times I had to ask Rosalee for help, but after a while Millie arrived and she took care of the orders. Relieved, I concentrated on my task. I wasn't sure that we needed Millie—we weren't actually that busy—but it was nice that I didn't have to keep running out front.

After I finished scooping the pie filling into the shells, Rosalee told me to roll out dough for lattice tops for three of the pies and make a crumb topping for the other two. I had to ask where the brown sugar was stored, but I was able to complete the rest of the job without asking anything else. I knew she was keeping an eye on me as she worked on making lemon cream pies.

As I rolled out dough for lattice tops, Millie poked her head into the kitchen. "Need any help back here?"

Rosalee frowned. "Is it slow out there?"

Millie nodded. "Not as slow as yesterday morning, though."

"How about if you clean out front? Give all the tables a good scrubbing. Then the walls."

Millie nodded and headed for the storage room. I craned my neck to see in the door as she entered, knowing I wanted to get a closer look in there later. Because the bakery had once been the *daadi haus*, I thought perhaps Sarah had stashed her paintings here in some secret spot. Millie emerged with rags and a spray bottle filled with blue liquid and headed back out front.

Once she was gone, Rosalee whispered, "She's great with the customers but not so good with the baking." She sounded so matter-of-fact that it didn't even sound critical. I sorely hoped she would never say I wasn't good with the baking.

I finished the crumb toppings and then wove the lattice design over the rest of the pies. Rosalee whisked them into the oven before I reached the sink to wash my hands.

"Now start on another batch of sticky buns," she said.

The recipe was also on the board but written in a hand easier to read—Rosalee's, I assumed. As she and I worked together, I asked her about what businesses in the area she'd approached about carrying her product.

"None. The bread distributor approached me. Other than that, I haven't been doing any selling—except here, on site. We have a big order from time to time, but we're just starting to distribute."

"Why haven't you before now?"

She scraped the metal bowl of lemon cream with a spatula. "I'd rather build up the business by word of mouth and get people to come out here."

"Do you have a brochure? Or a card?"

"*Ya*, a card. But that's all."

"Could I get some of your cards and take them around in town? Starting with the café?" I was pretty sure Wes would be happy not to have to make his own pies, and once he tasted Rosalee's other delicious items, it would be hard for him to resist those too. "Maybe we could offer a free sticky bun to business owners just to get them to come out and sample your products."

"How would you get into town? I can't spare Luke to take the time off to drive you."

"Penny's bike."

"What about deliveries?"

She had a good point. Maybe I could get a little trailer to pull behind the bike. I smiled at the thought. "We could see how many orders we get. I could drive the buggy." I knew I could, even though I hadn't ever driven one before. Once again wishing I had a license and a car, I added, "Or it might be worth it to hire a driver." I thought of Penny again. Delivering baked goods around Nappanee might be right up her alley. I smiled at the thought of her in her Volvo SUV delivering for Plain Treats.

Rosalee was quiet, but then she said, "It would be fine for you to pass my card around and try to drum up more business. It's no secret we need it."

We worked quietly after that until ten thirty, when she said I needed to go in the house and start our lunch.

"What should I fix?"

"It doesn't matter," she answered. "Take a look around. Make sure it's enough to feed the five of us, though, in an hour."

My stomach had started growling a while ago. I could only imagine, with breakfast at five, how hungry Eddie was by now. And Luke too.

"And then after lunch you can weed the garden while Luke finishes in the field."

"What about going into town?" I hoped my voice didn't sound whiny.

"Wait a few days, until you can talk about the bakery with more knowledge. But call the Penny woman about taking you to South Bend. Do that now—on your way to the house."

I left the bakery a few minutes later, checking my phone as I walked. I had a text from Zed. *Mom said to tell you she got your message and that she and Mammi both think the baking course is the best option for you right now.* I didn't bother to text back. Instead, I dialed Penny's number as I walked. She answered after the first ring. When I told her I needed a ride to visit the baking school after all, she answered she would love to drive me to South Bend.

"We can go tomorrow," she said.

"How about in the afternoon? After two?" That would give me time to do more weeding, if that's what Rosalee asked of me.

"Perfect."

I gave her the address of the Home Place.

I thought through lunch as I walked, feeling as if I was on one of those cooking shows where they give you three ingredients to make a meal. That perked me up a little. I knew there was leftover ham and hash browns. I would make a ham hash.

I pinched several stems of chives and a few sprigs of thyme on my way to the house, washed them clean, and then found stewed tomatoes and onions in the pantry. After chopping up the herbs and ham, I melted the butter in the cast iron skillet and then cooked the onion until it was soft. I added the leftover potatoes, ham, corn, and the jar of tomatoes, heating the hash until it started to bubble, and then I added the herbs and salt and pepper. While the flavors mixed, I sliced a loaf of homemade bread and placed it in the oven to toast. I needed something more, maybe applesauce or—I looked at the fruit bowl on the small table under the window—just apples. I cut four up quickly and then sliced white cheddar cheese I found in the fridge. It was more of a breakfast, but the astonished and delighted looks on everyone's faces as they took their first bites confirmed what I suspected.

It was delicious, even if I did say so myself.

Sixteen

The next afternoon, Luke and Eddie were on the tractor and on their way to the field when I headed back down to the bakery after cleaning up from lunch. The little guy waved enthusiastically while Luke just nodded at me.

His shyness was getting a little old. He definitely wasn't my type. Just being around him made me miss Ezra.

As I turned the corner to the bakery, I saw Penny's car in the parking lot. She was early. I hurried through the door and found her at the counter, the only customer in the store, buying a blueberry pie.

Millie was boxing up one with the crumb topping, and when I told Penny I had made that one myself, she gushed, "It looks incredible!"

Rosalee said I was free to go, so Penny and I started for South Bend. We zigzagged our way over to Highway 119 and then headed north, running parallel to the train tracks. The day was overcast and was growing more and more dreary as the miles ticked away. We chatted about the bakery.

"It looks like a wonderful place to work," Penny said. "I've always dreamed of owning something like that."

I shared my idea about marketing the bakery to local restaurants and stores, though I didn't mention the part about her being our delivery person. She suggested we stop by the café on the way home.

"I'm sure Wes and Kendra are approached by all sorts of home-based businesses, but you never know."

We rode along in silence after that, which made me drowsy, and then I fell asleep. When I awoke we were in South Bend. Penny drove right to the downtown area and then parked the car. Across the street was a sign with a fleur-de-lis on it that read "Petit Paris, Boulangerie and Patisserie." Underneath in smaller letters was another sign. "Culinary and Baking School, Classes by Pierre Baptiste and Elizabeth Elgin."

There were a few customers sitting at tables when we entered. The scent of coffee was strong and a hint of cinnamon hung in the air, mixed with the aromas of chocolate and baking bread. A waitress passed us with a bowl of soup in one hand and a salad in the other. The dining room was painted in warm golds and yellows, with a border of brown tiles. The display case was filled with rustic breads and fancy pastries. It was an absolute feast for my eyes.

A middle-aged woman was behind the counter. She wore a white apron, and her hair was covered with a net.

"May I help you?"

"I'm interested in the school." I held up the packet.

"*Oui.*" The woman smiled. "I'm Elizabeth. I'm in charge of the culinary school. And Pierre teaches the baking classes."

"I'm interested in baking," I said, glancing at Penny.

"Likewise," she chimed in.

A look of disappointment passed over the woman's face as she said, "I'll get Pierre." She spoke without any hint of an accent and looked more like a regular Midwest mom than a French chef.

She disappeared through a door, and I glanced around again. The ceiling was high with crown molding around the top. The tables and chairs were dark wood, and the floor was stone tile. Tall, leafy plants graced two corners, and black-and-white photos of loaves of bread, pastries, and cakes hung on the walls. There was also a series of group shots of people holding up what looked like diplomas.

The woman returned. "Pierre is busy right now. He wants to know if you can come back tomorrow."

"We're from out of town," Penny said, smiling hopefully.

The woman frowned.

For a moment I wondered if there was a Pierre at all. Maybe there was a Midwestern man named Peter. Maybe it was some sort of scam. But then she said, *"Bien.* Come with me."

We followed her through the door and into a cavernous kitchen. "He's back here, teaching."

My jaw fell. There was stainless steel table after table. Each had a mixer, a hot plate, and a set of utensils. On the far wall was a row of ovens. Back in a corner of the room, a group of people gathered around a table. As we neared it, I saw each had a round cake.

It seemed to be a school after all. As I stepped closer, I recognized Pierre from his photo on the website. He was shorter than I thought he'd be, though, shorter than me and rounder too. His brown eyes were lively as he spoke. He had his dark hair pulled back in a short ponytail, and he wore a double-breasted white coat with brass buttons.

"Everyone, hold up your cake." He spoke with an accent. "This is your canvas. Think very carefully about what you want to create on it."

The woman nodded toward Penny and me. "They can't come back tomorrow."

Pierre made an exasperated face and stepped toward me. "Where are you from?"

"Lancaster County, Pennsylvania."

"Why do you want to come here?"

I wanted to tell him I wasn't sure I did.

"I'm staying in Nappanee but not for long. This is the closest cooking school, and everything I've read about it sounds wonderful."

He turned toward Elizabeth again. "Do we not have an information sheet you can give her?"

"You said you were going to update it."

"I have a packet." I held up the envelope. "And it seems my mother has already enrolled me. I just wanted to see the place. And to meet you."

He touched the top of his paper chef's hat. "Oh, I see," he said. "And your name is?"

"Ella Bayer."

"*Oui*." He grinned and shuffled his feet. "Welcome. You start with the next group, *non*?"

"It seems that way—"

"We begin with bread. Then pastries. Finally we do cakes. I will insert lectures on the business side of things—bookkeeping, insurance, employee matters, those sorts of concerns—along the way. Just a general overview, you understand"

I nodded, hoping I could supplement the information from that one session with what I'd be learning about the business from Rosalee.

"Unless you are interested in Elizabeth's cooking school." A concerned expression settled on his face.

"Oh, no. Baking. That's what I want."

"Are you sure?" He laughed, and pointing at me, he said, "I would take you for a cook instead. With your apron and head thing you look as if you are ready to make a big farm dinner." He chuckled again.

He turned toward Penny. "You are not Ella's mother, no? You don't like look her. You don't dress like her."

Penny simply said, "I'm a friend. I gave her a ride. And I'd like the same packet, please. I may be interested as well."

"Wonderful. We happen to have room, just for you." He smiled encouragingly at Penny and then waved us off. "As you can see, I am busy. See you in May." He turned to Elizabeth and said, "Sorry. Everyone wants to learn to bake."

She ignored him.

Pierre addressed his students again. "First, the cake must taste delicious. Then you can worry about decorating it, *non*? Who cares how pretty a cake is if it does not taste divine. That includes the frosting…"

We followed Elizabeth back through the kitchen and back to the front counter, where she retrieved a packet for Penny.

"I need a price sheet too," I said. Even though *Mammi* had already paid, I still wanted to know what her investment was.

After we thanked her, Penny said quietly, "Pierre seems a little disorganized."

She laughed. "*Oui*. But he really knows his stuff. He taught at the university for a couple of years. A lot of college students in the hospitality program take classes from him now."

"What about you?" Penny asked.

"*Moi?*" She laughed again. "I was born and raised here in South Bend, but I graduated from the Chicago Culinary School."

My eyebrows shot up.

"Have you heard of it?" Elizabeth asked.

"Of course."

"It's a good school. But ours is too, even though we're small and we don't have accreditation."

Penny and I both thanked her. I studied the price sheet. It was comparable to other programs I'd seen. More expensive than the community college in Lancaster but not outrageous. Not enough to make me feel guilty that *Mammi* was the one paying. After all, she'd paid for Ada to go to Switzerland. She could pay for me to go to baking school.

On the way home, Penny asked, "What would you think if I signed up and went with you?"

"I think that would be great." I meant it. If I stayed, I'd have a ride, and it would be nice to have someone to discuss the classes with. I had a feeling Rosalee wouldn't exactly be enthusiastic.

When we got back to Nappanee, Penny parked in front of the café and then walked in with me to talk with Kendra and Wes about carrying baked goods from Plain Treats in the restaurant. No one was in the dining hall, so we pushed through the kitchen door, Penny calling out, "Knock, knock!"

Both of my former bosses were sitting on stools and having a cup of coffee, but they seemed happy to see me and fine with the interruption.

I handed each of them a business card.

"Rosalee makes pies. Sticky buns. Rolls. Bread. Pastries. All homemade with farm-fresh ingredients from old Amish recipes."

"You are quite the saleswoman," Wes said. He stood and put his coffee cup on the butcher block in the middle of the kitchen. "What do you think?" he asked Kendra.

"It would save us some time." She turned toward me. "How are the prices?"

"Amazing. Rosalee's overhead is really low." At least I assumed it was. The building was paid for. My compensation was room and board. I had no idea what she paid Luke and Millie, but I couldn't imagine it was that much.

"I'll let you know," Kendra said.

Pleased with my first marketing venture, I told them I'd bring them a sample the next time I came in.

That evening I wrote a list of the pros and cons of going to Pierre's baking school. I was sure I would learn a lot. I wouldn't have to hear about Freddy if I stayed in Indiana, but at this point I wasn't sure it was worth being away from Ezra to do that. Working for Rosalee was a pro, but I probably wouldn't learn that much from her. It was more likely that it would simply confirm what I did know.

I did enjoy being at the Home Place, but I wasn't sure living here was going to help me decipher the rest of Sarah's book, even though *Mammi* seemed to think so. On the other hand, it was only for three months. It wasn't as though it was for an eternity. But when it came to a rocky relationship, which I considered Ezra's and mine to be right now, three months was a really long time.

Being away from Ezra, of course, was the biggest con. Missing him was an ache that didn't stop. Everything reminded me of him. The motorcycle that passed us on our way to the Home Place. Luke's straw hat. The alfalfa growing in the field. Every sticky bun in the bakery. The blue sky. The rain. Rosalee's milk cow mooing in the field.

That evening, because he hadn't returned any of my texts, I wrote a letter to him. I was chatty at first, explaining why I moved in with Rosalee. I told him I'd met Millie and Eddie but not Tom or their parents.

Honestly, I felt a little timid about meeting Darryl Kline, but I didn't say that.

Then I told him about the school in South Bend. *I'm not sure if I should go or not,* I wrote. *I'd like to come home as soon as I can. I'm so thankful you said you'd wait for me.*

Soon I was finished, but as I folded the letter and tucked it into an envelope, I thought suddenly of pretty Ruth Fry, Sally's cousin who had come out from Ohio to work as a mother's helper until Sally's baby was born. How thrilled she must be to have Ezra back in town—and all to herself, no less.

Swallowing hard, I said a quick prayer that Ezra would remain a man of his word. He'd said he'd wait for me.

Please, Lord, let it be so.

Seventeen

Three days later it was my birthday, but I didn't tell Rosalee. I didn't expect a gift from home because Mom didn't believe in birthday presents, but I thought maybe she would call. Or perhaps Ezra would.

After supper that night, Rosalee served one of the lemon meringue pies that hadn't sold. For a moment I thought maybe someone had told her it was my birthday, but it was soon obvious no one had. It was just a day like any other day, except that after I'd done the dishes I asked Luke if I could go back to the dairy with him and see inside the house, where my grandmother and my mother and her sisters had once lived.

"Take my coat, but don't be too long," Rosalee said from where she sat at the kitchen table, working on her books. "It will be dark soon."

Luke grabbed a flashlight from the shelf on the mud porch, and I picked up the wool coat on our way out. The evening was cold and growing colder. I hoped it wouldn't freeze. We passed the garden and walked along the trail beside the barn, silently. When we reached the woods, Luke took the lead. The breeze stirred the pine trees towering above us.

"That's the tallest one," he said, pointing upward. "It's a red pine, and taller than they usually get. It's probably two hundred years old or so."

The trunk was bare on the bottom half and then, about where the branches started, the bark had a reddish tinge to it. I squinted in the dim light. "Is that a nest up there?"

Luke nodded. "It belongs to a family of magpies. They can get pretty noisy." He started up the path again at a faster pace.

The trail stopped at a stream and Luke jumped across. He extended his hand to me and I took it. He blushed and let go as soon as I was safely on the other side.

When we reached the edge of the woods, he pointed to a gate and we headed toward it. He opened it by pulling on a handle contraption on the side.

"Did you design that?" I asked.

He nodded.

As we passed through, I caught a glimpse of the farmhouse. It looked even smaller than it had on Sunday when I'd come here with the flat tire, but I decided I was comparing it to the Home Place, which was huge by anyone's standards.

"Luke's brought a girl home," a manly voice called out.

I turned toward the barn. A tall, broad-shouldered young man was sauntering toward us. Eddie was skipping beside him.

"It's Ella!" Eddie rushed toward me and in a minute he had taken my hand.

Luke started to say something, but before he could the man had his hat off and his hand outstretched.

"I'm Tom," he said. "Luke's big brother."

He was a little taller than Luke and much broader. His hair was lighter than Luke's and his eyes a softer gray. He smiled at me. He didn't have the family dimples, but his eyes were bright and lively.

I introduced myself, explaining I was Rosalee's cousin.

"Oh, I've heard all about you," Tom answered, resting his hand on Eddie's head. "First from Ezra and then from Luke." He smirked. "I mean Eddie."

I winced, wondering what Ezra had told him, and what he meant by referencing both of his brothers. I ignored his comment.

"My mother lived here when she was little. I was eager to see the place, and Luke was kind enough to invite me."

"Ah, yes," Tom said. "The Lantz family. The one all the troubles started with."

I gave him a questioning look. "What kind of troubles?"

"You haven't heard?"

"The only trouble I know of is that my grandfather died here."

He nodded. "*Ya*, pulled to death by his team."

"Tom." Luke stepped a little closer. "She probably doesn't want to hear about all that."

Tom shrugged. "It was all downhill from there, from what I understand."

I glanced down at Eddie, who was looking up at Tom and hanging on every word.

"Why don't we discuss it some other time," I said, discreetly gesturing toward the little boy.

Catching on, Tom tousled his littlest brother's hair. "Isn't it about time for you to get to bed?"

"Nah," Eddie bellowed. "It's too early."

"Let's walk Ella to the house." Luke took Eddie's other hand. "And introduce her to *Mamm*."

"She's resting," Tom said.

"Where's *Daed*?"

"Working on the irrigation in the far field."

Luke nodded and started toward the house anyway. I told Tom it was nice to meet him, and then Eddie pulled me along to keep up with Luke.

There was a swing in the oak tree on the side yard that I hadn't seen the other day. Grape vines grew up a trellis next to a small outbuilding. Chickens poked around in the grass.

Luke gave me a quick look and blushed again. It was obvious he and Tom were nothing alike.

As we neared the back door, it opened and Millie stepped out, a throw rug in her hand.

"*Ach*!" she cried out. "You startled me."

Eddie laughed, but Luke reached up and patted her shoulder. "Sorry. I wanted to introduce Ella to *Mamm*."

"She's on the sofa."

Eddie snuck by Millie.

"Go on." She smiled at me as I passed by her. Even though it was cold out, she was sweating. I could see why once I entered the house. It was like an oven inside.

"*Mamm*'s been chilling," Millie explained.

I followed Luke through the kitchen. The table was small, only big enough for six people, and it had been completely cleared, the dishes drying in the rack.

I could hear Eddie's sweet voice, and when we entered the living room, I saw him kneeling beside the couch. He was talking to a small woman who was reclining there, her hand in her young son's.

"Who's here?" she asked.

"Ella," Eddie answered.

"*Mamm*, I brought Rosalee's cousin for you to meet." Luke stopped in the middle of the room.

His mother stirred a little and then shifted to her elbow.

"Well, hello," she said, rising to a sitting position. She pulled the quilt closer as she lowered her feet to the floor.

I said hello, offering her my hand. She took it, holding it gingerly for just a second.

"I'm Cora," she said. "So you're Ezra's friend?"

"*Ya*," I answered. "We've known each other since we were little."

"He seemed like a nice young man. We were sorry it didn't work out. We could have used the—" She stopped in midsentence, as if she just remembered why Ezra left.

Ignoring her irritating faux pas, I wanted to ask if I could look around the house, trying to imagine *Mammi* and Mom and Aunt Klara and Aunt Giselle living in the place. But that felt too forward, and no one offered me a tour. I did notice a stack of library books on a chair though, mostly because the top one was a how-to book on drawing.

Millie stepped into the room. "*Daed* and Tom are headed in for our Bible reading."

"I'd better walk you back," Luke said as he picked up the stack of books. I wasn't sure if he noticed me glancing at them or was picking them up because his father was on his way.

"I'll be fine on my own." I put out my hand for the flashlight.

Luke shook his head, opening the bottom door of a cupboard under the window. He stashed the books inside.

"But you'll miss your family time," I said.

He looked at his mother.

"Go ahead," she said. "It'll be all right this once."

Eddie hugged me goodbye, and I told Millie I'd see her the next day. As we walked down the back steps, I didn't see Tom or his father, but as we passed the barn I heard their voices, which were kind of loud. It wasn't as if they were arguing, maybe just having a lively discussion. Luke didn't say anything, and in a few minutes we were back in the woods.

It was growing dark in the shadows of the trees, and I realized I was glad I wasn't doing this alone after all. I startled as an owl hooted, probably the same one I'd heard outside my window at night. Luke smiled when I jumped, and then I laughed.

After we crossed the creek, I asked why he worked for Rosalee instead of for his *daed*.

"Rosalee pays me."

"But it sounds as though your family needs help"

"We do, but cash pays the bills. Some days I don't get to Rosalee's at all, but on all the days I do, I work for my *daed* when I get home."

"What sort of things can you do at night?"

"Tonight I'll work on the fence by lantern light."

"Oh," was all I could answer. After a moment of silence, I asked, "Is your *mamm* all right?"

"Mostly. She'll be fine for a year or two and then she'll have a bad spell. It comes and goes."

I thought of Ezra calling Luke's *daed* a tyrant, but I wasn't about to bring that up. When we reached the edge of the woods, I said I could make it the rest of the way to the house. Luke handed me the flashlight.

"Take it back with you," I said.

He smiled. "I don't need it."

He waved and started on this return trip home.

As he disappeared into the trees, my phone rang. I looked at it instantly, hoping someone had remembered my birthday. It was the number for

Will and Ada's barn phone. It was Ezra! I stayed put at the edge of the trees, not wanting Rosalee to overhear my part of the conversation.

My heart pounded at the sound of Ezra's hearty, "Happy birthday, Ella!"

"Oh, I'm so glad you called," I said, backing up against a tree to steady myself, surprised at the warm rush of tears that filled my eyes. "How are you?"

"Mostly fine," he said. "Everyone's still really annoyed with me."

"I take it you don't have your cell."

"*Ya*. Will took it. It's probably in his underwear drawer. Not that I'm going to go looking for it in there."

Or on his dresser where he could read my texts. I cringed. Hopefully the battery was long dead.

"I wrote you a letter," I said. "Did you get it?"

"Not yet. What did you say? Besides that you still love me?"

I couldn't help but smile. I told him what I'd written, that I couldn't decide about the baking classes.

The tone of his voice changed. "I thought you were going to stay and go to the school. That's what Ada said your *mammi* told her."

Once again impressed with the speed of the Amish grapevine, I explained that *Mammi* had paid my tuition, but I wondered if I should come back to Lancaster instead.

"But why, Ella? You've always wanted that."

"Not more than I want to come home."

"It's not a good idea, not now," he said.

Dumbfounded, I stuttered, "Mom will get over it. She'll have to let me home once I show up—"

"It's not that. Everyone is watching me like birds of prey. I'm that itty-bitty mouse they are ready to tear apart with their talons and beaks."

I knew he was exaggerating. "Ezra," I pled. "I can't take any drama right now."

"I'm not kidding. It's horrible around here."

"You don't want me to come home?"

"Of course I do. But you should wait. Why not do the cooking school? It's what you want, right? Deep down? And someone else is paying for it! It's a win-win situation."

"Except for not being around you." I wanted him more than school, truth be told.

"Nothing's going to change with me. I'm going to take classes to join the church. Sell my bike. We can figure the rest out when you come back."

"I don't know…"

"Please, Ella. If you come back now, it's only going to make things worse for both of us."

Instantly my eyes filled with tears, only this time they weren't the happy kind.

"Go to school. It's a great opportunity for you. Then come back here and open a business."

The tree trunk dug into my back, so I stood up straight. "Will you help me?"

"Sure. It will be a family business. Our kids can help. They can frost the cookies."

I brushed away my tears, trying to be brave, smiling at the thought of a bunch of little Ezras licking their fingers. The subject of kids must have made him think of his nieces, because he started describing the twins chasing kittens through the barn. We talked for a few more minutes, and then the owl hooted again, startling me again, and I stepped away from the trees.

"I need to go," he said. "Will's been getting me up at four."

"When will you call again?"

"Not for a while. Will looks at the phone bills pretty closely. I'll be in trouble for this as it is."

"Tell him it was my birthday. Maybe he'll understand."

"I doubt it."

"Write to me, then."

"Sure thing," he answered as someone called out his name in the background.

"Gotta go. Bye!"

He was gone before I could respond. I held my silent phone in my hand, wondering if I could survive three months without him. At least if we'd had texting, we could stay in touch all day long every day. But with nothing but an occasional phone call and the US mail, I felt further away from him than I ever had from anyone before.

I slipped the cell into my pocket and turned on the flashlight, blinking away the tears again. He didn't want me to come home.

I would take the baking class and learn everything I could to run my own business someday. And I would watch and see how Rosalee ran hers. I knew Ezra was right. It would be crazy for me to leave now.

Maybe I'd even be able to figure out the code in Sarah's book.

I turned toward the woods, bouncing the beam among the trees. As I did, I thought of *Mammi* traipsing through these very trees with Aunt Klara, Aunt Giselle, and Mom tagging along beside her, coming over to spend an hour, or a morning, or an entire day at the Home Place with Sarah in the *daadi haus*. How nice for her that her parents had lived so close. Maybe the little girls even came over by themselves.

I wished Mom had talked about her life growing up here in Indiana. But then I had never asked. As I turned toward the Home Place, a wave of loneliness swept over me. I didn't know anything about the past except what I'd read in Sarah's journal. I had no idea what I should do about the present.

And the future I wanted was as far away from me as I was from home.

EIGHTEEN

For the next few weeks I worked alongside Rosalee, learning the ins and outs of her bakery business. That, combined with doing farm chores, cooking, and cleaning, made the time pass quickly.

I had another ride tentatively lined up but was relieved when Penny called three days before the class started to say she'd signed up for it too. Just after lunch the next Tuesday, before she was scheduled to pick me up, I sat down with my notebook and read over my "Recipes for Life."

Find a job. Go to school. Open a bakery. Marry E. And then, *Visit the Home Place.*

How things had changed since I'd written that in January. I was living at the Home Place, but I would rather be back in Lancaster County. I was going to start baking school the next day, even though I was ambivalent about it. And Ezra was six hundred miles away.

I should have put marrying Ezra as the first thing on my list.

As I headed down to the bakery to meet Penny, Luke approached.

"Rosalee asked me to give this to you," he said, handing me an envelope. It was from Ezra. I tried not to act too thrilled as I slipped it into my pocket.

He eyed me suspiciously. I was beginning to think his shyness was simply a front for how judgmental he was.

"Ezra's a big boy," I said. "I'm not going to hurt him, I promise."

Blushing, Luke opened his mouth to say something and then stopped.

"Besides," I added, "I'm out here, and he's in Pennsylvania."

Luke ducked his head and turned toward the barn, not responding to me at all.

I was sure he probably thought the same way the Gundys did—that Ezra needed to be away from me. That the less contact we had, the better. That I was set on corrupting him and snatching him away from the Amish faith.

I wanted to read the letter but knew Penny was about to arrive, so I left it in my pocket and continued on to the bakery. When I got there, she was already waiting for me.

"I'll pick up a pie before we go," she said to Rosalee.

"You may have one. Consider it a gift for giving Ella a ride."

I thanked her, boxed it up quickly, grabbed my bag with a notebook and pen in it, and followed Penny out to the car. She chatted the entire way to South Bend. She couldn't believe she was going back to school, at her age, which she said was fifty-three. I couldn't believe she was either, except it seemed providential that she was able to give me a ride. The woman could talk more than I could, something I never would have believed a month ago.

"I've been thinking about opening that little café I've always dreamed of in a year or so," she said.

I nodded as I listened. Ahead, an Amish buggy turned onto the highway. Penny barely slowed as she zipped past it.

"After my husband left, I was pretty lost. But watching you go after your dream has encouraged me to go after my own."

I gave Penny a smile. Older people could be so cute sometimes. She didn't have a clue as to how I really felt about all of this.

Finally she stopped to take a breath, and I pulled out Ezra's letter. Obviously, writing wasn't his favorite thing, which made it all the more endearing. *It was good to talk with you. I have a buyer for the bike. Sad but necessary. I visited the dairy Daed and Will plan to buy. It's fine. I'm not crazy about cows and all that other stuff, but…oh, well. I'll start working there next week. There's a little outbuilding on the dairy that will work as a bakery. Maybe we can offer a special— milk and cookies. Ezra*

I wish he would have added an "I love you" or something reassuring like that, but the mention of a building that would work as a bakery was enough. He must have written it the day after we talked. Someday we would have our own Home Place. Someday soon. This was exactly the encouragement I needed on my first day of baking school.

When we reached Pierre's, Penny parked on a side street. As we moved along the sidewalk, she said, "I'm nervous. Are you?"

"Nah." In this situation I had nothing to lose either way. Maybe I'd do well and end up liking it, and the next three months would be worth it. But if not, or if I failed, I'd just be able to go home all the sooner. Either outcome was fine with me.

I held the door for Penny and then followed her in. Elizabeth was at the counter again.

"Do you teach today too?" I asked her as she opened the door to the kitchen.

"No, Mondays and Wednesdays," she said. "But I only have two students. Want to switch programs?" She smiled. "I'm always looking to steal students from Pierre."

"Oh, it's tempting," Penny said, grinning herself.

I took a seat on one of the stools at a metal table close to the front, and Penny sat on the stool next to me. There were eight other students: two young men, a woman about my age, four women who looked to be in their thirties, and an older man, although he was probably a decade younger than Penny.

It seemed like forever before Pierre appeared. When he did, he bustled into the room drying his hands on his apron. Elizabeth handed him a clipboard.

"*Bonjour!*" he called out. "*Bienvenue!*" He stopped and beamed at all of us. "We will all be together, every Tuesday and Thursday evenings, for the next many months." He clapped his hands together.

"Now," he said. "Let us introduce ourselves. Tell us your name." He was looking at me. "Where you are from. And why are you here."

I froze. He pointed at me as if he'd never met me before. "You."

I coughed a little. "Ella Bayer. I'm from Pennsylvania. And I would like to own a bakery someday in Lancaster County."

Pierre rolled his eyes. "You don't need my school to learn how to make shoofly pie."

I opened my mouth to explain myself, but nothing came out.

"Or cook for a bunch of kids and farmhands."

I glared at him.

"Next," he said, pointing to Penny.

I hardly heard a word any of the other students said. Maybe I shouldn't have worn my prayer covering. Maybe I should have worn jeans. Maybe my first meeting with Pierre wasn't the exception but the norm, which meant I was going to regret taking his classes. My face grew warm.

"First things first, which in culinary school is *mise en place*. This means 'putting in place' or 'everything in place.' First we assemble our ingredients and equipment and keep it all organized, all the time. *Comprendre?* No running around in the kitchen looking for this or that. No working ourselves into fits. No drama. Everything needs to be orderly and with purpose. *Oui?*"

A couple of the students mumbled "*oui*" in return.

Pierre held his hand to his ear. "*Pardon?*"

"*Oui*," we all called out in unison.

"*Très bien*. I said *mise en place* was the first item of business, but really we must learn how to wash our hands first." He laughed. "Here the government thinks they can protect you from everything. So we wash our hands twice."

Penny was the first off her stool and in line. I was the last. Pierre made a comment about my needing to wash extra good to get the "barnyard" out from under my fingernails. I ignored him, but Penny told him I actually worked in a bakery.

"A really good one outside Nappanee."

"I thought you were from Pennsylvania?" Pierre had his hands on his hips.

"Was," I answered. "Obviously I'm not commuting, am I?"

"Ah, sassy." He laughed. "That I like."

I pretended to focus on washing my hands. Sassy. I could definitely do that. And stubborn.

When Rosalee asked me how my class went that night when I returned, I told her it was fine. She pried for details. I told her I'd learned how to wash my hands and how to sift flour.

She frowned.

I blushed. "Thursday we learn how to make bread."

"Which you already know how to do too."

She was right. The first four weeks of the course would be spent on *l'art du pain.* I couldn't imagine eight classes on bread, but no doubt Pierre could stretch it out that far. Next would be a month of classes on pastries, *l'art de la pâtisserie*, and then a month of classes on *l'art du gateau*, or in English, cakes. That was twelve weeks of classes. I'd be done by the end of July. Twelve weeks to learn to bake. Twelve weeks to figure out how to break the code in Sarah's book.

"I'm tired," I said to Rosalee, standing. "I'll see you in the morning. I thought I'd make Dutch babies for breakfast."

Rosalee raised her eyebrows. "I haven't had those in years."

"I thought Eddie would like them." He had been coming with Luke nearly every morning for breakfast, while Millie stayed behind and cooked breakfast for her father, Tom, and her mother, who still wasn't feeling well.

"I'm sure Luke will too." Rosalee smiled. "Like the rest of us, he will like anything you make."

After I'd slipped into my nightgown, I pulled out my notebook. Under "School" I wrote:

One arrogant pastry chef.

I closed the book and started a letter to Ezra. I began it with, *I don't know if this is a good idea*, and then I went on to describe my first day. But after I wrote it, I knew I wouldn't send it. He wanted me to stay. He wanted me to go to baking school. Someday he would help me with my business. I turned off my lamp and settled under the covers.

Just as I was about to doze off my phone beeped with a text. Of course, in my half-asleep state, I hoped it was from Ezra. I fumbled it off the bedside table, knocking it to the floor. I felt around for a moment and finally found it under the bed.

It was from Zed. *I'm loving my film class.*

Cool, I texted back, which I meant. *And goodnight. Some people have to get up REALLY EARLY in the morning.*

No surprise. He didn't text me back.

Eddie loved the Dutch babies, and I was pretty sure Luke did too, although he didn't say much. Rosalee had fixed herself a bowl of oatmeal and gone to the bakery early to get the bread started.

Millie was going to work the counter while I finished cleaning up after breakfast. I'd take my turn in the bakery later.

I dried the last plate and put it away and then washed out the sinks, wiped down the counters, and rinsed the dishcloth. I was pretty sure the kitchen was looking cleaner than it had when I first arrived. Although the bakery was always spotless, the house had a shabbiness about it. Slowly, I was trying to clean and polish, a little at a time.

Everyone at home must have been thinking about me because that afternoon letters came from both Mom and *Mammi.* I didn't read them until that night when I was alone in my room by the light of my lamp. Mom's was scribbled on an unlined three by five card. She said she and Zed missed me and hoped I was doing well. She'd been busy with work, and Zed had another few weeks of school. He planned to take summer classes to graduate early, just like I did, although he was hoping to finish an entire year ahead of schedule. On the other side of the card she wrote that they had seen "Dad" the week before. He continued to work in the soup kitchen, and his health seemed to be the same. She finished with, *We enjoy the time we spend with him.*

I put the card down in disgust, skimming over *Love, Mom.*

Mammi's letter was written on lined notebook paper in her shaky handwriting. She asked how I was, wrote that she prayed for me every day, and said she enjoyed thinking of me in at the Home Place, one of her very favorite locations.

"So why did you leave?" I muttered.

I've been thinking more about my mother's artwork, hoping you can find it and that it will help you decipher the code. All I took with me was the recipe book. I know when I was growing up she kept her work in the front upstairs bedroom, but I don't have any idea where she kept it after I moved out. I imagine, once Gerry's family had the house and she moved into the daadi haus, her artwork went with her. Keep looking until you find it. And let me know once you break that code!

The front bedroom was the one that was entirely empty, and I'd searched the bakery and hadn't found a thing. Maybe Gerry had tossed it after all, as Rosalee suspected.

Please let me know how your classes go.

She signed it, *Love and Prayers, Mammi.*

I wrote her a quick letter, telling her about my first day of class with a positive spin and updating her about the Home Place and Plain Treats. I told her that Rosalee was kind and I was enjoying the Home Place, but I still longed to return to Lancaster County. I didn't mention Sarah's book or the code. There was nothing more for me to tell her about that.

My mother I didn't write to at all.

NINETEEN

Luke worked for Rosalee nearly every day, and Millie worked for her most days. Their mother was growing stronger and was able to take over more of their household duties. Eddie tagged along with his older siblings, and his comic relief definitely made the days go faster. Plus, he was good company for Luke in the fields.

One Wednesday afternoon, as Rosalee made apple streusel and I washed baking pans, she asked me if I'd heard from Ezra recently. I was a little taken aback. I'd assumed he and Rosalee hadn't met.

"Why do you ask?"

"He seemed so befuddled, that's all."

I must have had a funny look on my face as I rubbed the tip of my nose with my wrist because she added, "He stopped by with Luke one day. Had a sticky bun." She tilted her head as if thinking. "Actually two."

That figured. I turned back toward the sink full of dishes. I'd never known anyone to refer to Ezra as "befuddled."

"He called—" I caught myself before I said "on my birthday." "A while back. And I've had a letter."

I didn't add how short it had been.

"How is he?"

"Trying to fly under the radar."

"Or ride?" Her voice was playful.

I smiled. "Something like that."

"My Henry had a motorcycle when I first met him."

"Really?" The thought of Rosalee on the back of a bike made me grin.

"He was from Michigan and had cousins here. He used to ride down to court me. But then we both joined the church before we got married."

"And moved to Michigan? Where you were happy?"

She didn't answer, so I stole a glance at her. She was staring at me. "Yes and no," she finally said.

"No?"

She turned her attention back to streusel in front of her. "I thought we'd be happy. Why wouldn't I? We were both Amish. We believed exactly the same thing." She laughed. "Still, we butted heads. It's not that we fought. There was just an underlying conflict almost all the time. I don't know. Maybe we repeat the patterns we see as a child."

I was standing with my back to the sink now, drying a metal bowl to make more room in the rack and wondering why she was telling me this. I couldn't imagine Rosalee butting heads with anyone.

Thankfully, Ezra and I had never had any conflict. Well, just a little after we'd arrived in Indiana, but we'd worked through all of that. I was even showing, probably as much to my surprise as to everyone else's back home, that I could be submissive by staying at the Home Place as he requested until everything settled down.

"What I learned," Rosalee said, sealing the dough around the filling, "was that there were all sorts of things I should have learned before I became Henry's bride."

"Oh?" I put the bowl away and picked up another. "Like what?"

"How to trust God more."

I thought about that for a moment, wondering if she thought I wasn't trusting God. I hated how adults communicated. They seemed to strive to be sly.

And the thing was, I was trusting God with Ezra. Why else would I be willing to join the Amish church? I didn't tell Rosalee that, though.

I thought she was finished, but then she added, "It's better to stay single than to marry someone who doesn't share your faith, Ella. Being unequally yoked is even more difficult than it sounds."

I had no idea why she would bring that up. Of course Ezra and I shared the same faith, but I didn't say that. Instead, I smiled and thanked her for telling me her story.

That afternoon I rode my bike into town and delivered the last of Rosalee's business cards, at least the last of the ones she had given me. So far no one had come into the bakery for their free sticky bun and no one had ordered anything from us. I had borrowed saddlebags from Luke and had filled them with small boxes of buns and streusel, hoping I could convince someone to order once they had a taste of Plain Treats. It turned out to be a bad idea. Everything was on the flat side by the time I arrived. Thankfully, I checked before offering the samples.

As I was getting ready to leave town, I stopped by the café again. Deciding I had nothing to lose, I took in the samples for Kendra and Wes.

Kendra was making a BLT, obviously for herself, and Wes wasn't in sight.

"I brought you something," I said. "Samples." I placed the boxes on the worktable. "Everything's a little smushed, but it all still tastes really good."

She put tomato slices on top of the bacon. "Well, thanks, sweetheart. Wes and I still haven't decided. Want to stick around for a cup of coffee?"

"Can't," I said. "I'm on my bike and need to get back. Call me when you're ready to place an order." I grinned.

She shook her head and smiled. "You're too much."

I waved as I hurried out the back door.

On Thursday Pierre offered his first lesson on bread making. It was to be a simple loaf of French bread. I'd first made one when I was nine. Still, I listened attentively and even took notes. Although it was interesting to watch Pierre go through the steps, I didn't learn anything new.

On Friday Eddie asked me if I'd be going to church on Sunday. It was at their house. I told him I would consider it.

Millie hadn't been over to the bakery since Wednesday because she'd been home cooking and cleaning. On Saturday I made cookies—snickerdoodles, peanut butter, and chocolate chip—for the service, plus a big pot of bean soup and an industrial-sized tray of corn bread. Luke drove the food over that evening in Rosalee's buggy.

The next morning I decided to attend the service, mostly out of curiosity and because Eddie wanted me to. Rosalee and I walked through the woods together. The day was a sunny spring day, cool but with the promise of warmth to come. I was a bit nervous as Rosalee introduced me to members of her district. Some I recognized from the bakery, but many of them I didn't. One of the older people asked me about my grandmother, but it seemed most didn't know who I was. I'd learned from Rosalee that I didn't have many relatives left in the area. Quite a lot of the Mennonite offspring had moved west, and the only one of my grandmother's brothers who'd had children was Gerry.

Millie and Eddie greeted me warmly, and Luke gave me a shy smile. Their mother took my hand and squeezed it, thanked me for the cookies and soup, and then introduced me to her husband.

Darryl took off his hat, showing an almost entirely bald head with just a fringe of dark brown hair to match his long, full beard. He was tall and wide and seemed a little gruff, but he wasn't the ogre I expected. Ezra had been exaggerating.

As Rosalee and I took our seats on the women's side of the Klines' shed, toward the back, I began to relax. Because I was going to marry Ezra someday, I needed to become comfortable in an Amish church service. I also needed to work at learning Pennsylvania Dutch, something I hoped Eddie could help me with.

I estimated there were probably close to eighty people at the church service, maybe more. Of course, a large portion were children, sitting up on the backless benches, looking straight ahead. I knew, from going to services with *Mammi*, that sometime during the morning parents would take the most restless of the children out for a break, but the majority of them would endure the long stretches of songs, sermons, and prayers. I admired the stamina of Amish children.

The first song, from the *Ausbund*, was in German and lasted about twenty minutes—or at least it felt like it. The second one was no better. The Scripture reading was also in German. I could make out a few words here and there, but as the bishop started the teaching segment in Pennsylvania Dutch, my mind began to wander.

Zed and I had texted the night before, but he was giving me less and less information. I sensed it was because he was spending more time with Freddy and didn't want to divulge that, but when I asked about it he didn't give me an answer. Mom and Zed were beginning to feel more and more distant, as did all of Lancaster County.

The preacher's voice fell to a near whisper—obviously he was emphasizing something. He was fairly young and extra good looking with blond hair and dark eyes. I wished I could understand what he was saying because he sounded very kind and the others listened attentively—except for Eddie. He was making a face at me. I quickly looked away, determined not to encourage him. Two hours later, by the end of the long service, Eddie had his head tucked against Luke's side and was fast asleep.

When it finally ended, I went to the house with Rosalee to help Cora and Millie pull the meal together. Cora looked better than the evening I met her and seemed to be holding up fine.

The tables in the kitchen and living room were already set. Men started bringing in the benches from the service and putting one on each side of each table. I realized there were tables set up in the basement too when the men started hauling benches down there. It seemed Tom was in charge of that task because he stood at the door and directed the men. Darryl must still have been outside.

It wasn't long until it was time for the meal to be served. I knew the men and women sat at separate tables. I also knew that it usually took two seatings for the entire district to eat, and that was probably truer here at the Klines' than in most homes because their house was small.

I waited with Rosalee while the first group ate. We refilled water pitchers and then put the cookies and other desserts out on a long table. I knew she hadn't contributed any pies from the bakery, but it looked as if other women had purchased some of our pies and brought them along.

Finally, Rosalee, Cora, Millie, and I sat down together with our bowls of soup. When we were finishing up, Eddie wiggled onto the bench between Rosalee and me, looking up at me with his big gray eyes.

"Yep," he said in English. "I'm going to court you some day."

The women all laughed, and I gave his shoulder a squeeze, realizing I felt a sense of belonging that I hadn't experienced since I left Lancaster County. It was the way I once felt with Ezra's family. That made me sad.

When I returned, would they be accepting of me, both as a member of the church and as Ezra's wife?

I began gathering the empty bowls around me, and as I stood I realized Luke was standing in the doorway of the kitchen, watching me. He blushed and then walked through to the living room. As I began washing the dishes, he came back through with the first of the benches. Soon they would all be stacked back in the church wagon and on their way to the home where services would be held in two weeks.

It was plenty warm enough for people to visit outside, and after Millie and I had finished the last of the cleanup, we went out and sat with some of the younger people.

"Are you coming to the singing tonight?" one of the younger teen girls asked.

Millie said she wasn't sure; it depended on how her *mamm* was feeling. I could see that hosting the church service would tire Cora out.

"How about Luke?" the girl asked, but Millie only shrugged.

"Naomi will be there," the girl teased, but then, without missing a beat, she turned toward me. "Are you going, Ella?"

"Probably not," I answered, not wanting to explain that, first of all, I hadn't been invited, and second of all, even though I'd felt a sense of community I didn't feel as if I belonged.

As I loaded Rosalee's pots and pans into the buggy, a man's firm voice drew my attention.

It was Darryl, standing in the doorway of the shed.

"Eddie," he called out.

The boy was scampering across the barnyard, a kitten in his hands, toward the shed.

"I already asked you to sweep up once."

Eddie let the kitten go and walked toward his *daed*, his head down.

I walked back to the house for Rosalee but bumped into Luke.

"Oh, sorry," he said to me, stepping wide, but then he stopped, watching Eddie grab the broom.

"Everything okay?" I asked.

"Seems to be."

It was obvious Darryl ran a pretty tight ship.

Luke turned to me. "Have you met our minister?"

I shook my head.

"Preacher Jacob," he called out.

He was twenty feet away but hurried over, his hand outstretched.

"Welcome," he said, shaking my hand. He didn't seem to be thirty yet. His wife joined us. She was pretty, with blond hair and blue eyes. They didn't have any children with them.

"Could you understand the sermon?" the preacher asked.

I told him I could make out a few words.

"Feel free to have Rosalee translate next time. She can whisper as I speak."

"I don't want to be a nuisance," I said.

"You won't be. I'd rather have it that way. Or I can speak in English."

My eyes must have betrayed my surprise.

"It's not unheard of," he said. "If you have any questions, let me know. But please come back. We'd love to have you join us regularly."

His wife nodded.

"This is Marilyn." Jacob stepped back and put his hand on her elbow.

She took my hand too. She was probably not much older than Millie. I wondered how long they had been married.

"It's so nice to have you with us," she said. "And nice that Rosalee has you every day."

I thanked them both, and then, after exchanging goodbyes, I watched them walk toward their buggy. Jacob leaned toward his wife, whispering something to her. Her head tilted forward and she patted his arm. I felt a pang of envy. That was what I wanted, minus having a preacher for a husband. I couldn't imagine Ezra doing that and hoped the lot would never choose him. But I envied Jacob and Marilyn's closeness, their easiness with each other, how he seemed to absolutely adore her, and vice versa. He was young to be a preacher, yes, but clearly he was doing a good job.

Rosalee joined me. "He's a *gut* preacher," she said. "He's taught me so many things. He talks about God's love in ways I've never heard before. It's as if God speaks right through him."

TWENTY

That afternoon, while Rosalee rested, I saw my chance to thoroughly explore the farm. I'd been on the lookout ever since I arrived, searching everywhere I could, but I hadn't been able to do a methodical search to see where Sarah's artwork might be tucked away—if it hadn't been destroyed. I had even asked Luke a couple of times if he'd seen it. The second time he told me he understood what I was asking, but he hadn't seen any sort of artwork around the place.

I'd searched the bakery a second time. I knew it wasn't in the house—unless it was in Rosalee's room, which I doubted. It wasn't in the shed. I'd been in the barn a few times and looked through a downstairs tack room to no avail, but I'd never been in the loft. If I were going to hide artwork, I definitely wouldn't put it there. Barns tended to burn down. But still, I needed to look.

I sneezed a few times as I climbed the ladder. The straw was old and musty and needed to be changed. It was probably on Luke's long list of chores. The horse neighed in her stall below me, and Rosalee's cow mooed. It was nearly time for her to be milked.

Only a few rows of hay bales, stacked four high, were left in the loft. The floor was long plank boards balanced on beams, but as I looked closer, to my relief, I saw they were nailed down. I scanned the open area. There was nowhere anything could be hidden. I walked to the end of the loft and stood at the open window where they most likely brought the hay in, probably on a conveyor belt. I could see past the first field and on to the second. I hadn't been out there yet. I squinted, making out a willow tree bowing down toward a small pond, remembering *Mammi*'s story about her grandfather playing his alpine horn.

Discouraged, I left the barn thinking I would walk out to the field. But first I decided to look in the underground cellar. I hadn't been in it before. It seemed that Rosalee always went after the potatoes herself or sent Eddie. It was worth a try.

I hurried down the stone walkway, sure *Mammi*'s grandfather Gerard Gingrich had constructed it. The wooden door at the bottom was also made of planks. I grasped the handle and pressed against the latch, easing the door wide open to give myself some light as I stepped into the cold cellar. I exhaled, noting that my breath hung in the air. It was probably around forty degrees, even though it was close to seventy outside.

The odor was pungent, a mix of earth, onions, garlic, and other root vegetables. A small pile of potatoes was in the corner. There were also nearly empty bins of turnips, cabbage, yams, and onions. Strings of garlic hung from the low ceiling.

I turned on the flashlight app on my phone and shone it around the room. The ceiling was curved and constructed of bricks, which seemed to be quite an engineering feat. There were no cupboards or shelves built into the wall, but there was a space between where the stone wall ended and the bricks began, although not enough room for much of anything. I didn't want to run my hand along it. I stood on my tiptoes and strained to see on the ledge, hopping around the room as I did. When I got to the other side, I stopped. Something looked like a piece of dull metal. I reached up, tentatively, and then pulled down an old butter cookie tin that was icy cold against my hands. I brushed away the cobwebs and opened it.

Inside were five stacks of papers, two-inch squared I estimated, rubber banded together. Each of the top squares had a drawing on it. I picked up one with a bird, and started to take the rubber band off, but it broke in my hand. Each of the squares had a symbol on it—many were the same ones that were in Sarah's book. It was obvious she'd drawn these too. There was edelweiss, an alpine horn, a hen with a brood of chicks, a crow, an eagle, a small bird, a hound, a butter churn, a cow, a cat, a willow tree... then an owl and hawk. I closed the lid and left the cellar, taking the box with me and carefully latching the door. It wasn't what I was looking for, but still it was a find.

I decided to go on to the pasture and the pond. I walked around the edge of the field because Luke had seeded it not too long ago. I stayed along the fence line and then cut across the pasture. As I neared the pond, I realized the Klines' property was on the other side of it. I could see the cows in their pasture, and there was a gate between the two. One of the cows raised her head, as if she had noticed my approach in the distance.

I stopped under the graceful willow and sat down on a wide, flat root that was sticking out of the ground. Opening the tin, I took the rest of the rubber bands off the stacks of squares. I was more careful with these and they didn't break. It was hard to tell how old the paper was. I guessed the coldness of the root cellar had preserved the images more than if they had been in the house.

I thumbed through the pictures. There were probably fifty altogether. At first I thought the squares seemed as if they were made for a game like Memory, but there were no matches. Each symbol was different. There were more herbs. More household objects—a lamp, a pitcher, a ladle. There were raspberries, blueberries, peaches, and apples. There was also a Bible, a songbook, and a notebook. I stopped at the very last picture. It was a baby. I gasped. *Mammi* said her mother didn't draw people. But here was proof that she had. I went through the pictures again, one by one, and then stopped at the picture of the baby once more. The infant had curly hair and bright eyes and was smiling. I wondered if it was a particular baby or just a drawing of a random baby. If it was a specific one, I couldn't help but wonder who it was. My *mammi*? Rosalee's father, Gerry? Mom or one of her sisters? It could easily have been a boy or a girl. I puzzled over it as I put the rubber bands back on the stacks and then carefully tied the rubber band I broke. I put everything back in the box for safekeeping. Unfortunately, I didn't see how any of the drawings would help me figure out the code, but I was grateful to have found them, even though they only added to the mystery of Sarah's work.

The mooing over at the Klines' grew louder, and I realized someone was herding the cows toward their barn. I stood up and stepped away from the tree and pond. Standing on my tiptoes, I shielded my eyes. It was Luke. He spotted me and took his hat off and waved it at me. I waved back, smiling a little.

He was hard to figure out. I was never sure if he was happy to see me or not. I was surprised he was doing the milking. He would miss the singing if he didn't hurry.

By the time I got back to the barn, Rosalee was already milking Bossie, perched on the little stool, her head against the cow's flank. The ping of the milk against the galvanized bucket masked the sounds of my entrance, and I had to say hello twice before she heard me.

"Goodness," she said, turning her head toward me and stopping the milking as she did. "You startled me."

Her hands returned to her work, picking up the steady rhythm again of the milk against the pail, but she kept her eyes on me.

"What do you have in the box?"

"A sort of game, I think. I found it in the underground cellar." I hesitated. "I hope you don't mind that I was snooping around."

She smiled a little. "No, I told you to. I expected it."

Relieved, I continued, "I think Sarah must have made it." I opened it as I spoke. "It has many of the same symbols as in her book, plus more, but these don't seem to be tied to recipes." I held up a stack of cards, showing the willow tree on top. "Do you remember these?"

She shook her head. "But that's the willow in the field."

I nodded but was disappointed that she didn't remember the cards or if they were part of a game. I put the stack of symbols back inside and closed the box, deciding I'd go fix dinner.

First, though, I retreated to my room and sat down on the bed, placing the box beside me. I took out my phone and hit the speed dial key for Mom's number. For once she picked up right away. I didn't want to chat or hear about Freddy, so I jumped straight to my question, asking her about the squares with the pictures on them and told her Rosalee didn't remember them.

"Oh, my," she said. "I hadn't thought about that in years."

"You remember them?"

"Yes." She paused and then stammered, "Barely. Let's see…"

I waited as patiently as I could.

"It was a game *Mammi* Sarah made up. Like Concentration."

I was right!

"I used to play it for hours with Zed, but the one we had was just farm animals and we got it at a toy store. *Mammi* Sarah drew all the symbols," Mom said. "We would play at her house."

"The tin I found only has one set of symbols. There aren't any duplicates."

"That's funny…No, wait. It makes sense." She paused again.

"Mom." I knew my voice sounded impatient.

"We used to keep one of the tins at our house," she said. "I remember walking through the woods with it, going to the Home Place."

"Did you take that set with you to Pennsylvania?"

"I don't think so," she answered. "I don't remember having them after we left Indiana, and it's not surprising Rosalee doesn't remember them. She's older, probably a good ten years more than Klara. She was married and had moved to Michigan by the time *Mammi* Sarah played that game with us."

"You don't think she played games with Rosalee?"

"Not that game. That was for us—for Klara, Giselle, and me."

My voice increased in excitement at the thought of the game being special to our family. "Some of the symbols in her book represent different people—do you think it's the same in the game?"

"What book?" Mom asked.

I faltered. *Mammi* hadn't wanted me to tell anyone about the book. How stupid of me.

"It's a recipe book of hers…" Perhaps Mom would think I'd come across it here, in Indiana.

She didn't seem to notice my blunder. "I bet the other box is around there somewhere," she said. "Keep looking. But it was just a game, Ella.

Nothing more. As we got older she had us spell the names of the object. She was teaching us while we had fun."

"What about the birds? Do you think they could represent different people?"

"Such as?"

"Herself. Her children. Her husbands."

"Husbands?"

I took a deep breath. "She had three."

"I only knew about *Daadi* David."

"She had two husbands who died before she married him."

There was a pause and then, "Are you sure?"

"That's what *Mammi* told me." I didn't bother to say the book verified it. "She didn't have kids with either of them, of course. Only with David."

"Well, then…" Mom's voice trailed off.

"How about the herbs?"

"Besides using them in her cooking, she was a bit of a healer too," Mom said. "She always had a remedy for every little thing. People used to come to her from all over, and she'd mix them up something. She used to dry herbs in the attic of the Home Place, I remember that. Uncle Gerry didn't like it—and neither did his wife."

"Maybe that's where you got your medical sense." I wouldn't bother to tell Mom, not now, that her grandmother had studied to be a nurse and then worked as one. I'd tell her that sometime—probably when it was okay for me to tell her about the book.

The more I learned about my great-grandmother, the more I liked her.

"I certainly didn't get her love of cooking," Mom said. "She was amazing."

"The recipes in the book are mostly for baking."

"Really? Well, she probably had all the other recipes in her head. And she was always improvising."

"One of the pictures in the game is of a baby—the only drawing of a person."

"Oh?" Mom said.

"Do you think it's of a particular baby?"

Mom didn't answer.

"Mom?"

"Let me think about it," she said. "I'll get back to you on that."

I heard Rosalee coming in the back door and decided to use that as an excuse to end the conversation. I'd gotten the information I needed and didn't want the subject to change to Freddy. I said I needed to go and after a goodbye from Mom, I hung up and left my phone on my bureau, picking up the tin and the recipe book and hurrying down the hall to the kitchen.

Rosalee had the pail of milk on the counter, ready to separate.

"How about an omelet?" I asked.

"Oh, no. I'll make scrambled eggs. You sit and look at your things." She motioned toward the table as she pulled the separator out from under the kitchen sink.

I hesitated, knowing my omelet would be better, but I couldn't very well insist when it was her kitchen. I spread the symbols out and then matched them to what I found in the book. There were more herbs: lark-spur, evening primrose, anise, lavender, basil, lily of the valley, sage, and parsley—those were the ones I recognized or that she'd identified by name in the book.

"Look at all those birds," Rosalee said. She stepped closer, two eggs in each of her hands. "She always liked birds and had a ton of birdhouses. My *daed* took those down over the years. She liked watching birds. She said you could learn a lot from the way they acted. But she liked observing everything in nature. She said nature was God's canvas, and every time we made something—dinner, a table, a garden, a painting—we were continuing His creation."

She turned back to the stove.

"Do you think Sarah was right?" I asked.

Rosalee's glanced over her shoulder at me. "Well, it depends on whether I'm baking dessert or cooking dinner. That was the thing with *Mammi* Sarah—she was creative to the core and found such joy in all of it. But as far as her symbols and drawings, they are beyond me. Maybe they were entirely for herself."

When we were ready to eat, I moved the book and tin to the end of the table and Rosalee led us in a silent prayer. The scrambled eggs were overcooked and rubbery, and the tomato juice she'd canned last fall needed salt. But the apple streusel, pulled from the bakery shelf yesterday, was heavenly. By the time the meal was over, I felt thoroughly satisfied, not just in my stomach but throughout my being. I knew that feeling wouldn't last for very long—I missed Ezra too much for that—but in this moment, I allowed myself just to sit and take in my surroundings and think about how the Lord had turned so many of my problems into blessings.

Truly, God was good.

Twenty-One

Luke spent the middle week of May cultivating the corn while Millie and I tended the garden in the afternoons. Besides weeding, we harvested the early vegetables: radishes, lettuce, and spinach. I suggested we make a spinach quiche in the bakery because we had all the needed ingredients, including the eggs. Two slices sold, but we ended up eating the leftovers for breakfast, lunch, and dinner.

Often, in the early afternoon, Eddie would come sit in the bakery and have a glass of milk and a snack. I would sweep, wash tables, clean the windows, and do other tasks while he ate. Sometimes he would put two chairs together and curl up and take a nap. As much as I liked to bake, my favorite time of the day was when he was in the bakery with me. Every once in a while Luke would come in too. He'd have a cup of coffee and sit with Eddie. Sometimes I would catch him looking at me. He would blush and look away then. He wasn't talking with me any more than when I first came. In fact, there were times when I wondered if he resented my living with Rosalee altogether.

Business at the bakery was the slowest it had been since I'd started working there. Monday of the third week in May, Rosalee sent me out to work in the garden with Luke. Eddie was with him, and they both had hoes, so I headed to the toolshed and retrieved another one.

"Come work by me," Eddie said as I approached.

I made my way to a row of half-foot high potato plants next to him. Luke called out, without greeting me, "Mound the soil around the bases of the plants like you're building a hill. Just don't scrape down deep—you don't want to scar the roots."

"Got it," I said, watching Luke for a few moments. Turning my attention to the plant at my feet, I did the same.

Eddie missed a plant and I redirected him. We were now right by each other. He told me about feeding the calves at his place as we worked. "*Daed* says it's time to wean them," Eddie said, his voice sorrowful. "That's been my favorite job. That and sitting with *Mamm*."

"How she's doing?" I asked

Eddie stood up straight and rubbed his back like an old man. "She's tired."

"From what?"

Eddie shrugged and began hoeing again. "Life, I guess. It's been one thing after another." He sounded even more grown up than he usually did.

"Really?"

He nodded solemnly. "That's what I overheard *Daed* say. First the cows got diseased. Then the well broke."

"Eddie," Luke said, his voice low. "That happened a long time ago. Years before you were born."

His little brother either didn't hear him or else he ignored him. "Next the tractor couldn't be fixed. Then *Mamm* lost another—"

Luke's voice was still low but very firm. "Eddie."

"What?" The little boy spun around.

"That's enough."

"Ella don't care." Eddie swung his hoe back and forth as he spoke. "Right?"

I deferred to Luke, but when he didn't say anything I answered. "Of course I don't mind, but what Luke is saying is that some things are to be talked about only with family members and not outsiders."

"Well, no one in our family talks about this stuff. *Daed* just did one time, to Tom. And you're family? Right?"

I smiled at him. "Actually, no."

"You couldn't court her someday if she was," Luke said, a mischievous look on his face.

He grinned. "Got it!"

We continued to hoe as Eddie prattled on about the new chicks that had just been delivered to their farm. I thought about their *mamm* and what could be wrong with her. Perhaps she had one of those conditions that made a person tired all the time, like fibromyalgia or chronic fatigue syndrome. Or maybe she was depressed. It certainly sounded as though the family had had their fair share of troubles. But, on the other hand, they still had their dairy farm. And each other. And Rosalee for support. And their district. Things could be a whole lot worse.

After a while Eddie put down his hoe and wandered over to the tulip tree. It was in full bloom now, its pinkish flowers brightening the entire property. Eddie picked up one that had fallen and returned with it, handing it to me as he grinned.

"Thank you." I took it and, with a flourish, pushed back my head covering and tucked it behind my ear. "Tulip trees are my absolute favorite."

Eddie clapped.

"It's not actually a tulip tree," Luke said. "It's in the magnolia family."

I made a face at Eddie and then said, "Thank you, Professor Kline."

Luke leaned against his hoe. "Just thought you might want to know." His eyes sparkled again. "Wouldn't want you to be misleading Eddie or anything."

"No, we wouldn't want to do that." I patted the little guy on the shoulder, bumping his hat. "Now back to work."

A few hours later, after we'd had lunch and the dishes were done, I walked down to the bakery to relieve Millie, who had only been filling in for Rosalee because she'd gone into town to the bank. Eddie was at the counter, asking for a sticky bun.

"You just had lunch," Millie answered. "So the answer is no. You can either go out and help Luke or come back home with me."

"I want to rest here," he said. The bakery was shaded by the century-old trees that surrounded it and surprisingly cool, but it was the hottest day of the year so far and humid. He had his hat in his hand.

"It's fine with me, Millie," I said. "I'll keep an eye on him."

She sighed, and I regretted butting in. Eddie was her responsibility, not mine. She turned to her little brother. "Rest for just a bit. Then ask Ella what you can do to help. Or go find Luke."

The boy climbed onto a chair at the table closest to the counter. His face was red and his hair was damp. I thought of Zed when he was little and of that little boy smell—a mix of sweat and soil.

After Millie was out the door, Eddie asked me for a sticky bun.

"Later," I said. "For a midday snack. After you've rested and done more work."

For a six-year-old, even an Amish one, I was sure, Eddie did a lot of chores. He never shirked or complained. I thought Millie was a little harsh not to give him a treat, but I wasn't about to go against her wishes, especially after I'd already intervened when I shouldn't have. I poured him a glass of water and he drank half of it down quickly.

"Millie's mean to me," Eddie said.

"Why do you say that?" I was refilling the cookie trays in the case.

"She doesn't want me around."

"Oh, I think she does. She was happy for you to go back home with her."

He shook her head. "She'd rather I stay here with Luke. She says I make too much noise. That it's hard on *Mamm*."

"Have you told Millie how you feel? Or your *mamm*?"

He wrinkled his nose and then put his head down on his hands. In a few minutes, he was asleep, and I went back into the kitchen, taking the recipe Pierre had given all of us out of my apron pocket. *L'art du pain*. Making bread wasn't my favorite thing, but Pierre said it was the foundation of life. If we couldn't master bread, we wouldn't be successful at baking anything else. That's why we were going to spend four weeks loafing around. That had been Pierre's joke, not mine.

As I worked, I checked on Eddie every once in a while. The heat was keeping customers away—at least I hoped that was what it was—and only two trickled in. The boy didn't even stir when the bell chimed. Getting up at four thirty every morning made for a tired child by the afternoon. And a tired lady. I was certain Rosalee would go back to the house for a nap after returning from town.

Even though bread making didn't thrill me, it didn't take long for me to

Somehow I managed to catch them both and put them on the table in front of me.

"Explain yourself," he said.

I shrugged. I wasn't about to tell him about having to walk Eddie home or any of that.

"The kitchen was hotter than I anticipated."

"What were you using? A woodstove?" He smirked. "And let me guess, no central air, *oui*?"

"*Oui*," I whispered.

"*Pardon*?"

"*Oui*!" I didn't mean to shout. What kind of Plain woman was I that I couldn't bake a decent loaf of bread?

Next up was Penny. Her loaves were perfect. She received four and half points, nonetheless.

"I never give a five," Pierre explained.

Inwardly, I groaned.

By the time we were on the way home, Penny had forgotten about my humiliating experience, or perhaps it hadn't registered with her in the first place. She gushed about Pierre.

"Isn't he amazing?" She beamed as she spoke. "I feel so privileged to be taking this course. And to think I never would have done it if I hadn't met you. If you hadn't lived with me for that short time."

I nodded encouragingly. I could see how God had worked that out. I was happy for her—but not so happy for me.

"And you're more comfortable with your own people. Right?" She gave me a quick glance.

I wasn't sure how to explain that the Amish weren't *my* people, because in some ways they were, but in others they really weren't.

"It's a little hard getting used to not having electricity."

"And using a woodstove. I thought your bread turned out great, considering. And to think of the things you all make in that bakery!"

I laughed. "Actually, we have a regular oven." Although it wasn't very consistent. Rosalee needed to look into buying a new one.

"Oh," she said. "But I thought…"

"Pierre's the one who mentioned the woodstove."

"That's right."

We rode in silence for a few minutes.

"I've been thinking about taking Elizabeth's cooking class next session." Penny slowed for a tractor that hugged the shoulder ahead of us. "Want to join me?"

"I'll be back home by next session," I said. "But thanks anyway."

"Ah, so you and your boyfriend are still an item?"

"Pretty much," I said briefly. I didn't want to talk about Ezra.

She zipped around the tractor and a field of foot-high corn came into view. In no time we were speeding down the highway toward Nappanee again. But I was wishing I were speeding toward Lancaster County instead.

TWENTY-TWO

The next day, Eddie wasn't his usually bouncy self, but at least he wasn't running a fever. We thought he'd become overheated, so we had him drink more water and rest during the hottest part of the day. Millie continued to seem short with him, but I figured that was because of all the responsibilities she had.

On Sunday, because it was an off week from church, Rosalee visited with a widow in the next district, while I stayed at the Home Place. I had run out of spots to look for Sarah's artwork, but I did go through her recipe book again, taking out my magnifying glass and rereading the section about her second husband, Dr. Clive Chapman, starting with when she moved to Indianapolis to go to nursing school.

August 29, 1915—Now that I'm away from Alvin, I'm free from that tedious code. I'm living in a boarding house with a bathroom down the hall and dinner every night. Once I start doing my rotations, I'll have to pay for dinner at the hospital or take a sandwich. I hope I'm doing the right thing. The program will take two years—and then I'll have to decide whether to go back to the Home Place or not. I've tried to talk to God about it, but don't think He's listening. Of course, Mother and Father weren't happy with me and neither was Alvin. In fact, he was quite adamant that I should stay and was very loud about it.

Later, Mother and I were talking and she said Alvin can't always help himself, which I disagreed with. She said she's surprised I haven't realized that he isn't "quite right." She told me she's afraid it's her fault, going on to say when he was newly born she was quite sick and the neighbor woman cared for Alvin for a stretch of time. She said that by the time she recovered and Alvin came back he wasn't like her other children had been at that age. And he'd been slow ever since.

I thought of the hunting accident when Gus was killed and wondered if Alvin's disability had contributed to that.

I think Mother is feeling needlessly guilty. Perhaps whatever made her so sick impacted Alvin too, although she thinks it was exhaustion from a mixture of the flu, caring for such a large family, and childbirth in her early forties.

The next entry was about Dr. Chapman, who had asked her on a date for the third time. *He's English and he wears glasses. He's as different from Gus as could be. I do enjoy talking about medicine with him. He's inquisitive and always learning, and I can tell he cares about his patients.* She went on to say he was concerned about the war in Europe that had been going on for more than a year. *I hope it will end soon. Honestly, I don't like to hear about it. It makes me miss home and our nonresistant ways.*

On March 10, 1916, she wrote: *Dr. Chapman—although he insists I call him Clive—took me to the Art Association today. It was splendid. Drawings, paintings, sculptures. I showed him some of my work afterward. He said he wonders at my wanting to become a nurse. I told him I think it's all related. It's all nurturing either the body, mind, or soul. Nursing, cooking, baking, making remedies, singing, drawing, painting, listening. None are more important than the other. I feel that all of these things are about beauty, about sharing God's creation. It's a form of worship.*

I stopped and considered Sarah's philosophy. Plain people were known for being purposeful, but she took it beyond that. I wondered if my baking was a way of worshipping God.

I kept reading.

April 29, 1916—Clive is talking of returning to England and joining up with the Red Cross to take care of soldiers. He says it's his duty, and that we shouldn't expect young men to sacrifice their lives if we're not willing to care for them.

In the next entry, Sarah wrote that Clive had asked her to marry him. *I can't give him an answer yet. He thinks it's because he's Episcopalian. That's not it. I know he worships the same God I do. We believe mostly the same, except when it comes to war.*

The next set of recipes were quite interesting, as they were for all English foods: marmalade, trifle, scones, Irish soda bread, Scottish oat cakes, rock cakes, Yorkshire curd tart, English summer pudding, and shepherd's pie. More entries followed.

May 23, 1916—Clive challenges me in a way I never dreamed possible. I saw that today as we hiked. He knows so much about nature and a person's whole being. He presents it all as one. I've never felt so full. I drew an owl with Clive's eyes today. Then I told him I would marry him. It will be at the courthouse, just him and me. I'll write to Mother, Father, and Alvin afterward.

On June 10, 1916, she wrote: *I'm now Mrs. Clive Chapman. He doesn't want me to finish nursing school, but unless I'm blessed with a baby before he leaves, I will.*

Then on July 17, 1916: *Clive left yesterday on the train to New York. He'll board the first ship he can and go straight to France. Oh, how I hope this war ends soon.*

Wow. Looking back at the date of the previous entry, I realized they had only been living as husband and wife for a little more than a month before he went away. How awful! I couldn't imagine how difficult it must have been to tell each other goodbye. I continued reading.

July 30, 1916—No new role as mother hen for me—not now. I am overwhelmed by loneliness. Thank goodness I didn't quit the program. I must press on and learn all I can.

September 25, 1916—I had a letter from Clive. He is in northern France, near Flanders. That was all he could say, except that he loves me very much and dreams of me every night.

November 10, 1916—From the Scripture I read today: "The beast of the field shall honour me, the dragons and the owls: because I give waters in the wilderness, and rivers in the desert, to give drink to my people, my chosen" (Isaiah 43:30).

That is my prayer, that the Lord provides for Clive in this wasteland of war...

May 28, 1917—I finished my program and have been awarded my cap and pin. I've decided to stay on at the hospital, even though Mother and Father have asked me to come home. Alvin has taken over the farm, but Mother said they could use my help around the house. I wrote back and said I would stay put and hope my husband returns soon.

March 10, 1918—Clive's letters are few and far between. I believe, from what he writes, that many have never reached me. Also, many of mine apparently don't reach him. He said trench fever is rampant, and he's had to send several soldiers back because of shell shock. They have also had an epidemic of typhoid fever. I'm praying he doesn't get it. He says the sanitation is horrible.

On August 7, 1918, she wrote that a letter arrived from Clive saying he'd been treating soldiers for the Spanish flu. *He said he's never seen anything like it, and it's spreading fast. Worse than typhoid. Oh, how I wish I could have gone with him. I don't think it's too late. He wouldn't allow it if he knew, but perhaps if I just show up? I'm contacting the Red Cross tomorrow.*

August 8, 1918—I filled out my application with the Red Cross. Why didn't I do this as soon as we married? I could have been by my husband's side all along.

Then again, by tending to the wounds of war, will that make me a proponent of war? Of violence? These thoughts trouble me, and yet how could God, who indeed hates war, not want His precious children tended to in their pain, regardless of what brought them to that state? These are questions I will put to prayer as I wait to hear back about my application.

Even though I knew what was coming, I tensed as I read the next entry.

August 22, 1918—Clive has passed on, taken by the flu pandemic, somewhere on the western front. He was buried in France. A Red Cross worker came to the hospital today to tell me. I thought he had come to give me an assignment.

September 9, 1918—The Red Cross has put a hold on my application. The rumor is the war will end soon. It turns out Clive left a sizable bank account. I will not have to worry about money—although I feel as if I have been robbed.

October 20, 1918—The flu pandemic has reached Indiana. I am working

long shifts, nearly around the clock. This is what God has for me, for now. The war continues on...I've been reading in the book of Isaiah: "The wolf also shall dwell with the lamb, and the leopard shall lie down with the kid; and the calf and the young lion and the fatling together; and a little child shall lead them."
I long for that day.

November 11, 1918— Armistice Day. Thank God this horrid war has ended.

In January 1919 she wrote that the flu pandemic had returned with a vengeance.

Many say it's worse than the bubonic plague. How much more must we suffer? I've heard predictions that more will die from the flu than in the war.

April 12, 1919—I am worn out. I've been in Chicago for the last month, working at the Marine Hospital, taking care of veterans. Amputees, mustard gas wounds, and those with shell shock. One could drown in this sorrow.

The sound of the city grates on my nerves. I do not want another person to bump into me on the busy streets. I despise the factory whistles and the smoke pouring from the chimneys. I long for the country.

April 23, 1919—I am going home and never leaving again. I've lost two husbands—Gus, my adventuresome first love, and Clive, my intellectual match. I'll never love again, I know.

And because I'm going back and Alvin still hasn't found a wife and, according to Mother, he seems more out of sorts than ever, I'll write again in code.

I felt wrung out from the pain of her story, again. I couldn't imagine it. Couldn't quite imagine her loving someone more than Gus to start with, but then to have a second husband die too. And one who was so smart and daring, so well traveled and educated. I could see why she thought she would never love again.

No wonder she wanted to return to the Home Place, but to think she went from being married to someone who was so dashing to marrying a Plain man like David Berg. I was baffled. Did she love him? Enough to join the Amish? Oh, how I wished I could break the code and find the answer, but it was looking less and less likely.

The next week I worked in Plain Treats, did all the cooking, weeded the garden, baked more bread, and was ridiculed two more times by Pierre.

On Sunday I went to church with Rosalee again, this time at the home of a family about two miles away. The two of us rode in her buggy.

The Klines were already there when we arrived, and I noticed Millie talking with a tall young man beside a brand-new buggy. Judging by the way they were looking at each other, I had a feeling that not only did Millie have the responsibility of taking care of her family, but she was also courting. I wondered who would take care of the Klines after she married.

Jacob preached again, this time from First John 4:8. I listened closely as he read the Scripture in German. Thankfully, he followed with the English, "Whoever does not love does not know God, because God is love."

Rosalee began translating for me, so quietly I had to really concentrate to hear her. Jacob talked about a father's love, and how if one didn't have a loving father, it was sometimes harder to comprehend God's love. He said he wanted to make sure we understood what the perfect love of a father was. It wasn't someone waiting with a switch, ready to strike when we did something wrong. It wasn't someone who was always disappointed in us.

"Our Father God delights in His children." Jacob repeated this in English, perhaps just for me. "There are times when He must discipline His children, but He's thrilled with all they learn, all they create, all the relationships they forge. God longs to keep leading us, long after we are adults. Long after our earthly fathers have released us. God created us—and He wants to relate with us."

It reminded me of Sarah's writings about worshipping God through her work and art. I wondered if she felt she worshipped God through the work she put into her relationships too, although besides Alvin she didn't seem to have much conflict in her life, at least not the way I did.

Twenty-Three

My lessons of *l'art du pain* ended with baguettes, which I thought turned out perfectly. Pierre said they tasted like straw and asked if I'd used it as filler. He was the type of teacher who seemed to need to choose one student to target. I was the one with the bull's-eye on my forehead—or maybe on the top of my prayer covering. He threw darts during every class, sometimes lobbing them in my direction and sometimes sending zingers that caught me by surprise.

The truth was that I was learning much more from Rosalee than from Pierre, and my bread at the bakery always turned out beautifully, whether white, whole wheat, or French. So did my muffins, scones, pretzels, and biscuits at home.

On Monday of the first week of the pastry-making course, I decided to ride my bike into town again with business cards for Plain Treats, thinking I'd give it one more try, this time taking soft pretzels, which packed better. I stopped at all the same places I'd been to, including the café. I dropped off two pretzels for Wes and Kendra. They were happy to see me, and before I left, Wes said he'd decided to order a few pies and told me which ones they wanted. I was ecstatic. As I left, Wes winked at Kendra. I couldn't see her expression, but I was pretty sure she was smiling. I didn't care if she'd talked him into it. I loved to see them together and couldn't wait until Ezra and I could work someday the way they did, sharing inside jokes and knowing looks.

With Penny's help, I dropped off the pies the next day on the way to South Bend, hoping the delivery was the beginning of a profitable future for Rosalee and Plain Treats.

On Friday afternoon I noticed the corner of a piece of paper sticking out of Eddie's pocket.

"What's that?" I asked.

"Oh, something I found."

"May I see it?"

He handed it to me. It was folded in fourths and looked fragile.

I unfolded it carefully. It was a picture of a kitten and obviously drawn by Sarah. "Where did you find this?"

He blushed.

"It's okay, Eddie."

He hung his head. "There's a metal box in the floor of my room. It has a bunch of squares of paper. I like to play with them. It's like a game."

"Game?"

He nodded. "Kind of. I'll show you."

"I'd like that," I said, doing my hardest not to sound too eager. "After you nap and I close the bakery."

By the time Eddie woke up, the day had grown overcast and cool for June. Walking through the woods and then veering around the slash pile on the edge of the pasture that was growing larger from Darryl and Tom's logging, I rehearsed what I would say to Millie. It sounded so ludicrous. "I think the other half of a game my great-grandmother made years ago is hidden in Eddie's floor." That sounded ridiculous. And even if it was true, that didn't mean I had a right to it. It was their property. And their house.

Thankfully, Millie was at the house alone. Cora had gone to a quilting frolic. Eddie scampered ahead and up the stairs as I explained to her what was going on.

"I'll need to talk to *Daed*," she said. "I'll have to see what he says."

"I think Eddie's getting it right now. Is it okay if I have a look?"

"I suppose that wouldn't hurt."

Eddie hurried into the kitchen, a grin on his face, but it dissipated when he saw Millie's serious expression.

He handed me the box. It was also a cookie tin. I pried open the lid. The squares of paper were all loose. I estimated there weren't as many as I had, but that made sense. Children had been in charge of this one. There were the birds and household items and trees and a baby and herbs, just like the other set Sarah had done.

"Eddie, how long have you had this?" Millie was kneeling beside him.

He shrugged. "A while."

"It's definitely Sarah Berg's work. I found an identical set over at the Home Place."

"Well, I'll talk to *Daed*."

"Eddie," I said. "Is there anything else under your floor? Other drawings? Paintings? Anything like that?"

He shook his head solemnly.

I held the tin toward him. "You should put the kitten back with the others."

He did so reluctantly.

"Maybe we can play the game sometime," I said.

He nodded solemnly.

I ran my fingers through the squares again and then picked some more up, turning them right side up. There was the willow tree and a rosemary plant. I stared at the next one. I hadn't seen it before.

"This is odd: 1+1+1=1," I read out loud.

"There are two of that one," Eddie said, "but only one of all the rest."

Millie laughed. "Your great-grandmother wasn't very good at math."

"How strange," I said. I was certain Sarah Berg knew the right answer to that equation. Maybe this was part of her code with the numbers.

Millie held out her hand for the box, and I closed the lid and gave it to her.

"I'll let you know what *Daed* says."

I thanked her, told Eddie goodbye, and then headed back through

the woods. When I reached the Home Place, Luke was parking the tractor by the barn. I waited until he jumped down and then said there was
something I wanted to tell him about. I relayed the story of the two boxes.
When I explained Millie was going to talk with his *daed*, his face reddened.

"Do you think you could say something to him? I'd really like to have
the pictures."

He nodded but didn't speak.

A raindrop fell and then another. I thanked him.

Luke started toward the barn but then stopped and walked back
toward me.

"You should brace yourself," he said. "*Daed* doesn't think very highly
about things like that." He kicked at a rock with his boot. "He doesn't like
it when I get drawing books from the library, even though I use them to
draw inventions—like the gate latch."

I nodded. I remembered. More raindrops fell.

"*Daed* thinks things are pretty black and white."

I shaded my eyes. "And Tom agrees with him, right?"

"Two peas in a pod is what *Mamm* says." Luke had a pained expression
on his face. "*Daed* and Tom have always gotten along."

"And you and he haven't?"

"Oh, he loves me all right. I know that. But we don't have much in
common."

"Is that why Rosalee wanted you to work at her place?" I realized my
hand was balled in my apron pocket, wadding the fabric.

"I suppose so," he answered. "Plus, considering Tom will take over the
dairy someday, she probably thought working here would give me extra
experience to hire out."

"That hardly seems fair—"

He held up his hand. "It's fine. Really. God will provide." With that
he turned and walked away again.

I was pretty sure that was the most he'd ever said to me. It was certainly
the most he had ever said to me about himself.

I slept fitfully that night. Though they might not seem important
to Darryl, the drawings were priceless to me and, of course, irreplaceable. Before dawn I woke for what seemed like the tenth time that night.

I decided to go ahead and dress. I might as well head down to the bakery with Rosalee to start the bread for the day. But first, kneeling at the bedroom window, I prayed more than that God's will would be done—I prayed that He would soften Darryl's heart.

I said "amen" out loud and then stared off into the trees. At first I thought my eyes were playing tricks. In the dim light it looked as if a strong wind was blowing through the woods. Then I saw a faint orange glow that seemed to come from over on the Klines' side.

I was pretty sure Darryl and Tom were burning their slash pile. I stood, catching a whiff of smoke through the three inches of open window. It wouldn't hurt to go see if they were burning—I wouldn't get close enough for them to see me. I just wanted to make sure that the fire was intentional, not accidental.

By the time I reached the woods, the smoke was more noticeable. When I reached the creek, more flames were darting up from where the slash pile was. I moved quickly but quietly, expecting to see the men any minute. The wind grew stronger, and in the dark shadows of the trees I stumbled over a root, catching myself before I fell. The flames were larger now, and I moved to the left. Before I reached the edge of the woods, it was obvious the slash pile was on fire. A moment later it was also clear no one was attending it, at least not now. The pile was damp, as if water had been poured on it, but the wind was fanning the flames into the grass and the fire was creeping toward the woods. Sparks from the crackling pine needles in the pile were flying up toward the branches of the closest trees. If one tree caught fire, the whole woods could be engulfed in flames.

There wasn't a shovel in sight so I dashed up the back steps and pounded on the back door so hard my fist throbbed. Though it only took a few minutes for Darryl to answer, it seemed like forever before he appeared looking tired and grumpy, pulling his suspenders over his shoulders.

Before he could speak, I yelled "Fire!" and pointed to the slash pile.

"Tom! Luke! Now!" he bellowed.

Darryl grabbed a shovel from the side of the house and took off running toward the woods. A second later, Luke dashed out the door, his boots in his hands. He hopped a few times, slipping them onto his feet. He ran to the barn and then back out with a big shovel.

Tom followed a minute later. "Grab the hose on the side of the house," he said to me. "And meet me by the barn."

I did as I was told. By the time I was running toward the barn, the hose slung over my shoulder, Eddie was in the front yard of the house, barefoot.

"Don't come any closer," I said.

Tom had two other hoses hooked together and quickly attached the one I brought.

"Turn on the spigot!" he yelled at me.

I did and then followed him as he ran toward the fire.

Luke and Darryl were digging a trench on the tree side of the flames.

Tom started spraying water over the fire, blanketing it as he moved the nozzle of the hose back and forth, over and over. Darryl and Luke kept digging as Tom splattered them with wet ashes. As the flames subsided, Tom soaked the surrounding pasture and then the closest trees.

I stood staring at the pile, aware that dawn had broken, aware that Eddie, Millie, and Cora were all standing behind me, aware that Darryl now had a pitchfork and was sifting through the pine needles to make sure every spark was out. As I watched the steam and ashes rise from the pile, I noticed a small piece of paper float up and then fall to the ground a few feet away. I picked it up, and though its edges were charred, I could still make out $1 + 1 + 1 = 1$. If Darryl had thrown this innocent card on the pile to be burned, then surely he had burned the whole set of Sarah's pictures. Eddie quietly reached out and took my hand. Luke didn't look at me, but I saw a brief flicker of anger in his eyes as he glanced toward his father.

I squeezed Eddie's hand, let go, and then stumbled back through the woods in a daze.

I didn't go down to the bakery. Instead, I made breakfast, but it was just Rosalee and me this morning. I gave her the short version of what happened, leaving out the part about Darryl burning Sarah's pictures. I don't know why I couldn't tell her that. I think I was afraid if I said it out loud I might fully realize it was true.

On the way down to the bakery I had a text from Zed. *Summer school is great. I'm taking another film class.* I wondered if Mom knew. I felt too emotionally drained to respond and slipped my phone back into my pocket.

Within a half hour we were finishing up the order for the distributor—an order that grew a little larger each week—when Luke poked his head into the kitchen, telling Rosalee he'd be working in the soybean field for the day. I started after him, banging through the kitchen door and then the dining room door, yelling, "Luke!"

He was almost to the tractor when he turned. "I'll talk to you later," he called out, pulling his hat down on his head.

I walked slowly back to the bakery.

He didn't join us for lunch, and Rosalee guessed he went back home. "Darryl probably has some work that's urgent," she said.

Around one, Millie and Eddie showed up at the bakery. "I promised him a sticky bun," she said.

I served one up immediately, delivering it to Eddie with a flourish.

He looked up at me, his eyes moist. "I'm sorry *Daed* burned the pictures."

"It was the picture of the baby," Millie said. "He has some ideas that way—not about babies, just about drawings of people."

I slumped down into a chair. "Oh."

"Are you okay?" Millie put a hand on my shoulder.

I nodded.

"I'm sorry," she said. "I should have just given them to you. I thought I was doing the right thing by talking to *Daed*. But it wouldn't have mattered."

Their father really was a tyrant, just as Ezra had said. Suddenly I felt overcome with sadness for Luke. Millie would marry and move away. Tom would get the dairy. But what about Luke? It wasn't as though his family could afford to buy him a place of his own like the Gundys were doing for Ezra. Luke had nothing. He would end up hiring out to people, unless the girl he was courting, Naomi it seemed, came from a family with money or an extra farm.

Eddie sniffled. "I wanted to play the game with you." His sticky bun sat untouched.

"I have the other set," I said quickly. "We could copy all of those, minus the baby."

He nodded solemnly.

"Then we can play the game, the way my mom and her sisters used to," I said.

"I'd like that," he answered.

"Me too." I tousled his hair. "Now eat."

I knew that as long as I didn't recreate the drawing of the baby, Darryl shouldn't object. Amish kids were allowed to play board games all the time.

I began copying the pictures on the squares in my spare time. I wasn't nearly as good as Sarah, but I was good enough that the pictures were definitely matchable. Although several times, I wondered why Darryl couldn't have just destroyed the picture of the baby and let me have the other ones. It took me several days to finish the copying, but when I did Eddie and I sat down at a table in the bakery and played the game. Eddie won the game by matching the two willows.

As we were putting it away, Luke came into the bakery.

"Time to go," he said to his little brother.

I put the lid on the tin. If Luke knew what we were doing, he didn't say anything.

"We need to get back home." Luke spun his straw hat on his finger. "Tom and *Daed* are gone for the day, so I have to do the milking."

Eddie's face lit up as he turned toward me. "Want to come help?"

It was a Friday, so I didn't have class until Tuesday. I glanced at Luke and he was actually smiling. "Let me check with Rosalee."

She was in the living room, dozing. She said to go and have fun. "Take the roast in the fridge to help with their dinner, would you? I'll make a sandwich."

Luke took the roast from me and led the way through the woods. Halfway there we stopped at the red pine and all looked up at the magpie nest.

"They're always fighting," Eddie said.

"Kind of like another family I know," Luke muttered. I don't think Eddie heard him, and I pretended not to.

When we reached their house, we greeted Millie, who was hanging wash on the line. I stayed out with her while Luke put the meat in the refrigerator.

Their mother appeared at the back door. "Thank you for the roast, Ella," she said. She seemed to be feeling fine.

A minute later Luke came out carrying a pair of rubber boots. "These are for you," he said.

I slipped off my shoes and pulled on the boots. Eddie was barefoot, as usual, and Luke wore his work boots.

As we headed toward the barn, Luke veered off to the field and began herding the cows toward the holding pen. He cornered one and directed her into the barn. I followed. The cow walked to the end of the row and stuck her head through the slats of the gate. Luke pulled on the gate to secure her and then, as he hooked her up to the machine, said, "Give her a half shovel of feed." Eddie pointed to a bin, where the feed was coming out of a chute.

I grabbed the shovel.

Soon cows were hooked up to all eight machines and milk was pumping through tubes to the vat in the adjacent room. Eddie ran back and forth between Luke, the vat, the cows, and me as if he were the supervisor.

After the first couple of cows were done, Luke unhooked them and ushered in the next ones. I scooped the feed into the trough and we kept going, cow after cow, with Eddie running around, just out of reach of the cows' hooves, his bare feet pattering on the cement.

It took an hour and a half to do all the milking, and by the time we were done, I was hungry.

"I just need to fill the water trough out in the pasture," Luke said. "Want to come along?"

"Sure," I said.

As we left the barn, Eddie between us, my phone beeped. I took it out. It was Zed. *Mom wants you to call her tonight.*

"*Daed* hates cell phones," Eddie said as we reached the pasture. I followed Luke through the gate.

"So I've heard." Embarrassed that I'd been so careless, I started to put it into my pocket but it buzzed again. I started to fumble the phone just as

Eddie darted in front of me toward the spigot. I tripped on his foot, sending the cell phone sailing. I grabbed for it, but it was already in flight, arcing toward the trough. It landed with a splash.

I plunged my arm in after it. The visibility was nil as I thrashed around.

Luke splashed both hands into the trough too, submerging himself up to his armpits, soaking his shirt as Eddie jumped around behind us.

"Got it!" Luke said, jumping to his feet, the phone in his hand.

As he gave it to me I thanked him, but of course it was ruined. I took the battery out immediately. "Do you have rice? If I put the phone in a bag of it, it might be okay." I'd heard of that working before.

They did have rice, and soon my phone and battery were buried in a plastic bag of it.

"Thanks," I said to Millie.

"Good thing *Daed* isn't here," she said.

"I know," I said, chastising myself. If I had been more respectful of Darryl Kline's rules, I wouldn't be wondering if my phone was going to still work or not.

I tried not to think about it as we sat down to dinner. Luke led the prayer. Eddie talked about how fun the milking was. Cora smiled as she looked at her youngest son. She seemed in good spirits. Millie seemed more relaxed than usual too.

After dinner Luke said he'd walk me back through the woods. I told him there was no need and then wished I hadn't. It seemed, perhaps, as if he had something to say to me.

By the time I reached my room, clutching the bag of rice to my chest, I was in tears. I knew I would need to give up my phone someday, but I wasn't ready to, not yet.

Twenty-Four

My new life started Monday morning. I waited that long to take the phone out of the rice. The battery and phone were totally dry, but there was nothing there. Absolutely nothing.

My contract wasn't up for six months, so it wasn't as though I could go get another one at a reduced price. No, I would be paying the big bucks, money I didn't have. After more than two years of having a cell phone, I was going without one cold turkey.

That morning I slipped the phone into the top drawer of my bureau next to Sarah's book, deciding to keep it as a memento of my previous life. If I was going to become Amish before I married Ezra, I might as well get used to it. Maybe this was God's way of preparing me.

We were busier in the bakery that day. An owner of a grocery in town stopped by to redeem the sticky bun offer I'd given him. He was a middle-aged man, and he ate slowly, as if he were really tasting each bite. I practically held my breath until he finished.

Once he had he approached the counter again. "Do you deliver?" he asked.

I nodded. "Bread. Pies. Streusel. Anything we make."

"I'll start with the buns," he said and placed an order.

When Millie came in mid morning, she said her *daed* and Tom returned home late the night before with a new tractor. They had driven it home from the other side of Nappanee. That was one of the differences between the Amish in Elkhart County and Lancaster— unlike the metal tires used in Lancaster County, the tractors here had regular tires and could be driven on the road.

"That will help," she said.

That night I wrote letters to Zed and Mom, Ezra, and Lexie, and explained that my phone was toast. Not that Ezra had called me since my birthday. Finally, I wrote to Ada. She'd sent me a letter after I moved to the Home Place, but I hadn't written her back. I wrote a quick note but didn't mention my phone. It was pretty unlikely she would ever try to reach me on it anyway.

The pastry-making lessons didn't go any better than bread making. I decided if I offered pastries through my business in Lancaster that they would be good old-fashioned Plain pastries, like tarts, not the fancy stuff Pierre was trying to teach me.

The very last lesson on *l'art de la patisserie* was the final. We were to choose a recipe and bake it at the school. I decided to take a risk and bake Rosalee's lemon tart. I told Pierre it was an old family recipe I had modified. By the time we all had our pastries out of the oven, the bakery smelled absolutely divine.

Pierre went around the room, tasting each sample. He made sparingly positive remarks to most of the students and then raved about Penny's éclairs. When he got to mine, he took a small bite.

"Better," he said and then shrugged. "Good enough, anyway, to pass this part of the class." He took another bite. "Hmmm," he said, taking a third forkful. "Ever heard the expression 'cook what you know'?"

I shook my head. Who would ever learn anything new if that was all we did?

"Well, it applies to you. If this is the sort of thing in your family's repertoire, why are you in my baking school?" He shrugged, as if blowing me off.

I shrugged back. He was such a demigod. My own little Napoleon.

The next morning Luke cut the alfalfa before we even had breakfast. He said mid-June was a little late for the first cutting, but not bad.

After breakfast the bakery was extra slow, so I helped him clean out the chicken coop again. I thought of my first day at the Home Place and how quiet he was. He wasn't much more talkative than he'd been then, but it felt more comfortable to be with him now, unlike it had that time.

When we were almost finished, I asked him how his mother was doing. "Better."

"What is wrong with her?" It couldn't hurt to ask.

"Female problems," he said. I expected him to blush but he didn't.

"What does the doctor say?"

He shook his head. "Different things different times. She lost a couple of babies, like Eddie said. Then she was anemic. Things like that. She kept hoping for another baby for years, but now I think she just hopes as she gets older the problems will stop."

Luke was twenty-one and Tom wasn't more than a year older, which meant Cora had to be at least forty, if not more.

"It must be hard on your family to have her sick so much."

"*Ya,*" he answered. "It's especially hard on my *daed*. He thinks he should be able to fix it, but he can't. I just figure every family has its problems. If it wasn't this it would be something else." Luke opened the door to the toolshed and put his shovel inside. Then he took mine and put it in too, as I thought about what he'd said.

I kept waiting for my family's problems to disappear—mainly for Freddy to go away—so we could get on with things. And then I expected things to be smooth as French silk pie after that. I gave Luke a sideways glance. He sounded like a pessimist, but then he said, "We've been trusting God for a long time. We'll keep doing that. It's all we can."

I gave him a wave as I started back to the house to scrub up, a little surprised at him talking about trusting God. It wasn't that I doubted it, but I was just surprised at his openness. I wondered how many babies Cora had lost, considering the wide gap between Millie and Eddie. Thirteen years was a long, long stretch. And now Eddie was six, and it sounded as though she'd lost a couple after him too.

The morning of the first class in *l'art de la gateau*, I pulled the pages of the bridal magazines I'd brought along out of my bottom drawer. Cake-making was the whole reason I was at baking school...well, that and hoping to learn how to run a business. Obviously I couldn't have a Plain bakery someday and make exquisite cakes, but in the meantime I wanted to make as many as possible to get it out of my system, so to speak. I decided to arrive with a fresh attitude and pretend it was the very first day—ever—with Pierre.

We all took our places and waited for him. And waited some more. Finally Elizabeth came in and said he was running late.

"Any of you want to take this chance to jump ship and take the third course of my cooking class?"

No one did, but Penny reminded her she would be taking her class next session.

Elizabeth turned toward me. "How about you, Ella? I've heard you're a great cook."

I blushed, wondering who would have told her that. It must have been Penny, although I hadn't cooked for her. "I'm going back to Lancaster County as soon as this class is done." That was my agreement with my mother. As soon as the end of July rolled around, I would be catching a bus home.

When Pierre finally showed up, he yawned and said he'd snuck home to take a nap. "Getting up at two every morning is getting old."

He looked around the room, taking us all in as if he'd never seen us before.

"So now you want to learn to make cakes. It is probably why you signed up for the class, *oui*? You like the rolled fondant. The ganache. The marzipan. Ha! You think you will be on TV next season on some cake competition. Well, let me tell you. Making cakes is not what it's—what are the words—cracked up to be? It's a one-shot deal. A flash in the pan. Baking bread and croissants and pastries...they are for every day. They are what is important. Cake making is solely to impress people, not to feed them."

I felt my body slump down on the stool. The next four weeks were going to be worse than the first eight. I wanted to go home now. Maybe I could take a cake class at the community college.

Pierre continued with his diatribe, belittling all of us for our interest in cakes, until finally he sighed and said we might as well get started. "We will begin with flavors," he said. "If you are going to make a cake, you had better make sure it tastes good, because in my class no one is going to bury it in American frosting." He made a face as if he'd just been forced to eat a Twinkie.

As the class progressed, he grew more and more cynical and cranky. Finally, I stopped taking notes and started drawing cakes. Funny, each one had birds on it. Hawks. Owls. Swallows. Chickens. Eagles. I wasn't aware Pierre was standing over me until he cleared his throat.

"Mademoiselle."

Startled, I raised my head and instinctively covered my notebook.

"My I see your notes?" He'd never asked such a thing before of anyone.

I moved my hand.

He turned his head and stared, finally saying, "I see." He met my gaze and then stepped away. Then he yawned again. "That's it for today. No homework. See you next Tuesday."

Disappointed, I closed my notebook. I was hoping for homework. I was hoping he'd show us tricks to rolling fondant. I wanted to work with marzipan. I knew there was only so much I could learn in four weeks, but it was the reason I'd stuck around so long. Now I was sure it hadn't been worth it. Not at all.

TWENTY-FIVE

On Saturday afternoon, after we'd closed the bakery, Eddie and I sat at a table and played the matching game. I thought of the baby card I had safely tucked away in Sarah's book now.

Eddie matched the willow tree, the rosemary bush, and then the little bird all in a row before he missed. As we played he taught me the Pennsylvania Dutch words for what he knew. *Bohm*. Tree. *Rauda-shtokk*. Herb plant. *Fokkel*. Bird.

I turned over the hawk and the owl. Eddie barely waited until I was done before he had the other owl.

"Let me see that," I said, taking the one Sarah had drawn. It was smudged a little and the eyes were a little blurry, but they were penetrated with pain. The drawing was so beautiful it made me shiver. I knew my Aunt Giselle was an artist, and I couldn't help but wonder what it was like for her to play with her grandmother's drawings when she was a child.

Eddie won by matching the two daisies. As we carefully put the squares of paper back in the tin, Eddie told me how much he liked the game.

"I see the pictures and then I see the stuff outside. The birds. The flowers. The herbs. It makes me look at everything more closely."

He carried the tin as we left the bakery, following me up to the house. I needed to change into my work dress to do the chores. He stopped at the herb garden.

"See. There's the rosemary. And the sage."

I nodded as a starling swooping out of the barn caught my attention. Luke was walking toward us, holding the mail in his hand.

"You had two letters in Rosalee's box," he called out.

Eddie put the tin down on the lawn that Luke had managed to keep green through the summer and collapsed beside it, under the tulip tree. It was mid afternoon and he was tired.

Luke reached us, handed me the letters, and then he sat down beside Eddie. The little boy snuggled against his brother, even though it was hot. His eyes were heavy and his body relaxed.

Neither letter was from Ezra. One was from Mom and one from Zed. I plopped down on the grass and opened Mom's first. She jumped right into what she was writing about, skipping all pleasantries.

I remembered more about the game. As we played, our grandmother talked about what it meant to be a friend, a wife, and a mother. I didn't want to talk about it over the phone, but the two cards I remember most had babies on them, and when one of us would match those cards, she'd talk about how every single baby was a gift from God and it was our job to love them and bring them up to know the Lord. I don't think the pictures were of a particular baby—I think they just represented babies in general. Do you have those two cards? I would really like to see them again.

She signed it, *Love, Mom.* That was it.

Zed wrote that summer school was going well. He was taking third-year German and it was nice to have an entire morning of it every day. He was taking a film course in the afternoons, for fun. Then he wrote about seeing Ada and Will and the girls the day before. *Christy's friend Izzy was there too. She's still helping Ada.* I wondered why Ada needed more help than Christy could offer now that she was out of school. Izzy seemed like a nice girl, and she was a couple of years older than Christy, so maybe she was more help. Zed said he really liked having a cell, and it was a bummer mine was fried.

One more thing, Zed wrote. *Dad isn't doing well. We found out what's been wrong with him. He was diagnosed with stomach cancer. He's doing chemo.*

I cringed.

Ella, there's a chance he won't make it and he really would like to see you. The treatments are hard on him—and they'll only get worse. I think you need to get back here soon. He went through rehab for alcohol a few years ago, and he says he's been sober since then and now goes to AA and stuff like that.

I crumbled the letter into a ball without realizing what I was doing.

"Bad news?"

I became conscious of Luke sitting beside me. It was the longest I'd seen him sit still, except at the dinner table. Eddie was asleep beside him.

I took a deep breath.

"Want to talk about it?"

I glanced sideways at him. "You want me to talk?"

"Sure. I'll listen."

"But you might have to talk back."

He raised his eyebrows.

"I was only teasing," I said, glancing at Eddie. He was sound asleep. Still I couldn't imagine Luke wouldn't tell me the same thing everyone else had. *Get over it. Let it be. Of course you should see Freddy. He's making an effort to change for the better.*

Even so, I started the story, saying my father had left when I was three, after my mother had adopted Zed, and how for the next fifteen years I hadn't heard from him once. Luke had a sympathetic expression on his face.

"Before I came out here, he showed back up in Lancaster."

"Is that why you wanted to come here?" Luke had pushed back his straw hat and his eyes were shining.

"Yes. That, and Ezra."

"Is that the reason you didn't go back home with him?"

I tilted my head. "No. I was determined to go back and avoid Freddy, but Mom didn't want me to come home right away. Everyone wants Ezra and me to be apart. They all seem to think I'm not good for him, even though I'm willing to join the Amish church."

"Oh."

"Anyway," I said. "Now he's—"

"Your father?"

I nodded and cringed at the same time. "He's been diagnosed with cancer. And I know that's bad. Apparently, he really wants to see me."

"Is he dying?"

"It seems that way…" Stomach cancer sounded pretty serious, though whether the time he had left was being measured in days or weeks or months, I wasn't sure.

Luke met my eyes and took a deep breath. Finally he said, "I'm sorry, Ella. That sounds really hard."

"It is," I whispered. And then I started to cry. Just as Luke reached his hand out toward me, Eddie stirred. I wiped my eyes quickly, and as I did I saw Rosalee on the porch, bracing herself against the rail, staring at the three of us.

It was just Rosalee and me at supper that evening, and after I'd finished the dishes I went out to weed the herb garden. I crushed a bloom of lavender between my fingers and then brought it to my nose. I smelled soap and lotion and pound cake, all in one sniff. According to Sarah's book, it could also be used for migraines, fainting, and dizziness, and as an antiseptic.

First I cultivated around the rosemary. The warm scent overpowered everything nearby. It added wonderful flavor to roasted potatoes, root vegetables, and chicken, but as a tincture, if too much was used, it could be deadly. Like so many things in life, it could be part of a recipe for success or for disaster.

I kept working until the sun started to disappear behind the woods. I stood stretching my back, shielding my eyes from the glare. I startled a little at the silhouette at the edge of the trees. It was Luke, watching me.

"Hello," I called out.

He waved. "I need to borrow Rosalee's fence post digger. Ours just broke." He started toward the house to ask her, I was sure, even though he knew what her answer would be. I made my way to the toolshed to put away my hoe and cultivator. I found the tool Luke was after, pulled it out of the shed, and headed toward the house with it.

We met halfway, by the herb garden.

"This is such a pretty spot," Luke said.

I nodded.

"And it always smells so fresh."

I didn't answer, hoping he would say more.

"God is good to make us such a beautiful world, *ya*?"

"*Ya*." I responded.

"Your great-grandmother's drawings do a fine job of capturing the beauty—but still, nothing can beat what God has done."

"But don't you think the drawings make us appreciate the beauty even more?"

He nodded. "Preacher Jacob talked about beauty a few months back. He said appreciating it is part of praising God. I was thinking about your father—and then my father. I think my *daed* has stopped seeing beauty. All he sees is how sick *Mamm* is and how the place is falling apart and how bad our finances are. He's turned everything into rules. It seems he thinks if we just figure out how to do things the 'right' way our troubles will stop." He paused, and then without looking at me he said, "That got me thinking about your father. Even if you don't want to see him, have you been able to forgive him?"

I bristled. I'd gone round and round on the forgiveness thing. I'd think I'd forgiven and then the same old feelings would come back.

"I know, I know," I said, "I'm supposed to forgive so God will forgive me. I keep trying."

"I think forgiving also frees us," he said, as if he hadn't heard me. "And the other person."

"Even if they never ask for our forgiveness?"

"In a way I don't understand, *ya*," he said. "Although I know forgiveness and reconciliation are two different things." He gave me a sympathetic look and said, "I heard once that to truly forgive means you no longer resent the person."

I took another step away. That was the most ridiculous thing I'd ever heard. How could I not resent Freddy Bayer for what he'd done to me? Wasn't it enough that I'd tried to forgive him? I should have known Luke wouldn't understand.

Twenty-Six

For the next several classes, Pierre taught lessons on fondant, ganache, frosting, icing, and marzipan. Then he let us start experimenting. I couldn't help but smile. Even without having his heart in it, he was showing us what we needed to know.

As I was working away, rolling fondant to put over the top of the brown-butter banana cake I had made, he stopped at my table.

"Why the fondant?" he asked. "How about a butter cream to go with that flavor?"

"I like fondant," I answered.

"Because it is pretty?"

I nodded.

"How about making something beautiful instead of pretty? Beauty. That is what you should strive for."

I kept rolling my fondant. Later, when I was sculpting eyes in the bird I'd made out of marzipan, he stopped again. "You should stick with something Plain," he said.

"This is," I answered. "I got the idea from my Amish great-grandmother."

"Well, then..." He took a closer look. "I will withhold judgment until you are finished."

I ended up squishing it. The eyes were all wrong. I left, discouraged.

That evening when I entered the kitchen at the Home Place, Rosalee was sitting at the table working on her books. She rubbed her eyes as she asked me how I was.

"Do you really want to know?" I sank down onto the chair across from her.

"Of course," she answered.

I told her about Pierre.

She raised her eyebrows. "You'll be done soon. Learn everything you can from him. He has a very successful business. No matter what, he has a lot to teach you."

I knew he did, but I didn't point out I'd learned just as much from her. I didn't want it to sound as if I didn't appreciate *Mammi*'s investment.

"He's just so sarcastic."

"Maybe that's his way." She picked up her pencil again.

I asked how things looked. "If that's any of my business," I quickly added. That was a part of running a bakery that I had no experience with, but I wasn't anticipating it would be too hard.

Rosalee peered at me. "Everyone says supporting a family costs way more than they anticipate, even for the Amish. That's how running this bakery is. I'll come up with a budget and then the price of sugar goes up. And the price of electricity. And the price of a new roof on the building."

"Really?"

She nodded. "But Luke thinks he can do the roofing for me. That will save some." She picked up her pencil. "There are times when I wonder how much longer I can keep going."

"Are you serious?"

"I'm just thinking out loud." She yawned. "I'm tired. And I'm getting old."

"You're not old," I said, even though I knew she was.

"I started this business hoping I could help out Luke and Millie. Maybe earn enough money to pay them wages..." Her eyes drifted toward the back door as if she were mentally headed to the bakery. She shook her head quickly and met my gaze again. "At least your drumming up business in town has helped. That's kept us in the black, barely."

That was the best news I'd heard in weeks.

"You have a letter," she said, looking back down at the books. "I put it on your dresser."

I hurried down the hall, hoping it would be from Ezra. It wasn't. It was from Freddy Bayer. My whole body grew cold as I sank down onto the bed. If there had been a woodstove in the house that was lit, I would have burned it without reading it, I was sure. But there wasn't, so I opened the envelope.

Dear Ella,

First, I want you to know how proud I am of you. Your mother speaks so highly of you, as does Zed. We all hoped you would return to Lancaster County, but the fact you stayed in Indiana and chose to go to baking school shows your strength and determination. You've had a good example of this in your mother, plus she has raised you right, I know. For that I am very grateful.

Second, I was disappointed not to be able to meet you, as you probably know. But I don't blame you for not wanting to see me. I was horrible to your mother, you, and Zed. I deeply regret what I did. Please forgive me, in time, if you can.

I am an alcoholic and have been in recovery for the last three years. One of the things I've been learning is to express my feelings. As a young man, I too was deeply betrayed by my father, but I was taught to ignore my pain and carry on. Instead I ended up committing the same sins he did. My prayer for you and Zed is that you will be able to express your pain and eventually heal. My hope is that the destructive cycle in our family will end.

When I joined the Mennonite church with your mother, I thought I knew what it meant to be a Christian—but I didn't. While in recovery, I've learned what it means to follow Jesus, to try to trust Him one day at a time. That's all I can do.

So I trust Him with you.

Love,
Dad

I crumpled the letter in my hand and curled onto the bed. The thickening in the back of my throat surprised me. I wasn't just angry—I was also really, really sad. The tears flowed like a flash flood. I pulled my knees to my chest and tightened my fist around the letter. My stoic mother had never told me emotions were bad, but she'd never encouraged them, either. Sobs shook me. I hadn't cried in years, and never like this.

A knock came on my door, followed by Rosalee's tentative voice. "Ella, are you all right?"

"*Ya*," I answered, trying hard to keep my voice even.

She hesitated and then said, this time a little louder, "Come get me if you need me."

"*Danke*," I answered. "I will."

I stayed that way until the room began to darken and then smoothed the letter out as best I could and read it again. No longer sad, I stopped on the words "our family." And then again on "Dad." How dare he think he could weasel his way back in and then refer to himself in such a familiar way? Mom and Zed were obviously gullible enough to buy into his scheme, but I could see how he was trying to manipulate me, saying Mom was proud of me. Not even mentioning his cancer. Writing about what he'd learned in recovery. He was trying to get me to go home without begging me to. It was probably some kind of reverse psychology. He hoped to have my forgiveness to make himself feel better.

I took a deep breath, relieved to feel only the old familiar anger. It felt so much better than the pain.

I waited until Rosalee was in bed, and then I tiptoed into the living room, taking a match from the mantle and lighting the letter and envelope on fire. I held it until the heat of the flames licked at my fingers before dropping it to the floor of the fireplace and watched it turn from paper to fire and finally to ashes.

I was in a funk all the next day as I waited on the customers at the front counter of Plain Treats. After we all ate leftover stew from the night before for our noon meal, Luke asked if I could help him load hay into the hayloft. Most of the hay was rolled into huge rounds and left in the fields, but he had a portion put in seventy-pound bales that were kept in the barn. As we walked, he asked me what was bothering me.

"Is it that obvious?"

"*Ya*, as a matter-of-fact it is."

I bit my lower lip and shook my head. "It's nothing." I wasn't about to set myself up for any more advice from him.

We worked in silence, him running up and down between the loft and the wagon, while I made sure the conveyor belt stayed in position. Once all the bales were in the loft, Luke said he would stack them later after he did the milking back home. His *daed* and Tom had gone into town.

"I'll see you tomorrow," he said.

I waved and headed toward the house, but then I turned and watched him walking toward the pasture. He'd been a good friend to me in his quiet way. I knew he had problems of his own, but his faith seemed to keep him in balance. I had never seen him in a dither or disrespectful with anyone.

As it turned out, I didn't see him the next day. It was the first time since I'd been at Rosalee's that he hadn't been at the Home Place for at least an hour or two.

"I told him to take the day off," Rosalee said. "He needs a break from us, don't you think?"

I nodded, but I knew she meant from *me*. She and Luke got along fabulously.

On the way to class that afternoon, Penny prattled away about the lemon-cherry pudding cake she had made the night before. I half listened and half thought about Freddy Bayer. Then my mind fell to Ezra. I hadn't had a letter from him, not even a paragraph, in several weeks.

A wave of relief washed over me as we arrived in South Bend. Cake making would take my mind off everything else. I knew it was prideful to think, but the truth was I was acing *l'art du gateau*. It was the last class before our final next week, and there was nothing Pierre could say to me that could make me think otherwise. He hardly ever had a negative comment to make concerning my work, except that it was too elaborate.

My cakes were delicious and moist. My fondant rolled out as if I'd been doing it my entire life. My frostings were tasty and manageable. Lesson after lesson, I led the class. Everything was going well except for my marzipan birds. As hard as I tried, I couldn't get them to look like Sarah's drawings. But that was a minor failure in the overall scope of the class. I'd redeemed myself. Even Pierre was impressed.

Our final was to bake and decorate a cake that was due the next week. I came up with a three-tiered white chocolate raspberry wedding cake topped with fondant. My plan was to use Rosalee's berries for the filling and then decorate the whole thing with marzipan birds inspired from Sarah's book, but simpler. I finally decided that the key was inspiration, not replication. I wanted to capture the essence of her art, not recreate it. All of the work had to be done at the school because I had no way of transporting a cake. Penny was making her cake at the school too, and Pierre said we could work Friday afternoon, late into the evening if we needed to.

Toward the end of class on Thursday, Pierre called me into his office. My heart raced, sure he'd turned back into the dictator he'd been and was going to come up with some reason to humiliate me—except he usually did that in front of all the others.

"Mademoiselle Ella," he said, sitting on the edge of his desk. "You have come so far, *oui*?"

I stayed silent.

"I have a proposition for you," he said. "If—and it is a big if—you can pull off this cake, and if it turns out the way you have described it to be, drawn it to be…Anyway, I would like…" He blinked rapidly. "Let me start over."

He took a deep breath. "I'm thinking about expanding."

I raised my eyebrows.

"I would like to add a wedding cake line. That has been missing from my bakery. Americans love their wedding cakes, and once a bride buys a cake she will come back for everything—bread, pastries, birthday cakes for the kids. Then wedding cakes for her daughters. See what I mean?"

I nodded. I understood customer loyalty. Especially when it came to a good experience on a woman's wedding day.

"So, I am thinking, if you are successful with your cake, I would like to hire you to work for me."

My hand went to my chest. "Me?"

"*Oui*," he said. "I know it is a surprise."

"But I was your worst student—"

"Yes, was," he said. "Although you will do better if you still believe that."

"What do you mean?"

"You did not take me seriously, did you? All that ribbing?"

"Actually, I did."

He smiled sarcastically. "I only treated you that way because I knew you were gifted."

"I beg your pardon?" He'd made my life miserable for almost three months. And for what?

"It is just my way," he declared. "So will you consider working for me?"

"Why would I want to?"

He sat up straight. "Because I am the best around, and you will have the chance to keep learning—but you will be paid to do it. I do not have the patience for cakes anymore—but you? You enjoy it."

"When do you need to know?"

He chuckled. "When I offer the position to you, depending on how your final goes."

My face grew warm. He'd already said that.

I thought about Pierre's possible offer as Penny drove home. There was no way I could work for Pierre. On the other hand, I'd be crazy not to.

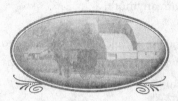

TWENTY-SEVEN

Pierre's offer was tempting, but I longed to be with Ezra. The next morning, I tried to call Mom's cell from the phone in Plain Treats, but she didn't answer so I called Zed.

"Ella!" He sounded so happy to hear from me.

"Is Mom around?"

"No. She's out on a call. You know how it goes." He sounded so grown up. "Want me to give her a message?"

"I want to talk with her about coming home."

"Well, yeah. About that. You're probably going to have to stay at *Mammi*'s."

"Stay at *Mammi*'s? I don't mean just for a visit. I'm coming for good." Or at least until I got married.

"For good?"

"Zed." My voice twanged with frustration. "What's going on?"

His voice quieted. "I moved into your room."

"Why?"

"Dad's staying in mine."

My knees practically buckled. Reaching out for the counter, I steadied myself before I spoke. "Dad?"

"Mom moved him in a couple of weeks ago. The chemo has been so hard on him that he needs to be taken care of."

"I don't have a room anymore..."

"There's the alcove."

Lexie slept on a bed in the alcove for the two months she stayed with us. Why she'd been willing to do that, I still couldn't understand.

"Although sometimes Izzy stays over. Then Mom sleeps in the alcove and Izzy uses her room."

"Why is Izzy staying over? I thought she was helping Ada."

"She's been helping with Dad some too," he said. "When Mom has an appointment and I have school."

"Freddy needs to leave."

"Ella..."

"What?"

"Mom's not going to do that. He's, uh, he's in hospice care."

Hospice. That meant he was dying. Pushing that thought from my mind, I responded, my voice growing shrill. "But I want to come home!"

"Did you understand what I said? He's dying," Zed whispered.

I swallowed hard, refusing to care. "So how come you're not at school right now?"

"I'm going in late. I'll leave once Izzy gets here."

I wound my index finger through the cord of the phone. "Why didn't you tell me this earlier?"

"I thought Mom had. Come home and stay with *Mammi*," Zed suggested. "I'll come out and see you."

"I have to go."

"I'll tell Mom you called."

"Don't bother," I answered, tears stinging my eyes.

"Ella—"

"Bye." I hung up without telling him I loved him, without even waiting for his farewell.

Maybe I could go home to visit, make sure things were okay with Ezra, and then come back and work for Pierre for a couple of months. Then I could return to Lancaster County for good.

Neither Millie, Luke, nor Eddie was around all morning, or for dinner, either. Rosalee and I didn't talk much. It was hot and humid and I looked forward to riding in Penny's air-conditioned car to South Bend. Even though Pierre's kitchen was hot, the place had air and was still cooler than Plain Treats or the Home Place.

After we were done eating, I waited for Penny in the shade of the tulip tree. She was late. Finally I sat down, crossing my legs under my dress, my book bag in my lap.

I heard a rustling behind me. It was Luke.

"Are you sneaking up on me?"

He held something wrapped in an old brown paper bag in his hand.

"Kind of," he said. "I know you're leaving soon—"

"Not until next week." I didn't add "Maybe."

"Oh." He stopped a foot from me. "Well, do you have a minute now?"

I glanced toward the driveway. "Until Penny gets here."

He nodded. "Okay. I should have gifen this to you three months ago, when you were asking if I'd seen any artwork around here."

I gasped in anticipation.

He knelt down beside me. "I found this in our house years ago, where Eddie found the game. I was just older than Eddie is now. I shared that room with Tom. We hadn't lived here long and I was exploring." He opened the bag as he talked. "I've hidden it from *Daed* all these years. It wasn't until he burned Eddie's half of the game that I realized you were looking for this. Then it took a while for me to be willing to part with it." He pulled a foot-by-foot canvas mounted on a square frame from the bag and then turned it over and handed it to me.

It was a painting of a baby, but not the baby in the game. The eyes were different and this one's face wasn't as full as the other one. And while I couldn't tell if the baby in the game was a boy or a girl, for some reason, this one looked like a boy. Was this a painting of *Mammi's* brother Gerry, Rosalee's father? I hesitated for a moment, wondering if I should chance showing it to Rosalee. I didn't think she would be offended by it, but it was hard to know for sure. The baby had dark curly hair and was smiling.

"He's beautiful," I whispered.

"I've always thought so too," Luke said. "Not as beautiful as a real baby is—but pretty close."

The background of the painting was green and texturized, like the woods, and a small bird was in the bottom right-hand corner.

"You think your great-grandmother painted it, *ya*?"

"Probably," I answered. "Though I don't know why it was over at the dairy. Which room was it in? I want to tell my mom about it."

He explained that the bedroom was at the top of the stairs, looking out on the backyard. It was a small room with a slanted roof, just big enough for a child or two.

A wave of appreciation for Luke swept over me. He had treasured the painting all these years. And he had kept it safe. Now, he hadn't given it to me impulsively, but had thought through his decision, long and hard, first.

"Thank you," I said, as the sound of tires rolled over the gravel. A quick glance and I knew Penny was arriving. "Thank you so much."

"I should have taken the game too," he said. "I didn't think it would be in danger." He sighed. "You know, not very many people in our district would have destroyed the game—or a painting like this either. Lots of the kids I know draw." He had a look of regret on his face.

"I'm just glad you saved the painting. This is absolutely amazing." I stared into the eyes of the baby. I didn't recognize them. I was certain they weren't replicated in Sarah's book. I stood, looking from Penny's SUV to Luke.

"Would you tell her I'll be right back? I need to run this to my room."

Luke started toward the driveway while I ran to the house, putting the painting in the drawer with the book, and I then hurried back out.

"Thanks again," I said to him as he handed me my bag.

Penny tapped her horn.

Impulsively, I reached out to hug him. He allowed me to and even gently hugged me back.

When we reached the bakery, Pierre welcomed us warmly. My plan was to bake my cakes, roll the fondant, and make the marzipan birds today. I would assemble everything tomorrow. On Monday Pierre would grade the cakes.

I started with mixing up my batter, and then as the cake was baking, I whipped up the filling from the fresh raspberries I'd brought from Rosalee's berry patch.

When that was done, I began molding the birds.

Pierre peered over my shoulder.

"Shoo," I said.

"Sassy, are we?"

"Yes, as a matter-of-fact, we are." I glared at him.

"Settle down, Ella. If we are going to work together, we had better find some peaceful ground." He was eyeing my raspberry filling as he spoke. "And besides," he said. "I have another proposition for you."

"Shouldn't you wait until you can fulfill the first one before adding another?"

"*Non*. They actually go together." He turned away from me. "Do you think your cousin—the one who owns the bakery—would let me carry some of her delicious things? Those sticky buns, perhaps."

"How do you know about the sticky buns?"

"Oh, I snuck in there one day. But you weren't working." A grin crept across his face.

"It's a little far for distribution."

"I know. I distribute out to Nappanee. It would not be a problem for the company I use to swing by."

I couldn't help but smile. That would open up all sorts of distribution possibilities.

"I'll talk to Rosalee," I said. "Thanks for asking."

I watched Pierre get ready to leave for the day. I really could work with him until things settled down back home…I caught that train of thought and then I frowned. Why was I trying to kid myself? I wouldn't be waiting for things to "settle down." I would be waiting for Freddy to die.

Pierre disappeared, although I didn't think he'd left. The restaurant was gearing up for the dinner rush, and Elizabeth and her cooks were busy in the kitchen, adjacent to the classroom. We could hear pans banging and an occasional shout through the wall. I liked the energy of it, and for the first time wondered about taking Elizabeth's class. Maybe I could work for Pierre and fit her classes in too. Maybe I could open up a café when I returned to Lancaster.

A few minutes later I heard Elizabeth's voice in the classroom. I looked over at her and noted she had a concerned look on her face just as I realized that Luke was behind her. Trailing him was Pierre.

I stepped around the table, sure something had happened to Rosalee. "What's wrong?"

"Your cousin called," Luke said.

"Is it my father?" He was probably dead, and I wondered why they thought it was worth all this trouble to let me know. Didn't they realize I didn't care?

Luke shook his head. "Your brother. He's been in an accident."

I grasped the edge of the table, feeling as if I might fall.

Luke spoke quickly. "He's in the intensive care unit."

"What happened?"

"He was hit by a car."

I dropped the sculpting tool and it clattered to the floor. "I need to go home."

"*Ya.*" Luke's voice was low and calm. He didn't have to say any more. I knew Zed was badly hurt.

"Ella, Ella." Pierre was at my side. "What about your final? Could you wait a couple of days? You know how these things go. In hospital one day, out the next."

Zed was my baby brother. I didn't care about my final.

"I have to go," I said.

"What about the cake?" Pierre took my elbow.

"It doesn't matter."

"What about your grade?" His voice was lower now, but not like Luke's.

"We can freeze her cake," Elizabeth said, shooting Pierre an exasperated look. "It's her baby brother, for goodness' sake. You sacrificed your family for your career, but that's not how Ella was raised."

I looked away from Pierre's pouty face as he said, "But you will return. Right?"

"I'll take you back to Nappanee," Penny offered.

"I hired a driver," Luke said. "And Rosalee packed a bag. I brought it with me. You can catch the bus from here."

I was overcome with gratitude for Luke and Rosalee as I followed him out the door, leaving Pierre staring at my cake.

On the way to the bus station, Luke told me Zed had been hit a couple of hours ago. He'd just gotten off the public bus at the stop close to home and had darted across the highway. I could just imagine it. My brilliant brother forgetting to look both ways.

In no time we reached the bus station and Luke pulled my bag from the trunk.

"Thank you," I said, taking it from him. "You've helped me so much."

But he wasn't leaving. He asked the driver to wait.

When we reached the counter, I took out my purse to pay and at the same time Luke handed me an envelope of money.

"I can cover it," I said.

"This is from Rosalee and me." He pushed the envelope toward me. "Just in case you need a little extra."

I thanked him, touched by their concern.

The next bus boarded in twenty minutes, but I wouldn't arrive in Lancaster until the afternoon of the next day.

After I paid for my ticket, I told Luke he should leave.

"Nah, I'll wait."

It wasn't until I sat down that I remembered the baby. "Oh, Luke," I said. "What if Rosalee does something with the painting?" I didn't think she would, but the thought made me gasp.

He nodded to my bag. I unzipped it quickly. On top, still wrapped in paper, was the baby. Underneath it was Sarah's book, and then the cookie tin with the matching game.

"Thank you," I whispered to him.

"Rosalee took the call. As soon as she told me, I raced to the house and grabbed these things before she packed your bag."

My eyes welled up at the thought of Luke watching out for me, and then a tear escaped at the thought of Zed being hit by a car.

"It will be all right," Luke said.

I nodded, but I could only hope he was right.

"Could we pray?" he asked.

I nodded again and we bowed our heads in silence. I tried to recite the Lord's Prayer, and yet again I got stuck on "Thy will be done."

Your will, I prayed, breathing in deeply. God gave us the gift of life. It was His will for Zed to live. He might decide to allow differently—and I might have to accept that. But right now I was going to ask for my brother to live.

"Please, Lord."

Luke reached for my hand, and I realized I'd spoken out loud. "Be with Ella," he prayed softly. "Heal Zed. Heal her family."

I jerked my hand away, not sure if I was reacting to the intimacy of the moment or Luke's praying out loud or his request for healing in my family, meaning with my father. A moment later the call for my bus came over the loudspeakers.

Luke didn't respond to me. He simply grabbed my bag and led the way to the door.

"Leave a message on Rosalee's phone," he said. "Let us know how you are." He paused. "And when you're coming back."

I nodded, took my bag, and thanked him sincerely.

TWENTY-EIGHT

By the time we reached Toledo I was famished. I bought a sandwich and a couple of bottles of water and climbed back on the bus to eat. Ahead of me, a woman chatted on her cell.

It dawned on me that I should have bought a prepaid one. I could call Mom at least, and she could get ahold of me. I hurried off the bus and searched the station but didn't see any for sale. Perhaps in Cleveland I'd be able to buy one.

As the bus pulled back onto the highway, despair overcame me. *Think about something happy,* I chided myself. Ezra. I would think about him.

Luke told me he would call Mom and tell her what time my bus was arriving. Ezra would be the perfect candidate to pick me up. Of course, he wouldn't be on his motorcycle because he wasn't driving it anymore, but he could hire a driver. And we could go straight to the hospital.

Somewhere in the middle of Ohio I fell asleep, not waking until we reached Cleveland. The bus depot there didn't have any prepaid phones for sale either, and I resigned myself to not being in contact with anyone until I reached Lancaster. I slept more, in fits through the night, trying to stay comfortable in my seat, thankful Rosalee had packed my cape. It worked well as a blanket. When the sun rose, I made my way to the lavatory and brushed my teeth, washed my face, brushed my hair, and then repositioned my head covering. With nothing to read, I stared out the window. As we stopped over and over, I was sure I could have made better time in a buggy. As we neared Lancaster, my heart began to race. Finally, we reached the station.

After stepping down from the bus, I scanned the sidewalk but didn't see anyone. It wasn't far to the hospital—if no one had come to get me, I would walk. I gathered my things and disembarked, looking around and hoping Ezra was close by. He wasn't. Only the muggy late-July afternoon greeted me. I folded my cape over my bag and pointed myself in the direction of the hospital. Feeling exhausted, lonely, dejected, and worried sick, I pressed on.

I was three blocks from the hospital when I heard my name. I turned. There were several people on the sidewalk, none of whom I recognized.

"Ella!" Someone was shouting my name, louder now. My heart raced. It was Ezra. He dodged around a woman carrying a large shopping bag, holding his straw hat atop his head as he ran. I stepped toward him and he swooped me up in a hug, my bag bouncing against him. I stayed in his arms for a long moment, taking in his scent, his strength, his intensity.

As he put me down, I stammered, "I didn't think anyone was going to meet me."

"Of course I'd be here," he answered. Under his hat, his hair was still cut in the traditional Amish style. "Your bus was early, but I figured you would start toward the hospital." He took my hand and pulled me back the way he came. "And Lexie's here too."

"She is?"

He pulled me around a man and a little girl. As we passed, the father lifted his daughter up onto his shoulders.

"She flew in this morning," Ezra said. "She's going to help your mom with her practice so she'll have more time to be with Zed." He led me around the corner to where Lexie was double-parked. A look of relief flooded her face as she saw us.

Ezra took my bag, flung it on the backseat, and jumped in after it. I climbed into the front and was engulfed in a quick hug from my cousin.

"Finally," she said. Her blond hair was in a knot on top of her head and her eyes were as kind as ever. "That must have been the longest day of your life. And without your cell. We were all worried sick."

"How's Zed?"

"Alive," Ezra said grimly.

Lexie shot him a look in the rearview mirror. "He's in pretty bad shape, sweetie. In fact, he's in a coma."

I gasped. Luke hadn't said anything about a coma.

"He was pretty banged up."

"How's his head?"

"Well, he definitely hit it pretty hard." Lexie concentrated on her turn onto Duke Street for a moment. "And he has a broken arm. Plus cracked ribs."

I winced. "What do the doctors say?"

"To wait and see," she answered, meeting my eyes with a brief glance.

"He's that bad?" My words came out in a wail.

She took my hand and squeezed it.

Mom was at Zed's side when I followed Lexie into his cubicle in the intensive care unit. She stood and hugged me, harder than she ever had in her life.

"I'm so glad you're here," Mom said, and when she pulled away, she ran a finger under her eye, corralling a tear that had escaped.

She looked as if she hadn't slept—but worse. There were plenty of times she didn't sleep for more than a day because of her job. The way she looked now was ten times scarier than any of those. Her face was ashen, and dark half circles had formed under her eyes.

I stepped to the side of the bed and reached across Zed's casted arm and stroked his chin.

His head was bandaged, he had a tube going up his nose, the side of his face was scraped raw, and wires were hooked up to his chest. When a monitor started to beep, I jumped.

"It's just taking his blood pressure," Lexie explained.

"Oh," I answered. I'd never liked hospitals. I could never be a nurse like Sarah or Lexie, or even a midwife like Mom. That was certain.

"He had an MRI yesterday," Lexie said. "He has a skull fracture and a bad concussion, but we won't know how serious the injury is until he comes out of the coma. He could wake up anytime or not for quite a while..."

"Oh," I answered again, understanding all too well.

Mom spoke in a faint voice. "At least he's young. His chances are better because of that."

"Did the car stop that hit him?"

"Oh, yes," Mom said. "It wasn't the driver's fault. Zed must have been in a hurry to get home. I was still out on a call, so Izzy was with Freddy." She took a raggedy breath. "The driver felt horrible, as you can imagine. He called nine-one-one. In fact I had a message from him today asking how Zed is."

We stood in silence for a moment, watching Zed breathe. At least he could do that on his own. That had to be a good sign.

"I'll go wait with Ezra," Lexie said after a few minutes.

"Ella." Mom turned toward me. "I want to ask you something." She sounded so serious. I couldn't imagine what it might be. "I need someone to sit with Freddy tonight."

"Mom."

It was as if she hadn't heard me. "Izzy is there right now, but she can't spend the night. She's a good help, but this is all too much for her, especially with Zed getting hit. Freddy stayed alone last night, but he shouldn't have. I don't want to leave him alone again." Her eyes, full of expectation, met mine.

I thought of the letter Freddy had sent. And then of Luke urging me to forgive him. I started shaking my head slowly at first, but then more adamantly.

"She'll give you instructions. What medicine. All of that."

"No," I managed to say. I wasn't ready to take care of Freddy Bayer.

"I'll be home by ten."

"No," I said again.

"Ella." Mom's voice was soft.

"No. Please, no. I'm staying here with Zed. You go home to Freddy."

"I should stay with Zed," Mom said.

"Then find someone else to stay with *him*." I knew my voice was full of resentment. But it was more than that. I had no reason to trust Freddy Bayer. There was no way I was going to take care of him. "Maybe someone else could do it. Like Lexie."

"There's a first-time mother in early labor."

"Maybe Ada could."

Mom shook her head and then cleared her throat. "Ada isn't in labor yet, but she could be any day now."

"What? I thought she lost the baby."

"I thought she would, that night," Mom said. "But she didn't. She's not due for another couple of weeks, but she keeps having contractions nonetheless."

I slumped down into the chair beside Zed, feeling overwhelmed. Ada was going to have a baby, but no one had told me until they had to. It looked as though she'd gotten her honeymoon baby—not that she'd had a real honeymoon—after all.

And it felt like such an Amish thing that Mom expected me to go take care of Freddy. More forgive and forget. And to think I was determined to become Amish.

"I can't do it." I met Mom's eyes and leaned forward. "I just can't."

I expected her to shame me into it—or bully me. But she didn't. "I shouldn't have asked," she said. "I'm tired. I need to find a nursing aide for Freddy. That will free us up to be here more without having to leave him home alone."

"Okay," I whispered. "But tonight, you go. I'll stay with Zed. And I'll call if anything happens." I stood, and Mom gave me a half hug, squeezing me tightly, bumping against my shoulder with her chin. Then she kissed Zed on the forehead and left the room. I was surprised when Ezra joined me a few minutes later.

"Are you staying?" I was overcome with relief.

He shook his head. "I wanted to tell you goodbye. Your mom's getting the car. She's going to give me a ride back because Lexie is headed the other direction."

Tears clogged my throat.

"I'll see you tomorrow, though," he said. "I'll call here in the morning."

"Thanks," I whispered.

"We'll make time to talk." He took my hand and held it as we both gazed at Zed. "Things will be okay." His voice was full of confidence. "I'm so glad you're home." He hugged me then, all of me. A long tender hug. As I melted against him, it was as if the last few months never happened.

"I'll see you tomorrow," he said, pulling away reluctantly. My heart pounded as I watched him go, his hat at his side, loping through the intensive care unit and out the door into the hall.

It wasn't until an hour later that I thought to leave a message for Luke and Rosalee. I nearly started crying as I called from the phone beside Zed, telling them I'd arrived. "Please pray," I added. Then I left the hospital number, telling Luke to feel free to call it if he wanted.

After that I slept for a few hours, waking to a nurse hovering over Zed.

"How is he?" I stammered, jumping to my feet.

"The same," she said, turning toward me. "How are you?"

"Hungry."

"Cafeteria's on the first floor."

"Thanks," I answered, gazing at Zed. He was still in the same position. His good hand remained on his chest, the IV taped to the back of it.

On the way to the cafeteria, I stopped by the gift store to see if they had any prepaid cell phones. They did, and I bought one and keyed in the code. By the time I reached the cafeteria I texted Mom with the number in case she wanted to reach me. I didn't know Ezra's number at the dairy where he was working. I'd have to wait until he called me in the morning. But I did call Plain Treats back, leaving the new number.

After a turkey sandwich and a bag of chips, I returned to Zed's room with a cup of coffee.

The next thing I knew it was morning and Mom was at my side, her hand against Zed's face.

"Who's with Freddy?" I asked.

"Izzy. I left messages at all the home health agencies. I expect I'll have an aide by this afternoon."

"Izzy must be really mature to handle this."

"I think she's sweet on Zed. She said she wanted to come and see him. She's been helping with Freddy for the last month while Zed was at school."

The picture was coming into focus for me. Freddy had been at the house longer than I thought. At first Zed and Mom had been able to care for him, leaving him alone when needed. But a month ago they had to pull in outside help.

"Did the mother who was in labor deliver?"

Mom nodded. "Lexie's back at the house, sleeping."

If Mom was sleeping in the alcove, then Lexie would be in Zed's room—meaning my room.

"I think once Lexie wakes up, Izzy will hire a driver to bring her into town to see Zed."

"Really?"

Mom took a deep breath and let it out slowly. "They've become close."

Izzy couldn't be more than fifteen. I sighed. The same age as Zed. He was so big now and acted so mature that I had to remind myself how young he really was.

My eyes landed on my brother. I'd missed a lot in the last few months. Zed was almost sixteen. Too young to be dating, but not too young to be interested. Except she was Amish. What was he thinking? A Mueller girl would never leave the church. And Zed would never join. Unlike me, he liked to travel. And unlike me, he was an academic.

"You should go home and get some sleep," Mom said.

Home? What was she thinking?

"I thought I'd stay here as much as possible, and then with *Mammi* if needed," I said, keeping my voice even, determined not to stir up any unneeded drama.

Mom didn't answer.

I wasn't sure how I would get back and forth if I did go to *Mammi's*. I'd probably have to hire a driver.

In the mid afternoon, Izzy tiptoed into the room. She whispered a hello to me, but that was all. Her eyes were entirely on Zed.

"Has he woken?"

"No," I answered.

She touched his good arm lightly and then put her hands back at her side. "Zed," she whispered. "It's time for you to wake up now. We need to know you're okay."

I stood and stepped away from her. Honestly, I felt a little miffed at her familiarity, but when Zed's arm twitched a little I let go of my pettiness.

"Keep talking to him," I said.

Izzy hesitated a moment, and then she said, "I finished the book you gave me. The one about the philosophers. I really liked it."

I raised my eyebrows toward Mom, trying to imagine what Peggy and Eli Mueller would think of Zed sharing such books with their Izzy.

"I was hoping we could talk about it." Izzy sat down in the chair I'd vacated. It looked as if she planned to stay a while. She leaned closer to the bed and Zed's arm twitched again.

"Your dad said to tell you hello and that he's praying for you."

It was my turn to twitch.

Izzy continued. "Lexie's with him now. She seems really nice."

Zed's hand flopped a little and then began to move around on the bed as if he were looking for something. Izzy sensed it too. In a moment, when she placed her hand over his, it was obvious what Zed was searching for. When he grasped her hand, Mom and I both startled, but Izzy prattled on, saying how much she liked Lexie, that Zed was right—his cousin rocked. Then she talked about the chickens and how out of sorts they were that morning. Zed didn't move anymore, but he kept holding her hand.

Somehow she jumped from the topic of the henhouse to Freddy. "He's really worried about you," Izzy said. "He feels it's his fault somehow, but I told him that was ridiculous. But that's sweet of him, isn't it?"

I thought of Izzy and Freddy in the cottage as Zed was hit. Did they hear the screeching of tires?

"You scared me to death," Izzy said. "I couldn't believe what happened. Do you remember me beside you? Somehow your dad managed to get out the door too. I was holding your head. I guess I shouldn't have done that—thank goodness you don't have a neck injury."

I swiped away a tear.

Izzy was silent for a moment. Maybe that was what it took—Zed wanting her to keep talking because he opened an eye, and he'd turned his head to the side, as if he were trying to focus on her. I stepped closer to the bed, trying to get in his line of vision. A smile slowly crept across his face, but it was more than apparent that it wasn't directed at me.

"I'll get the nurse," Mom said, slipping from the room.

I swiped at another tear. "Welcome back."

"Izzy," was what he said. "Izzy, Izzy, Izzy."

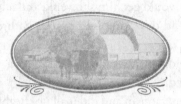

Twenty-Nine

Zed didn't speak again, but he smiled at Mom and reached for my hand once I had a chance to get close to him. The nurse was able to catch the doctor before he finished his rounds, and he checked Zed's eyes and gave him one instruction after another, all that he was able to follow. The doctor said the worst was most likely over but it was still too soon to predict Zed's recovery.

After the doctor left, Zed fell back to sleep, but it was obvious he'd just made an enormous leap in his healing.

An hour later I hitched a ride with Izzy's driver, hoping he could take me on to *Mammi's* house after he dropped Izzy off. She and I sat in the back and chatted. She said she didn't particularly like nursing, but she'd agreed to help Mom because her parents told her to. She was awfully glad she had.

"It's been a wonderful experience…until Zed got hit." She sat up a little straighter. "I hope to teach in a couple of years. That's why Zed has been giving me books to read. The latest was on the different philosophies of teaching."

"Oh," was all I could manage to say. I'd never heard of an Amish teacher reading about different philosophies, but then I'd never been interested in teaching.

"I don't think I can take care of your dad much longer, though," she said. "At first it was just to fix him lunch, do the housekeeping, and get dinner started. Zed would get him showered and all of that."

"He can go up and down the stairs?" The bathroom was on the second floor.

"Oh, no," Izzy said. "He uses the new bathroom. Downstairs."

My eyes narrowed.

"*Ya*, the carpenters came in and did it all up. Right off Zed's old room."

I was sure she meant Amish carpenters. They had probably done the whole thing in a day and only charged Mom the cost of the supplies.

"Anyway," Izzy said. "Freddy is getting weaker by the hour. And without Zed around, someone else is going to have to take care of him. Your *mamm* was going to. In fact, that's why Lexie came out, to free up your mother to care for him."

"Really?"

"*Ya.* Wasn't the timing something? That she was already on her way? And now you're here too."

I stared straight ahead. "Mom's trying to hire an aide to take care of him. Someone who is trained and can start right away."

After that, Izzy put her head back against the seat and closed her eyes. It looked as though I wasn't the only one who was exhausted.

When the driver stopped at the house, panic filled my entire body. Just getting this close to him was more than I could handle. I didn't open the door, couldn't open the door. One small part of me felt as if I should go in, but I just couldn't face the thought of seeing him.

Izzy put her hand on my arm. "It will be okay," she said.

I shook my head. "Tell my mother, when she gets home, that I'm at *Mammi*'s," I said. I would give Mom a call once I'd calmed down. "Tell her I'll be at the hospital tomorrow to sit with Zed."

Izzy said she would, but her voice had an element of hurt to it. Perhaps she'd imagined me taking care of Freddy while she sat with Zed.

I concentrated on the scenery on the way to *Mammi*'s, thankful for the air-conditioning inside the car. The heat rose off the highway. Waves of it settled over the cornfields. The cows and horses grazing in the pastures stood in the coolest spots they could find, next to ponds or under the shade of trees where they could. As much as I was trying to distract myself, I kept thinking about Freddy anyway. I regretted burning his letter. I should have saved it and read it again when I wasn't reacting so strongly. I remembered Izzy saying Freddy was praying for Zed. I couldn't help but be grateful for that. And impressed. Sure, I'd shot up quick prayers for Zed, but had I really come before God and taken the time to pray thoughtfully?

When the driver dropped me off, and I'd stepped back into the heat of the late afternoon, I stopped under the shade of the pine trees at the end of my aunt and uncle's drive. With my bag in my hands, I tilted my head back and looked straight up into the tallest tree. And then I prayed. For Zed. For Mom. For me. For Freddy.

"I don't know what You have in mind," I said to God. "But I want to be open."

I stepped to the walkway to Aunt Klara's, taking in the house for just a moment. The wisteria twisted around the balcony railing, still green and lush, although the blossoms were long gone. The flowerpots on the balcony were filled with red geraniums and lobelia that trailed down the outside. The French doors that led to Ada's old room where completely shut against the heat, and the exterior of the house was as immaculate as ever, as I knew the inside was too. I thought of all the family homes, from Abraham Sommers' childhood home down to mine. First was the bakery in Frutigen, then Amielbach, the family estate, both in Switzerland. Then there was the Home Place in Indiana. And the dairy. And my mother's cottage, here in Lancaster County. The cottage wasn't much. It was small and modest and maybe even a little threadbare. Still, I longed for it. Leaving it behind today had been hard.

I trudged up to Aunt Klara's door, finally overcome with the exhaustion that I'd been denying for the last day. I knocked once, and when no one answered, I knocked a second time, louder. I was about ready to turn around and walk around to *Mammi's daadi haus* when I heard footsteps, heavy footsteps. It seemed as though it took forever, but finally the doorknob turned.

"Ella!" Ada stood in front of me, as big as a barn, her arms pulling me into an awkward hug. "*Mamm* said you were home."

I hugged her, working around her humongous belly, but before I could say anything she pulled away and leaned against the open door.

"How is Zed?" Her face contorted as she spoke.

"He woke up for a few minutes. The doctor said the worst of it is over now, but he has a long road of recovery ahead of him." I could give her a more detailed version later. Right now I was concerned about her. "Are you all right? I thought you'd be home in bed."

"I'm okay."

"Ada," I said, my voice even. "It looks like you're having a contraction."

"I know." She met my gaze with a look of concern. "I felt fine when we came over. Better than I have in a couple of months. But then the contractions started again—stronger and closer together. *Mamm* took the girls to the barn to call Lexie and Will."

It was my turn for wide eyes. "Shouldn't you be getting home?"

"I'm hoping Lexie can take us."

"Good idea," I said. She wouldn't want to be stuck in a buggy with her girls. "But isn't the baby early?"

"Just a couple of weeks now. We should be fine." She wiped her face with the hem of her apron.

I followed her into the house, but before I could even drop my bag the back door slammed open and the twins, Mat and Mel, bolted into the living room.

"*Daed*'s on his way!" Mel shouted.

"Oh, no, he should stay there."

Aunt Klara was right behind them. "He thinks you should stay here. The trip home might be too much for you."

Ada didn't look happy about that, but she didn't say anything.

"Lexie said she'd be here within twenty minutes..." Aunt Klara's voice trailed off as she saw me. "Ella."

"Hi."

After she gave me a hug, I told her I was hoping to stay at *Mammi*'s for a few days when I wasn't at the hospital.

"I'm sure that'll be fine, but why aren't you staying at home?"

I shrugged. "It's pretty crowded there. What with Lexie staying and all."

"I see," Klara answered. I was sure she did.

"I'll go out to the *daadi haus* now," I said. I felt like the biggest intruder ever.

"Actually, would you be willing to help us out with the girls? In case Lexie doesn't let me go home?" Ada had her hand against her belly. "Christy's over at Lydia's parents' for the day. I thought I still had a week or two."

I nodded. I knew Lydia's family did everything they could to stay connected to the girls. I thought it was nice that Christy was having some time with her maternal grandparents alone, without the twins.

"I'll just take my things out and say hello to *Mammi*. Maybe grab a quick shower, if you don't mind? I've been on a bus…"

Ada smiled. "Of course. Take a shower." Pinching her nose, she added, "*Please* take a shower."

We both chuckled.

I hoped Lexie would say Ada was fine to travel back home because I knew she would rather have her baby there. Besides, not to be selfish, but if her labor and delivery lasted a long time, that meant I would be going without much sleep for the third night in a row.

Mammi was sitting in her chair reading when I walked into her little house.

She squinted, as if it was hard to see at first.

"It's me, *Mammi*. Ella," I said, dropping my bag and hurrying forward to see her.

As she peered over her reading glasses, she broke into a big smile. Her face looked thinner, but her coloring was good. She put her book on the table beside her chair, and pressed down, making the recliner slip into the upright position. By the time I reached her, she was struggling to her feet. I helped her up and then hugged her. When I let go, she stood steady.

"Is your balance better?" I held onto her shoulders.

"I believe it is," she said.

I told her Ada thought she might be in labor, and that I was going to go help with the girls.

"I'll go too," she said. "They can sit and do a puzzle with me."

I wanted to show her the painting and ask her more about Sarah, but it wouldn't be worth it to upset her before we were going over to help with the twins. Regardless of my plans, she broached the subject of Sarah's book.

"Tell me what you've discovered about the code," she said, her voice full of enthusiasm.

"Nothing."

Her face fell.

"I'm sorry, *Mammi*. I've tried."

She swallowed and then said, "No matter. At least you gave it your best shot, eh?"

I nodded. "We can talk about it more later and take a look at the book together again."

"I'd like that."

I would also show her the painting. At least I had that to give her.

I took a quick shower and changed my clothes, and then *Mammi* and I went over to the big house together. When we came inside, Aunt Klara told us that Lexie had arrived and was upstairs with Ada, checking to see how far along she was in labor.

Before *Mammi* even suggested a puzzle, Mel went over to the bookcase on the other side of the fireplace and picked one out. Mat was sitting at the table, ready, by the time *Mammi* settled into the head chair. "Which one did you pick?"

"The ponies!" Mel called out.

"Isn't that more than a hundred pieces?" *Mammi*'s voice was full of mock surprise.

"*Ya!*" Mat answered, her hand flying up into the air.

I settled down on the couch and without intending to, dozed until I heard the sputter of a motorcycle outside the house. In a daze, thinking perhaps I'd dreamed it, I rose to my feet and shuffled to the window. Sure enough, Ezra was climbing off his bike, swooping off his helmet at the same time. Will, no helmet in sight, was already halfway up the steps. In a second he burst into the house.

"Ada!" he called out.

"Upstairs," I said. "With Lexie."

He didn't say hello to me or acknowledge his girls or *Mammi*. His steps sounded like a derailing train as he hurried up the stairs.

I went to the door and stood on the porch. Ezra was stepping away from his bike.

"I thought you'd sold it."

He grinned. "The buyer backed out. Good thing I just got it again, huh? Will was beside himself as it was, fretting he wouldn't get here in time in the buggy. Can't imagine what he would have done if I couldn't have given him a ride."

"Have you looked for another buyer?"

Ezra shrugged as he bounded up the steps. "I've been meaning to do that." He reached out for me, taking my arm. "Want to go for a ride?" he whispered.

"Not really," I lied. In fact, I desperately wanted to. "Come on in the house."

He looked from me to the motorcycle and then back at me again, a grin on his face. "Come on," he said, reaching for my hand.

"Maybe later," I teased, pulling him toward the door.

Will was coming down the stairs as we came through the door.

"We're staying," he said. "Lexie said it's not safe for Ada to go home." He was more flustered than I'd ever seen him. I wondered if he'd been this way when Lydia had been in labor, but then, feeling like a fool, I realized why he was unsettled. The last birth he'd been to had ended with the deaths of both his wife and son.

I sank down onto the couch. Ezra sat beside me.

"We're not needed here," he said, quietly. "Come with me. We can go to a friend's place."

I shook my head. "I want to stay." I wanted to know that Ada was okay. I wanted to be able to help with the twins. I wanted to be able to help Aunt Klara— The ringing of my disposable cell interrupted my thoughts.

I answered it quickly.

"I know you don't want to do this." It was Mom. "But I really need your help. Izzy isn't feeling well and needs to go home. But Zed is fully awake now—"

I knew what she was going to ask me.

"I'll go," I said, remembering my prayer under the pines as I looked at Ezra. "I can get a ride. Tell me what I need to do."

"Oh, thank you, Ella." At that my stoic, nonemotional mother began to cry.

"Mom?"

"I'm sorry," she gasped. "Give me a sec."

"Are you okay?"

Another sob racked her, but then she managed to say, "Yes." There was another pause and then she said, "Thank you. Freddy will tell you what he needs. All of his meds are on the counter with a chart. Izzy can show that to you. I have an aide lined up for tomorrow. Call me if you have any questions."

I told her I would.

"Ella?" she said after I told her goodbye.

"Yes?"

"I mean it. Thank you." She hung up then, while I held the phone at my ear, feeling emotionally spent.

"You're going to take care of your dad?" Ezra leaned back against the arm of the couch.

I nodded. "Can you give me a ride?"

"Sure…"

I found Aunt Klara in the kitchen. I told her what I needed to do. She hugged me and said, "I'll be praying."

"Thanks," I answered. "I'm praying for Ada too."

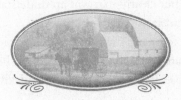

THIRTY

Ten minutes later Ezra pulled into the driveway of the cottage. He turned sharply, positioning the bike perpendicular to the walkway that led to the front door. It was obvious he didn't plan to come in with me.

"Where are you going?" I pulled the helmet off my head and straightened my head covering.

"Bishop Fisher's house. To talk to him about us."

I blushed.

"About you joining the church, all of that. We're still planning on that, right?"

I nodded. "But what if Will needs you tonight?" *What if I need you?*

Ezra smiled. "He won't. Alexander's there. And everyone else. They'll be fine."

I cleared my throat.

"I'll come by in a couple of hours. To check in."

"Thanks..." I expected him to be more of a help. A year ago, he would have done better.

He flashed me his killer smile. "Your dad doesn't need me around, right? Neither does Ada. I'll be back. I promise." He waved and then sped away. By the time he reached the highway, a car was pulling into the driveway. Most likely Izzy's driver.

I climbed the steps and let myself in.

Izzy was huddled on the couch, wrapped in a blanket. Mom had said she didn't feel well, but clearly that was an understatement. Izzy looked terribly ill—and I said as much to her now.

"I know. I have a fever and my throat is killing me. I just hope I didn't expose Zed." As an afterthought, she added, "And I hope it's not strep."

I wrinkled my nose. It had come on pretty quickly, which I knew strep could do.

"Guess I'll find out soon. The driver is taking me straight to the doctor."

"Good idea," I said.

"Your mom wrote out all the instructions. They are on the counter. He's having a hard time getting out of bed. You'll have to help him."

I must have wrinkled my nose again because she said, "Don't worry. He's still getting himself to the bathroom. Your mom said the aide will start tomorrow."

"So I've heard," I said.

"Freddy's sleeping now. He has a bell to ring when he needs something."

After she left I found a can of disinfectant under the kitchen sink and sprayed it everywhere. Then I ventured upstairs to my old room. Zed's clothes were on the pegs, but the quilt *Mammi* had made me was still on the bed and the rag rug was on the floor.

I noticed Lexie's suitcase in the corner, zipped up tight.

I headed back downstairs and settled into the wingback chair in the living room, not wanting to risk any of Izzy's lingering germs on the couch. I fell asleep immediately.

When I awoke, the cottage was dark, my cell phone was ringing, and a faint sound from a bell tinkled from faraway.

I pulled the cell from my apron pocket as I made my way to Zed's old room.

"How are things?" It was Mom on the phone.

"Good," I said. "I think Freddy just woke up. How's Zed?" I passed through the kitchen and rapped quickly on the bedroom door just off of it.

The ring of the bell grew louder. I eased the door open.

"He was awake again for a little bit. He asked about you."

My eyes filled with tears. "When will you be home?" I stood in the doorway of what had been Zed's room, not wanting to go any farther.

"Late," Mom said.

"Izzy?" Freddy's voice sounded confused.

"I'd better go," I said to my mother. "Call me back."

I took a deep breath as I stepped into the room.

It smelled stale with a hint of antiseptic. Freddy squinted up at me in the dim light from a hospital bed.

He was bald, his hair probably taken from him by the chemo. His skin was pale, and he was thin. I searched his face, looking for some sort of resemblance. Had I inherited his chin? His eyes? I couldn't see anything noticeable. Zed looked far more like him than I did. No sense of connection swept over me. I felt absolutely numb as I stared at the man who had fathered me.

"You must be the home health nurse."

I hesitated for a moment. I could tell him I was filling in for Izzy without ever admitting who I was. I took a step toward the bed. "Actually—"

He looked spent.

"The aide is coming tomorrow. I'm just filling in." It wasn't a lie. Not at all.

"Could you help me?" He slipped his feet over the side of the bed and sat up straight. He wore sweatpants and a long-sleeved nightshirt, even though the room was warm.

I pretended he was *Mammi*, the way she was a few years ago, and put my arms around him, set my feet, and lifted. I could feel his shoulder blades through his cotton shirt. I waited until I felt him catch his balance and then let go. He shuffled toward the door where Zed's closet was. Except it wasn't a closet anymore—it was the new bathroom. I followed, walking behind him, in case he started to fall.

I thought of Luke saying that to truly forgive someone meant to no longer resent them. I sighed as Freddy closed the door behind him. I was beginning to understand what Luke meant—but I wasn't there yet.

After Freddy came out of the bathroom, he crawled back into bed. I asked him if he wanted something to eat.

He nodded. "And my pain medicine."

I returned with a ramekin of homemade custard I found in the fridge and his pills a few minutes later. His hand shook as he lifted the spoon to his mouth, and then he laid back, his head on his pillow, extending the empty cup for me to take. I waited a moment and then held the glass of water, positioning the straw so he could take his pills.

As he swallowed, his eyes met mine. He coughed a little and then said, "So you're just filling in?"

I nodded. "Just for today. Because Izzy is sick."

"When will Marta be back?"

"Tonight," I answered.

"Do you know how Zed is?"

"Better," I answered. "He was awake again not too long ago." I knew Izzy would have told Freddy about Zed having come out of the coma. I glanced at the bell beside the bed. "Ring if you need anything."

He put the glass down and settled his head back on his pillow. "If Marta calls, tell her I want to talk with her before she comes home. I want to ask her something about Ella."

"Ella?" I tried to keep my voice even.

"Our daughter," he said. "She doesn't want to see me." He took a deep breath and held it for a moment, startling me, and then he exhaled and turned away. "She's out in Indiana right now."

"Oh?" So Mom hadn't told him I'd returned.

He didn't answer for a long moment. Finally he said, "Just let me know if Marta calls."

I stepped out of the room, my heart racing.

I scrubbed the kitchen counters and then started a pot of soup, using a ham bone I found in the refrigerator. Next I baked a lemon chiffon cake, Zed's favorite. I'd take him a piece the next day, God willing.

I was scrubbing the mixing bowl when I heard the bell. I rinsed my hands, flung the dishtowel over my shoulder, and went to see what Freddy needed.

"I can't seem to get comfortable," he said.

All I could think of to do was fluff his pillows. Then I remembered the nurse changing Zed's position every few hours.

"How about if we raise the bed a little and put a pillow under your knees?"

"The pain is definitely worse," he said.

"I'm sorry." I genuinely was. I wished I could help him. Maybe the next time the hospice nurse came, she could increase his meds.

He wiggled his legs under the covers and then flopped his head to the side, away from me.

I started toward the door, at a loss of what to do, but then I stopped. Maybe talking would help distract him.

"I heard you haven't been in Lancaster long," I said. "Where did you come from?"

He turned his head back toward me and squinted. I wasn't sure if he was going to answer me or not, but finally he spoke.

"I was working near Chicago, doing construction, lucky to have a job at all, when I started feeling bad. The doctors thought it was one thing and then another. An allergy. Acid reflux. Then an ulcer. I'm an alcoholic, and although I hadn't had a drink for a few years, I thought maybe I was paying the piper for all of that. Soon I was missing work and could hardly keep any food down. That's when I decided to come back here."

He took a shallow breath and then exhaled slowly. "I was a fool. Such a fool. Do you know my family very well?"

I shrugged.

"Marta was what I needed, but I couldn't see that. Instead, I was off chasing anything I could, Plain or fancy. I did exactly what my dad did—but worse." He paused again.

"I left. Even after Marta forgave me," he said. "What's amazing is she's forgiven me again. And Zed. I asked them to, that first night I saw them, and they did. And…" His eyes filled with tears. "They have taken me in." He was crying.

I pulled a tissue from the box and handed it to him, thinking I should pat his hand or something, but I couldn't bring myself to do it.

He sighed. "I thought Marta would blame me for Zed getting hit. I know he was rushing back because of me."

Or because of Izzy.

"But Marta hasn't held anything against me." He blew his nose. "I just wish my daughter would give me a chance."

I took a deep breath. The room was too warm. I wiped my hand on my apron and then raised it to my forehead. I'd just spun quite the little web by deceiving him.

He leaned back against the bed. "I finally understand God's love. Marta and Zed have shown it to me." He closed his eyes and was quiet for a long moment. Finally he said, "Thanks for listening," he said. "I'm going to try to rest now."

"Ring when you need me."

Ezra came back as I was taking the cake out of the oven. I offered him a bowl of soup, but he said he'd eaten with the Fishers. He leaned against the counter. "So the bishop says you need to go to the bishop in this district. Or else move over to ours."

"Okay…" Not even *Mammi* was in Ezra's district.

"I was thinking that maybe you could live with Will and Ada."

I grimaced. "I can't imagine Will being open to that."

"I think he would. Once he knows you're going to join the church for sure."

"Let's wait. I'm thinking Mom will need me here…" Soon we'd have Zed to take care of too, if Freddy lasted until he came home.

The handbell began to ring again.

"Want to come meet Freddy?" I put the oven mitts back in the drawer.

"Nah. I already have."

"Really?"

"*Ya*, a couple of times."

My stomach knotted. And he hadn't told me.

"I'm going to stop by my friend Jason's house. He's interested in buying the bike."

"Could you stay? Freddy seems pretty sick."

"Your mom will be home soon, right?"

I explained that she would be getting home late as the bell rang again.

"I'd better go see what he needs."

"I'll see you tomorrow." Ezra gave me a quick hug.

"I'll be at *Mammi's*."

"So will I," he said, starting toward the living room. "To see my new niece or nephew." He glanced over his shoulder, grinning at me, as if his smile alone could make everything all right. The sad thing was, I used to think that was true.

I heard the front door close as I stepped into Freddy's room.

"I'm sorry." He was sitting on the edge of the bed, his feet dangling. "I couldn't make it to the bathroom."

The custard had come back up, all over the front of his nightshirt.

"I'm sorry," he said again.

Convicted of my insensitivity, I shook my head. "It's not your fault. Let's get you cleaned up." I unbuttoned the shirt and slipped it off his arms as he told me to look in the top drawer of the dresser for a clean one. Next I ran warm water over a washcloth and then cleaned his face and chest. He was emaciated, and I could tell that just the touch of the cloth was painful.

When I'd finished, I asked if he needed help getting to the bathroom.

He answered that he didn't as he collapsed back on the bed. I suspected he needed more pain meds, especially after getting sick, but I wasn't sure how much was still in his system and therefore how much I should give him, so I didn't mention it.

I started to leave when he asked me to wait.

"You didn't tell me your name," he said.

I stopped and turned slowly.

"What is it?" He had his head turned toward me, his brown eyes wide.

I left the room. Feeling horrible, I collapsed into the wingback chair. Why hadn't Ezra stayed? I'd never felt so alone in my life.

Thy will be done. "What is Your will?" I whispered out loud. "Please show me Your will."

I peeked in on Freddy a little later, and his eyes were closed. I decided to make the frosting for the cake so I could ice it as soon as it had cooled. As I was beating the butter and sugar, my phone began vibrating in my pocket. I dug it out quickly, hoping it was Mom. It wasn't. The number that showed up was Rosalee's bakery.

I answered, anticipating Rosalee was calling to check on me and relieved that someone cared. I blurted out an eager "Hello."

"Ella, it's Luke."

"Oh, Luke," I said, tears filling my eyes.

"I was praying for you and decided to call—"

Before he could say another word, I was pouring out my story to him, blubbering on about Zed and Freddy.

"He doesn't know it's me," I said. "And I'm afraid he doesn't have much time left."

"I know this is hard for you," he said. "And I don't think before that I listened enough to how you felt—but if you're not honest with him tonight you might not have another chance."

"I know," I wailed.

"Do you feel that you could tell him? I'll pray. And then call me back. I'll wait until I hear from you."

"Are you sure?"

"Positive," he said.

I hung up and tiptoed back into Freddy's room. He opened his eyes when I stopped at the side of his bed. He tried to raise his head but couldn't. I wedged the pillow under it a little more, giving him some height.

"I didn't answer you," I said.

"I know," he whispered.

"My name is Ella."

"What a coincidence—" he stopped.

Even though it seemed as if he'd comprehended it on his own, I said, "Your daughter, Ella."

He stared at me for a long moment, our eyes locked. Tears welled up, and he swallowed hard before he spoke. "I'm sorry."

"I know."

"I'm so sorry." He reached out for my hand. I let him take it.

"I know."

He began to cry. "Did you get my letter?"

I nodded.

When I didn't say anything more, he continued, "I am so proud of you—and Zed. Walking away from all of you is the stupidest thing I could have ever done. Can you forgive me?"

"Yes," I answered. And I had. I realized that in the middle of changing his nightshirt the resentment was gone. He was a broken, dying, sorry man, one who had reached out and received God's grace.

God had forgiven him. How could I not do likewise?

I stayed in his room for a while, sitting on the chair that Mom, Zed, or Izzy must have occupied for the last few weeks. I didn't frost the cake. Or wash up the dishes. I just sat, holding his hand and watching him.

He told me how cute I was when I was little, how much I talked, and how smart I was. "You're wonderful now too," he said. "I see God's beauty in you."

I didn't know how to answer, but that didn't matter. He kept talking. "You had a right to stay away from me, to feel the way you did."

It was my turn to get emotional.

"I didn't blame you, not at all," he said. "I'm just thankful you were willing to see me now."

I nodded, and he closed his eyes. After he was finally asleep I went back to the living room and called Luke. I told him how it went.

He didn't say much, just that he thought I'd done the right thing and that I'd never regret it. I agreed.

Mom came home an hour later. She said Zed had been quite talkative the last time he awoke and was then resting well when she left. The doctor said it was possible he would make a full recovery. Right now they were most concerned about his concussion and keeping him calm. She told me to go to bed in her room because she was going to sleep on the couch and see to Freddy.

I asked about Ada.

"Her labor slowed. Last I heard she was about ready to push. It shouldn't be too much longer."

"Do you want to go over there? I can watch Freddy."

She gave me a funny look and then said, "No. I'd rather be here."

"Why didn't you tell him I was coming home?"

She rubbed her forehead. "I didn't want to disappoint a dying man." Her eyes locked on mine. "It was his last wish—his only wish." She reached out to me then, hugging me tightly. "I'm so proud of you, Ella. You've done a beautiful thing."

In the morning I woke to the slamming of car doors and footsteps on the porch. I hurried down the stairs in Mom's robe. There were two men dressed in suits standing in the living room with Mom.

She turned toward me. "Freddy passed during the night." Her voice shook.

"Why didn't you wake me?"

Her eyes filled with tears.

"Mom?"

She fell into my arms then. "He went quickly. I didn't expect it so soon." She took my hand and led me to his bed, while the two men stayed in the living room.

My father's eyes were closed, and his face was peaceful.

"He went in his sleep," she said. "I think he hung on until he saw you, and then he finally let go."

"But he was still able to walk last night. How could he be dead this morning?"

"It happens that way sometimes."

I stood beside the bed and began to weep. For Freddy. For Zed. For me. For Mom. She wrapped her arms around me and held me while I cried.

"He took so much from me," she said. "But he also gave me my two greatest gifts. I have no regrets. Only joy mixed in with sorrow."

THIRTY-ONE

The day was a blur. Ada had had a baby boy in the early morning, not long before Freddy passed. They named him Abraham after our great-great-great-grandfather from Switzerland, but said they would call him Abe. Will had phoned right after the undertakers left. Mom shared our sad news with him, saying what a blessing it was that Abe came into the world just as Freddy was leaving.

That morning Luke and Rosalee called, and I caught them up on things. It was good to hear from them both. Before lunch Mom and I went to the funeral home and planned a simple graveside service for my father. While we were there, Uncle Alexander called Mom's cell and offered a plot in the Amish cemetery near their house. He knew Freddy had died penniless, and buying a plot would be a tremendous strain on Mom's budget. He'd already talked it through with the bishop. Mom cried as she told him yes. After she hung up, I offered her the little bit of money I had in savings.

She shook her head. "Thank you, Ella, but this is my responsibility."

"You have Zed's medical bills too." I couldn't imagine what those would be. I knew Mom had health insurance, but her part of the hospital bill would still be a lot.

"I'm not going to worry about that," she said. "Not now."

Mom told Zed about Freddy's passing that afternoon. I told him about Freddy's concern for him and that I'd reconciled with our father before the end. Zed acknowledged what I said but didn't want to talk about it. I guessed it was all too much for him to process, considering his injuries.

He walked that afternoon with Mom and me at his side. Not long after we got him back into bed, Izzy called, and Zed waved us out of the room as he talked with her. When we came back, he said she did have strep but was on antibiotics and would come see him after a couple of days. He couldn't stop smiling as he told us that last part.

Mom and I stopped by Aunt Klara's on our way home to see Ada and little Abe. Lexie's rental car was still in the driveway. I hoped she'd been able to get some rest. The house was full of chaos with the twins running around in circles and Christy hollering at them to calm down.

"Where's your *daed*?" Mom asked Christy.

"At our house, choring. He'll be back."

I wondered where Ezra was. He should have been doing that for his brother.

Mom headed upstairs, where I assumed Lexie and Aunt Klara were helping Ada, and I settled the little girls down at the table, getting coloring books and crayons from the box Aunt Klara kept under the puzzles. I helped them for a few minutes until I heard Mom call my name from the stairs.

"Ada wants to see you."

"We'll go with you," Mel said, hopping down from the table.

"Not yet. Let me check and see how Ada is first," I said. "Color your picture so you can take it up to Abe after a while." I hurried up the stairs, heading down the landing to Ada's old room. The door was open, and I could see Lexie perched on the end of the bed. Aunt Klara was sitting beside Ada, who was holding the baby. He had a head full of curly hair.

I looked down at him, but something about him seemed familiar, for some reason, so familiar that I stared at him for a long moment before I remembered to gush.

"He's so cute," I said. And he really was. He was beautiful. "Oh, Ada, I'm so happy for you."

"Would you like to hold him?"

I nodded, taking him in my arms. His weight settled against me, and the longer I stared into his little face, the more familiar he seemed. He was awake, and he looked up at me with inky eyes. His face was round and full. He was small but alert, and his head full of curly dark hair made him appear much older than he was.

Aunt Klara was standing beside me, her eyes on the baby too. "I can't stop staring at him." She stroked the edge of his face. "I do believe he is the most beautiful baby I've ever seen."

"How did it go?" I glanced from Ada to Lexie and then caught the smile between them.

"Really well," Lexie said. "Ada did great."

Ada shook her head a little. "I did what I had to do."

"How's Will faring?"

Both women chuckled. "You'd think he had the baby himself for all his shenanigans," Lexie said.

I smiled. Turning to Aunt Klara, I asked, "Has *Mammi* seen him?"

"*Ya*," she said. "This morning. But then she went back out to her house. She said she wasn't feeling well."

That was when I realized whom Abe looked like.

The baby in the painting.

"I should go check on her," Aunt Klara said.

"No, you stay here. I can do that," I said.

She reached for the baby, and I slid him into her arms.

"The little girls are restless," I said to Ada. "They are coloring pictures for Abe."

"Good idea," she said. "Tell them to come on up—quietly—when they finish."

I relayed the message when I reached the dining room. Christy was coloring too now, and all of them seemed engrossed in their work, so I slipped out the back door to the *daadi haus*. When I entered, it was completely dark.

"*Mammi*?" I reached for the light switch. She wasn't in her chair, but my bag was exactly where I'd left it the day before, next to the wall of the kitchen. I headed down the hall, calling out her name again.

Her bedroom door was open. "*Mammi?*"

"Is that you, Giselle?" Her voice was so soft I could barely hear her.

"No, *Mammi*. It's Ella."

She struggled to sit up. She was on top of her quilt, blinking, confused, her dress and *kapp* still on. Aunt Giselle, *Mammi's* middle daughter, had been in Switzerland for more than twenty years.

"What's the matter?" I sat down on the bed beside her.

"Oh, nothing," she said. "I'm just resting." She blinked a few more times, and as she did, it was almost as if I could see her coming back to herself. "*Ella.* Of course. I'm sorry." She found my hand and gave it a squeeze.

"Why did you think I was Aunt Giselle?"

Mammi put her hand to her forehead. "Oh, my. I'm not sure. She's just been on my mind all day. I keep remembering when—" She covered her mouth with her hand. "When the girls were little."

I studied her features. "What do you think of little Abe?"

Pain filled her eyes. "He's beautiful, *ya?*"

"*Ya,*" I answered. "Aunt Klara said she's never seen a baby quite so beautiful."

Mammi was quiet for a moment then looked away. "I have."

"I have too." I crawled off the bed. "I'll be right back."

All along I had figured the baby in it was probably *Mammi's* brother Gerry. But now I had to wonder if the picture wasn't of an older brother but of a *younger* one. A younger brother who had died. *Mammi* must have been old enough when he was born that she still remembered him and what he looked like, even now.

Thinking of my love for Zed, I couldn't fathom the pain of losing him at a young age. Had Zed died as a babe, perish the thought, I, too, would have remembered his face and mourned his passing for the rest of my life.

I unzipped my bag and took out the painting, the game, and Sarah's book. When I crawled back on *Mammi's* bed, I put the book and cookie tin between us but placed the painting on the other side of myself.

I opened the tin first. "Do you remember this?"

She gasped, sitting up straighter. "Where did you find it?"

"The Home Place. In the root cellar."

"Oh, my," *Mammi* said. "The girls used to play this for hours."

I opened the book. "Many of the drawings on the cards are in here too. Except for this one." I took out the card of the baby that I'd tucked into the pages and handed it to *Mammi*. She held it in her hand a long time before she spoke.

"The game was more than *just* a game, you know," she said finally. "It was a teaching tool, a way for my mother to talk to the girls about important things."

I waited in silence for her to go on.

"She added this card after I'd had several miscarriages to help the girls understand about babies and life and death."

Mammi handed it back to me, and I tucked it into the book. Then, taking a deep breath, I told her there was one more thing. Though I was glad to get information about the babe on the card, I wanted to hear about the boy in the painting, about her baby brother.

Reaching around behind me, I picked it up and handed it to her.

"Oh, Ella," she gasped, taking the framed canvas from me carefully, caressing the edges. "Where did you get this?" she finally asked, her voice barely audible.

"It was at the dairy," I answered. "In the farmhouse. My friend Luke found it under the floorboards of his room when he was a little boy."

"The room at the top of the stairs?"

I nodded.

"That makes sense. That was Giselle's room."

I blinked. "Why would it have been in her room? She couldn't have painted it. She wasn't even alive back then."

Mammi looked at me, confused. "You're right that she didn't paint it. But you're wrong about the other. Of *course* she was alive then." Her eyes returned to the painting, she gazed at it tenderly as she added, "Giselle loved baby Paul. She was only ten, but she was like a second mother to him. Like you were with Zed, though of course you were much younger with your brother than Giselle was with hers."

It took me a long moment. It took longer than it should have. But then I finally got it. This painting, this baby named Paul, hadn't been a child of *Sarah*'s who had died.

He'd been a child of *Mammi*'s.

"No," I whispered, hand to my mouth.

"I couldn't seem to keep a baby to delivery, not for anything. I was always just so tired and worn out. But then finally it happened five years after your mother was born. I had one more child. A son. Paul."

Tears filled my eyes.

"All of us were so happy. Even Malachi became more bearable."

I shook my head, not wanting to hear what was coming next.

"Then when Paul was just four months old, we lost him. Our baby boy died." She swiped at her eye.

"What happened?" I whispered, imagining a tragedy—a fire, a buggy wreck, a horrible disease.

She met my eyes and then looked away.

"We never knew for sure. He wasn't exactly robust, but I blamed that on the fact that I'd had troubles nursing him and had had to put him on the bottle instead. Still, he would smile and coo. He slept well. One morning Giselle put him down for his nap. She'd done it many times before. She was always my little helper. I'd give him his bottle, and then she would change his diaper and put him in his cradle off the kitchen. It was our routine. She was so good with him." *Mammi* drew in a shaky breath. "That morning he slept longer than usual, and finally she went to check on him."

My eyes were wide, my heart pounding.

"I was in the garden, but I heard her scream as if she were beside me. Malachi heard it from the barn. Both of us went running. We found Giselle at the back door, Paul's lifeless body in her arms."

"Oh, *Mammi*."

"Malachi blamed her, even though the doctor said it wasn't Giselle's fault."

"What was it? What had happened?"

"The baby just died. In his cradle. In his sleep." She swallowed hard and then continued. "Malachi was sure Giselle put Paul's head against a blanket or that she should have checked him sooner. He blamed me too, saying I never should have trusted Giselle with the baby. And that if only I'd been able to nurse him…But I was so careful with his bottles. Always boiling the water first to mix with the formula. Taking extra care with everything."

"What did the doctor say?"

"That sometimes these things happen. And the bishop said it was God's will. That we needed to trust God to know what was best for our baby." At that a sob wracked my grandmother's chest.

"Oh, *Mammi*," I said, wrapping my arms around her.

After a few more sobs, she took a deep breath and then continued. She told how her mother came over and prepared the baby to be buried. She assured Giselle she was not to blame and *Mammi* too. Finally, a week after the funeral, when Malachi was ranting through the house, Sarah stood up to him.

"She told him she'd move me and the girls back to the Home Place if he continued. Furious, Malachi took off in the wagon, but he hadn't hitched it properly and the horses dragged him to death."

I could feel an actual ache in my heart. I knew Malachi had died around that same time, and I even knew how he had died, but to hear these details—and to know that it happened so soon after Paul's death—was almost too much to bear.

"I was beside myself, as you can imagine," *Mammi* said. "I sold the dairy. My oldest brother needed a housekeeper, and I decided to move to Lancaster County. My mother thought it was best for us. She encouraged me to take the girls and start anew. I think it must have broken her heart, though. She died soon after."

Her story told, *Mammi* settled back against the pillows and gazed at the painting some more.

"So when did Sarah paint his picture?" I asked gently, wondering if she'd done it before or after his death.

Mammi looked up at me in surprise. "My mother didn't paint this." She touched the swallow at the bottom right corner.

Startled, I sputtered, "Who did?" Sarah hadn't painted it. Aunt Giselle hadn't painted it. But there weren't any other artists in the family, and it was far too beautiful to have been done by just anyone.

Her hands held the canvas tenderly. I waited for her to answer me, but she again leaned her head back against the bedstead and closed her eyes.

"*Mammi?*"

"Give me some time, Ella. It's been a hard day."

I wanted to tell her she couldn't give me most of the story but not all. But I didn't. "Would you like me to leave the painting?"

"No," she said. "I don't want anyone asking questions. Bring it back when you come again though, *ya*?"

"*Ya*," I answered, kissing her forehead. I tiptoed from the room and collected my bag, willing myself to be patient.

THIRTY-TWO

As it turned out, Izzy didn't come to the hospital. Zed's recovery surprised all of us, especially the doctors, and he was released before she had a chance. Instead, her father, Eli, brought her to the cottage the evening before Freddy's service. Eli was a quiet man, and he sat on a dining room chair while Zed and Izzy sat on the couch together. Mom chatted with Eli, asking about his wife, Peggy, his youngest son, Thomas, and his other children. The oldest daughter had married the year before and his second daughter, Becky, was working as a teacher.

"*Ya*, she likes it," Eli said. "She's convinced Izzy it's the best job in the world. If all goes well, I imagine we'll have two teachers in the family soon." Those three sentences were the most I'd ever heard Eli say. He obviously thought Izzy would make a good teacher. I wondered what he thought of her visiting a Mennonite young man, but of course I didn't ask, and he didn't give any indication of what he might be feeling. I imagined it was a stretch for him to allow her this time with Zed, and it was probably out of compassion for our family.

I hadn't seen Ezra since the night before Freddy had died, but he assured me he would be at the service. He ended up coming late. Half of the congregation from our church was there, plus Will, Aunt Klara, and Uncle Alexander.

The service was short. The pastor from Mom's church said a few words about eternity and then read Psalm 23. None of us cried, although Zed sat with his head bowed the entire time. I mourned the father I'd only met long enough to forgive, but I was pretty sure Zed mourned the man he knew. Mom stared straight ahead, back to her stoic self.

After the service, Ezra asked if he could give me a ride home. I asked where his motorcycle was, and he said at his friend Jake's.

"So you sold it?"

"Nah," he answered, flashing a grin. "But it's hardly appropriate for a service."

Once we were settled in his buggy, I asked where he'd been the last three days.

"Working." He stared straight ahead.

"I thought maybe you would have come by."

He shrugged. "I thought you might need some space to be with your family."

I concentrated on the rhythm of the horse's hooves on the asphalt.

"I can see that living with Will and Ada wouldn't be the best. I imagine you want to be with your *mamm* and Zed now." He reached for my hand and held it tenderly. "I told the bishop of the district closest to you that we'd like to stop by tomorrow."

"All right," I said.

Bishop Schwartz turned out to be an older man, past fifty for sure, with a long, long beard.

"So you want to join the church," he said, peering at me over his glasses.

"Yes."

"And you grew up Mennonite?"

I nodded.

"But not Old Order?"

"That's right," I said. "But my mother grew up Old Order Amish, and most of my relatives on her side are Amish."

"So you speak Pennsylvania Dutch?"

"I'm learning," I said. "I've been living with an Amish woman in Nappanee, Indiana, for the last few months. I've been going to church with her."

He scowled. "*Ya*, I've heard." I wondered what else he'd heard about me—perhaps someone had told him about my going with Ezra to Indiana.

"I have a few concerns." He smiled then, the first time all evening. "I don't condone joining the church to marry, not even for Amish folk, but especially not for an outsider. And no other bishop should either."

Ezra pushed back his chair a little.

"If you want to join the church, by all means do. But I wouldn't be allowing a marriage anytime soon."

"That's ridiculous," Ezra blurted out.

The bishop folded his arms over his barrel chest.

Ezra kept talking. "And hypocritical. Most of the kids who join the church do so to get married."

Bishop Schwartz slowly shook his head. "Not in my district."

Ezra jumped to his feet.

I wanted to reach out for his hand and pull him back down, but I knew that wouldn't look good in front of the bishop.

Instead I said to him, "We'll take what you said into consideration." I stood. Ezra mumbled a farewell.

"What a crock," he said, too loudly once we were out the door.

"Shhh."

When we reached his buggy, he drove his horse hard down the lane. "Do you remember when I suggested going to Florida last winter?"

I nodded. He'd been joking.

"Well, it's sounding better and better." Ezra pulled his hat down on his head. "I know people there who could help us find work. We can take the bike again. But we'll stay this time."

I leaned back against the seat. "Are you serious?"

"I don't know." His voice was close to a wail. "I'm just so tired of all these hoops."

More than anything I wanted him to say, "Let's pray about it." But he didn't. I realized he and I had never prayed about anything together, not once.

He fumed some more. "He's the biggest stick-in-the-mud there is. All Amish bishops and preachers are."

"Ezra…" I put my hand on his arm. "That's not true." Preacher Jacob back in Indiana certainly wasn't. He was one of the kindest people I knew.

"No, it *is* true. I'm getting so tired of this. Will bosses me around. The bishop bosses us both around. Everyone kept you from moving back. It's like we can't have a life of our own. It's worse than when I was living at the Klines'." He took a quick breath. "I'm not sure I want to be shoveling you-know-what for the rest of my life."

I turned my head to the field next to us. The corn was shoulder high. I could make out each tassel.

It was obvious Ezra didn't like working on the dairy farm. I'd never seen him so miserable. He had changed in the last few months. We had both changed.

But in different ways.

That evening, as Lexie packed to return home, I sat on the bed in my old room and told her about what the bishop said.

"What will you do?" she asked.

"I don't know. I've always been so sure I was going to marry Ezra…"

"Wow." Lexie sat down and put her arm around me. "I know I'm meddling, but don't feel locked into a future together just because you're childhood sweethearts."

I thought of her and James. They had known each other since high school and they'd married. That was what I had wanted.

She squeezed my shoulder. I thought of what Rosalee had said. That it was better to stay single than to marry someone who didn't share your faith.

I shivered. That was the thing. For so long I thought I was the one who needed to convert to Ezra's faith, that my becoming Amish was all we needed. Now, I realized, the problem here was with Ezra's faith, not mine.

Our differing religions aside, if we weren't on the same page with Christ, we didn't belong together at all.

"Remember, Ella, you're only eighteen." Lexie let go of me and stood.

I grabbed the pillow and held it to my chest. "I know," I said. "I just wish I knew what was best—not for right now, but for the future." I hugged the pillow tighter.

"Do you want to stay here or return to Indiana?"

"Stay here…" I said. But I sounded about as sure as I felt.

"Well, if things don't work out with Ezra, at least you don't have to decide about joining the Amish church anymore." She lifted her roller bag off the end of the bed.

I didn't answer, but the truth was I wasn't so sure about that, either.

Lexie left the next morning, driving off in her rental car and waving as she went, on her way home to James and her childhood farm. She'd come to our rescue once again.

Zed had a doctor's appointment in town that afternoon and Mom took him, while I busied myself with housework. As I hung the wash on the line, a buggy turned into the driveway. Expecting one of Mom's clients, I walked toward it, a wet pillowcase in my hands. But it wasn't a pregnant mother. It was Bishop Schwartz.

Stepping down from the buggy, with a nod for a hello, he said, "I put some more thought into your problem."

My eyebrows shot up. I didn't realize the jury was still out.

"I talked with Ezra's bishop, and we both think it's best if you return to Indiana and join the church there, under that preacher. After that, once you return to Lancaster County and if you and Ezra are still intent on marrying, then so be it."

"Back to Indiana?" My head began to spin.

He nodded. "I spoke with your minister out there, and he also agrees this would be the best way to proceed." He turned as if to climb back into the buggy.

"Wait," I said. "What if Ezra and I didn't plan to marry? Then could I join?"

"Is this some sort of trick?" He held his hat against his chest.

"No."

"Go back to Indiana. That will reduce the concerns I have about you joining the church."

That evening Ezra came over and we walked down to the covered bridge. I told him what the preacher had said.

"Figures," he grunted. "So how long will that take?"

"I don't know. But there's more." We'd reached the middle of the bridge.

"More?"

The light was fading fast. "Why do you want to join the church?" I turned my face toward him, and his eyes met mine.

"Because it's the next step."

"But what about Christ? How does He play into your decision?"

"Nothing has changed there. He's the center of all of it, right? Jesus, others, you. That's what I've been taught my whole life." He shrugged. "What's the big deal?"

I wasn't exactly sure what the big deal was. I couldn't explain it to him. But something wasn't right. I wasn't judging him. Maybe he and I did share the same faith—but if he never talked about it, how could I know?

It took another week for me to sort things out. I called Pierre and explained what had happened here at home and why I left so suddenly. I asked if I could redo my final and, amazingly, he agreed. Then I called Rosalee and asked if I could return to the Home Place for however long it took me to join the church. Then I asked Mom to drive me out to the dairy where Ezra was working.

I have to admit, as we turned down the tree-lined lane, my heart nearly gave way. It was a beautiful farm with a charming two-story house and a huge dairy barn and a handful of outbuildings, including one in tip-top shape that would be perfect for a bakery, just as Ezra had said. I thought of the Home Place for a fleeting second and all of the upkeep it needed. The two farms were like night and day.

It was afternoon and Ezra came out of the shed when he heard the car. He waved, stepped back in, and then came back out with a blue rag in his hands. He must have been working on the tractor.

Mom waited in the car. I asked Ezra if there was somewhere we could talk in private.

He laughed and said we had seventy acres at our disposal. I glanced toward the dairy barn and then the house, thinking if he really saw a life for us together he would want to show me around. After all, this was where we would live someday if we married.

We stepped to the side of the shed, away from where Mom could see us. I told him I was going back to Indiana to finish school and join the church.

"And then you'll be back?" He raised his head and flashed me a grin.

I shook my head. "I'm not sure. Right now, I'm not sure of anything."

He stood up straight then.

I took his hand. "I don't think you are either."

He shook his head. "We really could go to Florida and leave this all behind."

"I want to join the Amish church, Ez. I really do."

"Ella, please. All of this isn't for either of us. I was a fool. I thought I could make it work—but I can't. My friend who left the church is headed to Florida. He has a brother down there. He said he could get us jobs. It's the right thing for us."

"I think we have to decide, on our own, what's right for each of us." I let go of his hand. "I don't want to go to Florida. And I don't want to be yoked unevenly."

I turned away and didn't look back, not even to say goodbye. And he didn't follow me. After I climbed into the passenger seat of Mom's car, I glanced at the shed. He stood in the open garage door, the blue rag back in his hand. He gave me a nod and a wave but that was all.

I was silent as Mom drove up the lane, the branches of the trees swaying gently as we passed in the early August heat, my window down because Mom's air had stopped working. This dairy farm would never be my home, but I sincerely doubted if it would be Ezra's either.

THIRTY-THREE

We drove straight on to *Mammi's*. I had already shown Mom the game with the card of the baby. When she parked under the pine trees in front of Klara's house, I showed her the painting of the baby too, pulling it from my bag.

She took it from me without speaking.

"*Mammi* says Sarah didn't paint it."

"I've never seen this before—the painting," she said. "But it's Paul. I'm sure it is. I was little when he died, but I remember exactly what he looked like. Come to think of it, he rather resembles little Abe, doesn't he? Probably because of the hair."

"Who do you think could have painted it?"

"I don't know," she replied, but from the look on her face, I could tell she had an idea.

We climbed from the car, me holding my bag, and headed straight to the *daadi haus*, moving alongside the climbing roses that clung to Aunt Klara's house and past the garden overflowing with produce. No one was in sight, and I suspected that my aunt was over at Ada's. Will had taken them back home a couple of days after the birth, and I knew Aunt Klara had been helping as much as she could. I was pretty sure that being a grandmother was the next best thing that had ever happened to her, aside from being a mom. And considering that Ada had married a widower who already had three children, Aunt Klara was especially blessed.

When we entered the *daadi haus*, the first thing I noticed was the bouquet of dahlias on the entryway table. As Mom called out a hello, I ran my fingers over the petals of a purple ball-shaped flower. Also mixed into the bouquet were red and yellow flowers.

Mammi was on her feet, standing in the kitchen. When she saw me, she said, "Aren't those beautiful? Will brought them by, in honor of my being a great-grandmother. I told him I'd already been one since his and Ada's wedding last November, but said I'd keep the flowers anyway." Her faded blue eyes twinkled.

I pulled the painting from the bag and unwrapped it again.

"Oh, you've brought it back," she said. "I've thought long and hard about what I want to tell you. Let me sit down."

We followed her into her living room, and once she'd settled into her chair, I handed her the painting.

She took it and again held it tenderly. As she stared at it, she said, "I've decided to tell you all I remember and not hold anything back. Isn't that what we all learned from our experience with Lexie and James?"

I glanced at Mom before looking back at *Mammi* and nodding, giving her an encouraging smile.

She took a deep breath and exhaled slowly. "Believe it or not, Malachi was very nice to me before we married. Afterward, though, he began to grow concerned about how we looked as a couple and then as a family. My mother and her 'ways' embarrassed him—how smart she was, how outspoken, how creative. He was always trying to make sure I wasn't like her at all.

"She told me then that since I was little she used to recite a verse from a psalm over me, the one that goes, 'Yea, the sparrow hath found an house, and the swallow a nest for herself, where she may lay her young, even thine altars.' She said it was her prayer for me, that I would make my spiritual home next to the altar of the Lord. That's why I put the swallow on the painting. It was my signature."

Mammi looked from Mom to me. Her eyes glistened as she spoke. "I painted this the night Paul died. I couldn't sleep. Giselle had brushes and supplies in her room that she kept hidden. I knew my mother had given her some canvases too. I found those under her bed, and then I painted in the kitchen by the light of the lamp.

"I couldn't bear the thought of someday forgetting what he looked like. I'd never have him with me as a boy or as a man." She looked at Mom. "Not like I have you and Klara and Giselle." She breathed in deeply and then exhaled. I wondered if she said all she was going to, but then she continued. "Anyway, I felt compelled to paint him. I worked fast and finished before Malachi got up to milk, but as I was hurrying up the stairs he heard me. I reached Giselle's room by the time he was on the landing, but he saw the canvas and the paints.

"He jumped to conclusions, though, thinking I was coming out of the room instead of going in and that Giselle had done the painting. He told me he'd instructed Giselle to get rid of all her art supplies. I said she would. He demanded the painting, but I turned it away from him and told him I'd take care of it. Ever the obedient wife, I did plan to destroy it…but I just needed some time. In his anger he grabbed it from me, and the paints fell to the floor in a clatter. He stomped down the stairs and Giselle came out of her room. I was overcome with grief. The back door banged shut."

She closed her eyes. "Oh, the things I can remember. Giselle in her white nightgown, tiptoeing down the stairs, her long blond hair hanging halfway to her waist. A minute later she returned with the painting, tears streaming down her face. She hugged me tightly and then slipped back into her room. I never asked her what she did with it. Malachi was furious. I simply told him it was gone, implying I'd destroyed it. That was after the milking. Thankfully the preacher arrived right then to talk about the burial.

"Then Malachi was killed so tragically a short time later, and regardless of all his faults, he was my husband. The next few weeks were a blur. I realized how big our debts were and that I had to sell the dairy. I had to take care of the girls. I wanted more than anything to escape all the grief around me. Then we moved to Lancaster. Mother encouraged us to go. She wasn't well, and we both knew she couldn't give me the help I needed.

"It wasn't until we were here that I remembered the painting. I asked Giselle about it, hoping she'd brought it with her. The look on her face told me she hadn't. I was harsh with her, which was so unfair of me. In all my grief I'd forgotten it too.

"I wrote to my mother, asking her to retrieve it for us, to make some excuse to the new owners, but she had passed by the time the letter arrived. I'm sure my brother Gerry intercepted it, but I never heard from him about it."

She held the painting out so she could see it more clearly. "And now, here it is, after all these years. I can remember now, plain as day what Paul looked like, when I haven't been able to recall him for years. Funny how seeing little Abe brought it all back, though. Isn't that something? How we can see the past in the present?"

She handed the painting back to me. "I want you to keep it."

"*Mammi*, no," I said. "You should have it."

"No. I'll look at little Abe and remember Paul. It's all I need," she said. "It's yours now."

I turned toward Mom and she nodded.

"Thank you," I whispered. "It was so amazing to see this after finding the game and going through Sarah's book—" I clamped my hand over my mouth, realizing I'd mentioned the book in front of my mother.

"It's all right," *Mammi* said. "We need to talk more about that, now that you know about Paul." She nodded toward my bag. "Go ahead and show the book to your mother."

I retrieved it and handed it to Mom.

Mammi cleared her throat and then said, softly, "Ella, the reason I was hoping you could break the code has to do with Paul."

I looked at her, eyes wide. "What about him?"

"I think my mother knew why he died."

Mom's head shot up.

Mammi continued. "A few years after we lost him a woman here, an English neighbor, lost a baby to crib death. I began wondering if that was what it was. But the more I thought about it, the more I think my mother suspected something else. She had a brother, Alvin, who wasn't quite right. Of course, mother always told us what a blessing he was and how much she learned about life from loving him, but through the years I've wondered if Paul had something like what was wrong with Alvin."

"*Mamm*, why do you think that?" Mom asked.

"Oh, I don't know. He wasn't like you girls were by the time he died. He wasn't as alert. He wasn't as strong."

Mom shook her head. "There are some things we can never know. Even if it was crib death—it's called sudden infant death syndrome now—there's no known cause for it. It wouldn't have been anything anyone did."

I thought of Malachi blaming Giselle.

"I know," *Mammi* said, her eyes watering. "I would just like to know what my mother thought. I think she would have told me in time, had she lived." She turned toward me. "Anyway, that was what I was hoping for."

Mom must have found the code because she was turning the book on its side.

"I bet Zed could help me figure it out," I said.

"Don't ask him now," Mom said. "Wait a few months. Until he's healed."

I agreed.

Mammi sighed. "I hope I'm still around then."

For a second none of us said anything, and then all at once all three of us started laughing. She'd been saying that sort of thing for the last several years, but the truth was she kept getting better—not worse.

After we told her goodbye and headed out to Mom's car, I realized I had another clue—a big one—to Sarah's book. *Mammi* was the swallow. Sarah had borrowed a symbol from the Bible and then prayed for *Mammi* based on that verse.

Zed still wasn't allowed on the computer because of his concussion, so I had it all to myself that evening. First, I viewed the raw footage he'd put together for his film class, at his request, while he rested on the couch. It started out with a still photo of Lexie's box with Amielbach carved on the top and then a photo of Abraham Sommers.

"Where did you get this photo?" I called out. The man had dark hair, a beard, and intense eyes. He wore a suit with a thin tie.

"Herr Lauten sent it to me."

There was footage of the box with the Frutigen bakery on it, a still of my box with the Home Place, then the outside of our cottage and Aunt

Klara's house, and then scenes from Lexie's wedding and our train trip out to Oregon and back. He'd included the footage of Freddy, along with a close-up of his face I hadn't seen before. He had footage of the back of an Amish girl—Izzy, I was sure—toward the end.

"What are you going to do with it?"

"Take another film class next year," he said. "I have to figure out what my story is."

"Good luck," I muttered. He definitely had a lot to work with, but I didn't envy him figuring out how it all fit together. Designing a cake was obviously a whole lot easier than putting together a film, even a short one.

Next, I pulled up an online Bible concordance and started looking up different birds. Both the sparrow and swallow were referenced in the verse in Psalms. There was a reference to a hen and her brood in the New Testament. There were quite a few references to hawks, owls, and eagles. I had already decided the last one represented David. I wasn't sure about the crow, though.

I wished I could just mention the secret code to Zed to see if he had any ideas, but there was no way I would. I just hoped there was someway we could figure it out for *Mammi*'s sake, now more than ever, knowing why she so desperately wanted to find out what Sarah had written.

Thirty-Four

Rosalee told me she would send a driver to pick me up at the bus station in Nappanee. As I stepped off the bus, I looked for someone familiar—one of the drivers she sometimes used. Or even Penny. But no one was there. As the bus driver hoisted my bag out of the luggage compartment, I was just about to reach for it, when an Amish man stepped forward, his back toward me.

"Pardon me," I said. "That's mine."

As he turned toward me, I realized it was Luke. A smile spread slowly across his face, but at the sight of him I began to cry.

He blushed as he directed me away from the bus with the nod of his head.

I wanted so badly for him to hug me, but I knew he wouldn't, certainly not in public and probably not even in private. He put my bag in the back of his buggy and then helped me up to the bench, squeezing my hand before letting it go.

After he climbed in, he turned toward me. I'd found a tissue in my purse and was blowing my nose.

"Are you all right?"

"Yes," I answered. "Just emotional."

"I really am sorry about your *daed*. And Zed. And Ezra."

I started to cry again. All the tears I'd been holding in came rushing out. Luke put his arm around me, a little awkwardly, but still it felt comforting.

"Someone will see," I said.

"*Ach*," he replied. "It doesn't matter."

I leaned against him then, gently, and cried some more.

He waited quietly, and once I'd stopped and he eased the buggy onto the road, he urged me to talk as we slowly made our way to the Home Place. He asked a question now and then. By the time we reached the lane, I'd dried my tears. By the time we reached the bakery, I was smiling. By the time I saw Eddie on the lawn of the Home Place, jumping up and down, waving his arms at me, I was laughing.

I redid my final with Pierre, using one of Sarah's cake recipes, the sour cream spice cake, and a simpler design than the first one. I only used swallows instead of all the birds in Sarah's book, but even at that I was pretty sure it was the last fancy cake I would ever do.

Pierre groaned when he saw it and said, "Not this fowl cake again." Then he laughed at his pun. He grew serious and added, "Such a waste of talent. You could do so much better."

"I like it," I answered.

He gave me a mark of eighty-five out of a hundred and then offered me the job anyway.

"No, thank you," I answered. "Your shop is too fancy for me."

"So you're sticking with that little backwater bakery? Where the fanciest thing is a turnover?"

"Pretty much," I said.

"Such a waste," he said again.

I thanked him for all he taught me, knowing I'd learned far more than he intended.

"Why?" He threw up his arms. "You won't use a fraction of it!"

"I will," I said. "Wait and see. Somehow I will."

Then he touched my sleeve. "I still see you as a cook. Making big farm breakfasts. Feeding a family. Lots of homemade breads and soups and stews. Then a pie to top it all off." He sighed. "Just know, even though I teased you, how important that work is. What I wouldn't give to have a family to feed. There is nothing more important."

"Where's your family?" I knew it wasn't any of my business, but I asked anyway.

"Outside Paris. I have two boys. They are grown now. Raised by their *mère* and *beau-père*—stepfather."

"How long has it been since you've seen them?"

He shrugged.

My eyes stung as I realized that was Pierre's unfulfilled recipe for life. Baking and teaching and a successful enterprise were all rewarding, but now I realized what he'd given up to have it.

"This business is hard on a family. Long hours. Lots of wine. Too many beautiful women." He shrugged. "After my family disintegrated, I fled France. I meant to go back…" His voice trailed off.

"Do you have time for a story?" I asked, chancing his ridicule.

He nodded.

I told him about Freddy and how his asking for my forgiveness had freed both him and me. "We found our *mise en place*," I added.

Pierre patted my hand, thanked me, and said he'd think about it.

"How sweet you have become," he added, and then he winked at me. "Just do not lose that spice. And remember, I expect you to fill my order for one hundred sticky buns a week, maybe more. My drivers will do the pickups on Wednesday and Friday mornings, six a.m. sharp."

After I was two weeks back in Indiana, I realized I had no desire to return to Lancaster. I missed Ezra, and even more I missed the dream of the life I thought we would have, but I didn't regret breaking things off with him. Not once. I missed Mom and Zed, but I enjoyed being with Rosalee, Eddie, and Luke more than ever.

One evening when Luke was working in the shop, fixing a sprinkler head, I brought the carved box and Sarah's book out to him, hoping he might have an idea about the code and wondering why I hadn't asked him months ago.

The carving of the Home Place was as familiar to me now as my own hands, but I remembered when Ada first gave it to me and how impressed

I was with it. Although Luke had seen it before, he took a closer look now, marveling over the craftsmanship. When I opened the box and pulled out the book, he stepped to the utility sink and washed his hands.

Once he was done, I pointed out the tiny code and explained I thought Sarah had scrambled the numbers, that they had to correlate with letters, but I just couldn't figure it out.

"Do you have any idea how to break it?"

He tilted his head as he studied it. "What about the weird writing?"

"I think that's just a ruse," I said. "I've done some reading about number codes way back before I came out here the first time."

He flipped through the book, looking at several entries. "Was Sarah left-handed by any chance?"

"I don't know." No one had ever said, one way or the other.

"Let me think about it," he said. "Show me again tomorrow."

The next day, in the afternoon, he rode his bike into town without telling me why and when he returned he had a book with him.

"I read this a few years ago," he said. "I wonder if it might help."

It was a library book on Leonardo da Vinci. Granted, Sarah was gifted, but not in a Renaissance man sort of way, I knew. It turned out I was wrong, at least partly.

"Go get her book," Luke said. "And a mirror."

The only mirror I had was the magnified handheld one I packed in the box I'd sent ahead to Penny's house when I first came to Indiana. I retrieved that from my bottom drawer and pulled Sarah's book from the top of the dresser.

Luke was on the porch, the library book open on the picnic table. "Da Vinci was a mirror writer. He wrote what wasn't intended for other people to read from the right side of the page to the left, backward. Of course, he wrote in Italian, but I wonder if Sarah did the same in English."

I sat down beside him. "Wouldn't that be really hard?" I asked, imagining holding a mirror as one wrote, trying to get it right.

"No. Apparently, a small percentage of people can mirror-write naturally, without any effort. Perhaps she was one of them." He nodded to the mirror. "Want to give it a try?"

I opened the book up to a line written in code, and held the mirror below it. It was still hard to read, small and scribbled like all of her writing with upside-down numbers inserted randomly through the words, but with the magnified mirror I could make out *Gus Stoll.*

"Oh, my!" I moved the mirror to the next passage. *What if Gus wasn't Mennonite? Would I be thinking of marrying him?* And then: *Hunting with him today. I found a sassafras tree. Also some wild dill. As we walked, a hawk circled overhead. I teased Gus that he was like a hawk. He is. Smart. Keen. Alert. Powerful. Determined. He got a buck, a four-point.*

Luke was looking over my shoulder. "Try it on the picture of the hawk."

I did, holding the mirror below the drawing. Embedded in the feathers was a *G.*

"For Gus," I said out loud.

I moved it to the next passage. *Doth the hawk fly by thy wisdom, and stretch her wings toward the south? Job 39:26*

And then, *I can't imagine not spending the rest of my life with Gus. He is so full of life. So determined. I think a Christmas wedding is what we'll do. Alvin will no longer be able to call me an old maid at 21.*

I skimmed the next entries not written in code, after she married Gus and didn't think she had any reason to hide her writing, about them praying for a baby, Alvin accidentally shooting Gus when they were hunting, Gus dying, and Sarah moving back to the Home Place.

She wrote: *November 3, 1911—I caught Alvin with my book. He's 25. Much too old for that. I guess it's back to the code.* The next entries were all in code, starting with, *I do wish he would grow up. I think he feels somehow responsible for me now, but the truth is I'm much more capable than he is. It doesn't help that Mother babies him.*

The next entries were also written in code and were about how much she missed Gus and the children she thought they would have together. She wrote she was drawing more and studying about herbs and fowl. *I think I will increase the flock of chickens to earn some money of my own and dry more herbs and start making more tinctures too. I found Alvin pawing through some of my drawings. I'd done a crow with his eyes, and I think he recognized himself. He is a crow, going forth to and fro like it says in the Bible, with no direction, no purpose.*

I put the mirror under the picture of the crow and sure enough there was an "A" drawn into its chest. She wrote about doing domestic work for other people, selling eggs, raising chickens, and drying herbs to sell. By 1915 she had saved enough money to move to Indianapolis to go to nursing school at Robert W. Long Hospital.

The next set of entries I'd already read, all about Clive and the war and the flu pandemic and her decision to return to the Home Place. Sure enough, there was an upside down *C* in the feathers of the owl. I didn't even need the mirror to spot it.

Now I was on to one of the sections I was most curious about. Why Sarah joined the Amish church. I positioned the mirror on the last section of the April 12, 1919, entry. It read: *If God ever does still bless me with a brood of chicks, however that may be, I'm never going to risk them going off to war. Ever, ever, ever. If I join the Mennonites, I may choose to leave again. Or think I want to take up nursing in a hospital again and meet another doctor. If I am blessed with children, boys in particular, they may end up in some future war. I have no doubt this was NOT the war to end all wars. Mankind is too fallen for that.*

If I join the Amish, I'll never leave. I've already written Bishop Berg, telling him of my intentions.

She didn't join the Amish to marry David after all. My growing suspicions were correct, but I never guessed her reason was because of her nonresistant beliefs. I moved the mirror to the next line and kept on going.

June 1, 1920—A new year. A new church. A new life—except I am still at the Home Place. However, maybe not for long. David Berg lost his wife six years ago in childbirth. He has proposed marriage to me, saying he knows I would make a good wife to him. I know I do not love him, but I do respect him. I do love his eight-year-old son, Caleb, though. If, as is a possibility, I'm never able to conceive, this is the one way I can be a mother.

I have known young love. I have known all-encompassing love. I am fine with platonic love. I can be a wife to David. And a mother to his son.

She wrote that she was learning to trust God as never before in a calm and steady way. *I felt He failed me when Gus died. I bargained with Him over Clive. I wanted His protection, but I didn't want to take the time to truly trust Him. Now, I'm willing to ask Him each day what He has for me.*

A month later she wrote: *I have been honest with D. about how I feel.*

He is in agreement. He also says I can continue with my art as long as I don't draw people. That is fine with me.

Next was the picture of a flock of geese, flying in formation, with just one side of their bodies shown. The second one had the same eye as the hen.

Then the next entry was the one, not in code, that I'd read many times before: *October 3, 1920—Hang the bird feeder. Finish quilt. Sort the herbs. Marry D.*

There was nothing until March, 4 1923. I moved the mirror down and deciphered, *Caleb has found my book, so I will keep writing in code.* She went on to write that her brother Alvin died. *He'd never been strong, but he'd been especially weak all winter, short of breath and with swelling in his legs. I'm wondering if Mother was right all along, that something had damaged him. I think he died of kidney failure, but the doctor said he couldn't be sure.*

I wondered if that was what Sarah thought Paul had died from too. If Luke wasn't with me, I would have flipped ahead to find out but I liked the fact that we were reading it together. It made it easier to bear the hard parts.

Mother and Father are beside themselves. D. and Caleb and I are moving to the Home Place, and D.'s brother will take over their family farm. I am going home. Haymet. What a beautiful word.

I knew *haymet* meant home. It was one of the words Eddie had taught me.

I kept reading. *Three times now I couldn't wait to leave the Home Place. Now I can't wait to return. I am going to have a boppli. It is true. Soon I will be the mother of two—my own little brood of chicks.*

I skimmed through the recipes written in her small script I had read before. Sour cream spice cake. Snow biscuits. Baked rice pudding.

The next entry written in code was on June 12, 1923. She'd had a baby boy, but he was stillborn. *He came three months early or thereabouts. These are times when it's hard to trust the Lord, but what other choice do I have?*

Next was the entry about Enoch being born and her father dying, both not in code, and then an entry in code about her brother. *I've been missing Alvin. As my boys grow older I think of him more. I never blamed him for Gus's death, but I wasn't kind to him about it either. I know he carried that burden heavily. And I did hold it against him. Now it's too late to release him from the pain of that. I wish I would have been gentler with him and more understanding, and not just about that but about all the challenges he faced.*

The next entry was Gerry's birth and then Frannie's. In code she wrote: *My Frannie. I pray she will grow up like the swallow in the temple, in a nest next to the altar of the Lord. Mother is overjoyed. The boys adore her.*

Caleb is nineteen and planning on going to Pennsylvania to work with a friend. We will miss him. He has visited twice now and although he hasn't said, I believe he is sweet on a girl there.

There were more recipes and then, in code, *January 17, 1939—Mother passed away yesterday. She was 88. My, the changes she saw in this lifetime. Frannie is beside herself with grief. The only thing that comforts her is the carved box of Amielbach that Mother gave her. I haven't told her the place will belong to her someday. That's more than a nine-year-old should know.*

"What's Amielbach?" Luke asked.

"A family property in Switzerland. *Mammi* sold it when my cousin Ada was a baby. It's kind of a long story…" I would tell him later. I jumped to the next entry in code, June 30, 1944, and then gasped. *We received word today that Enoch was killed in France. Oh, the horror of it. We didn't know until three months ago that he'd joined up. My heart is broken. Oh, my son.*

"Oh, wow," Luke said.

Mammi had never told me about her brother who was killed in battle. She would have been fourteen. If I'd had a brother killed when I was fourteen, I don't think I would have ever stopped talking about it—but I couldn't know for sure. And besides, *Mammi* and I were obviously very different people.

From mourning Enoch, Sarah went to lamenting not being a better wife to David. In code she wrote, *I was afraid to be hurt again. All these years, I kept my heart from him. Now as he grieves for Enoch, I see I've robbed him of a deeper love that might be of help to him now. Instead, he is the one who is strong for me. The truth is I do love him. I've been with him twenty-four years. He IS the true love I always wanted, the day-to-day, year-after-year love. If only I can return that love to him now. I realize he has been the eagle all these years, waiting upon the Lord. I pray I'll be able to help renew his strength as he has mine.*

*D. said a funny thing last night, that 1+1+1=1. I laughed, but then I real-
ized he was referring to the three-strand cord mentioned in Ecclesiastes.*

I thought of the card in the game. It finally made sense. I imagined her
explaining it to Mom and her sisters. I think Aunt Klara in her relationship with Uncle Alexander must have been the only one to really experience it—and not fully until just a few years ago.

Sarah included the verse from Isaiah 40:31, about waiting upon the
Lord and mounting up with wings as eagles. On December 10, 1944, she
wrote, *D. is ill. The doctor thinks it is cancer. I'm doing all I can. The doctor
said there is no cure. All I can do is love him.*

May 10, 1945—D. died today. I am a widow again.

*The war in Europe has ended, or so they say. Too late for Enoch. And David.
Only God, now.*

"Isn't it sad?" I whispered. Luke agreed.

I thumbed through the book. There were still several pages of code.

"I should get dinner ready," I said, even though I was desperate to find
out if Sarah wrote more about what she thought Alvin had died from, and
if she thought it was what Paul died from too.

"We could finish it tomorrow. I'm sure Rosalee would be fine if we took
an hour after lunch," Luke said.

I nodded. I wouldn't go through the rest of it tonight. I'd wait for Luke.

It was harder than I thought it would be not to keep reading. Both at
bedtime and when I awoke, I was tempted. Then all morning as I made
pies and waited on customers I thought about Sarah's story. After lunch,
I got the book and mirror, and Luke followed me down to the bakery. As
soon as we settled down at a table we started decoding again.

Sarah wrote about Frannie bringing Malachi Lantz home. *He seems to
be a nice young man. I was afraid she might decide on someone outside our
faith. I'm relieved she's choosing wisely.*

The next entry was written normally. Frannie had married Malachi.
The next one was back in code. I wasn't sure, at this point, why she still
felt it necessary. There was only a year, 1953, but no date. *It's been five
years now and still no baby for Frannie. They are living at his parents' place,*

farming. *Frannie spends time with me when she can. Sometimes we paint and draw. Gerry and his wife, Sharon, have the Home Place now and I'm in the daadi haus.*

Ah, that was probably the reason for the code—she was afraid Gerry or Sharon might stumble across her book. *They've blessed me with a grand-daughter, Rosalee. Such a sweet thing. Quiet and compliant. I have to say she takes after her mother's side of the family.*

Luke and I both smiled. We continued reading. *Gerry doesn't approve of my artwork. He says D. put up with it when he shouldn't have. One son lost to Lancaster County. One son lost to war. The last lost to legalism. At least I have Frannie.*

Sometime in 1956 she wrote, *I'm trusting God with a family for Frannie. I was so sure Malachi was a good match for her, but with time he has grown harsh. Maybe God is waiting to bless them with children until Malachi learns to be the husband—and father—God wants him to be.*

The next entries were in her tiny script, but normal, announcing the arrival of Aunt Klara in 1958, Aunt Giselle in 1961, and Mom in 1966. The next was in code, explaining that Malachi had purchased the dairy on the other side of the woods and how nice it was to have Frannie and her girls close. The next one, also in code, read, *1970—Frannie is with child again after several miscarriages. She's been staying with me the last couple of months, as are the girls. Gerry tells me I'm meddling. I do not care. I'm delighted to have all of them here. We play the matching game. I added a card of a baby— the only human I've ever drawn. I know God doesn't mind.*

She wrote she had been building Frannie's strength with her remedies. *I've told her I think their well is bad from all the chemicals Malachi uses, but she doesn't believe me.*

Luke's head and my head popped up at the same time.

"Oh, my goodness," I said. "Do you think…" His mom had had multiple miscarriages too.

Luke shook his head. "We have our well tested every year. It's fine."

"Whew," I said. We went back to reading. Sarah also wrote that she'd been painting with Giselle and hadn't been so happy in years.

I moved the mirror down through the next entries. *February 21, 1971— Frannie delivered a boy and named him Paul. He is perfect in every way. I'm* disappointed that the birth of a boy is what it took for Malachi to be the husband and father he was meant to be, but it seems that is the case. He even drilled a new well.

I met Luke's eyes. I could tell he was just as relieved as I was.

Next was the Home Place "Recipe" page with symbols already used in the book drawn among the words "hope," "trust," "love," "cherish," "believe," and "forgive."

Then on June 10, 1971, she wrote, *Paul has died. Crib death is what the doctor suspects, but I didn't tell Frannie that. She feels as if she's done something wrong. If she knew about the possibility of crib death, I think she'd assume it was her fault and heap even more guilt on herself. However, I'm not convinced Paul died from that. I keep thinking about the neighbor taking care of Alvin when he was a baby. And how I suspected all along the well water might be causing Frannie's miscarriages. It feels as if all the grief in the world has fallen on our little family.*

June 13, 1971—I'm afraid I've had a stroke, though not a bad one. I must stay strong for Frannie and the girls. Malachi is beside himself, and Gerry is of little help. He seems to think people "get what they deserve."

June 19, 1971—Malachi was dragged to death by his team two days ago. He failed to hitch them properly. Poor Frannie is our own Job, I'm afraid. I don't know what more she can bear.

August 1, 1971—I've not been feeling right, and the doctor says it's probably only a matter of time. The dairy has sold, and I think I've convinced Frannie to go to Caleb's in Lancaster. He needs a housekeeper because his wife passed on last year. He would be good to Frannie and the girls, I know. He is the most like his father.

I talked with the new owners of the dairy yesterday and told them about my concerns about the old well water. They said the new well had been drilled but never hooked up. I'm flabbergasted Malachi didn't do it. I told the new people to do it right away.

I came home and cried. Frannie asked me what was wrong, and I simply told her I was tired.

And I am. But I was crying because I'm sure I know what injured Alvin's brain and killed Paul. I went into town to the library this morning and looked up nitrate poisoning. Blue baby syndrome. The blood is unable to carry enough oxygen throughout the body. Alvin's brain and his kidneys were damaged. Paul's oxygen was completely shut off. Frannie thought she was doing the right thing by boiling the water for the bottles but now I see that only made the nitrate more concentrated!

The older couple who took care of Alvin wouldn't have been impacted. Neither would Frannie, Malachi, and the girls. Nitrate poisoning only affects babies six months and younger.

The old well was surely shallow and full of nitrates. I hadn't seen Paul for a couple of weeks before he died because I was trying to stay out of Malachi's way. But afterward, Frannie said his complexion hadn't been good. That she'd planned to bring him over that afternoon to have me look at him.

I will never tell Frannie what I suspect. It would break her heart—for good. Her husband's actions—or lack of action, as the case may be—killed her son.

I looked up at Luke again but he'd continued reading. I couldn't help but wonder about the two wells at the dairy. But if theirs was tested every year, surely there wasn't a correlation. I focused on the book again.

August 29, 1971—I'll tell my precious swallow and her baby birds goodbye tomorrow. It will be the hardest thing I've ever had to do, but I am trusting God completely with them. I have known the love of three good men, but God's love has outlasted all of them. In the end, I am His bride alone.

I just wish I could have shown His love fully to others—to Alvin, to David, especially to Malachi. I know he's at peace in heaven, all that was broken in him finally mended. Soon it will be the same for me…

I am thankful I can send the deed to Amielbach with Frannie. When the time comes, she will be able to sell it. That's what my Grandfather Abraham would have wanted. If none of us ever return to Switzerland, so be it.

I turned the page to the maze, eyeing the route again. The edelweiss, the alpine horn, the crow, the hen, the hawk, the city, the owl, the nurse's cap, the eagle, the swallow, and finally, the Home Place. Underneath she'd written *Haymet*. And then *Himmel*.

"Heaven," Luke whispered.

The very last entry was also written in code, in block letters. *I SING IN THE SHADOW OF YOUR WINGS. PSALM 63:7*

I wiped a tear from my eye and leaned back against the chair.

"Did you find what you wanted?" Luke's voice was quiet, as always, but the most tender I'd ever heard it.

"*Ya.*" I wiped away another tear. "I did." I just didn't know how I was going to tell *Mammi*.

"Your great-grandmother was some kind of lady." He smiled at me, his dimples flashing.

"*Ya.* She was, wasn't she?" I wasn't sure why my face grew warm as I spoke. It was a beautiful Indian summer day, but I knew my response was more than that.

"I like the geese the best," Luke said.

"Why?" I asked.

He looked at me and smiled again. "They fly together."

THIRTY-FIVE

That night I called Mom from the bakery and told her what I'd learned, with Luke's help. Unlike Sarah, she felt *Mammi* had a right to know the truth. Mom assured me she would talk with her, that it wasn't my responsibility.

"But I'm afraid it will make her so sad."

"*Ya*," Mom answered. "I'm sure it will. But she wants the truth, Ella. And, in a way, I actually think this is a blessing. She spent her whole life feeling guilty, wondering if Paul died because of something *she* did. As heartbreaking as the truth is, I think knowing it was the well and not her actions will bring her tremendous relief."

I agreed.

After I hung up I went to my room and wrote a long letter to Aunt Giselle, copying many of the entries of the Recipes for Life book and explaining all I had learned. I mailed it the next day, asking God to use my words to bless the aunt I'd never met. I hoped someday she would come to visit because chances of me ever making it to Switzerland were pretty slim.

I thought about Sarah and her granddaughters—Rosalee, the baker; Klara, the cook; Giselle, the artist; and Marta, the midwife. Each one of them had followed in her footsteps in an area in which she excelled. She really was a remarkable woman.

The next day, as I was fixing lunch, I thought of Sarah and her husbands, and then of Alvin and Malachi, and now my father, too, all in heaven. And then I had the strangest sense of them all together, having lunch, telling stories. All healed. All whole. The brokenness a distant memory. All with baby Paul.

What I didn't expect was that Sarah's book would also bring healing to Luke's family. His suspicions matching mine, he began snooping around the two wells at the dairy. The new one was above the dairy barns. It was the one that was tested every year, by law. The old one was hooked up to the windmill behind the house, downhill from the barn. He asked his father about the history of the wells because Luke thought, when the new well broke, that his *daed* had hooked up the old one for a short time. Darryl explained that what he did was have the old one redrilled, for the house, while using the new one solely for the dairy—the one that was tested every year by law.

Luke didn't challenge his father. He rode into town and bought a ten-dollar kit to check the well. It was no surprise that it was high in nitrates.

The next day Darryl shut off the old well for good and he, Luke, and Tom worked together to get the line from the new well to the house repaired.

And unlike Malachi, who was driven primarily by selfishness, and Gerry, who was driven primarily by legalism, Darryl—who had tendencies toward both—was apparently driven primarily by the one desire we all strived for, to be Christlike. When everything came to light, somehow that difficult man, the one Ezra had called a tyrant, found it within himself to sit down with his family and ask their forgiveness for his oversight with the well and the heartache it had caused.

When Luke told me about that moment later, he said it was the first time he'd ever seen his father cry. And when his mother took her husband's hand and told him all was forgiven and forgotten, that it wasn't his fault, Luke said it was as though God laid a healing balm over all of them.

As the psalmist said, *He healeth the broken in heart, and bindeth up their wounds.*

The family chose to focus on the positive, on God's goodness, mainly that Eddie had survived both Cora's pregnancy and his infancy. Perhaps the nitrate level in the well wasn't as high during that time. Or maybe it was as simple as God stepping in and allowing Eddie to live.

I wondered if he would have mental problems similar to Alvin's, but I suspected, based on how bright the little boy was, that he wouldn't. Sure, he'd had a few difficulties learning, but all in all he was catching on. As far as his physical health, at least his parents knew what he may have been exposed to and could keep that in mind when dealing with any future medical issues.

Mom called me a couple of evenings after we'd talked to let me know she'd spent the day at *Mammi*'s. She said her mother was sad, yes, but very grateful for the information and the work I'd done for her.

"She said to thank your friend—this Luke," Mom said.

I smiled, grateful she couldn't see me.

"And that she'd like to meet him some day."

I didn't respond.

"And I'm thinking I would too. When you're ready."

"It's not like that," I said. "I'm really not boy crazy anymore. Tell *Mammi* that, okay?"

Mom laughed a little and said she would.

The next Sunday I spoke with Preacher Jacob about taking the classes to join the church. When he asked me why, I said I wanted to be the bride of Christ. He smiled, and said he'd heard about what happened in Lancaster. I told him I could assure him, without a shadow of a doubt, that my desire to join the church had nothing to do with getting married—it had everything to do with following Christ. Eddie joined us then and as I reached down for his hand, he told the preacher he was teaching me to speak Pennsylvania Dutch.

"And she's helping me with my English, from school," he said. "The writing and reading parts." I tousled his hair and agreed we had a deal.

Preacher Jacob taught the classes to the join the church, and as I worked through them, any remaining doubts I had faded away. I needed community to live the life God had called me to. I needed the structure and security of like-minded believers to live out my faith. I needed to make a firm commitment and to be held accountable. I needed the Amish church. I knew it wasn't what everyone needed—but it was right for me.

After a month back in Indiana, I called Mom to talk with her about my wanting to stay indefinitely. She sounded sad at first, but by the time I told her how contented I felt, she agreed it was a good idea. Before we hung up she said she had a bit of news she felt compelled to share and hoped I wouldn't take it as gossip. She said Ezra had left for Florida the week before.

I gasped.

"Do you know anything about this?" Mom asked.

"Maybe," I answered. "He mentioned Florida, but I didn't think he was serious." Foolishly, I'd thought he would go only if I went with him.

"He never did sell his motorcycle. He has a job down there working on a dock. It sounds as if he doesn't plan to ever join the church."

My heart sank. *Oh, Ezra.*

"Are you okay, sweetie?" Mom's voice was full of kindness.

"I just hope he's okay," I said.

"We all do…" Her voice trailed off. "Keep him in your prayers."

"And to think all of you put out such an enormous effort to keep me from corrupting him." I shook my head, even though she couldn't see it.

"Is that what you thought?"

"Well, sure."

"Actually," she said. "*Mammi* and I were more interested in keeping Ezra away from *you*."

"What?"

"Once the truth came out, I learned *Mammi* also had an ulterior motive with Sarah's book, but at the time that's why she said she wanted to pay for baking school, to help keep Ezra from being such an influence on you. We wanted you to stay in Indiana to give you some distance."

"But what about the Gundys? Isn't that's why they sent Ezra away in the first place? To keep us apart?"

"Well," Mom said, "I can't speak for the Gundys, but I know *Mammi* and I weren't nearly as concerned with you being around Ezra as we were with Ezra being around you. And for good reason."

"What's that?"

She took a deep breath and blew it out. "Both your grandmother and

I married men who didn't love the Lord with all their hearts. I'm not saying Ezra would have turned mean or cheated on you, but I think his relationship with the Lord was more about family and culture than devotion to God. Frankly, I think the main reason Ezra was joining the church was because that's what was expected of him."

"Well, duh. It *is* what was expected of him."

"I know, but joining the church, expected or not, should be about far more than that. It should be a step of faith, not just of tradition."

I didn't have to be able to see my mother to imagine the exasperated look on her face.

"But you," she added, her voice softening. "Your decision is completely unexpected—which makes it all the more real, I'm sure."

The middle of October, six weeks after I returned to Indiana, I approached Rosalee and asked if she would consider me as a business partner. I would invest the money I had saved, making repairs and updating the equipment for a fourth of the profits.

"I realize, in time," I said, "that you'll sell the Home Place."

She opened her mouth as if to speak, but then she didn't say anything.

"But I'm willing to cut my losses if the new owner won't allow me to continue with the bakery."

I was going to be a single Amish woman without close family nearby. I would need a way to support myself. But by the time she sold the Home Place, I hoped to have enough saved to lease a shop in town. Maybe by then I could bring Penny in on my business.

After a few days of prayer and consulting with the bishop, Rosalee agreed to take me on as a partner. She also told me her plans had always been to leave the Home Place to Luke.

We were in the bakery kitchen and I stepped backward, bumping against the worktable. "Does he know it?"

"*Ya*, I told him yesterday."

My heart swelled for my friend. It didn't matter that Tom would get the dairy. God had provided a place for Luke, the place he loved most on earth. I regretted ever spending an ounce of time worrying about Luke's position in life. He'd been right. It wasn't my concern.

He'd known to trust God all along.

I made a batch of caramel apple dumplings to celebrate and then had a heart-to-heart talk with Luke, explaining that I had no expectation that I would keep working at the bakery after he took over the farm. I knew he would marry someday and have a family of his own. I had no intention of being the old-maid cousin by marriage, hanging around, making everyone uncomfortable.

He listened and then said, "So be it." He was quiet for a few days after that, but soon we were back to talking every afternoon as always. He would come into the bakery at closing time, and I would pour him a cup of coffee and serve him the best of what was left. Sometimes I would talk through improvements with him. Sometimes we would still be talking when Eddie arrived from school and then I would help him with his English and both he and Luke would help me with my Pennsylvania Dutch.

The first of November, as I walked from the bakery to the house, Eddie called out to me from the edge of the woods. "Come play with us!" He and Luke had left the bakery about a half hour earlier, and I thought they had gone home.

"Hide-and-seek," he said. "With me and Luke."

I couldn't help but grin as I hurried toward him. "Who's it?"

He pointed back into the woods, which was a blaze of red, yellow, and orange leaves against the dark green of the pines and firs.

"Luke." Eddie cupped his hands around his mouth, as he turned, and shouted, "Ella's playing too!"

I followed Eddie to the right, behind the smokehouse, but when he took a trail toward the creek, I opted to hide in the brush that was turning scarlet from the late autumn cold, behind the red pine tree. It wasn't too long until I heard the little boy shout, indicating he'd been caught. I crouched down farther and pulled the brush in front of me.

After a while I heard footsteps. I shifted my head. Eddie led the way along the trail, followed by Luke.

"Where is she?" Eddie's tone was exasperated.

"She's pretty good at this, huh?" Luke stopped in the middle of the path, took his straw hat off, and ran his hand through his dark hair. His gray eyes twinkled.

"Let's give up," Eddie said.

"Nah," Luke said. "Let's keep trying."

There was something about his words—and his tone—that made my heart skip a beat. He turned around then, his eyes practically locking with mine. My heart skipped another beat. And then another, terrifying me. What was I feeling?

Luke was my best friend. I couldn't feel anything more for him.

They continued down the path, or so I thought, until a minute later when Luke's hand darted through the shrubs and slid across my back.

"You're it," he said as Eddie's laughter rang through the woods.

I wondered about my feelings for Luke over the next weeks. Was I transferring all of my emotion from Ezra on to him? I knew enough time had passed that this wasn't a rebound thing, but was it that "got to have a boyfriend" thing, even though I'd vowed to give that up? I'd told Mom I wasn't boy crazy anymore. And I was so sure I wasn't.

I prayed about it every morning and night and thought about it off and on each day.

About a week later, after Luke had his cup of coffee in the afternoon plus several of my orange frosted cookies, he asked me if something was wrong.

"No," I was quick to answer. "Why do you ask?"

"You've been acting funny. Kind of cold."

"To you?"

He nodded.

"No, nothing's wrong." I grabbed the cloth and began wiping off the counter, turning away from him, my heart pounding, praying for God to take my feelings away. I didn't want to ruin what we had. I didn't want to lose my best friend.

Fall turned into winter. I was able to make a brief but lovely trip home for Christmas without missing any of my classes to join the Amish church. The very last class was held the end of January, and then the next church meeting was held at the Home Place, the second Sunday of February. Rosalee and I spent the week cleaning and cooking and baking. The service was long, and the living room grew hot with so many bodies in the house on what turned out to be an unseasonably warm day. Then, at the end, Preacher Jacob said we would be having a baptism.

He called me up and I kneeled, bowing my head, barely able to comprehend his words. Thankfully I'd listened closely in class. When it was time, the water splashed over my *kapp*, over my forehead, rushing down my face. I tipped my head upward, smiling. When I stood and started back to my seat, brushing the wetness from my face, I caught Luke's eye. He nodded solemnly.

Rosalee and I, with help from the other women, readied the food while Luke directed the rearranging of the benches around tables. After the meal was served, I found my way out to the lawn and leaned against the bare tulip tree. A group of girls was out there, most a few years younger than me. I said hello and they returned the greeting, but then all of their eyes fell behind me. I turned. Luke was coming down the steps.

I gazed at the girls again, recognizing Naomi from all those months ago when I first arrived in Indiana. She must have been visiting a friend in our district. I couldn't help but wonder if Luke had his eye on her too. He could easily marry now that he knew he would have a place of his own.

"Ella," he was behind me and I turned around. "May I speak with you?"

The girls stirred, but I didn't dare look at them. Luke stepped toward the driveway and I followed. Overhead, a flock of geese flew south.

Luke's hand bumped against mine as we walked, unintentionally I was sure. It was a minute before he spoke, until we were definitely out of hearing from the others.

"I was wondering," he said, stopping and turning toward me. "If you would go to the singing with me tonight."

"Me?"

He nodded.

I wiped the palms of my hands on my apron as my face grew warm. I knew it was flushed, most likely beet red by now.

"Are you sure that's a good idea?"

"Why wouldn't it be?"

My head pounded. Why was he asking me this? Did he want me to meet some of the other young men in the area? Was he hoping I'd get married and out of his way, sooner rather than later?

"*Ya*," I answered, trying to keep the sadness from my voice. "I'll go."

I sat behind the girls from church that evening, while Luke sat at a table on the other side of the Yoders' barn. The evening was crisp and cold, but my nerves kept me warm. I did my best not to work myself into a dither. I sang along to the songs I knew and sort of hummed the others.

Luke chatted with one of the other young men for a few minutes when the singing ended, while I stood by myself, watching the other girls. It wasn't long until he was ready to go and we were back in his family's buggy.

"That was fun," I said, wondering if I would ever fit in with people my own age. At least I had Rosalee and Eddie.

Luke glanced at me. "I've never really liked the singings."

"So why do you go?"

He chuckled. "I usually don't."

"Really?"

He nodded.

All this time I'd imagined him living it up on Sunday nights.

"But you have your eye on one of the girls, right? Maybe on Naomi." It wasn't as if I'd ever seen them together, but that wasn't unusual for an Amish couple.

"Whatever gave you that idea?"

"From the first time I visited the dairy. Remember? She and her sister gave me a ride. And later you said you had…" What had he said?

"You asked if I was going to the singing that night. That was all."

"Oh," I answered. Maybe I'd just assumed that's whom he was going with.

He chuckled again and shook his head. "I actually do have my eye on someone."

A fist wrapped around my heart, and it was all I could do not to moan.

We rode along in silence as we passed under the train trestle, me trying to figure out if I wanted to know who it was. I was pretty sure I wanted things to stay as they were—or as they had been five minutes ago, rather—forever.

But nothing ever stays the same. Somehow, I would get over this and go on, just as all of the women in my family had persevered in spite of their pain.

"So who do you have your eye on, then?" I asked, my own voice sounding foreign in my ears.

He turned his head toward me, fully, his lively eyes locking on mine as he stopped the horse at the highway. "You."

My hand went to my neck. "Me?"

He nodded, his face serious now.

"For how long?"

"The first day I met you. In the café. Couldn't you tell how nervous I was?"

"Why did you wait so long to tell me?"

"Well, you had a boyfriend. You weren't Amish. You weren't going to stay in Indiana…"

"Oh, Luke."

"Today really was my first opportunity…"

"Oh, Luke."

"…to court you." He turned right onto the highway. Looking straight ahead again, he said, "Would you like to go to the singing next week?"

As much as I didn't like the singings, I knew it was the way things were done.

"*Ya*," I said. "I'd like that ever so much." And I left it at that, determined to trust God as best I could.

Epilogue

As always, life with Luke moved at an even pace as he improved the farm and slowly renovated the outbuildings and then the house. In the meantime, I kept working on the bakery, ordering a new stove, working on the marketing, and trying out new recipes. Rosalee still opened the shop every morning, but most days she only worked a few hours. After six months she turned the books over to me. Luke helped me expand the distribution, and he began helping me with a business plan too. Pierre even started ordering more than just sticky buns and actually made a request for one of my Plain cakes.

"For a very simple wedding I'm catering," he told me.

Our courting moved at the same even pace. We were pretty much friends during the week, and a little more than that on Saturday and Sunday evenings. Even on those times when he came to Rosalee's for a snack after a singing, he was still reserved with me, though. And as much as I wanted to declare my love to him, I knew I couldn't. I had to wait until he was ready. And if he wasn't—or never would be—I'd trust God for my future. For a recovering boy-crazy girl, it wasn't easy. But the funny thing was, the more I depended on God, the better I became at it.

I also grew closer to Luke's family. Of course, my relationship with

Eddie was as easy as ever, and Millie and I continued to grow our friendship. She did marry but continued to help with the bakery, taking over the orders and overseeing the distribution, including to Penny's Luncheonette, as she called it, so as not to compete too much with Kendra and Wes's Downtown Café.

Cora's health improved once the well water situation was taken care of. At the age of forty-one she had her fifth baby. A little girl and a blessing to all, especially her next oldest brother. Shortly after the baby was born, Darryl came into the bakery and asked to talk to me. I felt puzzled by his uncharacteristic shyness.

"I want to thank you for the information about the well." He paused, then took a deep breath and exhaled slowly. "And I want to say I'm sorry. I've wanted to tell you for a long time. I know I hurt you when I burned those drawings. I thought doing God's will meant keeping all the rules, but in doing that I forgot about God's command to love my neighbor as myself. You've been a *gut* neighbor to my family, and I thank you for that."

He left quickly, before I could tell him I'd made my peace with him in my heart long ago.

I began to see things more from Darryl's point of view once I could appreciate how different Luke was from him and from Tom. I could see that Darryl loved both of his sons, even though he had trouble understanding one of them. And I knew Darryl felt deeply responsible for raising his children to follow God and the traditions of the church.

I wanted to be with Luke more and more. Not because of the bakery or because the Home Place would be his or because he was strong and grew more handsome with each passing day. I wanted to be with Luke because he was kind and loving. Because he prayed with me. Because he showed me the love of Christ. Because there was no one else in the world I wanted to tell about my day and how I felt and what I thought. There was no one who listened to me more honestly than Luke.

But it wasn't just that. There was no one else I wanted to have tell me about his day, either. No one. Not one single friend I'd ever had.

There were plenty of times I wished he talked more. And there were times I wished he didn't move at a snail's pace, especially when it came to our relationship. But then, after a year and a half of going to singings and volleyball games with him, on a Sunday evening in early August at Rosalee's under the canopy of the tulip tree, he took my hand in an unusual gesture of affection.

I leaned toward him as he spoke.

"Are you staying?" he asked, peering at me from under the brim of his straw hat.

"In Indiana?"

He shook his head. "In the church." With his free hand he straightened one of the ties of my *kapp*. Then he met my gaze.

"*Ya.*" My pulse quickened as I spoke. "Why do you ask?" After courting for so long, I could only hope another question was coming.

Luke tightened his hold on my hand. "I just wanted to make sure your commitment was true."

"It is," was my simple reply.

"Because if you plan to stay, then I hope you'll stay with me."

My heart began to pound. My eyes locked on his. But in one of those rare times in my life, words failed me.

Turning more fully toward me, he took my other hand. "Will you marry me, Ella?"

My eyes filled with tears. "*Ya,*" I answered, as sure as I'd ever been in my entire life. "I will."

He leaned forward and touched his lips to mine, tentative at first. Then he took me in his arms and kissed me with surprising intensity. I met his passion in return, knowing this was exactly where I belonged, for a lifetime.

All the months of courting, of waiting, of wondering fell away.

Our kisses, our embrace, our commitment, all of it felt so right, so full of passion and tenderness and promise. In that moment, the world seemed to disappear—except for Luke and me and the Home Place all around us.

As he pulled away, his eyes danced. "You'd best be deciding where you want to marry. Here or in Lancaster. But don't tell me now. Talk to your *mamm* first."

I would talk to my *mamm*, but I already knew. I had it all planned. Mom and Zed would come. And Izzy too, considering from Zed's letters it was obvious they were still spending a lot of time together. Ada and Will and their family would all come as well. Little Abe was toddling after his sisters now, and I was anxious to see him. I knew for sure Lexie and James would come from Oregon. Knowing Penny and Rosalee, they would insist on hosting all of them. I could only hope that *Mammi* could also make it, accompanied by Aunt Klara and Uncle Alexander, not only because I wanted her here for me but because she needed to come for herself. To make peace. To close this chapter of her life.

I knew it was a long shot, but I even hoped Aunt Giselle would come from Switzerland. I longed for a reunion for all of us, all together before *Mammi* passed on. A homecoming was what we needed. What better place to have it than at the Home Place?

I was blessed beyond belief that it would be my permanent home. My *haymet*. And I would begin the rest of my life with Luke here.

That night I drew a new maze in my notebook. I kept the cottage and motorcycle, the box and book. But I added a cake, a creek, two geese, and a red pine tree. At the center was the Home Place. But instead of putting it in a daisy, as Sarah had done with hers and I had copied all those months ago, I drew mine in a hand.

It was the hand of the One who had a plan for me all along.

DISCUSSION QUESTIONS

1. Ella is hurt that her mother didn't tell her who Zed's birth mother and father were sooner. Was Marta right to withhold the information from Ella as long as she did?

2. Ella describes herself as "boy crazy." What has made her that way? What about Ezra is so attractive to her?

3. Sarah's book resonates with Ella. Are there documents, artifacts, or stories passed down through your family that have impacted your life?

4. Why is Rosalee willing to take Ella into her home? What does the Home Place come to mean to Ella?

5. In what ways is Luke different than Ezra? How does Luke view his father? How does Luke respond to his father? How does Luke view his future?

6. Freddy's return to Lancaster County turns Ella's world upside down. Why doesn't she want any contact with him? What happens later in the story that leads her to change her mind? What changes in Freddy make reconciliation between the two a possibility?

7. What does Ella learn from her relationship with Ezra that helps her to become a more mature follower of Christ? What changes within Ella as far as her desire to join the Amish church? Which characters influence her decision?

8. How does Ella's relationship with Luke differ from her relationship with Ezra?

9. Ella realizes that her mother and two aunts were each molded in very individual ways by their grandmother, Sarah, and her interests. Are there ways that your grandmother impacted you?

10. Ella has a rocky relationship with her mother throughout most of the story. What assumptions does she make about her mother? Did you identify more with Ella or with Marta? Why?